General Editor: *David Stuart Davies*

THE TEMPLE OF DEATH

*Ghost stories of A. C. Benson
and R. H. Benson*

THE TEMPLE OF DEATH

Ghost stories of A. C. Benson
and R. H. Benson

Selected and introduced by
David Stuart Davies

WORDSWORTH EDITIONS

In loving memory of
MICHAEL TRAYLER
the founder of Wordsworth Editions

1

Readers who are interested in other titles from
Wordsworth Editions are invited to visit our website at
www.wordsworth-editions.com

For our latest list and a full mail-order service contact
Bibliophile Books, 5 Thomas Road, London E14 7BN
Tel: +44 0207 515 9222 Fax: +44 0207 538 4115
e-mail: orders@bibliophilebooks.com

This edition published 2007 by
Wordsworth Editions Limited
8B East Street, Ware, Hertfordshire SG12 9HJ

ISBN 978 1 84022 547 1

Typeset in Great Britain by Chrissie Madden
Printed by Clays Ltd, St Ives plc

CONTENTS

To

MARK VALENTINE

*A Gentleman and
a Scholar*

INTRODUCTION

The instance of there being two sibling writers in the same family is not as rare as one might think, but for there to be three authors all of the same generation is exceptional. The most famous case, of course, is the Bronte sisters, Charlotte, Emily and Anne. Less well known, but still of great interest, are the Benson brothers, Arthur Christopher (1862–1925), Edward Frederic (1867–1940) and Robert Hugh (1871–1914). Between them their literary output consisted of over a hundred books, both fiction and non-fiction. While works in the supernatural genre formed only a small part of their individual output, each brother during his writing career created chilling and engrossing ghost stories.

The Benson brothers' early life was as dramatic and sensational as the dramatic and sensational gothic novels that they devoured in their childhood. Their father, Edward White Benson, began his working life as a schoolmaster at Rugby School, but later became one of Queen Victoria's favourite archbishops after serving a term as the Bishop of Truro. He married his bride, the sexually overwrought Mary Sidgwick, when she was just eighteen. They had six children in all, two of whom died in childbirth. The only surviving girl, Maggie, also an author and artist, became totally insane and on one occasion attempted to murder her own mother. It has been suggested that this homicidal attack was prompted by her mother's lesbian affair with one of Maggie's friends. With his marriage in tatters, Edward White Benson, disappointed, disillusioned and somewhat mentally disturbed by events, took revenge on the world through the ill-treatment of his sons. He was brutish and cruel to them. It may well be that experiencing such a wild and upsetting domestic situation in their youth contributed to the fact that none of the brothers ever married. Another suggested explanation for this aspect of their lives is that they were all homosexual, but there has been no concrete evidence to support this theory.

Arthur became a teacher, first of all at Eton from 1885 to 1903, and later becoming master of Magadelene College Cambridge. His unhappy childhood is reflected in his observation concerning his approach to teaching:

> I am sure it is one's duty as a teacher to try to show boys that no opinions, no tastes, no emotions are worth much unless they are one's own. I suffered acutely as a boy from the lack of being shown this.

A. C. Benson was a large man with a sharp tongue, and suffered from long bouts of manic depression, probably inherited from his father. He was also a compulsive writer. Words just poured from him. His poems, works of fiction and numerous volumes of essays such as *From a College Window*, were well known and highly praised in their day. He also left one of the longest diaries ever written, said to run to over four million words, although only extracts have ever been published. Today he is perhaps best remembered for providing the lyrics to fit Edward Elgar's music for the rousing patriotic song, *Land of Hope and Glory*.

The middle brother, Edward Frederic (Fred) Benson, proved to be the most famous and perhaps the most accomplished author of the family. Following the success of his early novel, *Dodo*, he became a full time writer. Nowadays he is largely known for his whimsical 'Mapp and Lucia' series of six novels about Emmeline 'Lucia' Lucas and Elizabeth Mapp. The principal setting for four of the Mapp and Lucia novels is a town called Tilling, which is recognisably based on Rye in East Sussex, where E. F. Benson lived for many years and served as Mayor. As well as penning a series of autobiographies and memoirs, including one of Charlotte Brontë, he achieved some notoriety as a writer of ghost stories.

Initially Robert Hugh Benson achieved fame by means of a scandal. He was ordained as a priest in the Church of England by his father in 1896, but several years later, after his father's death, he renounced this faith and became a Catholic priest. The news that the son of an Archbishop of Canterbury was rejecting his father's religious beliefs and embracing Catholicism caused shock waves in the Anglican community. It was as though he at last had the courage and opportunity to rebel against his father's tyranny. Like his brothers, R. H. Benson was also a prolific writer who produced works of great variety including science fiction, historical dramas, religious plays, children's tales and of course supernatural stories.

It is interesting to note that while the scope of the three brothers' *oeuvre* is very wide and diverse, each of them experienced the need and the inspiration to create weird tales of ghosts, hauntings and unnatural events. Again one must look to the influence of their dark father, for he had a liking for such material. It is said that on one occasion Edward White Benson told Henry James a simple, rather inexpert story that he had heard concerning the ghosts of evil servants who tried to lure young children to their deaths. James made a note of the tale and eventually used it as the basis for his classic spooky story, *The Turn of the Screw*.

Apart from their father, there was one other major influence on the supernatural fiction of two of the brothers. Both Arthur and Fred were acquainted with the master of the ghost story, M. R. James, whose scholarly style and reserved descriptions infuse some of their writings. Indeed, while at Eton Arthur contributed to James's ghost story sessions with a few examples of his own.

However it has to be said that each brother was prompted to write ghost stories for different reasons. For Fred, the professional writer, it was for his personal satisfaction and in particular for money that he created his creepy narratives. Most of Arthur's successful published pieces helped him to work through his own confused ideas concerning his religious beliefs. However, many of his tales were never published and only came to light after he was dead. It would seem that he penned the darker material for his own private pleasure. Hugh wrote his stories as a kind of glorification of the Catholic faith, a glorification that at times, it has to be said, interfered with the suspense of the narrative.

For E. F. Benson, his ghost stories, like his other fiction, became well known and have been anthologised in many collections. As a result, the work of his two brothers has been undeservedly over-shadowed, neglected by publishers and therefore also by readers. It is the purpose of this collection to redress the balance in some small measure. This dark banquet of tales has been prepared from the various volumes produced by A. C. and R. H. Benson in an attempt to introduce their work to devoted readers of strange and chilling fiction.

It is fair to say that of the two, A. C. Benson's tales fall more naturally into the realm of ghost fiction or strange tales. A great number of his best stories were written when he was a master at Eton. It is clear that he viewed the students in his charge as the main audience for his fiction. He designed the stories to provide examples and lessons to show the youngsters how to cope with the moral dilemmas that confront us along the journey through life. He observed that:

> I used to shape a tale in which a figure might leave an arresting or restraining thought in their minds; or even touch with a light of romance some of the knightly virtues which are apt to be dulled into the aspect of commonplace and uninteresting duties. I chose, not deliberately but instinctively, the old romantic form for the setting of these tales, a semi-medieval atmosphere such as belongs to the literary epic; some of the stories are pure fantasy; but they all aim more or less directly at illustrating the stern necessity for moral choice; the difficulty is to get children to believe, at the brilliant outset of life, that it will not do to follow the delights of impulse.

However, we must not be misled into thinking that because of the moral tone and the reserved and archaic pitch of the language in these stories, they cannot therefore chill or surprise the reader. Rest assured, they can and, indeed, they do.

The first story, 'The Temple of Death', which gives this collection its title, resembles the form of a moral allegory in outline, but the actual content of the narrative with its tense bleakness, the strange slavering beast which we encounter and the dramatic dénouement do more than place it firmly within the realms of a ghostly horror fiction.

With 'The Closed Window', A.C. Benson proves to be one of the writing pioneers who took the idea that by passing through some seemingly ordinary portal – in this case a window – one can enter a frightening and alien parallel world. Imagine Stephen King writing *The Lion, the Witch and the Wardrobe*!

A different kind of portal is presented in 'The Hill of Trouble', one that reveals the future. The central character, the scholar Gilbert, like Dickens's Ebenezer Scrooge in *A Christmas Carol*, is shown his own future. It is a vision that drives him to despair, but as the mystic who gave him this dubious privilege observes, 'A man who pulls open the door which leads from the present into the future must not be vexed if he sees the truth.'

The majority of A.C. Benson's stories in this collection were published around the turn of the twentieth century and are full of visions, dusty old churches and mysterious spiritual places. The tales are taken from two collections, *The Hill of Trouble* (1903) and *The Isles of Sunset* (1904). Each of the narratives contains moments which are surprisingly weird and unnerving. For example, in 'Out of the Sea', a grim tale of revenge, we encounter a strange goat-like creature which after it has completed its mission remains 'snuffing at the sand'; in 'The Grey Cat' a pool of water writhes with 'large and luminous worms'; and in 'The Slype House' we witness the destructive power of black magic.

After Arthur's death in 1926, his brother Fred discovered a stash of unpublished stories amongst his papers. Choosing the two he regarded as the best, 'Basil Netherby' and 'The Uttermost Farthing', Fred arranged for their publication. We reproduce these rare tales in this collection. They are more subtle, restrained, and therefore more frightening, than Arthur's early work. What happened to the rest of the stories is anyone's guess.

In 'Basil Netherby' Arthur returned to a theme touched on in his earlier tale, 'The Open Window': the entry into a darker and morally corrupt world by means of a mundane doorway. In Netherby's case it is through music and for his folly he pays a terrible price. 'The Uttermost Farthing' is a slow burner, but stay with it for it turns into one of the greatest of British ghost stories, albeit heavily influenced by M. R. James in content and description.

Robert Hugh Benson's tales are more esoteric and heavily influenced by the Catholic fervour that infused all of his writing, but to say that they are less effective than those of his brothers is to undervalue the cool menace he is able to instil into much of his prose. Reading his stories with care and attention brings its rewards. His observations about ghost story fiction and the effects it attempts to achieve are incredibly perceptive and telling: 'It is like looking at the backs of a crowd; they are attending to something else, not us at all. Just occasionally we catch the eye of someone who turns round – but that is all.' Certainly in this observation we can detect the influence, yet again, of M. R. James.

The stories of R. H. Benson selected for this collection are mainly from two books: *The Light Invisible* (1903) and *A Mirror of Shallott* (1907). The earlier volume was written while he was an Anglican, and still in the midst of the convulsive throes of spiritual conversion. The book takes the form of a series of tales, almost anecdotes, told to the unnamed narrator by an old priest recounting a series of supernatural experiences. While at the heart of all of these narratives there is a wild array of emotive mysticism – a confession of faith amidst

xii   THE TEMPLE OF DEATH & OTHER STORIES

the confusion of doubt, mirroring the author's wavering religious beliefs, some of the tales also contain strong elements of the ghost or horror story.

The second volume, *The Mirror of Shallott*, made up of a series of tales told by a group of priests, is much darker. In essence they are campfire tales meant to chill in that inexplicit manner that is at the heart of all good ghost stories. For instance in 'The Watcher' the author hints in a wonderfully subtle fashion that something bestial lies in the heart of man. However, R. H. Benson's *pièce de résistance* is 'The Traveller', a chillingly unemotional account of the ghost of one of Thomas à Becket's murderers. The cool, precise prose works effectively to create uneasy feelings in the reader.

It has been a great pleasure to put together this strange brew of stories by two men who, had they been born into separate families, might be more widely known today. Certainly by the uncertain and fleeting standards of the twenty-first century, these stories are strange, archaic and unworldly, but as exercises in the art of luring the reader into a state of unease, they are as potent as they were when the ink was barely dry on the page.

DAVID STUART DAVIES

THE TEMPLE OF DEATH

*Ghost stories of A. C. Benson
and R. H. Benson*

The Temple of Death

A. C. BENSON

It was late in the afternoon of a dark and rainy day when Paullinus left the little village where he had found shelter for the night. The village lay in a great forest country in the heart of Gaul. The scattered folk that inhabited it were mostly heathens, and very strange and secret rites were still celebrated in lonely sanctuaries. Christian teachers, of whom Paullinus was one, travelled alone or in little companies along the great high roads, turning aside to visit the woodland hamlets, and labouring patiently to make the good news of the Word known.

They were mostly unmolested, for they travelled under the powerful name of Romans, and in many places they were kindly received. Paullinus had been for months slowly faring from village to village, without any fixed plan of journeying, but asking his way from place to place, as the Spirit led him. He was a young man, a very faithful Christian, and with a love of adventure and travel which stood him in good stead. He carried a little money, but he had seldom need to use it, for the people were simple and hospitable; he did not try to hold assemblies, for he believed that the Gospel must spread like leaven from quiet heart to quiet heart. Indeed he did not purpose to proclaim the Word, but rather to prepare the way for those that should come after. He was of a strong habit, spare and upright; when he was alone he walked swiftly, looking very eagerly about him. He loved the aspect of the earth, the green branching trees, the wild creatures of the woodland, the voices of birds and the sound of streams. And he had too a great and simple love for his own kind, and though he had little eloquence he had a plentiful command of friendly and shrewd talk, and even better than he loved to speak, he loved to listen. He had a sweet and open smile, that drew the hearts of all whom he met to him, especially of the children. And he loved his wandering life in the free air, without the daily cares of settled habit.

He had spent the night with an old and calm man, who had been a warrior in his youth, but who could now do little but attend to his farm. Paullinus had spoken to him of the love of the Father and the tender care that Jesus had to His brothers on earth; the old man had listened courteously, and had said that it sounded fair enough, but that he was too old to change, and must stand in the ancient ways. Paullinus did not press him; his custom was never to do that. In the morning he had gone to and fro in the village, and it was late before he thought of setting out; the old man had pressed him to stay another night, but something in Paullinus' heart had told him that he must not wait, for it seemed to him that there was work to be done. The old man came with him to the edge of the forest, and gave him very particular directions to the village he was bound for, which lay in the heart of the wood. 'Of one thing I must advise you,' he said. 'There is, in the wood, some way off the track, a place to which I would not have you go – it is a temple of one of our gods, a dark place. Be certain, dear sir, to pass it by. No-one would go there willingly, save that we are sometimes compelled.' He broke off suddenly here and looked about him fearfully; then he went on in a low voice: 'It is called the Temple of the Grey Death, and there are rites done there of which I may not speak. I would it were otherwise, but the gods are strong – and the priest is a hard and evil man, who won his office in a terrible way, and shall lose it no less terribly. Oh, go not there, dear stranger;' and he laid his hand upon his arm.

'Dear brother,' said Paullinus, 'I have no mind to go there – but your words seem to have a dark meaning behind them. What are these rites of which you speak?' But the old man shook his head.

'I may not speak of them,' he said, 'it is better to be silent.'

Then they took a kind leave of each other, and Paullinus said that he would pass again that way to see his friend, 'for we are friends, I know.' And so he went into the wood. It was a wood of very ancient trees, and the dark leaves roofed over the grassy track making a tunnel. The heavens too grew dark above, and Paullinus heard the drops patter upon the leaves. Generally he loved well enough to walk in the woodways, but here it seemed different. He would have liked a companion. Something sinister and terrible seemed to him to hide within those gloomy avenues, and the feeling grew stronger every moment. But he said to himself some of the simple hymns with which he often cheered his way, and felt again that he was in the hands of God.

Presently he passed a little forest pool that was one of the marks of his way. Upon the further bank he was surprised to see a man sitting, with a rod or spear in his hand, looking upon the water. He was glad to see another man in this solitude, and hailed him cheerfully, asking if he was in the right way. The man looked up at the sound. Paullinus saw that he was of middle age, very strong and muscular – but undoubtedly he had an evil face. He scowled, as though he were vexed to be interrupted, and with an odd and angry gesture of the hand he stepped quickly within the wood and disappeared. Paullinus felt in his mind that the man wished him evil, and went on his way somewhat heavily. And now the sun began to go down and it was darker than ever in the forest; Paullinus came to a place where the road forked, and thinking over his note of the way, struck off to the left, but as he did so he felt a certain misgiving which he could not explain. He now began to hurry, for the light failed every moment, and the colour was soon gone out of the grass beneath his feet, leaving all a dark and indistinguishable brown. Soon the path forked again, and then came a road striking across the one that he had pursued of which he did not think he had been told. He went straight forward, but it was now grown so dark that he could no longer see his way, and stumbled very sadly along the wet path, feeling with his hand for the trees. He thought that he must by this time have gone much further than the distance between the villages, and it was clear to him that he had somehow missed the road.

He at last determined that he would try to return, and went slowly back the way that he had come, till at last the night came down upon him. Then Paullinus was struck with a great fear. There were wolves in those forests he knew, though they lived in the unvisited depths of the wood and came not near the habitations of men unless they were fierce with famine. But he had heard several times a strange snarling cry some way off in the wood, and once or twice he had thought he was being softly followed. So he determined to go no further, but to climb up into a tree, if he could find one, and there to spend an uneasy night.

He felt about for some time, but could discover nothing but small saplings, when he suddenly saw through the trees a light shine, and it came across him that he had stumbled as it were by accident upon the village. So he went forward slowly towards the light – there was no track here – often catching his feet among brambles and low plants, till the gloom lifted somewhat and he felt a freer air, and saw that he was in a clearing in the wood. Then he discerned, in front of him, a

space of deeper darkness against the sky, what he thought to be the
outline of the roofs of buildings; then the light shone out of a
window near the ground; but presently he came to a stop, for he saw
the light flash and gleam in the ripples of a water that lay in his path
and blocked his way.

Then he called aloud once or twice; something seemed to stir in
the house, and presently the light in the window was obscured by the
head and shoulders of a man, who pressed to the opening; but there
was no answer. Then Paullinus spoke very clearly, and said that he
was a Roman, a traveller who had lost his way. Then a harsh voice
told him to walk round the water to the left and wait awhile; which
Paullinus did.

Soon he heard steps come out of the house and come to the water's
edge. Then he heard sounds as though someone were walking on a
hollow board – then with a word of warning there fell the end of a
plank near him on the bank, and he was bidden to come across. He
did so, though the bridge was narrow and he was half afraid of
falling; but in a moment he was at the other side, a dark figure beside
him. He was bidden to wait again, and the figure went out over the
water and seemed to pull in the plank that had served as a bridge; and
then the man returned and bade him to come forward. Paullinus
followed the figure, and in a moment he could see the dark eaves of a
long, low house before him, very rudely but strongly built; then a
door was opened showing a lighted room within, and he was bidden
to step forward and enter.

He found himself in a large, bare chamber, the walls and ceiling of
a dark wood. A pine torch flared and dripped in a socket. There were
one or two rough seats and a table spread with a meal. At the end of
the room there were some bricks piled for a fireplace with charred
ashes and a smouldering log among them, for though it was still
summer the nights began to be brisk. On the walls hung some
implements; a spade and a hoe, a spear, a sword, some knives and
javelins. He that inhabited it seemed to be part a tiller of the soil and
part a huntsman; but there were other things of which Paullinus
could not guess the use – hooks and pronged forks. There were skins
of beasts on the floor, and on the ceiling hung bundles of herbs and
dried meats. The air was pungent with pine-smoke. He recognised
the man at once as the same that he had seen beside the pool; and he
looked to Paullinus even stranger and more dangerous than he had
seemed before. He seemed too to be on his guard against some
terror, and held in his hand a club, as though he were ready to use it.

Presently he said a few words in a harsh voice: 'You are a Roman,' he asked; 'how may I know it?' 'I do not know,' said Paullinus, trying to smile, 'unless you will believe my word.' 'What is your business here?' said the man; 'are you a merchant?' 'No,' said Paullinus, 'I have no business, I travel, and I talk with those I meet – perhaps I am a teacher – a Christian teacher.' At this the man's sternness seemed a little to relax. 'Oh, the new faith?' he said, rather contemptuously; 'well, I have heard of it – and it will never spread; but I am curious to know what it really is, and you shall tell me of it.' But suddenly his angry terrors came upon him again, and he said, with a frown, 'But where were you bound, and whence come you?'

Paullinus, with such calmness as he could muster, for he felt himself to be in some danger, he scarcely knew what, mentioned the names of the villages. 'Well, you have missed your way,' said the man. 'Why did you come here to the Temple of Death?' Paullinus had a sudden access of dread at the words. 'Is this the Temple?' he said; 'it is the place I was bidden to avoid.' At this the man gave a fearful kind of smile, like a flash of lightning out of a sombre cloud, and he said, with a certain dark pride, 'Ay, there are few that come willingly; but now you must abide with me tonight – unless,' he added, with a savage look, 'you have a mind to be eaten by wolves.' 'I will certainly stay,' said Paullinus, 'I am not afraid – I serve a very mighty God myself, who guards his servants if they guard themselves.' 'Ay, does He?' said the man, with a flash of anger, 'then He must needs be strong – but I wish you no evil,' he added in a moment. 'I think you are a brave man, perhaps a good one – I fear you not.' 'There is no need for you to fear me,' said Paullinus, 'my God is a God of peace and love – and indeed,' he added with a smile, looking at the man's great frame, 'I should have thought there was little need for you to fear anyone.' This last word seemed to dissolve the man's evil mood all at once, for he put away the club he held, in a corner of the room, and bade Paullinus eat and drink, which he did gladly. The meat was a strongly flavoured kind of venison, and there was a rough bread, and a drink that seemed both sweet and strong, and had the taste of summer flowers. He praised the food, and the man said to him, 'Ay, I have learnt to suit it to my taste. I live here in much loneliness, and there is none to help me.'

After the meal the man asked him to tell him something of the new faith, and Paullinus very willingly told him as simply as he could of the Way of Christ.

The man listened with a sort of gloomy attention. 'So it is this,' he said at last, 'which is taking hold of the world! Well, it is pretty enough – a good faith for such as live in ease and security, for women and children in fair houses; but it suits not with these forests. The god who made these great lonely woods, and who dwells in them, is very different' – he rose and made a strange obeisance as he talked. 'He loves death and darkness, and the cries of strong and furious beasts. There is little peace here, for all that the woods are still – and as for love, it is of a brutish sort. Nay, stranger, the gods of these lands are very different; and they demand very different sacri-fices. They delight in sharp woes and agonies, in grinding pains, in dripping blood and death-sweats and cries of despair. If these woods were all cut down, and the land ploughed up, and peaceful folk lived here in quiet fields and farms, then perhaps your simple, easy-going God might come and dwell with them – but now, if he came, he would flee in terror.'

'Nay,' said Paullinus, but somewhat sadly, for the man's words seemed to have a fearful truth about them, 'the Father waits long and is kind; the victory of love is slow, but it is sure.'

'It is slow enough!' said the man; 'these forests have grown here beyond the memory of man, and they will stand long after you and I have been turned to a handful of dust – and so I will serve my gods while I live. But you are weary,' he added, 'and may sleep; fear not any hurt from me; and as for the way you speak of, well, I will say that I should be content if it had the victory. I am sick at heart of the hard rule of these gods – but I fear them, and will serve them faithfully till I die.'

And then he brought some skins of beasts and heaped them in a corner of the room for Paullinus, who lay down gladly, and from mere weariness fell asleep. But the priest sat long before the fire in thought; and twice he went to the door and looked out, as if he were waiting for some tidings.

Once the opening of the door aroused Paullinus; and he saw the dark figure of the priest stand in the doorway, and over his head and shoulders a dark still night, pierced with golden stars; and once again, when he opened the door a second time, the pure gush of air into the close room woke Paullinus from a deep sleep; again he saw the priest stand silent in the door, with his hands clasped behind him; and through the door Paullinus could see the dim ring of dewy woods, that seemed to sleep in quiet dreams; and over the woods a great pale light of dawn that was coming slowly up out of the east.

But Paullinus fell back into sleep again from utter weariness, as a man might dive into a pool. And when at last he opened his eyes, he saw that day was come with an infinite sweetness and freshness; the birds called faintly in the thickets; and the priest was going slowly about his daily task, preparing food; and Paullinus, from where he lay, smiled at him, and the priest smiled back, as though half ashamed, and presently said, 'You have slept deeply, sir; and to sleep as you have done shows that a man is brave and innocent.'

Then Paullinus rose, and would have helped him, but the man said, 'Nay, you are my guest; and besides, I do things in a certain order, as all do who live alone, and I would not have anyone to meddle with me.' He spoke gruffly, but there was a certain courtesy in his manner.

Presently the priest asked him to come and eat, and they sat together eating in a friendly way. The priest was silent, but Paullinus talked of many things – and at last the priest said, 'I thought I loved my loneliness, but it seems that I am pleased to have a companion. I believe,' he added, 'that I would be content if you would dwell with me.' And Paullinus smiled in answer, and said, 'Ay, it is not good to live alone.'

A little while after Paullinus said that he must set out on his way, and that he was very grateful for so gentle a welcome; but the priest said, 'Nay, but you must see the sights of my house and of the temple. Few folk have seen it, and never a foreign man. It is not a merry place,' he added, 'but it will do to make a traveller's tale.'

So he led him to the door, and they went out. Paullinus saw that the house where he had spent the night stood on a little square island, with a deep moat all round it, filled with water; the island was all overgrown with bushes and tall plants, except that in one place there were some pens where sheep and goats were kept; and a path led down to the landing-place where he had crossed it the night before. But what at once seized and held the eyes and mind of Paullinus was the temple. He thought he had never seen so grim a place; it rose above the bushes and above the house. It was of very rough stone, all blank of windows, with a roof of stone; the blocks were very large, and Paullinus wondered how they had been brought there. In front there was a low door, and over it a hideous carving, that seemed to Paullinus to be the work of devils. Apart from the temple, rising among the bushes, stood a rude sculptured figure, with a leering evil face, very roughly but vigorously cut, with an arm raised as though beckoning people to the temple. This

figure, of a kind of reddish stone, seemed horrible beyond words to
Paullinus. It seemed to him like a servant of Satan, if not Satan
himself, frozen into stone.

The priest looked at Paullinus, who could not help showing his
horror, with a kind of pride. Then he said, 'Will you go further?
Will you enter the temple with me, and see what is therein? Perhaps you will after all bow your head to the gods of the forest.' And
Paullinus said, 'Yes, I will go,' and he said a silent prayer to the
Lord Christ that He would guard him well. Another path paved
with stone led from the landing-place to the temple, along which
they went slowly, the priest leading. Arrived at the door, the priest
made another strange obeisance, lifting his hands slowly above his
head and closing his eyes; then he opened the door into the temple
itself. There came out a foul and heavy smell that shuddered in the
nostrils of Paullinus and left him gasping somewhat for breath. The
priest looked at him with a sort of curious wonder, which made
Paullinus determine to go further.

The temple itself was large and dark, a sickly light only filtering in
through a hole in the roof. The floor was paved, and the roof was
supported by great wooden columns, the trunks of large forest trees.
The greater part of the building was shut off by a large wooden
screen, about the height of a man, close to them, so that they stood
in a kind of vestibule. The whole of the building, walls, roof, and
floor, had been painted at some time or other a black colour, which
was now faded and looked a dark slatey grey. Over the screen in
the centre was seen the head of what seemed an image, very great
and horrible. The light, which came from an opening immediately
above the image, showed a horned and bearded head, misshapen and
grotesque. Possibly at another time and place Paullinus might have
smiled at the ugly thing; but here, peering at them over the screen, in
the fetid gloom, it froze the blood in his veins.

And now behind the screen were strange sounds as well, a kind of
heavy breathing or snorting, and what seemed the scratching of
some beast. The priest went up to the screen and opened a sort of
panel in it; this was followed by a hoarse and hideous outcry within,
half of fear and half of rage. The priest took from an angle of the
wall a long pole shod with iron, and leaned within the opening,
saying in a stern tone some words that Paullinus did not understand. Presently the noises ceased, and the priest, using a great
effort, seemed to pull or push at something with the pole, and there
was the sound as of a great gate turning on its hinges. Then he drew

his head and arms out, and said to Paullinus, 'We may enter.' He then threw a door open in the middle of the screen and went in. Paullinus followed.

In front of them stood a great statue on a pedestal; the figure of a thing, half-man half-goat, crouched as though to spring. The smell was still more horrible within, and it became clear to Paullinus that he was in the lair of some ravenous and filthy beast. There lay a mess of bones underneath the statue. To the left, in the wall, there was a strong oaken door, made like a portcullis, which seemed to close the entrance of a den; something seemed to move and stir in the blackness, and Paullinus heard the sound of heavy breathing within. The priest, still holding the pole in his hand, led the way round to the back of the statue. Here, set into the wall, were a number of stone slabs, with what seemed to be a name upon each, rudely carved.

The priest pointed to these and said, 'Those are the names of the priests of this shrine. And now,' he went on, 'I will tell you a thing which is in my mind – I know not why I should wish to say it – but it seems to me that I have a great desire to tell you all and keep nothing back; and I tell you this, though you may turn from me with shame and horror. We have a law that if a man be condemned to death for a certain crime – if he have slain one of his kin – he is bound to a tree in the forest to be devoured piecemeal by the wolves. But if there seem to be cause or excuse for the deed that he has done, then he is allowed to purchase his life on one condition – he may come to this place and slay the priest who serves here, if he can, or himself be slain. And if he slay him he reigns in his stead until he himself be slain. And the rites of this place are these: all of this tribe who may be guilty of the slaying of a man by secret or open violence without due cause are offered here as sacrifice to the god – and that is the task that I have done and must do till I am myself slain. And here in a den dwells a savage beast – I know not its name and its age is very great – that slays and devours the guilty. What wonder if a man's heart grows dark and cruel here; I can only look into my own heart, black as it is, and wonder that it is not blacker. But the gods are good to me, and have not cursed me utterly.

'And now I will tell you that when I saw you by the pool, and when you called to me in the night, I thought that perchance you had come to slay me – and then I saw that you were alone, and not guarded as a prisoner would be; but even then my heart was dark, because the god has had no sacrifice for many a month, and seems to call upon me for a victim – so I had it in my heart to slay you here. And now,' he said, 'I have opened the door of my heart, and you have seen all that is to be seen.'

And then he looked upon Paullinus as if to know his judgment; and Paullinus, turning to the priest, and seeing that in his heart he desired what was better, and abode not willingly in the ways of death, said, 'Brother, with all my heart I am sorry for you – and I would have you turn your heart away from these dark and evil gods – who are indeed, I think, the very spirits of hell – and turn to the Father of mercy of whom I spoke, with whom there is forgiveness and love for all His sons, when once they turn to Him and ask His help.'

The priest looked very gently at Paullinus as he spoke; but there came a horrible roaring out of the den, and the beast flung himself against the bars as if in rage.

Then the priest said, 'For twenty years I have heard no speech like this; for twenty years I have lived with death and done wickedness, and all men turn from me with fear and loathing, and speak not any word to me: I have never looked in a kindly human eye, nor felt the hand of a friend within my own. Judge between me and my sin. I had a brother, an evil man, who made it his pleasure to trouble me. I was stronger than he, and he feared me. I loved a maiden of our tribe, and she loved me; and when my brother knew it he went about to do her a hurt, that it might grieve me. One day she went through the forest alone, and never returned, and I, in madness ranging the wood to find her, found the mangled bones of her body. I knew it by the poor torn hair – she had been devoured by wolves – but burying the bones I saw that the feet were tied together with a cord, and then I knew that someone had bound her by violence and left her to be devoured.

'Then as I returned from burying her, I came upon my brother in a glade of the wood; and he looked upon me with an evil smile, and said, "Hast thou found her?" And I knew in my heart what he had done, and I slew him where he stood – and then I returned and said what I had done. Then they imprisoned me – for my brother was older than myself, and my enemies said that I had done it to win his inheritance – and at last, after long consulting, they gave me the choice to be devoured of wolves or to become the priest of Death. I chose the latter, because I was mad and hated all mankind. I came to this place at sundown, and my guards left me. I swam the ditch, and knocked at the priest's door; he was an old man and piteous, who abhorred his trade – and there I seized him and slew him with my hands – he was weak and made no resistance – and I flung his body to the beast and carved his name. That is my bitter story – and since then I have lived, accursed and dreaded. These gods are hard taskmasters.' He made a wild gesture of the hand and turned his bright eyes upon Paullinus, who stood aghast.

'The tale is told,' said the priest. 'I who have kept silence all these years have babbled my story to a stranger. Why did I tell you? I thought that with all your talk of mercy and forgiveness you might have a message for my bitter and tired heart – but you shrink from me, and are silent.'

'Nay,' said Paullinus, 'shrink from you! – not so – nay, I cling to you more than ever; come and claim your part in the forgiveness that waits for all – you have suffered, you have repented – and the God whom I serve has comfort and peace for you and for all; His love is wide and deep – claim your share in it.' And he took the priest's hand in both of his own.

There was a horrible roaring behind them as they stood: the great beast behind them struck at the bars, but the priest took no heed.

'If I could,' he said, with his eyes fixed on Paullinus' face.

'Nay then,' said Paullinus, 'if you would it is done already, for He reads the very secrets of the heart.'

There broke out a loud fierce crashing sound behind them; the great oaken gate heaved and splintered, and a monstrous beast as huge as a horse appeared at the mouth of the den; his small head was laid back on his hairy shoulders, his little eyes gleamed wickedly, and his red mouth opened snarling fiercely. The priest turned, and met the rush of the beast full. In a moment he was flung to the ground with a dreadful rending sound. 'Save yourself!' he cried. The huge brute glared, with his foot upon the fallen form, and seemed to hesitate whether to attack his second foe. Paullinus, hardly knowing what he did, seized the great iron-pointed pole, and with a firmness of strength which he had not known himself to possess drove it full into the monster's great throat as it opened its mouth towards him. It made a wild and sickening cry; it raised one foot as though to strike, then it beat the air and struck once at the head of the prostrate form; then, with a gurgling sound, spitting out a flood of hot blood, it collapsed, rolled slowly on one side. Paullinus, watching it intently and still holding the pole, thrust it further in with all his might. It quivered all over, and in a moment lay still. Paullinus made haste to drag the priest out from beneath – but he saw that all was over; the last blow of the beast had battered in the skull – and besides that the body was horribly mangled and crushed. The limbs of the priest were heavy and relaxed; his hands were folded together as though in prayer, and he drew one or two little fluttering breaths, but never opened his eyes.

Paullinus was like one in a dream at this sudden horror; but he kept his senses; once or twice the great beast moved, and drummed on the pavement with a horny paw. So Paullinus drew the prostrate body of the priest outside the screen and closed the door. Then he went with swift steps out of the temple and to the water's edge; he drew up a little water in his hand, looking into the dark and cool moat. Then he came back with a purpose in his mind. He sprinkled the water on the poor mangled brow; and then, choosing the name of the Apostle whom Jesus most loved, he said, 'John, I baptize thee, *in nomine*, &c.' It was like a prisoner's release; the straining hands relaxed, and with a sigh the new-made Christian presently died. 'I doubt I have done right,' said Paullinus to himself. 'He was coming to the Saviour very swiftly, and I think was at His feet; and if he was not in heart a Christian, the Lord will know when he meets Him in the heavenly places.'

When Paullinus went back to the hut he found a rough mattock. First he dug a great hole; the earth was black and soft, and water oozed soon into the depths; then with much painful labour he dragged the great beast thither, and covered him in from the eye of day; and then he toiled to dig a grave for the priest – once he stopped to eat a little food, but he worked with unusual ease and lightness. But the night came down on the forest as he finished the grave – for he did not wish that the priest should lie within the dreadful temple.

Then he went back, very weary but not sad; his terrors and distresses had drawn slowly off from his mind, as he worked in the still afternoon, under the clear sky, all surrounded by woods; the earth seemed like one who had come from a bath, washed through and through by the drench of wholesome rains, and the smell of the woods was sharp and sweet.

Paullinus slept quietly that night, feeling very close to God; but in the morning, when the dawn was coming up, he was awakened by a shouting outside. His sleep had been so deep and still that he hardly knew at first where he was, but it all came swiftly back to him; and then the shouting was repeated. Paullinus rose to his feet and went slowly out.

On the edge of the water, where the causeway crossed it, he saw two men standing, that from their dress seemed to be great chiefs.

Behind them, with his hands bound, and attached by a rope held in the hand of one of the chiefs, was a young man of a wild and fierce aspect, in the dress of a serf, a rough tunic and leggings. His head was bare, and he looked around him in dismay, like a beast in a trap. Behind, at the edge of the clearing, stood four soldiers silent, with bows strung and arrows fitted to the string. Over the whole group there seemed to be the shadow of a stern purpose. At the appearance of Paullinus, the two chiefs hurriedly bent together in talk, and looked at him with astonishment. Paullinus came down to the water's edge, when one of the chiefs said, 'We have come for the priest; where is he? For he must do his office upon this man, who hath slain one of his kin by stealth.'

'It is too late,' said Paullinus; 'he is dead, and waits for burial.'

Then the chiefs seemed again to confer together, and one of them, with a strange reverence, said, 'Then you are the new priest of the temple? And yet it seems strange, for you are not of our nation.'

'Nay,' said Paullinus, 'I am a wanderer, a Roman. It was not I who slew him – it was the great beast who lived in the den yonder; and the beast have I slain – but come over and let me tell you all the tale.'

So he made haste to put out the bridge, and the two chiefs came over in silence, leaving the prisoner in the hands of the guards who surrounded him. Paullinus led them to the temple, which he could hardly prevail upon them to enter, and showed them the dead body, which was a fearful sight enough; then he showed them the broken gate and the empty den, and then he led them to the mound where the beast lay buried, and offered if they would to uncover the body. 'Nay, we would not see him,' said the elder chief in a low voice; 'it is enough.'

Paullinus then led them to the hut and told them the story from beginning to end. The chiefs looked at him with surprise when he told them of the beast's death, and one of them said, 'I doubt, sir, you slew him by Roman magic – for he was exceedingly strong, and you look not much of a warrior.' 'Nay,' said Paullinus, smiling, 'I doubt he was his own death, as is often the end of evil – he leapt upon the pole: I did but hold it, and the Lord made my hand strong.'

When he had done the story the chiefs spoke together a little in a low tone. Then one of them said, 'This is a strange tale, sir. And it seems to us that you must be a man whom the gods love, for you stayed here a night with the priest – who was a fierce man and no friend of strangers – and received no hurt. And then you have slain the Hound of Death, unarmed. But we will ask you to go with us, for we cannot decide so grave a matter until we have taken counsel with our tribe. Be assured that you shall be used courteously.'

'I will go very willingly,' said Paullinus. 'My God did indeed send me hither to do a work which He had prepared for me to do, and I would serve His will in all things.'

So they first buried the body of the priest in his grave, and then they went together to the village, and messages were sent to the chiefs of the tribe, who came in haste, ten great warriors; and they sat and debated long in low voices. And Paullinus sat without wondering that he could feel so calm, for he knew that he was in jeopardy.

So when they had talked a long while they called Paullinus into the council, and the oldest chief, an ancient warrior with silver hair, much bowed with age, told him that they saw that he was a man favoured of God. 'I hide it not from you,' he said, 'that some of my brethren here would have it that death should be your portion, because you have meddled with sacred and secret things. But I think that it is clear that you have done no wrong, or otherwise you would have been slain; you spoke but now of the God you serve, and we would hear of Him; for now that the priest is dead and the beast dead, we say with reverence that a cloud is lifted from us, and that we have served dark gods too long.'

So Paullinus spoke of the Father's love and the coming of the Saviour on to the earth; and when he had finished the chiefs thanked him very courteously, and then they asked him to abide with them and speak again of the matter. So Paullinus abode there and made many friends, as his manner was.

Then came a day when the chiefs again held council, and they told Paullinus that if he would, he should be the priest of the temple and teach what he would there, and that the temple should be cleansed; and they said that they would not ask him to be the slayer of such as had killed a man, for that, they said, seems to belong rather to a warrior than a priest.

So Paullinus said that he would abide with them, but that he must first go and be made a priest after his own order; and he departed, but soon returned, and the Temple of Death was made a Church of Christians.

Paullinus is an old man now; you may see him walk at evening beside the water, under the shadow of the church. The images have been broken and defaced; but Paullinus often stops beside a mound, and thinks of the bones of the great beast that lie whitening below – and then he stands beside a grave which bears the name of John, and knows that his brother, that did evil in the days of his ignorance, but that suffered sore, will be the first to meet him in the heavenly country, with the light of God about him; 'and perhaps,' says Paullinus to himself, 'he will bear a palm in his hand.'

The Closed Window

A. C. BENSON

The Tower of Nort stood in a deep angle of the downs; formerly an old road led over the hill, but it is now a green track covered with turf; the later highway choosing rather to cross a low saddle of the ridge, for the sake of the beasts of burden. The tower, originally built to guard the great road, was a plain, strong, thick-walled fortress. To the tower had been added a plain and seemly house, where the young Sir Mark de Nort lived very easily and plentifully. To the south stretched the great wood of Nort, but the Tower stood high on an elbow of the down, sheltered from the north by the great green hills. The villagers had an odd ugly name for the Tower, which they called the Tower of Fear; but the name was falling into disuse, and was only spoken, and that heedlessly, by ancient men, because Sir Mark was vexed to hear it so called. Sir Mark was not yet thirty, and had begun to say that he must marry a wife; but he seemed in no great haste to do so, and loved his easy, lonely life, with plenty of hunting and hawking on the down. With him lived his cousin and heir, Roland Ellice, a heedless good-tempered man, a few years older than Sir Mark; he had come on a visit to Sir Mark, when he first took possession of the Tower; and there had seemed no reason why he should go away; the two suited each other; Sir Mark was sparing of speech, fond of books and of rhymes. Roland was different, loving ease and wine and talk, and finding in Mark a good listener. Mark loved his cousin, and thought it praise-worthy of him to stay and help to cheer so sequestered a house, since there were few neighbours within reach.

And yet Mark was not wholly content with his easy life; there were many days when he asked himself why he should go thus quietly on, day by day, like a stalled ox; still, there appeared no reason why he should do otherwise; there were but few folk on his land, and they were content; yet he sometimes envied them their bondage and their round of daily duties. The only place where he could else have been was with the army, or even with the Court; but Sir Mark was no soldier, and even less of a courtier; he hated tedious gaiety, and it was a time of peace. So because he loved solitude and quiet he lived at home, and sometimes thought himself but half a man; yet was he happy after a sort, but for a kind of little hunger of the heart.

What gave the Tower so dark a name was the memory of old Sir James de Nort, Mark's grandfather, an evil and secret man, who had dwelt at Nort under some strange shadow; he had driven his son from his doors, and lived at the end of his life with his books and his own close thoughts, spying upon the stars and tracing strange figures in books; since his death the old room in the turret top, where he came by his end in a dreadful way, had been closed; it was entered by a turret-door, with a flight of steps from the chamber below. It had four windows, one to each of the winds; but the window which looked upon the down was fastened up, and secured with a great shutter of oak.

One day of heavy rain, Roland, being wearied of doing nothing, and vexed because Mark sat so still in a great chair, reading in a book, said to his cousin at last that he must go and visit the old room, in which he had never set foot. Mark closed his book, and smiling indulgently at Roland's restlessness, rose, stretching himself, and got the key; and together they went up the turret stairs. The key groaned loudly in the lock, and, when the door was thrown back, there appeared a high faded room, with a timbered roof, and with a close, dull smell. Round the walls were presses, with the doors fast; a large oak table, with a chair beside it, stood in the middle. The walls were otherwise bare and rough; the spiders had spun busily over the windows and in the angles. Roland was full of questions, and Mark told him all he had heard of old Sir James and his silent ways, but said that he knew nothing of the disgrace that had seemed to envelop him, or of the reasons why he had so evil a name. Roland said that he thought it a shame that so fair a room should lie so nastily, and pulled one of the casements open, when a sharp gust broke into the room, with so angry a burst of rain, that he closed it again in haste; little by little, as they talked, a shadow began to fall upon their spirits, till Roland declared that there was still a blight upon the place; and Mark told him of the death of old Sir James, who had been found after a day of silence, when he had not set foot outside his chamber, lying on the floor of the room, strangely bedabbled with wet and mud, as though he had come off a difficult journey, speechless, and with a look of anguish on his face; and that he had died soon after they had found him, muttering words that no-one understood. Then the two young men drew near to the closed window; the shutters were tightly barred, and across the panels was scrawled in red, in an uncertain hand, the words CLAUDIT ET NEMO APERIT, which Mark explained was the Latin for the text, *He shutteth and none openeth*. And then Mark said that the story went that it was ill for the man that opened the window, and that shut it should remain for him. But Roland girded at him for his want of curiosity, and had laid a hand upon the bar as though to open it, but Mark forbade him urgently. 'Nay,' said he, 'let it remain so – we must not meddle with the will of the dead!' and as he said the word, there came so furious a gust upon the windows that it seemed as though some stormy thing would beat them open; so they left the room together, and presently descending, found the sun struggling through the rain.

But both Mark and Roland were sad and silent all that day; for though they spake not of it, there was a desire in their minds to open the closed window, and to see what would befall; in Roland's mind it was like the desire of a child to peep into what is forbidden; but in Mark's mind a sort of shame to be so bound by an old and weak tale of superstition.

Now it seemed to Mark, for many days, that the visit to the turret-room had brought a kind of shadow down between them. Roland was peevish and ill-at-ease; and ever the longing grew upon Mark, so strongly that it seemed to him that something drew him to the room, some beckoning of a hand or calling of a voice.

Now one bright and sunshiny morning it happened that Mark was left alone within the house. Roland had ridden out early, not saying where he was bound. And Mark sat, more listlessly than was his wont, and played with the ears of his great dog, that sat with his head upon his master's knee, looking at him with liquid eyes, and doubt-less wondering why Mark went not abroad.

Suddenly Sir Mark's eye fell upon the key of the upper room, which lay on the window-ledge where he had thrown it; and the desire to go up and pluck the heart from the little mystery came upon him with a strength that he could not resist; he rose twice and took up the key, and fingering it doubtfully, laid it down again; then suddenly he took it up, and went swiftly into the turret-stair, and up, turning, turning, till his head was dizzy with the bright peeps of the world through the loophole windows. Now all was green, where a window gave on the down; and now it was all clear air and sun, the warm breeze coming pleasantly into the cold stairway; presently Mark heard the pattering of feet on the stair below, and knew that the old hound had determined to follow him; and he waited a moment at the door, half pleased, in his strange mood, to have the company of a living thing. So when the dog was at his side, he stayed no longer, but opened the door and stepped within the room.

The room, for all its faded look, had a strange air about it, and though he could not say why, Mark felt that he was surely expected. He did not hesitate, but walked to the shutter and considered it for a moment; he heard a sound behind him. It was the old hound who sat with his head aloft, sniffing the air uneasily; Mark called him and held out his hand, but the hound would not move; he wagged his tail as though to acknowledge that he was called, and then he returned to his uneasy quest. Mark watched him for a moment, and saw that the old dog had made up his mind that all was not well in the room, for he lay down, gathering his legs under him, on the threshold, and watched his master with frightened eyes, quivering visibly. Mark, no lighter of heart, and in a kind of fearful haste, pulled the great staple off the shutter and set it on the ground, and then wrenched the shutters back; the space revealed was largely filled by old and dusty webs of spiders, which Mark lightly tore down, using the staple of the shutters to do this; it was with a strange shock of surprise that he saw that the window was dark, or nearly so; it seemed as though there were some further obstacle outside; yet Mark knew that from below the leaded panes of the window were visible. He drew back for a moment, but, unable to restrain his curiosity, wrenched the rusted casement open. But still all was dark without; and there came in a gust of icy wind from outside; it was as though something had passed him swiftly, and he heard the old hound utter a strangled howl; then turning, he saw him spring to his feet with his hair bristling and his teeth bare, and next moment the dog turned and leapt out of the room.

Mark, left alone, tried to curb a tide of horror that swept through his veins; he looked round at the room, flooded with the southerly sunlight, and then he turned again to the dark window, and putting a strong constraint upon himself, leaned out, and saw a thing which bewildered him so strangely that he thought for a moment his senses had deserted him. He looked out on a lonely dim hillside, covered with rocks and stones; the hill came up close to the window, so that he could have jumped down upon it, the wall below seeming to be built into the rocks. It was all dark and silent, like a clouded night, with a faint light coming from whence he could not see. The hill sloped away very steeply from the tower, and he seemed to see a plain beyond, where at the same time he knew that the down ought to lie.

In the plain there was a light, like the firelit window of a house; a little below him some shape like a crouching man seemed to run and slip among the stones, as though suddenly surprised, and seeking to escape. Side by side with a deadly fear which began to invade his heart, came an uncontrollable desire to leap down among the rocks; and then it seemed to him that the figure below stood upright, and began to beckon him. There came over him a sense that he was in deadly peril; and, like a man on the edge of a precipice, who has just enough will left to try to escape, he drew himself by main force away from the window, closed it, put the shutters back, replaced the staple, and, his limbs all trembling, crept out of the room, feeling along the walls like a palsied man. He locked the door, and then, his terror overpowering him, he fled down the turret-stairs. Hardly thinking what he did, he came out on the court, and going to the great well that stood in the centre of the yard, he went to it and flung the key down, hearing it clink on the sides as it fell. Even then he dared not re-enter the house, but glanced up and down, gazing about him, while the cloud of fear and horror by insensible degrees dispersed, leaving him weak and melancholy.

Presently Roland returned, full of talk, but broke off to ask if Mark were ill. Mark, with a kind of surliness, an unusual mood for him, denied it somewhat sharply. Roland raised his eyebrows, and said no more, but prattled on. Presently after a silence he said to Mark, 'What did you do all the morning?' and it seemed to Mark as though this were accompanied with a spying look. An unreasonable anger seized him. 'What does it matter to you what I did?' he said. 'May not I do what I like in my own house?'

'Doubtless,' said Roland, and sate silent with uplifted brows; then he hummed a tune, and presently went out.

They sate at dinner that evening with long silences, contrary to their wont, though Mark bestirred himself to ask questions. When they were left alone, Mark stretched out his hand to Roland, saying, 'Roland, forgive me! I spoke to you this morning in a way of which I am ashamed; we have lived so long together – and yet we came nearer to quarrelling today than we have ever done before; and it was my fault.'

Roland smiled, and held Mark's hand for a moment. 'Oh, I had not given it another thought,' he said; 'the wonder is that you can bear with an idle fellow as you do.' Then they talked for a while with the pleasant glow of friendliness that two good comrades feel when they have been reconciled. But late in the evening Roland said, 'Was there any story, Mark, about your grandfather's leaving any treasure of money behind him?'

The question grated somewhat unpleasantly upon Mark's mood; but he controlled himself and said, 'No, none that I know of – except that he found the estate rich and left it poor – and what he did with his revenues no-one knows – you had better ask the old men of the village; they know more about the house than I do. But, Roland, forgive me once more if I say that I do not desire Sir James's name to be mentioned between us. I wish we had not entered his room; I do not know how to express it, but it seems to me as though he had sate there, waiting quietly to be summoned, and as though we had troubled him, and – as though he had joined us. I think he was an evil man, close and evil. And there hangs in my mind a verse of Scripture, where Samuel said to the witch, "Why hast thou disquieted me to bring me up?" Oh,' he went on, 'I do not know why I talk wildly thus'; for he saw that Roland was looking at him with astonishment, with parted lips; 'but a shadow has fallen upon me, and there seems evil abroad.'

From that day forward a heaviness lay on the spirit of Mark that could not be scattered. He felt, he said to himself, as though he had meddled lightheartedly with something far deeper and more danger-ous than he had supposed – like a child that has aroused some evil beast that slept. He had dark dreams too. The figure that he had seen among the rocks seemed to peep and beckon him, with a mocking smile, over perilous places, where he followed unwilling. But the heavier he grew the lighter-hearted Roland became; he seemed to walk in some bright vision of his own, intent upon a large and gracious design.

One day he came into the hall in the morning, looking so radiant that Mark asked him half-enviously what he had to make him so glad. 'Glad,' said Roland, 'oh, I know it! Merry dreams, perhaps. What do you think of a good grave fellow who beckons me on with a brisk smile, and shows me places, wonderful places, under banks and in woodland pits, where riches lie piled together? I am sure that some good fortune is preparing for me, Mark – but you shall share it.' Then Mark, seeing in his words a certain likeness, with a difference, to his own dark visions, pressed his lips together and sate looking stonily before him.

At last, one still evening of spring, when the air was intolerably languid and heavy for mankind, but full of sweet promises for trees and hidden peeping things, though a lurid redness of secret thunder had lain all day among the heavy clouds in the plain, the two dined together. Mark had walked alone that day, and had lain upon the turf of the down, fighting against a weariness that seemed to be poisoning the very springs of life within him. But Roland had been brisk and alert, coming and going upon some secret and busy errand, with a fragment of a song upon his lips, like a man preparing to set off for a far country, who is glad to be gone. In the evening, after they had dined, Roland had let his fancy rove in talk. 'If we were rich,' he said, 'how we would transform this old place!'

'It is fair enough for me,' said Mark heavily; and Roland had chidden him lightly for his sombre ways, and sketched new plans of life.

Mark, wearied and yet excited, with an intolerable heaviness of spirit, went early to bed, leaving Roland in the hall. After a short and broken sleep, he awoke, and lighting a candle, read idly and gloomily to pass the heavy hours. The house seemed full of strange noises that night. Once or twice came a scraping and a faint hammering in the wall; light footsteps seemed to pass in the turret – but the tower was always full of noises, and Mark heeded them not; at last he fell asleep again, to be suddenly awakened by a strange and desolate crying, that came he knew not whence, but seemed to wail upon the air. The old dog, who slept in Mark's room, heard it too; he was sitting up in a fearful expectancy. Mark rose in haste, and taking the candle, went into the passage that led to Roland's room. It was empty, but a light burned there and showed that the room had not been slept in. Full of a horrible fear, Mark returned, and went in hot haste up the turret steps, fear and anxiety struggling together in his mind. When he reached the top, he found the little door broken forcibly open, and a light within. He cast a haggard look round the room, and then the crying came again, this time very faint and desolate.

Mark cast a shuddering glance at the window; it was wide open and showed a horrible liquid blackness; round the bar in the centre that divided the casements, there was something knotted. He hastened to the window, and saw that it was a rope, which hung heavily. Leaning out he saw that something dangled from the rope below him – and then came the crying again out of the darkness, like the crying of a lost spirit.

He could see as in a bitter dream the outline of the hateful hillside; but there seemed to his disordered fancy to be a tumult of some kind below; pale lights moved about, and he saw a group of forms which scattered like a shoal of fish when he leaned out. He knew that he was looking upon a scene that no mortal eye ought to behold, and it seemed to him at the moment as though he was staring straight into hell.

The rope went down among the rocks and disappeared; but Mark clenched it firmly and using all his strength, which was great, drew it up hand over hand; as he drew it up he secured it in loops round the great oak table; he began to be afraid that his strength would not hold out, and once when he returned to the window after securing a loop, a great hooded thing like a bird flew noiselessly at the window and beat its wings.

Presently he saw that the form which dangled on the rope was clear of the rocks below; it had come up through them, as though they were but smoke; and then his task seemed to him more sore than ever. Inch by painful inch he drew it up, working fiercely and silently; his muscles were tense, and drops stood on his brow, and the veins hammered in his ears; his breath came and went in sharp sobs. At last the form was near enough for him to seize it; he grasped it by the middle and drew Roland, for it was Roland, over the window-sill. His head dangled and drooped from side to side; his face was dark with strangled blood and his limbs hung helpless. Mark drew his knife and cut the rope that was tied under his arms; the helpless limbs sank huddling on the floor; then Mark looked up; at the window a few feet from him was a face, more horrible than he had supposed a human face, if it was human indeed, could be. It was deadly white, and hatred, baffled rage, and a sort of devilish malignity glared from the white set eyes, and the drawn mouth. There was a rush from behind him; the old hound, who had crept up unawares into the room, with a fierce outcry of rage sprang on to the window-sill; Mark heard the scraping of his claws upon the stone. Then the hound leapt through the window, and in a moment there was the sound of a heavy fall outside. At the same instant the darkness seemed to lift and draw up like a cloud; a bank of blackness rose past the window, and left the dark outline of the down, with a sky sown with tranquil stars.

The cloud of fear and horror that hung over Mark lifted too; he felt in some dim way that his adversary was vanquished; he carried Roland down the stairs and laid him on his bed; he roused the household, who looked fearfully at him, and then his own strength failed; he sank upon the floor of his room, and the dark tide of unconsciousness closed over him.

Mark's return to health was slow. One who has looked into the Unknown finds it hard to believe again in the outward shows of life.

His first conscious speech was to ask for his hound; they told him that the body of the dog had been found, horribly mangled as though by the teeth of some fierce animal, at the foot of the tower. The dog was buried in the garden, with a slab above him, on which are the words:

EUGE SERVE BONE ET FIDELIS

A silly priest once said to Mark that it was not meet to write Scripture over the grave of a beast. But Mark said warily that an inscription was for those who read it, to make them humble, and not to increase the pride of what lay below.

When Mark could leave his bed, his first care was to send for builders, and the old tower of Nort was taken down, stone by stone, to the ground, and a fair chapel built on the site; in the wall there was a secret stairway, which led from the top chamber, and came out among the elder-bushes that grew below the tower, and here was found a coffer of gold, which paid for the church; because, until it was found, it was Mark's design to leave the place desolate. Mark is wedded since, and has his children about his knee; those who come to the house see a strange and wan man, who sits at Mark's board, and whom he uses very tenderly; sometimes this man is merry, and tells a long tale of his being beckoned and led by a tall and handsome person, smiling, down a hillside to fetch gold; though he can never remember the end of the matter; but about the springtime he is silent or mutters to himself: and this is Roland; his spirit seems shut up within him in some close cell, and Mark prays for his release, but till God call him, he treats him like a dear brother, and with the reverence due to one who has looked out on the other side of Death, and who may not say what his eyes beheld.

The Slype House

A. C. BENSON

In the town of Garchester, close to St Peter's Church, and near the river, stood a dark old house called the Slype House, from a narrow passage of that name that ran close to it, down to a bridge over the stream. The house showed a front of mouldering and discoloured stone to the street, pierced by small windows, like a monastery; and indeed, it was formerly inhabited by a college of priests who had served the Church. It abutted at one angle upon the aisle of the church, and there was a casement window that looked out from a room in the house, formerly the infirmary, into the aisle; it had been so built that any priest that was sick might hear the Mass from his bed, without descending into the church. Behind the house lay a little garden, closely grown up with trees and tall weeds, that ran down to the stream. In the wall that gave on the water, was a small door that admitted to an old timbered bridge that crossed the stream, and had a barred gate on the further side, which was rarely seen open; though if a man had watched attentively he might sometimes have seen a small lean person, much bowed and with a halting gait, slip out very quietly about dusk, and walk, with his eyes cast down, among the shadowy byways.

The name of the man who thus dwelt in the Slype House, as it appeared in the roll of burgesses, was Anthony Purvis. He was of an ancient family, and had inherited wealth. A word must be said of his childhood and youth. He was a sickly child, an only son, his father a man of substance, who lived very easily in the country; his mother had died when he was quite a child, and this sorrow had been borne very heavily by his father, who had loved her tenderly, and after her death had become morose and sullen, withdrawing himself from all company and exercise, and brooding angrily over his loss, as though God had determined to vex him. He had never cared much for the child, who had been peevish and fretful; and the boy's presence had done little but remind him of the wife he had lost; so that the child had lived alone, nourishing his own fancies, and reading much in a library of curious books that was in the house. The boy's health had been too tender for him to go to school; but when he was eighteen, he seemed stronger, and his father sent him to a university, more for the sake of being relieved of the boy's presence than for his good. And there, being unused to the society of his equals, he had been much flouted and despised for his feeble frame; till a certain bitter ambition sprang up in his mind, like a poisonous flower, to gain power and make himself a name; and he had determined that as he could not be loved he might still be feared; so he bided his time in bitterness, making great progress in his studies; then, when those days were over, he departed eagerly, and sought and obtained his father's leave to betake himself to a university of Italy, where he fell into somewhat evil hands; for he made a friendship with an old doctor of the college, who feared not God and thought ill of man, and spent all his time in dark researches into the evil secrets of nature, the study of poisons that have enmity to the life of man, and many other hidden works of darkness, such as intercourse with spirits of evil, and the black influences that lie in wait for the soul; and he found Anthony an apt pupil. There he lived for some years till he was nearly thirty, seldom visiting his home, and writing but formal letters to his father, who supplied him gladly with a small revenue, so long as he kept apart and troubled him not.

Then his father had died, and Anthony came home to take up his inheritance, which was a plentiful one; he sold his land, and visiting the town of Garchester, by chance, for it lay near his home, he had lighted upon the Slype House, which lay very desolate and gloomy; and as he needed a large place for his instruments and devices, he had bought the house, and had now lived there for twenty years in great loneliness, but not ill-content.

To serve him he had none but a man and his wife, who were quiet and simple people and asked no questions; the wife cooked his meals, and kept the rooms where he slept and read, clean and neat; the man moved his machines for him, and arranged his phials and instruments, having a light touch and a serviceable memory.

The door of the house that gave on the street opened into a hall; to the right was a kitchen, and a pair of rooms where the man and his wife lived. On the left was a large room running through the house; the windows on to the street were walled up, and the windows at the back looked on the garden, the trees of which grew close to the casements, making the room dark, and in a breeze rustling their leaves or leafless branches against the panes. In this room Anthony had a furnace with bellows, the smoke of which discharged itself into the chimney; and here he did much of his work, making mechanical toys, as a clock to measure the speed of wind or water, a little chariot that ran a few yards by itself, a puppet that moved its arms and laughed – and other things that had wiled away his idle hours; the room was filled up with dark lumber, in a sort of order that would have looked to a stranger like disorder, but so that Anthony could lay his hand on all that he needed. From the hall, which was paved with stone, went up the stairs, very strong and broad, of massive oak; under which was a postern that gave on the garden; on the floor above was a room where Anthony slept, which again had its windows to the street boarded up, for he was a light sleeper, and the morning sounds of the awakening city disturbed him.

The room was hung with a dark arras, sprinkled with red flowers; he slept in a great bed with black curtains to shut out all light; the windows looked into the garden; but on the left of the bed, which stood with its head to the street, was an alcove, behind the hangings, containing the window that gave on the church. On the same floor were three other rooms; in one of these, looking on the garden, Anthony had his meals. It was a plain panelled room. Next was a room where he read, filled with books, also looking on the garden; and next to that was a little room of which he alone had the key. This room he kept locked, and no-one set foot in it but himself. There was one more room on this floor, set apart for a guest who never came, with a great bed and a press of oak. And that looked on the street. Above, there was a row of plain plastered rooms, in which stood furniture for which Anthony had no use, and many crates in which his machines and phials came to him; this floor was seldom visited, except by the man, who sometimes came to put a box there; and the spiders had it to themselves; except for a little room where stood an optic glass through which on clear nights Anthony sometimes looked at the moon and stars, if there was any odd misadventure among them, such as an eclipse; or when a fiery-tailed comet went his way silently in the heavens, coming from none might say whence and going none knew whither, on some strange errand of God.

Anthony had but two friends who ever came to see him. One was an old physician who had ceased to practise his trade, which indeed was never abundant, and who would sometimes drink a glass of wine with Anthony, and engage in curious talk of men's bodies and diseases, or look at one of Anthony's toys. Anthony had come to know him by having called him in to cure some ailment, which needed a surgical knife; and that had made a kind of friendship between them; but Anthony had little need thereafter to consult him about his health, which indeed was now settled enough, though he had but little vigour; and he knew enough of drugs to cure himself when he was ill. The other friend was a foolish priest of the college, that made belief to be a student but was none, who thought Anthony a very wise and mighty person, and listened with open mouth and eyes to all that he said or showed him. This priest, who was fond of wonders, had introduced himself to Anthony by making believe to borrow a volume of him; and then had grown proud of the acquaintance, and bragged greatly of it to his friends, mixing up much that was fanciful with a little that was true. But the result was that gossip spread wide about Anthony, and he was held in the town to be a very fearful person, who could do strange mischief if he had a mind to; Anthony never cared to walk abroad, for he was of a shy habit, and disliked to meet the eyes of his fellows; but if he did go about, men began to look curiously after him as he went by, shook their heads and talked together with a dark pleasure, while children fled before his face and women feared him; all of which pleased Anthony mightily, if the truth were told; for at the bottom of his restless and eager spirit lay a deep vanity unseen, like a lake in woods; he hungered not indeed for fame, but for repute – *monstrari digito*, as the poet has it; and he cared little in what repute he was held, so long as men thought him great and marvellous; and as he could not win renown by brave deeds and words, he was rejoiced to win it by keeping up a certain darkness and mystery about his ways and doings; and this was very dear to him, so that when the silly priest called him Seer and Wizard, he frowned and looked sideways; but he laughed in his heart and was glad.

Now, when Anthony was near his fiftieth year, there fell on him a heaviness of spirit which daily increased upon him. He began to question of his end and what lay beyond. He had always made pretence to mock at religion, and had grown to believe that in death the soul was extinguished like a burnt-out flame. He began, too, to question of his life and what he had done. He had made a few toys, he had filled vacant hours, and he had gained an ugly kind of fame – and this was all. Was he so certain, he began to think, after all, that death was the end? Were there not, perhaps, in the vast house of God, rooms and chambers beyond that in which he was set for a while to pace to and fro? About this time he began to read in a Bible that had lain dusty and unopened on a shelf. It was his mother's book, and he found therein many little tokens of her presence. Here was a verse underlined; at some gracious passages the page was much fingered and worn; in one place there were stains that looked like the mark of tears; then again, in one page, there was a small tress of hair, golden hair, tied in a paper with a name across it, that seemed to be the name of a little sister of his mother's that died a child; and again there were a few withered flowers, like little sad ghosts, stuck through a paper on which was written his father's name – the name of the sad, harsh, silent man whom Anthony had feared with all his heart. Had those two, indeed, on some day of summer, walked to and fro, or sate in some woodland corner, whispering sweet words of love together? Anthony felt a sudden hunger of the heart for a woman's love, for tender words to soothe his sadness, for the laughter and kisses of children – and he began to ransack his mind for memories of his mother; he could remember being pressed to her heart one morning when she lay abed, with her fragrant hair falling about him. The worst was that he must bear his sorrow alone, for there were none to whom he could talk of such things. The doctor was as dry as an old bunch of herbs, and as for the priest, Anthony was ashamed to show anything but contempt and pride in his presence.

For relief he began to turn to a branch of his studies that he had long disused; this was a fearful commerce with the unseen spirits. Anthony could remember having practised some experiments of this kind with the old Italian doctor; but he remembered them with a kind of disgust, for they seemed to him but a sort of deadly juggling; and such dark things as he had seen seemed like a dangerous sport with unclean and coltish beings, more brute-like than human. Yet now he read in his curious books with care, and studied the tales of necromancers, who had indeed seemed to have some power over the souls of men departed. But the old books gave him but little faith, and a kind of angry disgust at the things attempted. And he began to think that the horror in which such men as made these books abode, was not more than the dark shadow cast on the mirror of the soul by their own desperate imaginings and timorous excursions.

One day, a Sunday, he was strangely sad and heavy; he could settle to nothing, but threw book after book aside, and when he turned to some work of construction, his hand seemed to have lost its cunning. It was a grey and sullen day in October; a warm wet wind came buffeting up from the west, and roared in the chimneys and eaves of the old house. The shrubs in the garden plucked themselves hither and thither as though in pain. Anthony walked to and fro after his midday meal, which he had eaten hastily and without savour; at last, as though with a sudden resolution, he went to a secret cabinet and got out a key; and with it he went to the door of the little room that was ever locked.

He stopped at the threshold for a while, looking hither and thither; and then he suddenly unlocked it and went in, closing and locking it behind him. The room was as dark as night, but Anthony going softly, his hands before him, went to a corner and got a tinder-box which lay there, and made a flame.

A small dark room appeared, hung with a black tapestry; the window was heavily shuttered and curtained; in the centre of the room stood what looked like a small altar, painted black; the floor was all bare, but with white marks upon it, half effaced. Anthony looked about the room, glancing sidelong, as though in some kind of doubt; his breath went and came quickly, and he looked paler than was his wont.

Presently, as though reassured by the silence and calm of the place, he went to a tall press that stood in a corner, which he opened, and took from it certain things – a dish of metal, some small leathern bags, a large lump of chalk, and a book. He laid all but the chalk down on the altar, and then opening the book, read in it a little; and then he went with the chalk and drew certain marks upon the floor, first making a circle, which he went over again and again with anxious care; at times he went back and peeped into the book as though uncertain. Then he opened the bags, which seemed to hold certain kinds of powder, this dusty, that in grains; he ran them through his hands, and then poured a little of each into his dish, and mixed them with his hands. Then he stopped and looked about him. Then he walked to a place in the wall on the further side of the altar from the door, and drew the arras carefully aside, disclosing a little alcove in the wall; into this he looked fearfully, as though he was afraid of what he might see.

In the alcove, which was all in black, appeared a small shelf, that stood but a little way out from the wall. Upon it, gleaming very white against the black, stood the skull of a man, and on either side of the skull were the bones of a man's hand. It looked to him, as he gazed on it with a sort of curious disgust, as though a dead man had come up to the surface of a black tide, and was preparing presently to leap out. On either side stood two long silver candlesticks, very dark with disuse; but instead of holding candles, they were fitted at the top with flat metal dishes; and in these he poured some of his powders, mixing them as before with his fingers. Between the candlesticks and behind the skull was an old and dark picture, at which he gazed for a time, holding his taper on high. The picture represented a man fleeing in a kind of furious haste from a wood, his hands spread wide, and his eyes staring out of the picture; behind him everywhere was the wood, above which was a star in the sky – and out of the wood leaned a strange pale horned thing, very dim. The horror in the man's face was skilfully painted, and Anthony felt a shudder pass through his veins. He knew not what the picture meant; it had been given to him by the old Italian, who had smiled a wicked smile when he gave it, and told him that it had a very great virtue. When Anthony had asked him of the subject of the picture, the old Italian had said, 'Oh, it is as appears; he hath been where he ought not, and he hath seen somewhat he doth not like.' When Anthony would fain have known more, and especially what the thing was that leaned out of the wood, the old Italian had smiled cruelly and said, 'Know you not? Well, you will know some day when you have seen him;' and never a word more would he say.

When Anthony had put all things in order, he opened the book at a certain place, and laid it upon the altar; and then it seemed as though his courage failed him, for he drew the curtain again over the alcove, unlocked the door, set the tinder-box and the candle back in their place, and softly left the room.

He was very restless all the evening. He took down books from the shelves, turned them over, and put them back again. He addressed himself to some unfinished work, but soon threw it aside; he paced up and down, and spent a long time, with his hands clasped behind him, looking out into the desolate garden, where a still, red sunset burnt behind the leafless trees. He was like a man who has made up his mind to a grave decision, and shrinks back upon the brink. When his food was served he could hardly touch it, and he drank no wine as his custom was to do, but only water, saying to himself that his head must be clear. But in the evening he went to his bedroom, and searched for something in a press there; he found at last what he was searching for, and unfolded a long black robe, looking gloomily upon it, as though it aroused unwelcome thoughts; while he was pondering, he heard a hum of music behind the arras; he put the robe down, and stepped through the hangings, and stood awhile in the little oriel that looked down into the church. Vespers were proceeding; he saw the holy lights dimly through the dusty panes, and heard the low preluding of the organ; then, solemn and slow, rose the sound of a chanted psalm on the air; he carefully unfastened the casement which opened inward and unclosed it, standing for a while to listen, while the air, fragrant with incense smoke, drew into the room along the vaulted roof. There were but a few worshippers in the church, who stood below him; two lights burnt stilly upon the altar, and he saw distinctly the thin hands of a priest who held a book close to his face. He had not set foot within a church for many years, and the sight and sound drew his mind back to his childhood's days. At last with a sigh he put the window to very softly, and went to his study, where he made pretence to read, till the hour came when he was wont to retire to his bed. He sent his servant away, but instead of lying down, he sate, looking upon a parchment, which he held in his hand, while the bells of the city slowly told out the creeping hours.

At last, a few minutes before midnight, he rose from his place; the house was now all silent, and without the night was very still, as though all things slept tranquilly. He opened the press and took from it the black robe, and put it round him, so that it covered him from head to foot, and then gathered up the parchment, and the key of the locked room, and went softly out, and so came to the door. This he undid with a kind of secret and awestruck haste, locking it behind him. Once inside the room, he wrestled awhile with a strong aversion to what was in his mind to do, and stood for a moment, listening intently, as though he expected to hear some sound. But the room was still, except for the faint biting of some small creature in the wainscot.

Then with a swift motion he took up the tinder-box and made a light; he drew aside the curtain that hid the alcove; he put fire to the powder in the candlesticks, which at first spluttered, and then swiftly kindling sent up a thick smoky flame, fragrant with drugs, burning hotly and red. Then he came back to the altar; cast a swift glance round him to see that all was ready; put fire to the powder on the altar, and in a low and inward voice began to recite words from the book, and from the parchment which he held in his hand; once or twice he glanced fearfully at the skull, and the hands which gleamed luridly through the smoke; the figures in the picture wavered in the heat; and now the powders began to burn clear, and throw up a steady light; and still he read, sometimes turning a page, until at last he made an end; and drawing something from a silver box which lay beside the book, he dropped it in the flame, and looked straight before him to see what might befall. The thing that fell in the flame burned up brightly, with a little leaping of sparks, but soon it died down; and there was a long silence, in the room, a breathless silence, which, to Anthony's disordered mind, was not like the silence of emptiness, but such silence as may be heard when unseen things are crowding quietly to a closed door, expecting it to be opened, and as it were holding each other back.

Suddenly, between him and the picture, appeared for a moment a pale light, as of moonlight, and then with a horror which words cannot attain to describe, Anthony saw a face hang in the air a few feet from him, that looked in his own eyes with a sort of intent fury, as though to spring upon him if he turned either to the right hand or to the left. His knees tottered beneath him, and a sweat of icy coldness sprang on his brow; there followed a sound like no sound that Anthony had ever dreamed of hearing; a sound that was near and yet remote, a sound that was low and yet charged with power, like the groaning of a voice in grievous pain and anger, that strives to be free and yet is helpless. And then Anthony knew that he had indeed opened the door that looks into the other world, and that a deadly thing that held him in enmity had looked out. His reeling brain still told him that he was safe where he was, but that he must not step or fall outside the circle; but how he should resist the power of the wicked face he knew not. He tried to frame a prayer in his heart; but there swept such a fury of hatred across the face that he dared not. So he closed his eyes and stood dizzily waiting to fall, and knowing that if he fell it was the end.

Suddenly, as he stood with closed eyes, he felt the horror of the spell relax; he opened his eyes again, and saw that the face died out upon the air, becoming first white and then thin, like the husk that stands on a rush when a fly draws itself from its skin, and floats away into the sunshine.

Then there fell a low and sweet music upon the air, like a concert of flutes and harps, very far away. And then suddenly, in a sweet clear radiance, the face of his mother, as she lived in his mind, appeared in the space, and looked at him with a kind of heavenly love; then beside the face appeared two thin hands which seemed to wave a blessing towards him, which flowed like healing into his soul.

The relief from the horror, and the flood of tenderness that came into his heart, made him reckless. The tears came into his eyes, not in a rising film, but a flood hot and large. He took a step forwards round the altar; but as he did so, the vision disappeared, the lights shot up into a flare and went out; the house seemed to be suddenly shaken; in the darkness he heard the rattle of bones, and the clash of metal, and Anthony fell all his length upon the ground and lay as one dead.

But while he thus lay, there came to him in some secret cell of the mind a dreadful vision, which he could only dimly remember afterwards with a fitful horror. He thought that he was walking in the cloister of some great house or college, a cool place, with a pleasant garden in the court. He paced up and down, and each time that he did so, he paused a little before a great door at the end, a huge blind portal, with much carving about it, which he somehow knew he was forbidden to enter. Nevertheless, each time that he came to it, he felt a strong wish, that constantly increased, to set foot therein. Now in the dream there fell on him a certain heaviness, and the shadow of a cloud fell over the court, and struck the sunshine out of it. And at last he made up his mind that he would enter. He pushed the door open with much difficulty, and found himself in a long blank passage, very damp and chilly, but with a glimmering light; he walked a few paces down it. The flags underfoot were slimy, and the walls streamed with damp. He then thought that he would return; but the great door was closed behind him, and he could not open it. This made him very fearful; and while he considered what he should do, he saw a tall and angry-looking man approaching very swiftly down the passage. As he turned to face him, the other came straight to him, and asked him very sternly what he did there; to which Anthony replied that he had found the door open. To which the other replied that it was fast now, and that he must go forward. He seized Anthony as he spoke by the arm, and urged him down the passage. Anthony would fain have resisted, but he felt like a child in the grip of a giant, and went forward in great terror and perplexity. Presently they came to a door in the side of the wall, and as they passed it, there stepped out an ugly shadowy thing, the nature of which he could not clearly discern, and marched softly behind them. Soon they came to a turn in the passage, and in a moment the way stopped on the brink of a dark well, that seemed to go down a long way into the earth, and out of which came a cold fetid air, with a hollow sound like a complaining voice. Anthony drew back as far as he could from the pit, and set his back to the wall, his companion letting go of him. But he could not go backward, for the thing behind him was in the passage, and barred the way, creeping slowly nearer. Then Anthony was in a great agony of mind, and waited for the end.

But while he waited, there came someone very softly down the passage and drew near; and the other, who had led him to the place, waited, as though ill-pleased to be interrupted; it was too murky for Anthony to see the newcomer, but he knew in some way that he was a friend. The stranger came up to them, and spoke in a low voice to the man who had drawn Anthony thither, as though pleading for something; and the man answered angrily, but yet with a certain dark respect, and seemed to argue that he was acting in his right, and might not be interfered with. Anthony could not hear what they said, they spoke so low, but he guessed the sense, and knew that it was himself of whom they discoursed, and listened with a fearful wonder to see which would prevail. The end soon came, for the tall man, who had brought him there, broke out into a great storm of passion; and Anthony heard him say, 'He hath yielded himself to his own will; and he is mine here; so let us make an end.' Then the stranger seemed to consider; and then with a quiet courage, and in a soft and silvery voice like that of a child, said, 'I would that you would have yielded to my prayer; but as you will not, I have no choice.' And he took his hand from under the cloak that wrapped him, and held something out; then there came a great roaring out of the pit, and a zigzag flame flickered in the dark. Then in a moment the tall man and the shadow were gone; Anthony could not see whither they went, and he would have thanked the stranger; but the other put his finger to his lip as though to order silence, and pointed to the way he had come, saying, 'Make haste and go back; for they will return anon with others; you know not how dear it hath cost me.' Anthony could see the stranger's face in the gloom, and he was surprised to see it so youthful; but he saw also that tears stood in the eyes of the stranger, and that something dark like blood trickled down his brow; yet he looked very lovingly at him. So Anthony made haste to go back, and found the door ajar; but as he reached it, he heard a horrible din behind him, of cries and screams; and it was with a sense of gratitude, that he could not put into words, but which filled all his heart, that he found himself back in the cloister again. And then the vision all fled away, and with a shock coming to himself, he found that he was lying in his own room; and then he knew that a battle had been fought out over his soul, and that the evil had not prevailed.

He was cold and aching in every limb; the room was silent and dark, with the heavy smell of the burnt drugs all about it. Anthony crept to the door, and opened it; locked it again, and made his way in the dark very feebly to his bed-chamber; he had just the strength to get into his bed, and then all his life seemed to ebb from him, and he lay, and thought that he was dying. Presently from without there came the crying of cocks, and a bell beat the hour of four; and after that, in his vigil of weakness, it was strange to see the light glimmer in the crevices, and to hear the awakening birds that in the garden bushes took up, one after another, their slender piping song, till all the choir cried together.

But Anthony felt a strange peace in his heart; and he had a sense, though he could not say why, that it was as once in his childhood, when he was ill, and his mother had sate softly by him while he slept.

So he waited, and in spite of his mortal weakness that was a blessed hour.

When his man came to rouse him in the morning, Anthony said that he believed that he was very ill, that he had had a fall, and that the old doctor must be fetched to him. The man looked so strangely upon him, that Anthony knew that he had some fear upon his mind. Presently the doctor was brought, and Anthony answered such questions as were put to him, in a faint voice, saying, 'I was late at my work, and I slipped and fell.' The doctor, who looked troubled, gave directions; and when he went away he heard his man behind the door asking the doctor about the strange storm in the night, that had seemed like an earthquake, or as if a thunderbolt had struck the house. But the doctor said very gruffly, 'It is no time to talk thus, when your master is sick to death.' But Anthony knew in himself that he would not die yet.

It was long ere he was restored to a measure of health; and indeed he never rightly recovered the use of his limbs; the doctor held that he had suffered some stroke of palsy; at which Anthony smiled a little, and made no answer.

When he was well enough to creep to and fro, he went sadly to the dark room, and with much pain and weakness carried the furniture out of it. The picture he cut in pieces and burnt; and the candles and dishes, with the book, he cast into a deep pool in the stream; the bones he buried in the earth; the hangings he stored away for his own funeral.

Anthony never entered his workroom again; but day after day he sate in his chair, and read a little, but mostly in the Bible; he made a friend of a very wise old priest, to whom he opened all his heart, and to whom he conveyed much money to be bestowed on the poor; there was a great calm in his spirit, which was soon written in his face, in spite of his pain, for he often suffered sorely; but he told the priest that something, he knew not certainly what, seemed to dwell by him, waiting patiently for his coming; and so Anthony awaited his end.

The Red Camp

A. C. BENSON

It was a sultry summer evening in the old days, when Walter Wyatt came to the house of his forefathers. It was in a quiet valley of Sussex, with the woods standing very steeply on the high hillsides. Among the woods were pleasant stretches of pasture, and a little stream ran hidden among hazels beside the road; here and there were pits in the woods, where the men of ancient times had dug for iron, pits with small sandstone cliffs, and full to the brim of saplings and woodland plants. Walter rode slowly along, his heart full of a happy content. Though it was the home of his family he had never even seen Restlands – that was the peaceful name of the house. Walter's father had been a younger son, and for many years the elder brother, a morose and selfish man, had lived at Restlands, often vowing that none of his kin should ever set foot in the place, and all out of a native malice and churlishness, which discharged itself upon those that were nearest to him. Walter's father was long dead, and Walter had lived a very quiet homely life with his mother. But one day his uncle had died suddenly and silently, sitting in his chair; and it was found that he had left no will. So that Restlands, with its orchards and woods and its pleasant pasture-lands, fell to Walter; and he had ridden down to take possession. He was to set the house in order, for it was much decayed in his uncle's time; and in a few weeks his mother was to follow him there.

He turned a corner of the road, and saw in a glance a house that he knew must be his; and a sudden pride and tenderness leapt up within his heart, to think how fair a place he could call his own.

An avenue of limes led from the road to the house, which was built of ancient stone, the roof tiled with the same. The front was low and many-windowed. And Walter, for he was a God-fearing youth, made a prayer in his heart, half of gratitude and half of hope.

He rode up to the front of the house, and saw at once that it was sadly neglected; the grass grew among the paving-stones, and several of the windows were broken. He knocked at the door, and an old serving-man came out, who made an obeisance. Walter sent his horse to the stable; his baggage was already come; and his first task was to visit his new home from room to room. It was a very beautiful solidly built house, finely panelled in old dry wood, and had an abundance of solid oak furniture; there were dark pictures here and there; and that night Walter sate alone at his meat, which was carefully served him by the old serving-man, his head full of pleasant plans for his new life; he slept in the great bedroom, and many times woke wondering where he was; once he crept to the window, and saw the barns, gardens, and orchards lie beneath, and the shadowy woods beyond, all bathed in a cold clear moonlight.

In the morning when he had breakfasted, the lawyer who had charge of his business rode in from the little town hard by to see him; and then Walter's happiness was a little dashed, for though the estate brought in a fair sum, yet it was crippled by a mortgage which lay upon it; and Walter saw that he would have to live sparely for some years before he could have his estate unembarrassed; but this troubled him little, for he was used to a simple life. The lawyer indeed had advised him to sell a little of the land; but Walter was very proud of the old estate, and of the memory that he was the tenth Wyatt that had dwelt there, and he said that before he did that he would wait awhile and see if he could not arrange otherwise. When the lawyer was gone there came in the bailiff, and Walter went with him all over the estate. The garden was greatly overgrown with weeds, and the yew hedges were sprawling all uncut; they went through the byre, where the cattle stood in the straw; they visited the stable and the barn, the granary and the dovecote; and Walter spoke pleasantly with the men that served him; then he went to the ploughland and the pastures, the orchard and the woodland; and it pleased Walter to walk in the woodpaths, among the copse and under great branching oaks, and to feel that it was all his own.

At last they came out on the brow of the hill, and saw Restlands lie beneath them, with the smoke of a chimney going up into the quiet air, and the doves wheeling about the cote. The whole valley was full of westering sunshine, and the country sounds came pleasantly up through the still air.

They stood in a wide open pasture, but in the centre of it rose a small, dark, and thickly grown square holt of wood, surrounded by a high green bank of turf, and Walter asked what that was. The old bailiff looked at him a moment without speaking and then said, 'That is the Red Camp, sir.' Walter said pleasantly, 'And whose camp is it?' but it came suddenly into his head that long ago his father had told him a curious tale about the place, but he could not remember what the tale was. The old man answering his question said, 'Ah, sir, who can say? Perhaps it was the old Romans who made it, or perhaps older men still; but there was a sore battle hereabouts.' And then he went on in a slow and serious way to tell him an old tale of how a few warriors had held the place against an army, and that they had all been put to the sword there; he said that in former days strange rusted weapons and bones had been ploughed up in the field, and then he added that the Camp had ever since been left desolate and that no-one cared to set foot within it; yet for all that it was said that a great treasure lay buried within it, for that was what the men were guarding, though those that took the place and slew them could never find it; 'and that was all long ago,' he said.

Walter, as the old man spoke, walked softly to the wood and peered at it over the mound; it was all grown up within, close and thick, an evil tangle of plants and briars. It was dark and even cold looking within the wood, though the air lay warm all about it. The mound was about breast high, and there was a grass-grown trench all round out of which the earth had been thrown up. It came into Walter's head that the place had seen strange things. He thought of it as all rough and newly made, with a palisade round the mound, with spears and helmets showing over, and a fierce wild multitude of warriors surging all round; the Romans, if they had been Romans, within, grave and anxious, waiting for help that never came. All this came into his mind with a pleasant sense of security, as a man who is at ease looks on a picture of old and sad things, and finds it minister to his content. Yet the place kept a secret of its own, Walter felt sure of that. And the treasure, was that there all the time? buried in some corner of the wood, money lying idle that might do good things if it could but get forth? So he mused, tapping the bank with his stick. And presently they went on together. Walter said as they turned away, 'I should like to cut the trees down, and throw the place into the pasture,' but the old bailiff said, 'Nay, it is better left alone.'

The weeks passed very pleasantly at first; the neighbours came to see him, and he found that an old name wins friends easily; he spent much of the day abroad, and he liked to go up to the Red Camp and see it stand so solitary and dark, with the pleasant valley beneath it. His mother soon came, and they found that with her small jointure they could indeed live at the place, but that they would have to live very sparely at first; there must be no horses in the stable, nor coach to drive abroad; there must be no company at Restlands for many a year, and Walter saw too that he must not think awhile of marriage, but that he must give all his savings to feed the estate.

After a while, when the first happy sense of possession had gone off, and then life had settled down into common and familiar ways, this began to be very irksome to Walter; and what made him feel even more keenly his fortune was that he made acquaintance with a squire that lived hard by, who had a daughter Marjory, who seemed to Walter the fairest and sweetest maiden he had ever seen; and he began to carry her image about with him; and his heart beat very sharply in his breast if he set eyes on her unexpectedly; and she too, seemed to have delight in seeing Walter, and to understand even the thoughts that lay beneath his lightest word. But the squire was a poor man, and Walter felt bound to crush the thought of love and marriage down in his heart, until he began to grow silent and moody; and his mother saw all that was in his heart and pitied him, but knew not what to do; and Walter began even to talk of going into the world to seek his fortune; but it was little more than talk, for he already loved Restlands very deeply.

Now one day when Walter had been dining with the Vicar of the parish, he met at his table an old and fond man, full of curious wisdom, who took great delight in all that showed the history of the old races that had inhabited the land; and he told Walter a long tale of the digging open of a great barrow or mound upon the downs, which it seemed had been the grave of a great prince, and in which they had found a great treasure of gold, cups and plates and pitchers all of gold, with bars of the same, and many other curious things. He said that a third of such things by rights belonged to the King; but that the King's Grace had been contented to take a rich cup or two, and had left the rest in the hands of him whose land it was. Then the old scholar asked Walter if it were not true that he had in his own land an ancient fort or stronghold, and Walter told him of the Red Camp and the story, and the old man heard him with great attention saying, 'Ay, ay,' and 'Ay, so it would be,' and at the last he said that the story of the treasure was most likely a true one, for he did not see how it could have grown up otherwise; and that he did not doubt that it was a great Roman treasure, perhaps a tribute, gathered in from the people of the land, who would doubtless have been enraged to lose so much and would have striven to recover it. 'Ay, it is there, sure enough,' he said.

Walter offered to go with him to the place; but the old Vicar, seeing Walter's bright eye, and knowing something of the difficulties, said that the legend was that it would be ill to disturb a thing that had cost so many warriors their lives; and that a curse would rest upon one that did disturb it. The old scholar laughed and said that the curses of the dead, and especially of the heathen dead, would break no bones – and he went on to say that doubtless there was a whole hen-roost of curses hidden away in the mound upon the downs; but that they had hurt not his friend who had opened it; for he lived very delicately and plentifully off the treasure of the old prince, who seemed to bear him no grudge for it. 'Nay, doubtless,' he said, 'if we but knew the truth, I dare say that the old heathen man, pining in some dark room in hell, is glad enough that his treasure should be richly spent by a good Christian gentleman.'

They walked together to the place; and the old gentleman talked very learnedly and showed him where the gates and towers of the fort had been – adding to Walter, 'And if I were you, Mr Wyatt, I would have the place cleared and trenched, and would dig the gold out; for it is there as sure as I am a Christian man and a lover of the old days.'

Then Walter told his mother of all that had been said; and she had heard of the old tales, and shook her head; indeed when Walter spoke to the old bailiff of his wish to open the place, the old man almost wept; and then, seeing that he prevailed nothing, said suddenly that neither he nor any of the men that dwelt in the village would put out a hand to help for all the gold of England. So Walter rested for awhile; and still his impatience and his hunger grew.

Walter did not decide at once; he turned the matter over in his mind for a week. He spoke no more to the bailiff, who thought he had changed his mind; but all the week the desire grew; and at last it completely overmastered him. He sent for the bailiff and told him he had determined to dig out the Camp; the bailiff looked at him without speaking. Then Walter said laughing that he meant to deal very fairly; that no-one should bear a hand in the work who did not do so willingly; but that he should add a little to the wages of every man who worked for him at the Camp while the work was going on. The bailiff shrugged his shoulders and made no reply. Walter went and spoke to each of his men and told them his offer. 'I know,' he said, 'that there is a story about the place, and that you do not wish to touch it; but I will offer a larger wage to every man who works there for me; and I will force no man to do it; but done it shall be; and if my own men will not do it, then I will get strangers to help me.' The end of it was that three of his men offered to do the work, and the next day a start was made.

The copse and undergrowth was first cleared, and then the big trees were felled and dragged off the place; then the roots were stubbed up. It was a difficult task, and longer than Walter had thought; and he could not disguise from himself that a strange kind of ill-luck hung about the whole affair. One of his men disabled himself by a cut from an axe; another fell ill; the third, after these two mishaps, came and begged off. Walter replaced them with other workers; and the work proceeded slowly, in spite of Walter's great impatience and haste. He himself was there early and late; the men had it in their minds that they were searching for treasure and were well-nigh as excited as himself; and Walter was for ever afraid that in his absence some rich and valuable thing might be turned up, and perhaps concealed or conveyed away secretly by the finder. But the weeks passed and nothing was found; and it was now a bare and ugly place with miry pools of dirt, great holes where the trees had been; there were cart tracks all over the field in which it lay, the great trunks lay outside the mound, and the undergrowth was piled in stacks. The mound and ditch had all been unturfed; and the mound was daily dug down to the level, every spadeful being shaken loose; and now they came upon some few traces of human use. In the mound was found a short and dinted sword of bronze, of antique shape. A mass of rusted metal was found in a corner, that looked as if it had been armour. In another corner were found some large upright and calcined stones, with abundance of wood-ashes below, that seemed to have been a rude fireplace. And in one part, in a place where there seemed to have been a pit, was a quantity of rotting stuff, that seemed like the remains of bones. Walter himself grew worn and weary, partly with the toil and still more with the deferred hope. And the men too became sullen and ill-affected. It surprised Walter too that more than one of his neighbours spoke with disfavour of what he was doing, as of a thing that was foolish or even wrong. But still he worked on savagely, slept little, and cared not what he ate or drank.

At last the work was nearly over; the place had been all trenched across, and they had come in most places to the hard sandstone, which lay very near the surface. In the afternoon had fallen a heavy drenching shower, so that the men had gone home early, wet and dispirited; and Walter stood, all splashed and stained with mud, sick at heart and heavy, on the edge of the place, and looked very gloomily at the trenches, which lay like an ugly scar on the green hilltop. The sky was full of ragged inky clouds, with fierce lights on the horizon.

As he paced about and looked at the trenches, he saw in one place that it seemed as if the earth was of a different colour at the side of the trench; he stepped inside to look at this, and saw that the digging had laid bare the side of a place like a pit, that seemed to have been dug down through the ground; he bent to examine it, and then saw at the bottom of the trench, washed clear by the rain, something that looked like a stick or a root, that projected a little into the trench; he put his hand down to it, and found it cold and hard and heavy, and in a moment saw that it was a rod of metal that ran into the bank. He took up a spade, and threw the earth away in haste; and presently uncovered the rod. It was a bar, he saw, and very heavy; but examining it closely he saw that there was a stamp of some sort upon it; and then in a moment looking upon a place where the spade had scratched it, he saw that it was a bright yellow metal. It came over him all at once, with a shock that made him faint, that he had stumbled upon some part of the treasure; he put the bar aside, and then, first looking all round to see that none observed him, he dug into the bank. In a moment his spade struck something hard; and he presently uncovered a row of bars that lay close together. He dragged them up one by one, and underneath he found another row, laid crosswise; and another row, and another, till he had uncovered seven rows, making fifty bars in all. Beneath the lowest row his spade slipped on something round and smooth; he uncovered the earth, and presently drew out a brown and sodden skull, which thus lay beneath the treasure. Below that was a mass of softer earth, but out of it came the two thigh-bones of a man.

The sky was now beginning to grow dark; but he dug out the whole of the pit, working into the bank; and he saw that a round hole had been dug straight down from the top, to the sandstone. The bones lay upon the sandstone; but he found other bones at the sides of where the gold had lain; so that it seemed to him as though the gold must have been placed among dead bodies, and have rested among corruption. This was a dim thought that lurked in an ugly way in his mind. But he had now dug out the whole pit, and found nothing else, except a few large blurred copper coins which lay among the bodies. He stood awhile looking at the treasure; but together with the exultation at his discovery there mingled a dark and gloomy oppression of spirit, which he could not explain, which clouded his mind. But presently he came to himself again, and gathering the bones together, he threw them down to the bottom of the pit, as he was minded to conceal his digging from the men. While he did so, it seemed to him that, as he was bending to the pit, something came suddenly behind him and stood at his back, close to him, as though looking over his shoulder. For a moment the horror was so great that he felt the hair of his head prickle and his heart thump within his breast; but he overcame it and turned, and saw nothing but the trenches, and above them the ragged sky; yet he had the thought that something had slipped away. But he set himself doggedly to finish his task; he threw earth into the holes, working in a kind of fury; and twice as he did so, the same feeling came again that there was someone at his back; and twice turning he saw nothing; but the third time, from the West came a sharp thunder-peal; and he had hardly finished his work when the rain fell in a sheet, and splashed in the trenches.

Then he turned to the treasure which lay beside him. He found that he could not carry more than a few of the bars at a time; and he dared not leave the rest uncovered. So he covered them with earth and went stealthily down to the house; and there he got, with much precaution, a barrow from the garden. But the fear of discovery came upon him; and he determined to go into the house and sup as usual, and late at night convey the treasure to the house. For the time, his trove gave him no joy; he could not have believed it would have so weighed on him – he felt more like one who had some guilty secret to conceal, than a man to whom had befallen a great joy.

He went to the house, changed his wet clothes, and came to supper with his mother. To her accustomed questions as to what they had found, he took out the coins and showed them her, saying nothing of the gold, but with a jesting word that these would hardly repay him for his trouble. He could scarcely speak at supper for thinking of what he had found; and every now and then there came upon him a dreadful fear that he had been observed digging, and that even now some thief had stolen back there and was uncovering his hoard. His mother looked at him often, and at last said that he looked very weary; to which he replied with some sharpness, so that she said no more.

Then all at once, near the end of the meal, he had the same dreadful fear that he had felt by the pit. It seemed to him as though someone came near him and stood close behind him, bending over his shoulder;

and a kind of icy coldness fell on him. He started and looked quickly round. His mother looked anxiously at him, and said, 'What is it, dear Walter?' He made some excuse; but presently feeling that he must be alone, he excused himself and went to his room, where he sate, making pretence to read, till the house should be silent.

Then when all were abed, at an hour after midnight, he forced himself to rise and put on his rough clothes, though a terror lay very sore upon him, and go out to the garden, creeping like a thief. He had with him a lantern; and he carried the barrow on his shoulders for fear that the creaking of the wheel should awake someone; and then stumbling and sweating, and in a great weariness, he went by woodpaths to the hilltop. He came to the place, and having lit his lantern he uncovered the bars, and laid them on the barrow; they were as he had left them. When he had loaded them, the same fear struck him suddenly cold again, of something near him; and he thought for a moment he would have swooned; but sitting down on the barrow in the cool air he presently came to himself. Then he essayed to wheel the barrow in the dark. But he stumbled often, and once upset the barrow and spilled his load. Thus, though fearing discovery, he was forced to light the lantern and set it upon the barrow, and so at last he came to the house; where he disposed the bars at the bottom of a chest of which he had the key, covering them with papers, and then went to bed in a kind of fever, his teeth chattering, till he fell into a wretched sleep which lasted till dawn.

In his sleep he dreamed a fearful dream; he seemed to be sitting on the ground by the Camp, holding the gold in his arms; the Camp in his dream was as it was before he had cleared it, all grown up with trees. Suddenly out from among the trees there came a man in rusty tarnished armour, with a pale wild face and a little beard, which seemed all clotted with moisture; he held in his hand a pike or spear, and he came swiftly and furiously upon Walter as though he would smite him. But it seemed as though his purpose changed; for standing aside he watched Walter with evil and piercing eyes, so that it seemed to Walter that he would sooner have been smitten. And then he woke, but in anguish, for the man still seemed to stand beside him; until he made a light and saw no-one.

He arose feeling broken and ill; but he met his mother with a smile, and told her that he had determined to do what would please her, and work no more at the Camp. And he told the men that he would dig no more, but that they were to level the place and so leave it. And so they did, murmuring sore.

The next week was a very miserable one for Walter; he could not have believed that a man's heart should be so heavy. It seemed to him that he lay, like the poor bones that he had found beneath the treasure, crushed and broken and stifled under the weight of it. He was tempted to do wild things with the gold; to bury it again in the Camp, to drop it into the mud of the pool that lay near the house. In fevered dreams he seemed to row himself in a boat upon a dark sea, and to throw the bars one by one into the water; the reason of this was not only his fear for the treasure itself, but the dreadful sense that he had of being followed by someone who dogged his footsteps wherever he went. If ever he sate alone, the thing would draw near him and bend above him; he often felt that if he could but look round swiftly enough he would catch a glimpse of the thing, and that nothing that he could see would be so fearful as that which was unseen; and so it came to pass that, as he sate with his mother, though he bore the presence long that he might not startle her, yet after a time of patient agony he could bear it no more, but looked swiftly behind him; he grew pale and ill, and even the men of the place noticed how often he turned round as he walked; till at last he would not even walk abroad, except early and late when there would be few to see him.

He had sent away his labourers; but once or twice he noticed, as he went by the Camp, that someone had been digging and grubbing in the mire. Sometimes for an hour or two his terrors would leave him, till he thought that he was wholly cured; but it was like a cat with a mouse, for he suffered the worse for his respite, till at last he fell so low that he used to think of stories of men that had destroyed themselves, and though he knew it to be a terrible sin to dally with such thoughts, he could not wholly put them from him, but used to plan in his mind how he could do the deed best, that it might appear to be an accident. Sometimes he bore his trouble heavily, but at others he would rage to think that he had been so happy so short a while ago; and even the love that he bore to Marjory was darkened and destroyed by the evil thing, and he met her timid and friendly glances sullenly; his mother was nearly as miserable as himself, for she knew that something was very grievously amiss, but could not divine what it was. Indeed, she could do nothing but wish it were otherwise, and pray for her son, for she knew not where the trouble lay, but thought that he was ill or even bewitched.

At last, after a day of dreadful gloom, Walter made up his mind that he would ride to London and see to the disposing of the treasure. He had a thought often in his mind that if he replaced it in the Camp, he would cease to be troubled; but he could not bring himself to that; he seemed to himself like a man who had won a hard victory, and was asked to surrender what he had won.

His intention was to go to an old and wise friend of his father's, who was a Canon of a Collegiate Church in London, and was much about the court. So he hid the treasure in a strong cellar and padlocked the door; but he took one bar with him to show to his friend.

It was a doleful journey; his horse seemed as dispirited as himself; and his terrors came often upon him, till he was fearful that he might be thought mad; and indeed what with the load at his heart and the short and troubled nights he spent, he believed himself that he was not very far from it.

It was with a feeling of relief and safety, like a ship coming into port, that he stayed his horse at the door of the college, which stood in a quiet street of the city. He carried a valise of clothes in which the bar was secured. He had a very friendly greeting from the old Canon, who received him in a little studious parlour full of books. The court was full of pleasant sunshine, and the city outside seemed to make a pleasant and wholesome stir in the air.

But the Canon was very much amazed at Walter's looks; he was used to read the hearts of men in their faces like a wise priest, and he saw in Walter's face a certain desperate look such as he had seen, he said to himself, in the faces of those who had a deadly sin to confess. But it was not his way to make inquisition, and so he talked courteously and easily, and when he found that Walter was inclined to be silent, he filled the silence himself with little talk of the news of the town.

After the meal, which they took in the Canon's room – for Walter said that he would prefer that to dining in the Hall, when the Canon gave him the choice – Walter said that he had a strange story to tell him. The Canon felt no surprise, and being used to strange stories, addressed himself to listen carefully; for he thought that in the most difficult and sad tales of sin the words of the sufferer most often supplied the advice and the way out, if one but listened warily.

He did not interrupt Walter except to ask him a few questions to make the story clear, but his face grew very grave; and at the end he sate some time in silence. Then he said very gently that it was a heavy judgment, but that he must ask Walter one question. 'I do not ask you to tell me,' he said very courteously, 'what it may be; but is there no other thing in which you have displeased God? For these grievous thoughts and fears are sometimes sent as a punishment for sin, and to turn men back to the light.'

Then Walter said that he knew of no such sin by which he could have vexed God so exceedingly. 'Careless,' he said, 'I am and have been; and, father, I would tell you anything that was in my heart; I would have no secrets from you – but though I am a sinner, and do not serve God as well as I would, yet I desire to serve Him, and have no sin that is set like a wall between Him and me.' He said this so honestly and bravely, looking so full at the priest, that he did not doubt him, and said, 'Then, my son, we must look elsewhere for the cause; and though I speak in haste, and without weighing my words, it seems to me that, to speak in parables, you are like a man who has come by chance to a den and carried off for his pleasure the cubs of some forest beast, who returns and finds them gone, and tracks the robber out. The souls of these poor warriors are in some mansion of God, we know not where; if they did faithfully in life they are beaten, as the Scripture says, with few stripes; but they may not enjoy His blessed rest, nor the sweet sleep of the faithful souls who lie beneath the altar and wait for His coming. And now though they cannot slay you, they can do you grievous hurt. The Holy Church hath power indeed over the spirits of evil, the devils that enter into men. But I have not heard that she hath power over the spirits of the dead, and least of all over those that lived and died outside the fold. It seems to me, though I but grope in darkness, that these poor spirits grudge the treasure that they fought and died for to the hands of a man who hath not fought for it. We may think that it is a poor and childish thing to grudge that which one cannot use; but no discourse will make a child think so; and I reckon that these poor souls are as children yet. And it seems to me, speaking foolishly, as though they would not be appeased until you either restored it to them, or used it for their undoubted benefit; but of one thing I am certain, that it must not be used to enrich yourself. But I must ponder over the story, for it is a strange one, and not such as has ever yet come before me.'

Then Walter found fresh courage at these wary and wise words, and told him of his impoverished estate and the love he had to Marjory; and the priest smiled, and said that love was the best thing to win in the world. And then he said that as it was now late, they must sleep; and that the night often brought counsel; and so he took Walter to his chamber, a little precise place with a window on the court; and there he left him; but he first knelt down and prayed, and then laid his hand on Walter's head, and blessed him, and commended him to the merciful keeping of God; and Walter slept sweetly, and was scared that night by no dismal dreams; and in the morning the priest took him to the church, and Walter knelt in a little chapel while the old man said his mass, commending therein the burden of Walter's suffering into the merciful hands of God; so that Walter's heart was greatly lightened.

Then after the mass the priest asked Walter of his health, and whether he had suffered any visitation of evil that night; he said 'no,' and the priest then said that he had pondered long over the story, which was strange and very dark. But he had little doubt now as to what Walter should do. He did not think that the treasure should be replaced now that it was got up, because it was only flying before the evil and not meeting it, but leaving the sad inheritance for some other man. The poor spirit must be laid to rest, and the treasure used for God's glory. 'And therefore,' he said, 'I think that a church must be built, and dedicated to All Souls; and thus your net will be wide enough to catch the sad spirit. And you must buy a little estate for the support of the chaplain thereof, and so shall all be content.'

'All but one,' said Walter sadly, 'for there goes my dream of setting up my own house that tumbles down.'

'My son,' said the old priest very gravely, 'you must not murmur; it will be enough for you if God take away the sore chastening of your spirit; and for the rest, He will provide.'

'But there is more behind,' he said after a pause. 'If you, with an impoverished estate, build a church and endow a priest, there will be questions asked; it will needs be known that you have found a treasure, and it will come, perhaps, to the ears of the King's Grace, and inquisition will be made; so I shall go this morning to a Lord of the Court, an ancient friend of mine, a discreet man; and I will lay the story before him, if you give me leave; and he will advise.'

Walter saw that the priest's advice was good; and so he gave him leave; and the priest departed to the Court; but while he was away, as Walter sate sadly over a book, his terrors came upon him with fresh force; the thing drew near him and stood at his shoulder, and he could not dislodge it; it seemed to Walter that it was more malign than ever, and was set upon driving him to some desperate deed; so he rose and paced in the court; but it seemed to move behind him, till he thought he would have gone distraught; but finding the church doors open, he went inside and, in a corner, knelt and prayed, and got some kind of peace; yet he felt all the while as though the presence waited for him at the door, but could not hurt him in the holy shrine; and there Walter made a vow and vowed his life into the hands of God; for he had found the world a harder place than he had thought, and it seemed to him as though he walked among unseen foes. Presently he saw the old priest come into the church, peering about; so Walter rose and came to him; the priest had a contented air, but seemed big with news, and he told Walter that he must go with him at once to the Court. For he had seen the Lord Poynings, that was his friend, who had taken him at once to the King; and the King had heard the story very curiously, and would see Walter himself that day. So Walter fetched the bar of gold and they went at once together; and Walter was full of awe and fear, and asked the priest how he should bear himself; to which the priest said smiling, 'As a man, in the presence of a man.' And as they went Walter told him that he had been visited by the terror again, but had found peace in the church; and the priest said, 'Ay, there is peace to be had there.'

They came down to the palace, and were at once admitted; the priest and he were led into a little room, full of books, where a man was writing, a venerable man in a furred gown, with a comely face; this was the Lord Poynings, who greeted Walter very gently but with a secret attention; Walter shewed him the bar of gold, and he looked at it long, and presently there came a page who said that the King was at leisure, and would see Mr Wyatt.

Walter had hoped that the priest, or at least the Lord Poynings, would accompany him; but the message was for himself alone; so he was led along a high corridor with tall stands of arms. The King had been a great warrior in his manhood, and had won many trophies. They came to a great doorway, where the page knocked; a voice cried within, and the page told Walter he must enter alone.

Walter would fain have asked the page how he should make his obeisance; but there was no time now, for the page opened the door, and Walter went in.

He found himself in a small room, hung with green arras. The King was sitting in a great chair, by a table spread out with parchments. Walter first bowed low and then knelt down; the King motioned him to rise, and then said in a quiet and serene voice, 'So, sir, you are the gentleman that has found a treasure and would fain be rid of it again.' At these gentle words Walter felt his terrors leave him; the King looked at him with a serious attention; he was a man just passing into age; his head was nearly hairless, and he had a thin face with a long nose, and small lips drawn together. On his head was a loose velvet cap, and he wore his gown furred; round his neck was a jewel, and he had great rings on his forefingers and thumbs.

The King, hardly pausing for an answer, said, 'You look ill, Master Wyatt, and little wonder; sit here in a chair and tell me the tale in a few words.'

Walter told his story as shortly as he could with the King's kind eye upon him; the King once or twice interrupted him; he took the bar from Walter's hands, and looked upon it, weighing it in his fingers, and saying, 'Ay, it is a mighty treasure.' Once or twice he made him repeat a few sentences, and heard the story of the thing that stood near him with a visible awe.

At last he said with a smile, 'You have told your story well, sir, and plainly; are you a soldier?' When Walter said 'no,' he said, 'It is a noble trade, nevertheless.' Then he said, 'Well, sir, the treasure is yours, to use as I understand you will use it for the glory of God and for the peace of the poor spirit, which I doubt not is that of a great knight. But I have no desire to be visited of him,' and here he crossed himself. 'So let it be thus bestowed – and I will cause a quittance to be made out for you from the Crown, which will take no part in the trove. How many bars did you say?' And when Walter said 'fifty', the King said, 'It is great wealth; and I wish for your sake, sir, that it were not so sad an inheritance.' Then he added, 'Well, sir, that is the matter; but I would hear the end of this, for I never knew the like; when your church is built and all things are in order, and let it be done speedily, you shall come and visit me again.' And then the King said, with a kindly smile, 'And as for the maiden of whom I have heard, be not discouraged; for yours is an ancient house, and it must not be extinguished – and so farewell; and remember that your King wishes you happiness;' and he made a sign that Walter should withdraw. So Walter knelt again and kissed the King's ring, and left the chamber.

When Walter came out he seemed to tread on air; the King's gracious kindness moved him very greatly, and loyalty filled his heart to the brim. He found the priest and the Lord Poynings waiting for him; and presently the two left the palace together, and Walter told the priest what the King had said.

The next day he rode back into Sussex; but he was very sorely beset as he rode, and reached home in great misery. But he wasted no time, but rather went to his new task with great eagerness; the foundations of the church were laid, and soon the walls began to rise. Meanwhile

Walter had the gold conveyed to the King's Mint; and a message came to him that it would make near upon twenty thousand pounds of gold, a fortune for an earl. So the church was built very massive and great, and a rich estate was bought which would support a college of priests. But Walter's heart was very heavy; for his terrors still came over him from day to day; and he was no nearer settling his own affairs.

Then there began to come to him a sore temptation; he could build his church, and endow his college with lands, and yet he could save something of the treasure to set him free from his own poverty; and day by day this wrought more and more in his mind.

At last one day when he was wandering through the wood, he found himself face to face in the path with Marjory herself; and there was so tender a look in her face that he could no longer resist, so he turned and walked with her, and told her all that was in his heart. 'It was all for the love of you,' he said, 'that I have thus been punished, and now I am no nearer the end;' and then, for he saw that she wept, and that she loved him well, he opened to her his heart, and said that he would keep back part of the treasure, and would save his house, and that they would be wed; and so he kissed her on the lips.

But Marjory was a true-hearted and wise maiden, and loved Walter better than he knew; and she said to him, all trembling for pity, 'Dear Walter, it cannot be; this must be given faithfully, because you are the King's servant, and because you must give the spirit back his own, and because you are he that I love the best; and we will wait; for God tells me that it must be so; and He is truer even than love.'

So Walter was ashamed; and he threw unworthy thoughts away; and with the last of the money he caused a fair screen to be made, and windows of rich glass; and the money was thus laid out.

Now while the church was in building – and they made all the haste they could – Walter had days when he was very grievously troubled; but it seemed to him a different sort of trouble. In the first place he looked forward confidently to the day when the dark presence would be withdrawn; and a man who can look forward to a certain ending to his pain can stay himself on that; but, besides that, it seemed to him that he was not now beset by a foe, but guarded as it were by a sentinel. There were days when the horror was very great, and when the thing was always near him whether he sate or walked, whether he was alone or in company; and on those days he withdrew himself from men, and there was a dark shadow on his brow. So that there grew up a kind of mystery about him; but, besides that, he learnt things in those bitter hours that are not taught in any school. He learnt to suffer with all the great company of those who bear heavy and unseen burdens, who move in the grip of fears and stumble under the load of dark necessities. He grew more tender and more strong. He found in his hand the key to many hearts. Before this he had cared little about the thoughts of other men; but now he found himself for ever wondering what the inner thoughts of the hearts of others were, and ready if need were to help to lift their load; he had lived before in careless fellowship with light-hearted persons, but now he was rather drawn to the old and wise and sad; and there fell on him some touch of the holy priesthood that falls on all whose sadness is a fruitful sadness, and who instead of yielding to bitter repining would try to make others happier. If he heard of a sorrow or a distress, his thought was no longer how to put it out of his mind as soon as he might, but of how he might lighten it. So his heart grew wider day by day.

And at last the day came when the church was done; it stood, a fair white shrine with a seemly tower, on the hill-top, and a little way from it was the college for the priests. The Bishop came to consecrate it, and the old Canon came from London, and there was a little gathering of neighbours to see the holy work accomplished.

The Bishop blessed the church very tenderly; he was an old infirm man, but he bore his weakness lightly and serenely. He made Walter the night before tell him the story of the treasure, and found much to wonder at in it.

There was no part of the church or its furniture that he did not solemnly bless; and Walter from his place felt a grave joy to see all so fair and seemly. The priests moved from end to end with the Bishop, in their stiff embroidered robes, and there was a holy smell of incense which strove with the sharp scent of the newly-chiselled wood. The Bishop made them a little sermon and spoke much of the gathering into the fold of spirits that had done their work bravely, even if they had not known the Lord Christ on earth.

After all was over, and the guests were departed, the old Canon said that he must return on the morrow to London, and that he had a message for Walter from the King – who had not failed to ask him how the work went on – that Walter was to return with him and tell the King of the fulfilment of the design.

That night Walter had a strange dream; he seemed to stand in a dark place all vaulted over, like a cave that stretched far into the earth; he himself stood in the shadow of a rock, and he was aware of someone passing by him. He looked at him, and saw that he was the warrior that he had seen before in his dream, a small pale man, with a short beard, with rusty armour much dinted; he held a spear in his hand, and walked restlessly like a man little content. But while Walter watched him, there seemed to be another person drawing near in the opposite direction. This was a tall man, all in white, who brought with him as he came a strange freshness in the dark place, as of air and light, and the scent of flowers; this one came along in a different fashion, with an assured and yet tender air, as though he was making search for someone to whom his coming would be welcome; so the two met and words passed between them; the warrior stood with his hands clasped upon his spear seeming to drink in what was said – he could not hear the words at first, for they were spoken softly, but the last words he heard were, 'And you too are of the number.' Then the warrior kneeled down and laid his spear aside, and the other seemed to stoop and bless him, and then went on his way; and the warrior knelt and watched him going with a look in his face as though he had heard wonderful and beautiful news, and could hardly yet believe it; and so holy was the look that Walter felt as though he intruded upon some deep mystery, and moved further into the shadow of the rock; but the warrior rose and came to him where he stood, and looked at him with a half-doubting look, as though he asked pardon, stretching out his hands; and Walter smiled at him, and the other smiled; and at the moment Walter woke in the dawn with a strange joy in his heart, and rising in haste, drew the window curtain aside, and saw the fresh dawn beginning to come in over the woods, and he knew that the burden was lifted from him and that he was free.

In the morning as the old Canon and Walter rode to London, Walter told him the dream; and when he had done, he saw that the old priest was smiling at him with his eyes full of tears, and that he could not speak; so they rode together in that sweet silence which is worth more than many words.

The next day Walter came to see the King: he carried with him a paper to show the King how all had been expended; but he went with no fear, but as though to see a true friend.

The King received him very gladly, and bade Walter tell him all that had been done; so Walter told him, and then speaking very softly told the King the dream; the King mused over the story, and then said, 'So he has his heart's desire.'

Then there was a silence; and then the King, as though breaking out of a pleasant thought, drew from the table a parchment, and said to Walter that he had done well and wisely, and therefore for the trust that he had in him he made him his Sheriff for the County of Sussex, to which was added a large revenue; and there was more to come, for the King bade Walter unhook a sword from the wall, his own sword that he had borne in battle; and therewith he dubbed him knight, and said to him, 'Rise up, Sir Walter Wyatt.' Then before he dismissed him, he said to him that he would see him every year at the Court; and then with a smile he added, 'And when you next come, I charge you to bring with you my Lady Wyatt.'

And Walter promised this, and kept his word.

Out of the Sea

A. C. BENSON

It was about ten of the clock on a November morning in the little village of Blea-on-the-Sands. The hamlet was made up of some thirty houses, which clustered together on a low rising ground. The place was very poor, but some old merchant of bygone days had built in a pious mood a large church, which was now too great for the needs of the place; the nave had been unroofed in a heavy gale, and there was no money to repair it, so that it had fallen to decay, and the tower was joined to the choir by roofless walls. This was a sore trial to the old priest, Father Thomas, who had grown grey there; but he had no art in gathering money, which he asked for in a shamefaced way; and the vicarage was a poor one, hardly enough for the old man's needs. So the church lay desolate.

The village stood on what must once have been an island; the little river Reddy, which runs down to the sea, there forking into two channels on the landward side; towards the sea the ground was bare, full of sand-hills covered with a short grass. Towards the land was a small wood of gnarled trees, the boughs of which were all brushed smooth by the gales; looking landward there was the green flat, in which the river ran, rising into low hills; hardly a house was visible save one or two lonely farms; two or three church towers rose above the hills at a long distance away. Indeed Blea was much cut off from the world; there was a bridge over the stream on the west side, but over the other channel was no bridge, so that to fare eastward it was requisite to go in a boat. To seaward there were wide sands, when the tide was out; when it was in, it came up nearly to the end of the village street. The people were mostly fishermen, but there were a few farmers and labourers; the boats of the fishermen lay to the east side of the village, near the river channel which gave some draught of water; and the channel was marked out by big black stakes and posts that straggled out over the sands, like awkward leaning figures, to the sea's brim.

Father Thomas lived in a small and ancient brick house near the church, with a little garden of herbs attached. He was a kindly man, much worn by age and weather, with a wise heart, and he loved the quiet life with his small flock. This morning he had come out of his house to look abroad, before he settled down to the making of his sermon. He looked out to sea, and saw with a shadow of sadness the black outline of a wreck that had come ashore a week before, and over which the white waves were now breaking. The wind blew steadily from the north-east, and had a bitter poisonous chill in it, which it doubtless drew from the fields of the upper ice. The day was dark and overhung, not with cloud, but with a kind of dreary vapour that shut out the sun. Father Thomas shuddered at the wind, and drew his patched cloak round him. As he did so, he saw three figures come up to the vicarage gate. It was not a common thing for him to have visitors in the morning, and he saw with surprise that they were old Master John Grimston, the richest man in the place, half farmer and half fisherman, a dark surly old man; his wife, Bridget, a timid and frightened woman, who found life with her harsh husband a difficult business, in spite of their wealth, which, for a place like Blea, was great; and their son Henry, a silly shambling man of forty, who was his father's butt. The three walked silently and heavily, as though they came on a sad errand.

Father Thomas went briskly down to meet them, and greeted them with his accustomed cheerfulness. 'And what may I do for you?' he said. Old Master Grimston made a sort of gesture with his head as though his wife should speak; and she said in a low and somewhat husky voice, with a rapid utterance, 'We have a matter, Father, we would ask you about – are you at leisure?' Father Thomas said, 'Ay, I am ashamed to be not more busy! Let us go within the house.' They did so; and even in the little distance to the door, the Father thought that his visitors behaved themselves very strangely. They peered round from left to right, and once or twice Master Grimston looked sharply behind them, as though they were followed. They said nothing but 'Ay' and 'No' to the Father's talk, and bore themselves like people with a sore fear on their backs. Father Thomas made up his mind that it was some question of money, for nothing else was wont to move Master Grimston's mind. So he had them into his parlour and gave them seats, and then there was a silence, while the two men continued to look furtively about them, and the goodwife sate with her eyes upon the priest's face. Father Thomas knew not what to make of this, till Master Grimston said harshly, 'Come, wife, tell the tale and make an end; we must not take up the Father's time.'

'I hardly know how to say it, Father,' said Bridget, 'but a strange and evil thing has befallen us; there is something come to our house, and we know not what it is – but it brings a fear with it.' A sudden paleness came over her face, and she stopped, and the three exchanged a glance in which terror was visibly written. Master Grimston looked over his shoulder swiftly, and made as though to speak, yet only swallowed in his throat; but Henry said suddenly, in a loud and woeful voice: 'It is an evil beast out of the sea.'

And then there followed a dreadful silence, while Father Thomas felt a sudden fear leap up in his heart, at the contagion of the fear that he saw written on the faces round him. But he said with all the cheerfulness he could muster, 'Come, friends, let us not begin to talk of sea-beasts; we must have the whole tale. Mistress Grimston, I must hear the story – be content – nothing can touch us here.'

The three seemed to draw a faint content from his words, and Bridget began: 'It was the day of the wreck, Father. John was up betimes, before the dawn; he walked out early to the sands, and Henry with him – and they were the first to see the wreck – was not that it?' At these words the father and son seemed to exchange a very swift and secret look, and both grew pale. 'John told me there was a wreck ashore, and they went presently and roused the rest of the village; and all that day they were out, saving what could be saved. Two sailors were found, both dead and pitifully battered by the sea, and they were buried, as you know, Father, in the churchyard next day; John came back about dusk and Henry with him, and we sate down to our supper. John was telling me about the wreck, as we sate beside the fire, when Henry, who was sitting apart, rose up and cried out suddenly, "What is that?"'

She paused for a moment, and Henry, who sate with face blanched, staring at his mother, said, 'Ay, did I – it ran past me suddenly.'

'Yes, but what was it?' said Father Thomas trying to smile; 'a dog or cat, methinks.'

'It was a beast,' said Henry slowly, in a trembling voice – 'a beast about the bigness of a goat. I never saw the like – yet I did not see it clear; I but felt the air blow, and caught a whiff of it – it was salt like the sea, but with a kind of dead smell behind.'

'Was that all you saw?' said Father Thomas; 'belike you were tired and faint, and the air swam round you suddenly – I have known the like myself when weary.'

'Nay, nay,' said Henry, 'this was not like that – it was a beast, sure enough.'

'Ay, and we have seen it since,' said Bridget. 'At least I have not seen it clearly yet, but I have smelt its odour, and it turns me sick – but John and Henry have seen it often – sometimes it lies and seems to sleep, but it watches us; and again it is merry, and will leap in a corner – and John saw it skip upon the sands near the wreck – did you not, John?'

At these words the two men again exchanged a glance, and then old Master Grimston, with a dreadful look in his face, in which great anger seemed to strive with fear, said, 'Nay, silly woman, it was not near the wreck, it was out to the east.'

'It matters little,' said Father Thomas, who saw well enough this was no light matter. 'I never heard the like of it. I will myself come down to your house with a holy book, and see if the thing will meet me. I know not what this is,' he went on, 'whether it is a vain terror that hath hold of you; but there be spirits of evil in the world, though much fettered by Christ and His Saints – we read of such in Holy Writ – and the sea, too, doubtless hath its monsters; and it may be that one hath wandered out of the waves, like a dog that hath strayed from his home. I dare not say, till I have met it face to face. But God gives no power to such things to hurt those who have a fair conscience.' – And here he made a stop, and looked at the three; Bridget sate regarding him with a hope in her face; but the other two sate peering upon the ground; and the priest divined in some secret way that all was not well with them. 'But I will come at once,' he said, rising, 'and I will see if I can cast out or bind the thing, whatever it be – for I am in this place as a soldier of the Lord, to fight with works of darkness.' He took a clasped book from a table, and lifted up his hat, saying, 'Let us set forth.' Then he said as they left the room, 'Hath it appeared today?'

'Yes, indeed,' said Henry, 'and it was ill content. It followed us as though it were angered.'

'Come,' said Father Thomas, turning upon him, 'you speak thus of a thing, as you might speak of a dog – what is it like?'

'Nay,' said Henry, 'I know not; I can never see it clearly; it is like a speck in the eye – it is never there when you look upon it – it glides away very secretly; it is most like a goat, I think. It seems to be horned, and hairy; but I have seen its eyes, and they were yellow, like a flame.'

As he said these words Master Grimston went in haste to the door, and pulled it open as though to breathe the air. The others followed him and went out; but Master Grimston drew the priest aside, and said like a man in a mortal fear, 'Look you, Father, all this is true – the thing is a devil – and why it abides with us I know not; but I cannot live so; and unless it be cast out it will slay me – but if money be of avail, I have it in abundance.'

'Nay,' said Father Thomas, 'let there be no talk of money – perchance if I can aid you, you may give of your gratitude to God.'

'Ay, ay,' said the old man hurriedly, 'that was what I meant – there is money in abundance for God, if He will but set me free.'

So they walked very sadly together through the street. There were few folk about; the men and the children were all abroad – a woman or two came to the house doors, and wondered a little to see them pass so solemnly, as though they followed a body to the grave.

Master Grimston's house was the largest in the place. It had a walled garden before it, with a strong door set in the wall. The house stood back from the road, a dark front of brick with gables; behind it the garden sloped nearly to the sands, with wooden barns and warehouses. Master Grimston unlocked the door, and then it seemed that his terrors came over him, for he would have the priest enter first. Father Thomas, with a certain apprehension of which he was ashamed, walked quickly in, and looked about him. The herbage of the garden had mostly died down in the winter, and a tangle of sodden stalks lay over the beds. A flagged path edged with box led up to the house, which seemed to stare at them out of its dark windows with a sort of steady gaze. Master Grimston fastened the door behind them, and they went all together, keeping close one to another, up to the house, the door of which opened upon a big parlour or kitchen, sparely furnished, but very clean and comfortable. Some vessels of metal glittered on a rack. There were chairs, ranged round the open fireplace. There was no sound except that the wind buffeted in the chimney. It looked a quiet and homely place, and Father Thomas grew ashamed of his fears. 'Now,' said he in his firm voice, 'though I am your guest here, I will appoint what shall be done. We will sit here together, and talk as cheerfully as we may, till we have dined. Then, if nothing appears to us' – and he crossed himself – 'I will go round the house, into every room, and see if we can track the thing to its lair: then I will abide with you till evensong; and then I will soon return, and lie here tonight. Even if the thing be wary, and dares not to meet the power of the Church in the day-time, perhaps it will venture out at night; and I will even try a fall with it. So come, good people, and be comforted.'

So they sate together; and Father Thomas talked of many things, and told some old legends of saints; and they dined, though without much cheer; and still nothing appeared. Then, after dinner, Father Thomas would view the house. So he took his book up, and they went from room to room. On the ground floor there were several chambers not used, which they entered in turn, but saw nothing; on the upper floor was a large room where Master Grimston and his wife slept; and a further room for Henry, and a guest-chamber in which the priest was to sleep if need was; and a room where a servant-maid slept. And now the day began to darken and to turn to evening, and Father Thomas felt a shadow grow in his mind. There came into his head a verse of Scripture about a spirit which found a house 'empty, swept and garnished', and called his fellows to enter in.

At the end of the passage was a locked door; and Father Thomas said: 'This is the last room – let us enter.'

'Nay, there is no need to do that,' said Master Grimston in a kind of haste; 'it leads nowhither – it is but a room of stores.'

'It were a pity to leave it unvisited,' said the Father – and as he said the word, there came a kind of stirring from within.

'A rat, doubtless,' said the Father, striving with a sudden sense of fear; but the pale faces round him told another tale. 'Come, Master Grimston, let us be done with this,' said Father Thomas decisively; 'the hour of vespers draws nigh.'

So Master Grimston slowly drew out a key and unlocked the door, and Father Thomas marched in. It was a simple place enough. There were shelves on which various household matters lay, boxes and jars, with twine and cordage. On the ground stood chests. There were some clothes hanging on pegs, and in a corner was a heap of garments, piled up. On one of the chests stood a box of rough deal, and from the corner of it dripped water, which lay in a little pool on the floor. Master Grimston went hurriedly to the box and pushed it further to the wall. As he did so, a kind of sound came from Henry's lips. Father Thomas turned and looked at him; he stood pale and strengthless, his eyes fixed on the corner – at the same moment something dark and shapeless seemed to slip past the group, and there came to the nostrils of Father Thomas a strange sharp smell, as of the sea, only that there was a taint within it, like the smell of corruption.

They all turned and looked at Father Thomas together, as though seeking a comfort from his presence. He, hardly knowing what he did, and in the grasp of a terrible fear, fumbled with his book; and opening it, read the first words that his eye fell upon, which was the place where the Blessed Lord, beset with enemies, said that if He did but pray to His Father, He should send Him forthwith legions of angels to encompass Him. And the verse seemed to the priest so like a message sent instantly from heaven that he was not a little comforted.

But the thing, whatever the reason was, appeared to them no more at that time. Yet the thought of it lay very heavy on Father Thomas's heart. In truth he had not in the bottom of his mind believed that he would see it, but had trusted in his honest life and his sacred calling to protect him. He could hardly speak for some minutes – moreover the horror of the thing was very great – and seeing him so grave, their terrors were increased, though there was a kind of miserable joy in their minds that someone, and he a man of high repute, should suffer with them.

Then Father Thomas, after a pause – they were now in the parlour – said, speaking very slowly, that they were in a sore affliction of Satan, and that they must withstand him with a good courage – 'and look you,' he added, turning with a great sternness to the three, 'if there be any mortal sin upon your hearts, see that you confess it and be shriven speedily – for while such a thing lies upon the heart, so long hath Satan power to hurt – otherwise have no fear at all.'

Then Father Thomas slipped out to the garden, and hearing the bell pulled for vespers, he went to the church, and the three would go with him, because they would not be left alone. So they went together; by this time the street was fuller, and the servant-maid had told tales, so that there was much talk in the place about what was going forward. None spoke with them as they went, but at every corner you might see one check another in talk, and a silence fall upon a group, so that they knew that their terrors were on every tongue. There was but a handful of worshippers in the church, which was dark, save for the light on Father Thomas's book. He read the holy service swiftly and courageously, but his face was very pale and grave in the light of the candle. When the vespers were over, and he had put off his robe, he said that he would go back to his house, and gather what he needed for the night, and that they should wait for him at the churchyard gate. So he strode off to his vicarage. But as he shut to the door, he saw a dark figure come running up the garden; he waited with a fear in his mind, but in a moment he saw that it was Henry, who came up breathless, and said that he must speak with the

Father alone. Father Thomas knew that somewhat dark was to be told him. So he led Henry into the parlour and seated himself, and said, 'Now, my son, speak boldly.' So there was an instant's silence, and Henry slipped on to his knees.

Then in a moment Henry with a sob began to tell his tale. He said that on the day of the wreck his father had roused him very early in the dawn, and had told him to put on his clothes and come silently, for he thought there was a wreck ashore. His father carried a spade in his hand, he knew not then why. They went down to the tide, which was moving out very fast, and left but an inch or two of water on the sands. There was but a little light, but, when they had walked a little, they saw the black hull of a ship before them, on the edge of the deeper water, the waves driving over it; and then all at once they came upon the body of a man lying on his face on the sand. There was no sign of life in him, but he clasped a bag in his hand that was heavy, and the pocket of his coat was full to bulging; and there lay, moreover, some glittering things about him that seemed to be coins. They lifted the body up, and his father stripped the coat off from the man, and then bade Henry dig a hole in the sand, which he presently did, though the sand and water oozed fast into it. Then his father, who had been stooping down, gathering somewhat up from the sand, raised the body up, and laid it in the hole, and bade Henry cover it with the sand. And so he did till it was nearly hidden. Then came a horrible thing; the sand in the hole began to move and stir, and presently a hand was put out with clutching fingers; and Henry had dropped the spade, and said, 'There is life in him,' but his father seized the spade, and shovelled the sand into the hole with a kind of silent fury, and trampled it over and smoothed it down – and then he gathered up the coat and the bag, and handed Henry the spade. By this time the town was astir, and they saw, very faintly, a man run along the shore eastward; so, making a long circuit to the west, they returned; his father had put the spade away and taken the coat upstairs; and then he went out with Henry, and told all he could find that there was a wreck ashore.

The priest heard the story with a fierce shame and anger, and turning to Henry he said, 'But why did you not resist your father, and save the poor sailor?'

'I dared not,' said Henry shuddering, 'though I would have done so if I could; but my father has a power over me, and I am used to obey him.'

Then said the priest, 'This is a dark matter. But you have told the story bravely, and now will I shrive you, my son.' So he gave him shrift. Then he said to Henry, 'And have you seen aught that would connect the beast that visits you with this thing?'

'Ay, that I have,' said Henry, 'for I watched it with my father skip and leap in the water over the place where the man lies buried.'

Then the priest said, 'Your father must tell me the tale too, and he must make submission to the law.'

'He will not,' said Henry.

'Then will I compel him,' said the priest.

'Not out of my mouth,' said Henry, 'or he will slay me too.' And then the priest said that he was in a strait place, for he could not use the words of confession of one man to convict another of his sin. So he gathered his things in haste, and walked back to the church; but Henry went another way, saying 'I made excuse to come away, and said I went elsewhere; but I fear my father much – he sees very deep; and I would not have him suspect me of having made confession.'

Then the Father met the other two at the church gate; and they went down to the house in silence, the Father pondering heavily; and at the door Henry joined them, and it seemed to the Father that old Master Grimston regarded him not. So they entered the house in silence, and ate in silence, listening earnestly for any sound. And the Father looked oft on Master Grimston, who ate and drank and said nothing, never raising his eyes. But once the Father saw him laugh secretly to himself, so that the blood came cold in the Father's veins, and he could hardly contain himself from accusing him. Then the Father had them to prayers, and prayed earnestly against the evil, and that they should open their hearts to God, if He would show them why this misery came upon them.

Then they went to bed; and Henry asked that he might lie in the priest's room, which he willingly granted. And so the house was dark, and they made as though they would sleep; but the Father could not sleep, and he heard Henry weeping silently to himself like a little child.

But at last the Father slept – how long he knew not – and suddenly brake out of his sleep with a horror of darkness all about him, and knew that there was some evil thing abroad. So he looked upon the room. He heard Henry mutter heavily in his sleep as though there was a dark terror upon him; and then, in the light of the dying embers, the Father saw a thing rise upon the hearth, as though it had slept there, and woke to stretch itself. And then in the half-light it seemed softly to gambol and play; but whereas when an innocent beast does this in the simple joy of its heart, it seems a fond and pretty sight, the Father thought he had never seen so ugly a sight as the beast gambolling all by itself, as if it could not contain its own dreadful joy; it looked viler and more wicked every moment; then, too, there spread in the room the sharp scent of the sea, with the foul smell underneath it, that gave the Father a deadly sickness; he tried to pray, but no words would come, and he felt indeed that the evil was too strong for him. Presently the beast desisted from its play, and looking wickedly about it, came near to the Father's bed, and seemed to put up its hairy forelegs upon it; he could see its narrow and obscene eyes, which burned with a dull yellow light, and were fixed upon him. And now the Father thought that his end was near, for he could stir neither hand nor foot, and the sweat rained down his brow; but he made a mighty effort, and in a voice which shocked himself, so dry and husky and withal of so loud and screaming a tone it was, he said three holy words. The beast gave a great quiver of rage, but it dropped down on the floor, and in a moment was gone. Then Henry woke, and raising himself on his arm, said somewhat; but there broke out in the house a great outcry and the stamping of feet, which seemed very fearful in the silence of the night. The priest leapt out of his bed all dizzy, and made a light, and ran to the door, and went out, crying whatever words came to his head. The door of Master Grimston's room was open, and a strange and strangling sound came forth; the Father made his way in, and found Master Grimston lying upon the floor, his wife bending over him; he lay still, breathing pitifully, and every now and then a shudder ran through him. In the room there seemed a strange and shadowy tumult going forward; but the Father saw that no time could be lost, and kneeling down beside Master Grimston, he prayed with all his might.

Presently Master Grimston ceased to struggle and lay still, like a man who had come out of a sore conflict. Then he opened his eyes, and the Father stopped his prayers, and looking very hard at him he said, 'My son, the time is very short – give God the glory.'

Then Master Grimston, rolling his haggard eyes upon the group, twice strove to speak and could not; but the third time the Father, bending down his head, heard him say in a thin voice, that seemed to float from a long way off, 'I slew him . . . my sin.'

Then the Father swiftly gave him shrift, and as he said the last word, Master Grimston's head fell over on the side, and the Father said, 'He is gone.' And Bridget broke out into a terrible cry, and fell upon Henry's neck, who had entered unseen.

Then the Father bade him lead her away, and put the poor body on the bed; as he did so he noticed that the face of the dead man was strangely bruised and battered, as though it had been stamped upon by the hoofs of some beast. Then Father Thomas knelt, and prayed until the light came filtering in through the shutters; and the cocks crowed in the village, and presently it was day. But that night the Father learnt strange secrets, and something of the dark purposes of God was revealed to him.

In the morning there came one to find the priest, and told him that another body had been thrown up on the shore, which was strangely smeared with sand, as though it had been rolled over and over in it; and the Father took order for its burial.

Then the priest had long talk with Bridget and Henry. He found them sitting together, and she held her son's hand and smoothed his hair, as though he had been a little child; and Henry sobbed and wept, but Bridget was very calm. 'He hath told me all,' she said, 'and we have decided that he shall do whatever you bid him; must he be given to justice?' and she looked at the priest very pitifully.

'Nay, nay,' said the priest. 'I hold not Henry to account for the death of the man; it was his father's sin, who hath made heavy atonement – the secret shall be buried in our hearts.'

Then Bridget told him how she had waked suddenly out of her sleep, and heard her husband cry out; and that then followed a dreadful kind of struggling, with the scent of the sea over all; and then he had all at once fallen to the ground and she had gone to him – and that then the priest had come.

Then Father Thomas said with tears that God had shown them deep things and visited them very strangely; and they would henceforth live humbly in His sight, showing mercy.

Then lastly he went with Henry to the storeroom; and there, in the box that had dripped with water, lay the coat of the dead man, full of money, and the bag of money too; and Henry would have cast it back into the sea, but the priest said that this might not be, but that it should be bestowed plentifully upon shipwrecked mariners unless the heirs should be found. But the ship appeared to be a foreign ship, and no search ever revealed whence the money had come, save that it seemed to have been violently come by.

Master Grimston was found to have left much wealth. But Bridget would sell the house and the land, and it mostly went to rebuild the church to God's glory. Then Bridget and Henry removed to the vicarage and served Father Thomas faithfully, and they guarded their secret. And beside the nave is a little high turret built, where burns a lamp in a lantern at the top, to give light to those at sea.

Now the beast troubled those of whom I write no more; but it is easier to raise up evil than to lay it; and there are those that say that to this day a man or a woman with an evil thought in their hearts may see on a certain evening in November, at the ebb of the tide, a goatlike thing wade in the water, snuffing at the sand, as though it sought but found not. But of this I know nothing.

The Grey Cat

A. C. BENSON

The knight Sir James Leigh lived in a remote valley of the Welsh Hills. The manor house, of rough grey stone, with thick walls and mullioned windows, stood on a rising ground; at its foot ran a little river, through great boulders. There were woods all about; but above the woods, the bare green hills ran smoothly up, so high, that in the winter the sun only peeped above the ridge for an hour or two; beyond the house, the valley wound away into the heart of the hills, and at the end a black peak looked over. The place was very sparsely inhabited; within a close of ancient yew trees stood a little stone church, and a small parsonage smothered in ivy, where an old priest, a cousin of the knight, lived. There were but three farms in the valley, and a rough track led over the hills, little used, except by drovers. At the top of the pass stood a stone cross; and from this point you could see the dark scarred face of the peak to the left, streaked with snow, which did not melt until the summer was far advanced.

Sir James was a silent sad man, in ill-health; he spoke little and bore his troubles bitterly; he was much impoverished, through his own early carelessness, and now so feeble in body that he had small hope of repairing the fortune he had lost. His wife was a wise and loving woman, who, though she found it hard to live happily in so lonely a place with a sickly husband, met her sorrows with a cheerful face, visited her poorer neighbours, and was like a ray of sunlight in the gloomy valley. They had one son, a boy Roderick, now about fifteen; he was a bright and eager child, who was happy enough, taking his life as he found it – and indeed he had known no other. He was taught a little by the priest; but he had no other schooling, for Sir James would spend no money except when he was obliged to do so. Roderick had no playmates, but he never found the time to be heavy; he was fond of long solitary rambles on the hills, being light of foot and strong.

One day he had gone out to fish in the stream, but it was bright and still, and he could catch nothing; so at last he laid his rod aside in a hollow place beneath the bank, and wandered without any certain aim along the stream. Higher and higher he went, till he found, looking about him, that he was as high as the pass; and then it came into his mind to track the stream to its source. The Manor was now out of sight, and there was nothing round him but the high green hills, with here and there a sheep feeding. Once a kite came out and circled slowly in the sun, pouncing like a plummet far down the glen; and still Roderick went onwards till he saw that he was at the top of the lower hills, and that the only thing higher than him was the peak itself. He saw now that the stream ran out of a still black pool some way in front of him, that lay under the very shadow of the dark precipice, and was fed by the snows that melted from the face. It was surrounded by rocks that lay piled in confusion. But the whole place wore an air that was more than desolate; the peak itself had a cruel look, and there was an intent silence, which was only broken, as he gazed, by the sound of rocks falling loudly from the face of the hill and thundering down. The sun warned him that he had gone far enough; and he determined to go homewards, half pleased at his discovery, and half relieved to quit so lonely and grim a spot.

That evening, when he sate with his father and mother at their simple meal, he began to say where he had been. His father heard him with little attention, but when Roderick described the dark pool and the sharp front of the peak he asked him abruptly how near he had gone to the pool. Roderick said that he had seen it from a distance, and then Sir James said somewhat sharply that he must not wander so far, and that he was not to go near that place again. Roderick was surprised at this, for his father as a rule interfered little with what he did; but he did not ask his father the reason, for there was something peevish, even harsh, in his tone. But afterwards, when he went out with his mother, leaving the knight to his own gloomy thoughts, as his will and custom was, his mother said with some urgency, 'Roderick, promise me not to go to the pool again; it has an evil name, and is better left to itself.' Roderick was eager to know the story of the place, but his mother would not tell him – only she would have him promise; so he promised, but complained that he would rather have had a reason given for his promise; but his mother, smiling and holding his hand, said that it should be enough for him to please her by doing her will. So Roderick gave his promise again, but was not satisfied.

The next day Roderick was walking in the valley and met one of the farmers, a young good-humoured man, who had always been friendly with the boy, and had often been to fish with him; Roderick walked beside him, and told him that he had followed the stream nearly to the pool, when the young farmer, with some seriousness, asked him how near he had been to the water. Roderick was surprised at the same question that his father had asked him being asked again, and told him that he had but seen it from a hill-top near, adding, 'But what is amiss with the place, for my father and mother have made me promise not to go there again?'

The young farmer said nothing for a moment, but seemed to reflect; then he said that there were stories about the place, stories that perhaps it was foolish to believe, but he went on to say that it was better to be on the safe side in all things, and that the place had an evil fame. Then Roderick with childish eagerness asked him what the stories were; and little by little the farmer told him. He said that something dwelt near or in the pool, it was not known what, that had an enmity to the life of man; that twice since he was a boy a strange thing had happened there; a young shepherd had come by his death at the pool, and was found lying in the water, strangely battered; that, he said, was long before Roderick was born; then he added, 'You remember old Richard the shepherd?'

'What!' said Roderick, 'the old strange man that used to go about muttering to himself, that the boys threw stones at?'

'Yes,' said the farmer, 'the very same. Well, he was not always so – I remember him a strong and cheerful man; but once when the sheep had got lost in the hills, he would go to the pool because he thought he heard them calling there, though we prayed him not to go. He came back, indeed, bringing no sheep, but an altered and broken man, as he was thenceforth and as you knew him; he had seen something by the pool, he could not say what, and had had a sore strife to get away.'

'But what sort of a thing is this?' said Roderick. 'Is it a beast or a man, or what?'

'Neither,' said the farmer very gravely. 'You have heard them read in the church of the evil spirits who dwelt with men, and entered their bodies, and it was sore work even for the Lord Christ to cast them forth; I think it is one of these who has wandered thither; they say he goes not far from the pool, for he cannot abide the cross on the pass, and the church bell gives him pains.' And then the farmer looked at Roderick and said, 'You know that they ring the bell all night on the feast of All Souls?'

'Yes,' said Roderick, 'I have heard it ring.'

'Well, on that night alone,' said the farmer, 'they say that spirits have power upon men, and come abroad to do them hurt; and so they ring the bell, which the spirits cannot listen to – but, young master, it is ill to talk of these things, and Christian men should not even think of them; but as I said, though Satan has but little power over the baptized soul, yet even so, says the priest, he can enter in, if the soul be willing to admit him – and so I say, avoid the place! It may be that these are silly stories to affright folk, but it is ill to touch pitch; and no good can be got by going to the pool, and perhaps evil – and now I think I have told you enough and more than enough.' For Roderick was looking at him pale and with wide open eyes.

Is it strange that from that day the thing that Roderick most desired was to see the pool and what dwelt there? I think not; when hearts are young and before trouble has laid its heavy hand upon them, the hard and cruel things of life, wounds, blows, agonies, terrors, seen only in the mirrors of another spirit, are but as a curious and lively spectacle that feeds the mind with wonder. The stories to which Roderick had listened in church of men that were haunted by demons seemed to him but as dim and distant experiences on which he would fain look; and the fainter the thought of his promise grew, the stronger grew his desire to see for himself.

In the month of June, when the heart is light, and the smell of the woods is fresh and sharp, Roderick's father and mother were called to go on a journey, to see an ancient friend who was thought to be dying. The night before they set off Roderick had a strange dream; it seemed to him that he wandered over bare hillsides, and came at last to the pool; the peak rose sharp and clear, and the water was very black and still; while he gazed upon it, it seemed to be troubled; the water began to spin round and round, and bubbling waves rose and broke on the surface. Suddenly a hand emerged from the water, and then a head, bright and unwetted, as though the water had no power to touch it. Roderick saw that it was a man of youthful aspect and commanding mien; he waded out to the shore and stood for a moment looking round him; then he beckoned Roderick to approach, looking at him kindly, and spoke to him gently, saying that he had waited for him long. They walked together to the crag, and then, in some way that Roderick could not clearly see, the man opened a door into the mountain, and Roderick saw a glimmering passage within. The air came out laden with a rich and heavy fragrance, and there was a faint sound of distant music in the hill. The man turned and looked upon Roderick as though inviting him to enter; but Roderick shook his head and refused, saying that he was not ready; at which the man stepped inside with a smile, half of pity, and the door was shut.

Then Roderick woke with a start and wished that he had been bold enough to go within the door; the light came in serenely through the window, and he heard the faint piping of awakening birds in the dewy trees. He could not sleep, and presently dressed himself and went down. Soon the household was awake, for the knight was to start betimes; Roderick sate at the early meal with his father and mother. His father was cumbered with the thought of the trouble-some journey, and asked many questions about the baggage; so Roderick said little, but felt his mother's eyes dwell on his face with love. Soon after they rode away; Roderick stood at the door to see them go, and there was so eager and bright a look in his face that his mother was somehow troubled, and almost called him to her to make him repeat his promise, but she feared that he would feel that she did not trust him, and therefore put the thought aside; and so they rode away, his mother waving her hand till they turned the corner by the wood and were out of sight.

Then Roderick began to consider how he would spend the day, with a half-formed design in his mind; when suddenly the temp-tation to visit the pool came upon him with a force that he had neither strength nor inclination to resist. So he took his rod, which might seem to be an excuse, and set off rapidly up the stream. He was surprised to find how swiftly the hills rose all about him, and how easily he went; very soon he came to the top; and there lay the pool in front of him, within the shadow of the peak, that rose behind it very clear and sharp. He hesitated no longer, but ran lightly down the slope, and next moment he was on the brink of the pool. It lay before him very bright and pure, like a jewel of sapphire, the water being of a deep azure blue; he went all round it. There was no sign of life in the water; at the end nearest the cliff he found a little cool runnel of water that bubbled into the pool from the cliffs. No grass grew round about it, and he could see the stones sloping down and becoming more beautiful the deeper they lay, from the pure tint of the water.

He looked all around him; the moorland quivered in the bright hot air, and he could see far away the hills lie like a map, with blue mountains on the horizon, and small green valleys where men dwelt. He sate down by the pool, and he had a thought of bathing in the water; but his courage did not rise to this, because he felt still as though something sate in the depths that would not show itself, but might come forth and drag him down; so he sate at last by the pool, and presently he fell asleep.

When he woke he felt somewhat chilly; the shadow of the peak had come round, and fell on the water; the place was still as calm as ever, but looking upon the pool he had an obscure sense as though he were being watched by an unclosing eye; but he was thirsting with the heat; so he drew up, in his closed hands, some of the water, which was very cool and sweet; and his drowsiness came upon him, and again he slept.

When next he woke it was with a sense of delicious ease, and the thought that someone who loved him was near him stroking his hand. He looked up, and there close to his side sate very quietly what gave him a shock of surprise. It was a great grey cat, with soft abundant fur, which turned its yellow eyes upon him lazily, purred, and licked his hand; he caressed the cat, which arched its back and seemed pleased to be with him, and presently leapt upon his knee. The soft warmth of the fur against his hands, and the welcoming caresses of this fearless wild creature pleased him greatly; and he sate long in quiet thought, taking care not to disturb the cat, which, whenever he took his hand away, rubbed against him as though to show that it was pleased at his touch. But at last he thought that he must go homewards, for the day began to turn to the west. So he put the cat off his knee and began to walk to the top of the pass, as it was quicker to follow the road. For a while the cat accompanied him, sometimes rubbing against his leg and sometimes walking in front, but looking round from time to time as though to consult his pleasure.

Roderick began to hope that it would accompany him home, but at a certain place the cat stopped, and would go no farther. Roderick lifted it up, but it leapt from him as if displeased, and at last he left it reluctantly. In a moment he came within sight of the cross in the hilltop, so that he saw the road was near. Often he looked round and saw the great cat regarding him as though it were sorry to be left; till at last he could see it no more.

He went home well pleased, his head full of happy thoughts; he had gone half expecting to see some dreadful thing, but had found instead a creature who seemed to love him.

The next day he went again; and this time he found the cat sitting by the pool; as soon as it saw him, it ran to him with a glad and yearning cry, as though it had feared he would not return; today it seemed brighter and larger to look upon; and he was pleased that when he returned by the stream it followed him much farther, leaping lightly from stone to stone; but at a certain place, where the valley began to turn eastward, just before the little church came in sight, it sate down as before and took its leave of him.

The third day he began to go up the valley again; but while he rested in a little wood that came down to the stream, to his surprise and delight the cat sprang out of a bush, and seemed more than ever glad of his presence. While he sate fondling it, he heard the sound of footsteps coming up the path; but the cat heard the sound too, and as he rose to see who was coming, the cat sprang lightly into a tree beside him and was hidden from his sight. It was the old priest on his way to an upland farm, who spoke fondly to Roderick, and asked him of his father and mother. Roderick told him that they were to return that night, and said that it was too bright to remain indoors and yet too bright to fish; the priest agreed, and after a little more talk rose to go, and as his manner was, holding Roderick by the hand, he blessed him, saying that he was growing a tall boy. When he was gone – and Roderick was ashamed to find how eager he was that the priest should go – he called low to the cat to come back; but the cat came not, and though Roderick searched the tree into which it had sprung, he could find no sign of it, and supposed that it had crept into the wood.

That evening the travellers returned, the knight seeming cheerful, because the vexatious journey was over; but Roderick was half ashamed to think that his mind had been so full of his new plaything that he was hardly glad to see his parents return. Presently his mother said, 'You look very bright and happy, dear child,' and Roderick, knowing that he spoke falsely, said that he was glad to see them again; his mother smiled and asked him what he had been doing, and he said that he had wandered on the hills, for it was too bright to fish; his mother looked at him for a moment, and he knew in his heart that she wondered if he had kept his promise; but he thought of his secret, and looked at her so straight and full that she asked him no further questions.

The next day he woke feeling sad, because he knew that there would be no chance to go to the pool. He went to and fro with his mother, for she had many little duties to attend to. At last she said, 'What are you thinking of, Roderick? You seem to have little to say to me.'

She said it laughingly; and Roderick was ashamed, but said that he was only thinking; and so bestirred himself to talk. But late in the day he went a little alone through the wood, and reaching the end of it, looked up to the hill, kissing his hand towards the pool as a greeting to his friend; and as he turned, the cat came swiftly and lovingly out of the wood to him; and he caught it up in his arms and clasped it close, where it lay as if contented.

Then he thought that he would carry it to the house, and say nothing as to where he had found it; but hardly had he moved a step when the cat leapt from him and stood as though angry. And it came into Roderick's mind that the cat was his secret friend, and that their friendship must somehow be unknown; but he loved it even the better for that.

In the weeks that followed, the knight was ill and the lady much at home; from time to time Roderick saw the cat; he could never tell when it would visit him; it came and went unexpectedly, and always in some lonely and secret place. But gradually Roderick began to care for nothing else; his fishing and his riding were forgotten, and he began to plan how he might be alone, so that the cat would come to him. He began to lose his spirits and to be dull without it, and to hate the hours when he could not see it; and all the time it grew or seemed to grow stronger and sleeker; his mother soon began to notice that he was not well; he became thin and listless, but his eyes were large and bright; she asked him more than once if he were well, but he only laughed. Once indeed he had a fright; he had been asleep under a hawthorn in the glen on a hot July day; and waking saw the cat close to him, watching him intently with yellow eyes, as though it were about to spring upon him; but seeing him awake, it came wheedling and fondling him as often before; but he could not forget the look in its eyes, and felt grave and sad.

Then he began to be troubled with dreams; the man whom he had seen in his former dream rising from the pool was often with him – sometimes he led him to pleasant places; but one dream he had, that he was bathing in the pool, and caught his foot between the rocks and could not draw it out. Then he heard a rushing sound, and looking round saw that a great stream of water was plunging heavily into the pool, so that it rose every moment, and was soon up to his chin. Then he saw in his dream that the man sate on the edge of the pool and looked at him with a cold smile, but did not offer to help; till at last when the water touched his lips, the man rose and held up his hand; and the stream ceased to run, and presently his foot came out of the rock easily, and he swam ashore but saw no-one.

Then it came to the autumn, and the days grew colder and shorter, and he could not be so much abroad; he felt, too, less and less disposed to stir out, and it now began to be on his mind that he had broken his promise to his mother; and for a week he saw nothing of the cat, though he longed to see it. But one night, as he went to bed, when he had put out his light, he saw that the moon was very bright; and he opened the window and looked out, and saw the gleaming stream and the grey valley; he was turning away, when he heard a light sound of the scratching of claws, and presently the cat sprang upon the window-sill and entered the room. It was now cold and he got into bed, and the cat sprang upon his pillow; and Roderick was so glad that the cat had returned that while he caressed it he talked to it in low tones. Suddenly came a step at the door, and a light beneath it, and his mother with a candle entered the room. She stood for a moment looking, and Roderick became aware that the cat was gone. Then his mother came near, thinking that he was asleep, and he sate up. She said to him, 'Dear child, I heard you speaking, and wondered whether you were in a dream,' and she looked at him with an anxious gaze.

And he said, 'Was I speaking, mother? I was asleep and must have spoken in a dream.'

Then she said, 'Roderick, you are not old enough yet to sleep so uneasily – is all well, dear child?' and Roderick, hating to deceive his mother, said, 'How should not all be well?' So she kissed him and went quietly away, but Roderick heard her sighing.

Then it came at last to All Souls' Day; and Roderick, going to his bed that night, had a strange dizziness and cried out, and found the room swim round him. Then he got up into his bed, for he thought that he must be ill, and soon fell asleep; and in his sleep he dreamed a dreadful dream. He thought that he lay on the hills beside the pool; and yet he was out of the body, for he could see himself lying there. The pool was very dark, and a cold wind ruffled the waves. And again the water was troubled, and the man stepped out; but behind him came another man, like a hunchback, very swarthy of face, with long thin arms, that looked both strong and evil. Then it seemed as if the first man pointed to Roderick where he lay and said, 'You can take him hence, for he is mine now, and I have need of him,' adding, 'Who could have thought it would be so easy?' and then he smiled very bitterly. And the hunchback went towards himself; and he tried to cry out in warning, and straining woke; and in the chilly dawn he saw the cat sit in his room, but very different from what it had been.

It was gaunt and famished, and the fur was all marred; its yellow eyes gleamed horribly, and Roderick saw that it hated him, he knew not why; and such fear came upon him that he screamed out, and as he screamed the cat rose as if furious, twitching its tail and opening its mouth; but he heard steps without, and screamed again, and his mother came in haste into the room, and the cat was gone in a moment, and Roderick held out his hands to his mother, and she soothed and quieted him, and presently with many sobs he told her all the story.

She did not reproach him, nor say a word of his disobedience, the fear was too urgent upon her; she tried to think for a little that it was the sight of some real creature lingering in a mind that was wrought upon by illness; but those were not the days when men preferred to call the strange afflictions of body and spirit, the sad scars that stain the fair works of God, by reasonable names. She did not doubt that by some dreadful hap her own child had somehow crept within the circle of darkness, and she only thought of how to help and rescue him; that he was sorry and that he did not wholly consent was her hope.

So she merely kissed and quieted him, and then she told him that she would return anon and he must rest quietly; but he would not let her leave him, so she stood in the door and called a servant softly. Sir James was long abed, for he had been in ill-health that day, and she gave word that someone must be found at once and go to call the priest, saying that Roderick was ill and she was uneasy. Then she came back to the bed, and holding Roderick's hand she said, that he must try to sleep. Roderick said to her, 'Mother, say that you forgive me.' To which she only replied, 'Dear child, do I not love you better than all the world? Do not think of me now, only ask help of God.' So she sate with his hand in both of her own, and presently he fell asleep; but she saw that he was troubled in his dreams, for he groaned and cried out often; and now through the window she heard the soft tolling of the bell of the church, and she knew that a contest must be fought out that night over the child; but after a sore passage of misery, and a bitter questioning as to why one so young and innocent should thus be bound with evil bonds, she found strength to leave the matter in the Father's hands, and to pray with an eager hopefulness.

But the time passed heavily and still the priest did not arrive; and the ghostly terror was so sore on the child that she could bear it no longer and awakened him. And he told her in broken words of the terrible things that had oppressed him; sore fightings and struggles, and a voice in his ear that it was too late, and that he had yielded himself to the evil. And at last there came a quiet footfall on the stair, and the old priest himself entered the room, looking anxious, yet calm, and seeming to bring a holy peace with him.

Then she bade the priest sit down; and so the two sate by the bedside, with the solitary lamp burning in the chamber; and she would have had Roderick tell the tale, but he covered his face with his hands and could not. So she told the tale herself to the priest, saying, 'Correct me, Roderick, if I am wrong;' and once or twice the boy corrected her, and added a few words to make the story plain, and then they sate awhile in silence, while the terrified looks of the mother and her son dwelt on the old priest's strongly lined face; yet they found comfort in the smile with which he met them.

At length he said, 'Yes, dear lady and dear Roderick, the case is plain enough – the child has yielded himself to some evil power, but not too far, I think; and now must we meet the foe with all our might. I will abide here with the boy; and, dear lady, you were better in your own chamber, for we know not what will pass; if there were need I would call you.'

Then the lady said, 'I will do as you direct me, Father, but I would fain stay.'

Then he said, 'Nay, but there are things on which a Christian should not look, lest they should daunt his faith – so go, dear lady, and help us with your prayers.'

Then she said, 'I will be below; and if you beat your foot thrice upon the floor, I will come. Roderick, I shall be close at hand; only be strong, and all shall be well.' Then she went softly away.

Then the priest said to Roderick, 'And now, dear son, confess your sin and let me shrive you.'

So Roderick made confession, and the priest blessed him: but while he blessed him there came the angry crying of a cat from somewhere in the room, so that Roderick shuddered in his bed. Then the priest drew from his robe a little holy book, and with a reverence laid it under Roderick's hand; and he himself took his book of prayers and said, 'Sleep now, dear son, fear not.'

So Roderick closed his eyes, and being very weary slept. And the old priest in a low whisper said the blessed psalms. And it came near to midnight; and the place that the priest read was, *Thou shalt not be afraid for any terror by night, nor for the arrow that flieth by day; for the pestilence that walketh in darkness, nor for the sickness that destroyeth in the noonday;* and suddenly there ran as it were a shiver through his bones, and he knew that the time was come. He looked at Roderick, who slept wearily on his bed, and it seemed to him as though suddenly a small and shadowy thing, like a bird, leapt from the boy's mouth and on to the bed; it was like a wren, only white, with dusky spots upon it; and the priest held his breath: for now he knew that the soul was out of the body, and that unless it could return uninjured into the limbs of the child, nothing could avail the boy; and then he said quietly in his heart to God that if He so willed He should take the boy's life, if only his soul could be saved.

Then the priest was aware of a strange and horrible thing; there sprang softly on to the bed the form of the great grey cat, very lean and angry, which stood there, as though ready to spring upon the bird, which hopped hither and thither, as though careless of what might be. The priest cast a glance upon the boy, who lay rigid and pale, his eyes shut, and hardly seeming to breathe, as though dead and prepared for burial. Then the priest signed the cross and said 'In Nomine'; and as the holy words fell on the air, the cat looked fiercely at the bird, but seemed to shrink into itself; and then it slipped away.

Then the priest's fear was that the bird might stray further outside of his care; and yet he dared not try and wake the boy, for he knew that this was death, if the soul was thrust apart from the body, and if he broke the unseen chain that bound them; so he waited and prayed. And the bird hopped upon the floor; and then presently the priest saw the cat draw near again, and in a stealthy way; and now the priest himself was feeling weary of the strain, for he seemed to be wrestling in spirit with something that was strong and strongly armed. But he signed the cross again and said faintly 'In Nomine'; and the cat again withdrew.

Then a dreadful drowsiness fell upon the priest, and he thought that he must sleep. Something heavy, leaden-handed, and powerful seemed to be busy in his brain. Meanwhile the bird hopped upon the window-sill and stood as if preparing its wings for a flight. Then the priest beat with his foot upon the floor, for he could no longer battle. In a moment the lady glided in, and seemed as though scared to find the scene of so fierce an encounter so still and quiet. She would have spoken, but the priest signed her to be silent, and pointed to the boy and to the bird; and then she partly understood. So they stood in silence, but the priest's brain grew more numb; though he was aware of a creeping blackness that seemed to overshadow the bird, in the midst of which glared two bright eyes. So with a sudden effort he signed the cross, and said 'In Nomine' again; and at the same moment the lady held out her hand; and the priest sank down on the floor; but he saw the bird raise its wings for a flight, and just as the dark thing rose, and, as it were, struck open-mouthed, the bird sailed softly through the air, alighted on the lady's hand, and then with a light flutter of wings on to the bed and to the boy's face, and was seen no more; at the same moment the bells stopped in the church and left a sweet silence. The black form shrank and slipped aside, and seemed to fall on the ground; and outside there was a shrill and bitter cry which echoed horribly on the air; and the boy opened his eyes, and smiled; and his mother fell on his neck and kissed him. Then the priest said, 'Give God the glory!' and blessed them, and was gone so softly that they knew not when he went; for he had other work to do. Then mother and son had great joy together.

But the priest walked swiftly and sternly through the wood, and to the church; and he dipped a vessel in the stoup of holy water, turning his eyes aside, and wrapped it in a veil of linen. Then he took a lantern in his hand, and with a grave and fixed look on his face he walked sadly up the valley, putting one foot before another, like a man who forced himself to go unwilling. There were strange sounds on the hillside, the crying of sad birds, and the beating of wings, and sometimes a hollow groaning seemed to come down the stream. But the priest took no heed, but went on heavily till he reached the stone cross, where the wind whistled dry in the grass. Then he struck off across the moorland. Presently he came to a rise in the ground; and here, though it was dark, he seemed to see a blacker darkness in the air, where the peak lay.

But beneath the peak he saw a strange sight; for the pool shone with a faint white light, that showed the rocks about it. The priest never turned his head, but walked thither, with his head bent, repeating words to himself, but hardly knowing what he said.

Then he came to the brink; and there he saw a dreadful sight. In the water writhed large and luminous worms, that came sometimes up to the surface, as though to breathe, and sank again. The priest knew well enough that it was a device of Satan's to frighten him; so he delayed not; but setting the lantern down on the ground, he stood. In a moment the lantern was obscured as by the rush of bat-like wings. But the priest took the veil off the vessel; and holding it up in the air, he let the water fall in the pool, saying softly, 'Lord, let them be bound!'

But when the holy water touched the lake, there was a strange sight; for the bright worms quivered and fell to the depth of the pool; and a shiver passed over the surface, and the light went out like a flickering lamp. Then there came a foul yelling from the stones; and with a roar like thunder, rocks fell crashing from the face of the peak; and then all was still.

Then the priest sate down and covered his face with his hands, for he was sore spent; but he rose at length, and with grievous pain made his slow way down the valley, and reached the parsonage house at last.

Roderick lay long between life and death; and youth and a quiet mind prevailed.

Long years have passed since that day; all those that I have spoken of are dust. But in the window of the old church hangs a picture in glass which shows Christ standing, with one lying at his feet from whom he had cast out a devil; and on a scroll are the words, DE ◊ ABYSSIS ◊ TERRAE ◊ ITERUM ◊ REDUXISTI ◊ ME, the which may be written in English, *Yea, and broughtest me from the deep of the earth again.*

The Hill of Trouble

A. C. BENSON

There was once a great scholar, Gilbert by name, who lived at Cambridge, and was Fellow of St Peter's College there. He was still young, and yet he had made himself a name for learning, and still more for wisdom, which is a different thing, though the two are often confused. Gilbert was a slender, spare man, but well-knit and well-proportioned. He loved to wear old scholarly garments, but he had that sort of grace in wearing them that made him appear better apparelled than most men in new clothes. His hair was thick and curling, and he had small features clearly cut. His lips were some-what thin, as though from determined thought. He carried his eyes a little wrinkled up, as though to spare them from the light; but he had a gracious look which he turned on those with whom he spoke; and when he opened his eyes upon you, they were large and clear, as though charged with dreams; and he had a very sweet smile, trustful and gentle, that seemed to take any that spoke with him straight to his heart, and made him many friends. He had the look rather of a courtier than of a priest, and he was merry and cheerful in discourse, so that you might be long with him and not know him to be learned. It may be said that he had no enemies, though he did not conceal his beliefs and thoughts, but stated them so courteously and with such deference to opposite views, that he drew men insensibly to his side. It was thought by many that he ought to go into the world and make a great name for himself. But he loved the quiet College life, the familiar talk with those he knew. He loved the great plenty of books and the discourse of simple and wise men. He loved the fresh bright hours of solitary work, the shady College garden, with its butts and meadows, bordered by ancient walls. He loved to sit at meat in the cool and spacious hall; and he loved too the dark high-roofed College Church, and his own canopied stall with the service-books in due order, the low music of the organ, and the sweet singing of the choir. He was not rich, but his Fellowship gave him all that he desired, together with a certain seemly dignity of life that he truly valued; so that his heart was very full of a simple happiness from day to day, and he thought that he would be more than content to live out his life in the peaceful College that he loved so well.

But he was ambitious too; he was writing a great book full of holy learning; and he had of late somewhat withdrawn himself from the life of the College; he sate longer at his studies and he was seen less often in other Colleges. Ten years he gave himself to finish his task, and he thought that it would bring him renown; but that was only a far-off dream, gilding his studies with a kind of peaceful glory; and indeed he loved the doing of his work better than any reward he might get for it.

One summer he felt he wanted some change of life; the sultry Cambridge air, so dry and low, seemed to him to be heavy and lifeless. He began to dream of fresh mountain breezes, and the sound of leaping streams; so at last he packed his books into a box, and set off a long journey into the hills of the West, to a village where an old friend of his was the priest, who he knew would welcome him.

On the sixth day he arrived at the place; he had enjoyed the journey; much of the time he had ridden, but he often walked, for he was very strong and active of body; he had delighted in seeing the places he had passed through, the churches and the towns and the castles that lay beside the way; he had been pleased with the simple friendly inns, and as his custom was had talked with all travellers that he met. And most of all he had loved, as he drew nearer the West, to see the great green slopes of hills, the black heads of mountains, the steep wooded valleys, where the road lay along streams, that dashed among mossy boulders into still pools.

At last he came to the village which he sought, which lay with its grey church and low stone houses by a bridge, in a deep valley. The vicarage lay a little apart in a pleasant garden; and his friend the Vicar had made him greatly welcome. The Vicar was an old man and somewhat infirm, but he loved the quiet life of the country, and knew all the joys and sorrows of his simple flock. A large chamber was set apart for Gilbert, who ranged his books on a great table, and prepared for much quiet work. The window of the chamber looked down the valley, which was very still. There was no pattering of feet in the road, as there was at Cambridge; the only sounds were the crying of cocks or the bleating of sheep from the hill-pastures, the sound of the wind in the woods, and the falling of water from the hills. So Gilbert was well content.

For the first few days he was somewhat restless; he explored the valley in all directions. The Vicar could not walk much, and only crept to and fro in the town, or to church; and though he sometimes rode to the hills, to see sick folk on upland farms, yet he told Gilbert that he must go his walks alone; and Gilbert was not loth; for as he thus went by himself in the fresh air, a stream of pleasant fancies and gentle thoughts passed lightly through his head, and his work shaped itself in his brain, like a valley seen from a height, where the fields and farms lie out, as if on a map, with the road winding among them that ties them with the world.

One day Gilbert walked alone to a very solitary place among the hills, a valley where the woods grew thickly; the valley was an estuary, where the sea came up blue and fresh twice in the day, covering the wide sandbanks with still water that reflected the face of the sky; in the midst of the valley, joined with the hillside by a chain of low mounds, there rose a large round hill, covered with bushes which grew thickly over the slopes, and among little crags, haunted by hawks and crows. It looked a very solitary, peaceful hill, and he stopped at a farm beside the road to inquire of the way thither, because he was afraid of finding himself unable to cross the streams.

At his knock there came out an ancient man, with whom Gilbert entered into simple travellers' talk of the weather and the road; Gilbert asked him the name of the place, and the man told him that it was called the Gate of the Old Hollow. Then Gilbert pointing to the hill that lay in the midst, asked him what that was. The old man looked at him for a moment without answering, and then said in a low voice, 'That, sir, is the Hill of Trouble.'

'That is a strange name!' said Gilbert.

'Yes,' said the old man, 'and it is a strange place, where no-one ever sets foot – there is a cruel tale about it; there is something that is not well about the place.'

Gilbert was surprised to hear the other speak so gravely; but the old man, who was pleased with his company, asked him if he would not rest awhile and eat; and Gilbert said that he would do so gladly, and the more gladly if the other would tell him the story of the place. The old man led him within into a large room, with plain oak furniture, and brought him bread and honey and milk; and Gilbert ate, while the old man told him the legend of the Hill.

He said that long years ago it was a place of heathen worship, and that there stood a circle of stones upon it, where sacrifice was done; and that men, it was said, were slain there with savage rites; and that when the Christian teachers came, and the valley became obedient to the faith, it was forbidden the villagers to go there, and for long years it was desolate; but there had dwelt in the manor-house hard by a knight, fearless and rough, who regarded neither God nor man, who had lately wedded a wife whom he loved beyond anything in the world. And one day there was with the knight a friend who was a soldier, and after dinner, in foolish talk, the knight said that he would go to the Hill, and he made a wager on it. The knight's lady besought him not to go, but he girded on his sword and went laughing. Now at the time, the old man said, there was much fighting in the valley, for the people were not yet subject to the English king, but paid tribute to their own Lords; and the knight had been one that fought the best. What the knight saw on the hill no-one ever knew, but he came back at sundown, pale, and like a man that has been strangely scared, looking behind him as though he expected to be followed by some-thing; and from that day he kept his chamber, and would not go abroad, or if he went out, he went fearfully, looking about him; and the English men-at-arms came to the valley, but the knight that had ever been foremost in the fight would not ride out to meet them, but kept his bed. The manor lay off the road, and he ordered a boy to lie in the copse beside the way, and to come up to the house to tell him if any soldiers went by. But a troop of horse came secretly over the hill; and seeing the place lie so solitary and deserted, and being in haste, they came not in, but one of them shot a bolt at a venture; but the knight, it seemed, must have stolen from his bed, and have been peeping through the shutters; for the knight's lady who sate below in sore shame and grief for her husband's cowardice, heard a cry, and coming up found him in his bedgown lying by the window, and a bolt sticking in his brain.

Her grief and misery were so sore at this, that she was for a time nearly mad; they buried the knight in secret in the churchyard; but the lady sate for many days speaking to no-one, beating with her hand upon the table and eating little.

One day it seems that she had the thought to go herself to the Hill of Trouble, so she robed herself in haste, and went at early dawn; she went in secret, and came back at noon, smiling to herself, with all her grief gone; and she sate for three days thus with her hands folded, and from her face it was plain that there was joy in her heart; and on the third evening they found her cold and stiff in her chair, dead an hour since, but she was still smiling. And the lands passed to a distant kinsman. And since that day, said the old man, no-one had ever set foot on the Hill, except a child not long since that strayed thither, and came back in a great fear, saying that he had seen and spoken with an old man, that had seemed to be angry, but that another person, all in white, had come between them, and had led him by the hand to the right road; it could not be known why the child was frightened, but he said that it was the way the old man looked, and the suddenness with which he came and went; but of the other he had no fear, though he knew him not. 'And that, sir, is the tale.'

Gilbert was very much astonished at the tale, and though he was not credulous, the story dwelt strongly in his mind. It was now too late to visit the Hill, even if he had wished; and he could not have so vexed the old man as to visit it from his house. He stood for a while at the gate looking down at it. It was hot and still in the valley. The tide was out and the warm air quivered over the sandbanks. But the Hill had a stillness of its own, as though it guarded a secret, and lay looking out towards the sea. He could see the small crags upon it, in the calm air, and the bushes that grew plentifully all over it, with here and there a little green lawn, or a glade sloping down to the green flat in which it stood. The old man was beside him and said in his shrill piping voice, 'You are not thinking of going to the Hill, sir?'

'Not now, at all events,' said Gilbert, smiling.

But the old man said, 'Ah, sir, you will not go – there are other things in this world of ours, beside the hills and woods and farms; it would be strange if that were all. The spirits of the dead walk at noonday in the places they have loved; and I have thought that the souls of those who have done wickedness are sometimes bound to a place where they might have done good things, and while they are vexed at all the evil their hands have wrought, they are drawn by a kind of evil habit to do what they chose to do on earth. Perhaps those who are faithful can resist them – but it is ill to tempt them.'

Gilbert was surprised at this wise talk from so simple a man; and he said, 'How is it that these thoughts come into your mind?'

'Oh, sir,' said the other, 'I am old and live much alone; and these are some of the thoughts that come into my head as I go about my work, but who sends them to me I cannot tell.'

Then Gilbert said farewell, and would have paid for his meal, but the old man courteously refused, and said that it was a pleasure to see a stranger in that lonely place; and that it made him think more kindly of the world to talk so simply with one who was, he was sure, so great a gentleman.

Gilbert smiled, and said he was only a simple scholar; and then he went back to the vicarage house. He told the Vicar of his adventure, and the Vicar said he had heard of the Hill, and that there was something strange in the dread which the place inspired. Then Gilbert said, half-impatiently, that it was a pity that people were so ridden by needless superstition, and made fears for themselves when there was so much in the world that it was well to fear. But the old Vicar shook his head. 'They are children, it is true,' he said, 'but children, I often think, are nearer to heaven than ourselves, and perhaps have glimpses of things that it is harder for us to see as we get older and more dull.'

But Gilbert made up his mind as they talked that he would see the place for himself; and that night he dreamed of wandering over lonely places with a fear upon him of he knew not what. And waking very early, after a restless night, and seeing the day freshly risen, and the dewy brightness of the valley, he put on his clothes in haste, and taking with him a slice of bread from the table, he set out blithely for the Hill, with an eagerness of spirit that he had been used to feel as a child.

He avoided the farm, and took a track that seemed to lead into the valley, which led him up and down through little nooks and pastures, till he came to the base of the Hill. It was all skirted by a low wall of piled stones covered with grey lichens, where the brambles grew freely; but the grass upon the Hill itself had a peculiar richness and luxuriance, as though it was never trodden or crushed underfoot. Gilbert climbed the wall, but the brambles clung to him as though to keep him back; he disentangled them one by one, and in a moment he found himself in a little green glade, among small crags, that seemed to lead to the top of the Hill. He had not gone more than a few paces when the pleasure and excitement died out of his mind, and left him feeling weary and dispirited. But he said to himself that it was his troubled night, and the walk at the unusual hour, and the lack of food; so he took out his bread and ate it as he walked, and presently he came to the top.

Then he suddenly saw that he was at the place described; in front of him stood a tall circle of stones, very grey with age. Some of them were flung down and were covered with bushes, but several of them stood upright. The place was strangely silent; he walked round the circle, and saw that it occupied the top of the Hill; below him were steep crags, and when he looked over he was surprised to see all down the rocks, on ledges, a number of crows that sate silent in the sun. At the motion he made, a number of them, as though surprised to be disturbed, floated off into the air, with loud jangling cries; and a hawk sailed out from the bushes and hung, a brown speck, with trembling wings. Gilbert saw the rich plain at his feet and the winding creek of the sea, and the great hills on left and right, in a blue haze. Then he stepped back, and though he had a feeling that it would be wiser not to go, he put it aside and went boldly into the circle of stones. He stood there for a moment, and then feeling very weary, sate down on the turf, leaning his back against a stone; then came upon him a great drowsiness. He was haunted by a sense that it was not well to sleep there, and that the dreaming mind was an ill defence against the powers of the air – yet he put the thought aside with a certain shame and fell asleep.

He woke with a sudden start some time after; there was a chill in his limbs, not from the air which glowed bright in the steady sun, but a chill of the spirit that made his hair prickle in an unusual way. He raised himself up and looked round him, for he knew by a certain sense that he was not alone; and then he saw leaning against one of the stones and watching him intently, a very old and weary-looking man. The man was pale and troubled; he had a rough cloak such as the peasants wore, the hood of which was pulled over his head; his hair was white and hung about his ears; he had a staff in his hand. But there was a dark look about him, and Gilbert divined in some swift passage of the spirit that he did not wish him well. Gilbert rose to his feet, and at the same moment the old man drew near; and though he looked so old and feeble, Gilbert had the feeling that he was strong and even dangerous. But Gilbert showed no surprise; he doffed his hat to the old man, and said courteously that he hoped he had not wandered to some private place, where he ought not to be. 'The heat was great, and I slept unawares,' he said.

The old man at first made no answer, and then said in a very low and yet clear voice, 'Nay, sir, you are welcome. The Hill is free to all; but it has an evil name, I know, and I see but few upon it.'

Then Gilbert said courteously that he was but a passer-by, and that he must set off home again, before the sun was high. And at that the old man said, 'Nay, sir, but as you have come, you will surely wait awhile and speak with me. I see,' he added, 'so few of humankind, that my mind and tongue are alike stiff with disuse; but you can tell me something of your world – and I,' he added, 'can tell you some-thing of mine.'

Then there came suddenly on Gilbert a great fear, and he looked round on the tall stones of the circle that seemed to be like a prison. Then he said, 'I am but a simple scholar from Cambridge, and my knowledge of the world is but small; we work,' he said, 'we write and read, we talk and eat together, and sometimes we pray.'

The old man looked at him with a sudden look, under his brows, as he said the words; and then he said, 'So, sir, you are a priest; and your faith is a strong one and avails much; but there is a text about the strong man armed who is overcome of the stronger. And though the faith you teach is like a fort in an enemy's country, in which men may dwell safely, yet there is a land outside; and a fort cannot always hold its own.'

He said this in so evil and menacing a tone that Gilbert said, 'Come, sir, these are wild words; would you speak scorn of the faith that is the light of God and the victory that overcometh?'

Then the old man said, 'Nay, I respect the faith – and fear it even,' he added in a secret tone – 'but I have grown up in a different belief, and the old is better – and this also is a little stronghold, which holds its own in the midst of foes; but I would not be disputing,' he added – and then with a smile, 'Nay, sir, I know what is in your mind; you like not this place – and you are right; it is not fit for you to set your holy feet in; but it is mine yet; and so you must even accept the hospitality of the place; you shall look thrice in my glass, and see if you like what you shall see.' And he held out to Gilbert a small black shining thing. Gilbert would have wished to refuse it, but his courtesy bade him take it – and indeed he did not know if he could have refused the old man, who looked so sternly upon him. So he took it in his hand.

It was a black polished stone like a sphere, and it was very cold to the touch – so cold that he would fain have thrown it down; but he dared not. So he said with such spirit as he could muster, 'And what shall I see beside the stone? – It seems a fair and curious jewel – I cannot give it a name.'

'Nay,' said the old man sharply, 'it is not the stone; the stone is naught; but it hides a mystery. You shall see it in the stone.'

And Gilbert said, 'And what shall I see in the stone?' And the old man said, 'What shall be.'

So Gilbert looked upon the stone; the sun shone upon it in a bright point of light – and for an instant he saw nothing but the gleaming sides of the ball. But in a moment there came upon him a dizziness like that which comes upon a man who, walking on a hill-top, finds himself on the edge of a precipice. He seemed to look into a great depth, into the dark places of the earth – but in the depth there hung a mist like a curtain. Now while he looked at it he saw a commotion in the mist; and looking closer, he saw that it seemed to be something waving to and fro that drove the mist about; and presently he saw the two arms of a man; and then the mist parted, and he saw the figure of a man standing and waving with his arms, like a man who would fan smoke aside; and the smoke fled from the waving arms and rolled away; and the man stepped aside.

Then Gilbert looked beyond, and he saw a room with a low ceiling and a mullioned window; and he knew it at once for his room in St Peter's College. There were books on the table; and he saw what seemed like himself, risen to his feet, as though at a sound; and then he saw the door open and a man come in who made an obeisance, and the two seemed to talk together, and presently Gilbert saw the other man pull something from a cloth and put it in his own hands. And the figure of himself seemed to draw near the window to look at the thing; and though it was all very small and distant, yet Gilbert could see that he held in his hands a little figure that seemed a statue. And then the mist rolled in again and all was hid.

He came to himself like a man out of a dream, he had been so intent on what appeared; and he saw the hill-top and the circle of stones, and the old man who stood watching him with a secret smile upon his face. Then Gilbert made as though he would give the stone back, but before he could speak, the old man pointed to the stone again – and Gilbert looked again and saw the deep place, and the cloud, and the man part the cloud.

Then he saw within a garden, and he knew it at once to be the garden of St Peter's; it seemed to be summer, for the trees were in leaf. He saw himself stand, carrying something in his hand, and looking at a place in the garden wall. There was something on the wall, a patch of white, but he could not see what it was; and beneath it there stood a small group of men in scholars' dress who looked upon the wall, but he could not see their faces; but one whom he recognised as the Master of the College stood with a stick in his hand, and pointed to the white patch on the wall – and then something seemed to run by, a cat or dog, and all at once the cloud flowed in over the picture; and again he came to himself and saw the hill-top, and the stones, and the old man, who had drawn a little nearer, and looked at him with a strange smile. And again he pointed to the stone; and Gilbert looked again and saw the cloud work very swiftly and part, and the man who swept the clouds off came forth for an instant, and then was lost to view.

And Gilbert saw a very dark place, with something long and white, that glimmered faintly, lying in the midst; and he bent down to look at it, but could not discern what it was. Then he saw in the darkness which surrounded the glimmering thing some small threads of dusky white, and some small round things; and he looked at them long; and presently discerned that the round things were pebbles, and that the white threads were like the roots of trees; and then he perceived that he was looking into the earth; and then with a sickly chill of fear he saw that the long and glimmering thing was indeed the body of a man, wrapped in grave-clothes from head to foot. And he could now distinguish – for it grew more distinct – the sides of a coffin about it, and some worms that moved to and fro in their dark burrows; but the corpse seemed to shine with a faint light of its own – and then he could see the wasted feet, and the thin legs and arms of the body within; the hands were folded over the breast; and then he looked at the face; and he saw his own face, only greatly sunk and fallen, with a bandage that tied up the chin, and leaden eyes; and then the clouds swept in upon it; and he came to himself like a drowning man, and saw that he was in the same place; and his first thought was a thrill of joy to know that he was alive; but then he groaned aloud, and he saw the old man stand beside him with a very terrible look upon his face, holding out his hand for the stone in silence; so Gilbert gave him back the stone, and then with a fierce anger said, 'Why have you shown me this? For this is the trickery of hell.'

And the old man looked at him very sternly and said, 'Why then did you come to this place? You were not called hither, and they that pry must be punished. A man who pulls open the door which leads from the present into the future must not be vexed if he sees the truth – and now, sir,' he added very angrily, 'depart hence in haste; you have seen what you have seen.' So Gilbert went slowly from the circle, and very heavily, and as he stepped outside he looked back. But there was nothing there but the turf and the grey stones.

Gilbert went slowly down the Hill with a shadow upon him, like a man who has passed through a sudden danger, or who has had a sudden glimpse into the dark realities of life. But the whole experience was so strange and dreamlike, so apart from the wholesome current of his life, that his fears troubled him less than he had supposed; still, a kind of hatred for the quiet valley began to creep over him, and he found himself sitting long over his books, looking down among the hills, and making no progress. If he was not silent when in company with the old Vicar, it was because he made a strong effort, and because his courtesy came to his assistance. Indeed the old Vicar thought that he had never known Gilbert so tender or thoughtful as he had been in the last week of his visit. The truth was that it was an effort to Gilbert to talk about himself, and he therefore drew the old priest on to talk about the details of his own life and work. Thus, though Gilbert talked less himself, he was courteously attentive, so that the old man had a sense that there had been much pleasant interchange of feeling, whereas he had contributed the most of the talk himself. Gilbert, too, found a great comfort in the offices of the Church in these days, and prayed much that, whatever should befall him, he might learn to rest in the mighty will of God for himself, whatever that will might be.

Soon after this he went back to Cambridge, and there, among his old friends and in his accustomed haunts, the whole impression of the vision on the Hill of Trouble grew faint and indistinct, especially as no incident occurred to revive it. He threw himself into his work, and the book grew under his hands; and he seemed to be more eager to fill his hours than before, and avoided solitary meditation.

Some three years after the date of his vision, there was announced to him by letter the advent of a great scholar to Cambridge, who had read one of Gilbert's books, and was desirous to be introduced to him. Gilbert was sitting one day in his rooms, after a happy quiet morning, when the porter came to the door and announced the scholar. He was a tall eager man, who came forward with great friendliness, and said some courteous words about his pleasure at having met one whom he was so desirous to see. He carried something in his hand, and after the first compliments, said that he had ventured to bring Gilbert a little curiosity that had lately been dug up at Rome, and which he had been fortunate in securing. He drew off a wrapper, and held out to Gilbert a little figure of a Muse, finely sculptured, with an inscription on the pedestal. Gilbert stepped to the window to look at it, and as he did so it flashed across his mind that this was surely the scene that he had observed in the black stone. He stood for a moment with the statue in his hand, with such a strange look in his face, that the newcomer thought for an instant that his gift must have aroused some sad association. But Gilbert recovered himself in a moment and resolutely put the thought out of his mind, praised the statue, and thereupon entered into easy talk.

The great scholar spent some days at Cambridge, and Gilbert was much with him. They talked of learned matters together, but the great scholar said afterwards that though Gilbert was a man of high genius and of great insight into learning, yet he felt in talking with him as though he had some further and deeper preoccupation of thought.

Indeed when Gilbert, by laying of dates together, became aware that it was three years to a day since he had seen the vision in the stone, he was often haunted by the thought of his visit to the Hill. But this lasted only a few days; and he took comfort at the thought that he had seen a further vision in the stone which seemed at least to promise him three more peaceful years of unchanged work, before he need give way to the heaviness that the third vision had caused him. Yet it lay like a dark background in his thoughts.

He kept very much to his work after this event, and became graver and sterner in face, so that his friends thought that his application to study was harmful. But when they spoke of it to Gilbert, he used to say laughingly that nothing but work made life worthy, and that he was making haste; and indeed the great book grew so fast that he was within sight of the end. He had many wrestles within himself, about this time, as to the goodness and providence of God. He argued to himself that he had been led very tenderly beside the waters of comfort, that he had served God as faithfully as he could – and indeed he had little to reproach himself with, though he began to blame himself for living a life that pleased him, and for not going about more in the world helping weak brethren along the way, as the Lord Christ had done. Yet again he said to himself that the great doctors and fathers of the Church had deemed it praiseworthy that a man should devote all the power of his brain to making the divine oracle clear, and that the apostle Paul had spoken of a great diversity of gifts which could be used faithfully in the service of Christ. Still, he reflected that the truest glimpse into the unknown that he had ever received – for he doubted no longer of the truth of the vision – had come to him from one that was, he thought, outside the mercies of God, an unhallowed soul, shut off by his own will and by his wickedness from the fold; and this was a sore burden to him.

At last the book was done; and he went with it to a friend he had at Oxford, a mighty scholar, to talk over some difficult passages. The opinion of the scholar had been cordial and encouraging; he had said that the book was a very great and sound work, useful for doctrine and exhortation, and that many men had given their whole lives to

work without achieving such a result. Gilbert had some of the happiness which comes to one who has completed a lengthy task; and
though the time drew nigh at which he might expect a further
fulfilment of the vision, he was so filled with gratitude at the thought
of the great work he had done, that there was little fear or expect-
ation in his mind.

He returned one summer afternoon to Cambridge, and the porter
told him that the Master and several of the Fellows were in the
garden, and would fain see him on his arrival. So Gilbert, carrying a
little bundle which contained his precious book, went out there at
once. The Master had caused to be made a new sundial, which he
had affixed in such a way to the wall that those whose chambers
gave on the garden could read the time of day without waiting to
hear the bells.

When Gilbert came out he saw the little group of Fellows standing
by the wall, while the Master with a staff pointed out the legend on
the dial, which said that the only hours it told were the hours of
sunshine. It came upon Gilbert in a moment that this was the second
vision, and though two or three of the group saw him and turned to
him with pleasant greetings, he stood for a moment lost in the
strangeness of the thing. One of them said, 'He stands amazed at the
novelty of the design;' and as he said the words, an old grey cat that
belonged to the College, and lodged somewhere in the roofs, sprang
from a bush and ran past him. One of the Fellows said, 'Aha, cats do
not love change!' and then Gilbert came forward, and greeted his
friends; but there lay a cold and terrible thought in the background
of his mind, and he could not keep it out of his face; so that one of the
Fellows, drawing him aside, asked if he had a good verdict on the
book, for he seemed as one that was ill-pleased. And the Master,
fearing that Gilbert did not like the dial, came and said to him
courteously that he knew it was a new-fangled thing, but that it was
useful, and in itself not unpleasant, and that it would soon catch a
grace of congruity from the venerable walls around. 'But,' he added,
'if you do not like it, it shall be put in some other place.' Then
Gilbert bestirred himself and said that he liked the dial very well, so
that the Master was content.

But Gilbert, as soon as he was by himself, delivered his mind up to
heavy contemplation; the vision had twice fulfilled itself, and it was
hardly to be hoped that it would fail the third time. He sent his book
to be copied out fair, and when it was gone it was as though he had
lost his companion. The hours passed very slowly and drearily; he

wrote a paper, to fill the time, of his wishes with regard to what should be done with his books and little property after his death, and was half minded to tear it up again. And then after a few days of purposeless and irresolute waiting, he made up his mind that he must go again to the West, and see his friend the old priest. And though he did not say it to himself in words, yet a purpose slowly shaped itself in his mind that he must at all cost go to the Hill, and learn again what should be, and that thus alone could he break the spell.

He spent a morning in making his farewells; he tried to speak to his friends as usual, but they noticed long afterwards that he had used a special tenderness and wistfulness in all he said; he sate long in his own room, with a great love in his heart for the beautiful and holy peace of the place, and for all the happiness he had known there; and then he prayed very long and earnestly in the chapel, kneeling in his stall; and his heart was somewhat lightened.

Then he set off; but before he mounted his horse he looked very lovingly at the old front of the College, and his servant saw that his eyes were full of tears and that his lips moved; and so Gilbert rode along to the West.

His journey was very different from the same journey taken six years before; he spoke with none, and rode busily, like one who is anxious to see some sad errand through. He found the old Vicar still more infirm and somewhat blind; but the Vicar said that he was very happy to see him, as he himself was near the end of life, and that he could hope for but few years – adding that it was far different for Gilbert, who, he supposed, would very soon be a Dean with a Cathedral of his own, and would forget his humble friend the old Vicar. But Gilbert put the wit aside, and talked earnestly with the Vicar about the end of life and what might be hereafter. But the old Vicar said solemnly that he knew not, and indeed cared little. But that he would go into the dark like a child holding a loving hand, and would have no need to fear.

That night Gilbert lay in his bed awake, and very strange thoughts passed through his mind, which he strove to quiet by prayers; and so fell asleep; till at last in the dim dawn he awoke. Then after a moment's thought he took a paper and wrote on it, saying that he was gone out and knew not when he would return; but he prayed the Vicar that when he should find the paper, he should at once fall to prayer for him, for there was a sore conflict before him to fight out, both in soul and body, and what would be the issue he knew not. 'And if,' the end of the writing ran, 'I must depart hence, then pray

that my passage may be easy, and that I may find the valley bright.'
And he laid the paper upon the table. Then he dressed himself, and
went out alone into the valley, walking swiftly and intently – so
intently that when he passed the farm he marked not that the old
farmer was sitting in an arbour in the garden, who called shrilly to
him; but Gilbert heard not, and the old farmer was too weak to
follow; so Gilbert went down to the Hill of Trouble.

It lay, as it had lain six years before, very still and beautiful in the
breathless sunshine. The water was in the creek, a streak of sapphire
blue; the birds called in the crags, and the bushes and lawns glistened
fresh with dew.

But Gilbert, very pale and with his heart beating fast, came to the
wall and surmounted it, and went swiftly up the Hill, till he found
himself near the stones; then he looked once round upon the hills
and the sea, and then with a word of prayer he stepped within the
circle.

This time he had not long to wait. As he entered the circle he saw
the old man enter from the opposite side and come to meet him, with
a strange light of triumph in his eyes. Then Gilbert looked him in
the face with a rising horror, and said, 'Sir, I have come again; and I
doubt the truth of your vision no longer; I have done my work, and I
have twice seen the fulfilment – now therefore tell me of my end –
that I may be certified how long I have to live. For the shadow of the
doubt I cannot bear.'

And the old man looked at him with something of compassion and
said, 'You are young, and you fear the passage hence, knowing not
what may be on the other side of the door; but you need not fear.
Even I, who have small ground of hope, am ashamed that I feared it
so much. But what will you give me if I grant your boon?'

Then Gilbert said, 'I have nothing to give.'

Then the old man said, 'Think once more.'

Then was there a silence; and Gilbert said, 'Man, I know not what
or who thou art; but I think that thou art a lost soul; one thing I can
give thee. . . . I will myself intercede for thee before the Throne.'

Then the old man looked at him for a moment, and said, 'I have
waited long . . . and have received no comfort till now;' and then he
said, 'Wilt thou promise?'

And Gilbert said, 'In the name of God, Amen.'

Then the old man stretched out his hand and said, 'Art thou ready?
for the time is come; and thou art called now;' and he touched
Gilbert on the breast.

Gilbert looked into the old man's eyes, and seemed to see there an unfathomable sadness, such as he had never seen; but at the touch a pain so fierce and agonising passed through him, that he sank upon the ground and covered his face with his hands.

Just at this time the old priest found the paper; and he divined the truth. So he called his servant and bade him saddle his horse in haste; and then he fell to prayer.

Then he rode down the valley; and though he feared the place, yet he rode to the Hill of Trouble; and though his sight was dim and his limbs feeble, it seemed to him that someone walked beside the horse and guided him; and as he prayed he knew that all was over, and that Gilbert had peace.

He came soon to the place; and there he found Gilbert lying on the turf; and his sight was so dim that it seemed to him as though someone slipped away from Gilbert's side He put Gilbert on his horse, and held the poor helpless body thereon, but there was so gentle a smile on the face of the dead that he could not fear.

The body of Gilbert lies in the little churchyard; his great book keeps his memory bright; and on the top of the Hill of Trouble stands a little chapel, built out of the stones of the circle; and on the wall, painted at the old priest's charge, is a picture of the Lord Christ, with wounded hands and side, preaching to the disobedient spirits in prison; and they hear him and are glad.

Basil Netherby

A. C. BENSON

It was five o'clock in the afternoon of an October day that Basil
Netherby's letter arrived. I remember that my little clock had just
given its warning click, when the footsteps came to my door; and just
as the clock began to strike, came a hesitating knock. I called out,
'Come in', and after some fumbling with the handle there stepped
into the room I think the shyest clergyman I have ever seen. He
shook hands like an automaton, looking over his left shoulder; he
would not sit down, and yet looked about the room, as he stood, as
if wondering why the ordinary civility of a chair was not offered
him; he spoke in a husky voice, out of which he endeavoured at
intervals to cast some viscous obstruction by loud hawkings; and
when, after one of these interludes, he caught my eye, he went a
sudden pink in the face.

However, the letter got handed to me; and I gradually learnt from
my visitor's incoherent talk that it was from my friend Basil Netherby; and that he was well, remarkably well, quite a different man
from what he had been when he came to Treheale; that he himself
(Vyvyan was his name) was curate of St Sibby. Treheale was the
name of the house where Mr Netherby lived. The letter had been
most important, he thought, for Mr Netherby had asked him as he
was going up to town to convey the letter himself and to deliver it
without fail into Mr Ward's own hands. He could not, however,
account (here he turned away from me, and hummed, and beat his
fingers on the table) for the extraordinary condition in which he was
compelled to hand it to me, as it had never, so far as he knew, left his
own pocket; and presently with a gasp Mr Vyvyan was gone, refusing
all proffers of entertainment, and falling briskly down – to judge
from the sounds which came to me – outside my door.

I, Leonard Ward, was then living in rooms in a little street out of
Holborn – a poor place enough. I was organist of St Bartholomew's,
Holborn; and I was trying to do what is described as getting up

a connection in the teaching line. But it was slow work, and I must confess that my prospects did not appear to me very cheerful. However, I taught one of the Vicar's little daughters, and a whole family, the children of a rich tradesman in a neighbouring street, the piano and singing, so that I contrived to struggle on.

Basil Netherby had been with me at the College of Music. His line was composing. He was a pleasant, retiring fellow, voluble enough and even rhetorical in tête-à-tête talk with an intimate; but dumb in company, with an odd streak of something – genius or eccentricity – about him which made him different from other men. We had drifted into an intimacy, and had indeed lodged together for some months. Netherby used to show me his works – mostly short studies – and though I used to think that they always rather oddly broke down in unexpected places, yet there was always an air of aiming high about them, an attempt to realise the ideal.

He left the College before I did, saying that he had learnt all he could learn and that now he must go quietly into the country somewhere and work all alone – he should do no good otherwise. I heard from him fitfully. He was in Wales, in Devonshire, in Cornwall; and then some three months before the day on which I got the letter, the correspondence had ceased altogether; I did not know his address, and was always expecting to hear from him.

I took up the letter from the place where Mr Vyvyan had laid it down; it was a bulky envelope; and it was certainly true that, as Mr Vyvyan had said, the packet was in an extraordinary condition. One of the corners was torn off, with a ragged edge that looked like the nibbling of mice, and there were disagreeable stains both on the front and the back, so that I should have inferred that Mr Vyvyan's pocket had been filled with raspberries – the theory, though improbable, did not appear impossible. But what surprised me most was that near each of the corners in front a rough cross of ink was drawn, and one at the back of the flap.

I had little doubt, however, that Mr Vyvyan had, in a nervous and absent mood, harried the poor letter into the condition in which I saw it, and that he had been unable to bring himself to confess to the maltreatment.

I tore the letter open – there fell out several pages of MS. music, and a letter in which Basil, dating from Treheale, and writing in a bold firm hand – bolder and firmer, I thought, than of old – said that he had been making a good deal of progress and working very hard (which must account for his silence), and he ventured to enclose some of his last work which he *hoped* I would like, but he wanted a candid opinion. He added that he had got quarters at a delightful farmhouse, not far from Grampound. That was all.

Stay! That was not all. The letter finished on the third side; but, as I closed it, I saw written on the fourth page, very small, in a weak loose hand, and as if scribbled in a ferocious haste, as a man might write (so it came oddly into my head) who was escaped for a moment from the vigilance of a careful gaoler, a single sentence. 'Vyvyan will take this; and for God's sake, dear Leonard, if you would help a friend who is on the edge (I dare not say of what), come to me tomorrow, UNINVITED. You will think this very strange, but do not mind that – only come – *unannounced*, do you see . . .'

The line broke off in an unintelligible flourish. Then on each corner of the last page had been scrawled a cross, with the same ugly and slovenly haste as the crosses on the envelope.

My first thought was that Basil was mad; my next thought that he had drifted into some awkward situation, fallen under some unfortunate influence – was perhaps being blackmailed – and I knew his sensitive character well enough to feel sure that whatever the trouble was it would be exaggerated ten times over by his lively and apprehensive mind. Slowly a situation shaped itself. Basil was a man, as I knew, of an extraordinary austere standard of morals, singularly guileless, and innocent of worldly matters.

Someone, I augured, some unscrupulous woman, had, in the remote spot where he was living, taken a guileful fancy to my poor friend, and had doubtless, after veiled overtures, resolved on a bolder policy and was playing on his sensitive and timid nature by some threat of nameless disclosures, some vile and harrowing innuendo.

I read the letter again – and still more clear did it seem to me that he was in some strange durance, and suffering under abominable fears. I rose from my chair and went to find a timetable, that I might see when I could get to Grampound, when again a shuffling footstep drew to my door, an uncertain hand knocked at the panel, and Mr Vyvyan again entered the room. This time his confusion was even greater, if that were possible, than it had previously been. He had forgotten to give me a further message; and he thereupon gave me a filthy scrap of paper, nibbled and stained like the envelope, apologised with unnecessary vehemence, uttered a strangled cough and stumbled from the room.

It was difficult enough to decipher the paper, but I saw that a musical phrase had been written on it; and then in a moment I saw that it was a phrase from an old, extravagant work of Basil's own, a *Credo* which we had often discussed together, the grim and fantastic accompaniment of the sentence "He descended into hell."

This came to me as a message of even greater urgency, and I hesitated no longer. I sat down to write a note to the father of my family of pupils, in which I said that important business called me away for two or three days. I looked out a train, and found that by catching the 10 o'clock limited mail I could be at Grampound by 6 in the morning. I ordered a hasty dinner and I packed a few things into a bag, with an oppressive sense of haste. But, as generally happens on such occasions, I found that I had still two or three hours in hand; so I took up Netherby's music and read it through carefully.

Certainly he had improved wonderfully in handling; but what music it was! It was like nothing of which I had ever even dreamed. There was a wild, intemperate voluptuousness about it, a kind of evil relish of beauty which gave me a painful thrill. To make sure that I was not mistaken, owing to the nervous tension which the strange event had produced in me, I put the things in my pocket and went out to the house of a friend, Dr Grierson, an accomplished and critical musician who lived not far away.

I found the great man at home smoking leisurely. He had a bird-like demeanour, like an ancient stork, as he sat blinking through spectacles astride of a long pointed nose. He had a slight acquaintance with Netherby, and when I mentioned that I had received some new music from him, which I wished to submit to him, he showed obvious interest. 'A promising fellow,' he said, 'only of course too transcendental.' He took the music in his hand; he settled his spectacles and read. Presently he looked up; and I saw in the kind of shamefaced glance with which he regarded me that he had found something of the same incomprehensible sensuality which had so oddly affected myself in the music. 'Come, come,' he said rather severely, 'this is very strange stuff – this won't do at all, you know. We must just hear this!' He rose and went to his piano; and peering into the music, he played the pieces deliberately and critically.

Heard upon the piano, the accent of subtle evil that ran through the music became even more obvious. I seemed to struggle between two feelings – an overpowering admiration, and a sense of shame at my own capacity for admiring it. But the great man was still more moved. He broke off in the middle of a bar and tossed the music to me.

'This is filthy stuff,' he said. 'I should say to you – burn it. It is clever, of course – hideously, devilishly clever. Look at the progression – F sharp against F natural, you observe' (and he added some technical details with which I need not trouble my readers).

He went on: 'But the man has no business to think of such things. I don't like it. Tell him from me that it won't do. There must be some reticence in art, you know – and there is none here. Tell Netherby that he is on the wrong tack altogether. Good heavens,' he added, 'how could the man write it? He used to be a decent sort of fellow.'

It may seem extravagant to write thus of music, but I can only say that it affected me as nothing I had ever heard before. I put it away and we tried to talk of other things; but we could not get the stuff out of our heads. Presently I rose to go, and the Doctor reiterated his warnings still more emphatically. 'The man is a criminal in art,' he said, 'and there must be an end once and for all of this: tell him it's abominable!'

I went back; caught my train; and was whirled sleepless and excited to the West. Towards morning I fell into a troubled sleep, in which I saw in tangled dreams the figure of a man running restlessly among stony hills. Over and over again the dream came to me; and it was with a grateful heart, though very weary, that I saw a pale light of dawn in the east, and the dark trees and copses along the line becoming more and more defined, by swift gradations, in the chilly autumn air.

It was very still and peaceful when we drew up at Grampound station. I enquired my way to Treheale; and I was told it was three or four miles away. The porter looked rather enquiringly at me; there was no chance of obtaining a vehicle, so I resolved to walk, hoping that I should be freshened by the morning air.

Presently a lane struck off from the main road, which led up a wooded valley, with a swift stream rushing along; in one or two places the chimney of a deserted mine with desolate rubbish-heaps stood beside the road. At one place a square church-tower, with pinnacles, looked solemnly over the wood. The road rose gradually. At last I came to a little hamlet, perched high up on the side of the valley. The scene was incomparably beautiful; the leaves were yellowing fast, and I could see a succession of wooded ridges, with a long line of moorland closing the view.

The little place was just waking into quiet activity. I found a bustling man taking down shutters from a general shop which was also the post-office, and enquired where Mr Netherby lived. The man told me that he was in lodgings at Treheale – 'the big house itself, where Farmer Hall lives now; if you go straight along the road,' he added, 'you will pass the lodge, and Treheale lies up in the wood.'

I was by this time very tired – it was now nearly seven – but I took up my bag again and walked along a road passing between high hedges. Presently the wood closed in again, and I saw a small plastered lodge with a thatched roof standing on the left among some firs. The gate stood wide open, and the road which led into the wood was grass-grown, though with deep ruts, along which heavy laden carts seemed to have passed recently.

The lodge seemed deserted, and I accordingly struck off into the wood. Presently the undergrowth grew thicker, and huge sprawling laurels rose in all directions. Then the track took a sudden turn; and I saw straight in front of me the front of a large Georgian house of brown stone, with a gravel sweep up to the door, but all overgrown with grass.

I confess that the house displeased me strangely. It was substantial, homely, and large; but the wood came up close to it on all sides, and it seemed to stare at me with its shuttered windows with a look of dumb resentment, like a great creature at bay.

I walked on, and saw that the smoke went up from a chimney to the left. The house, as I came closer, presented a front with a stone portico, crowned with a pediment. To left and right were two wings which were built out in advance from the main part of the house, throwing the door back into the shadow.

I pulled a large handle which hung beside the door, and a dismal bell rang somewhere in the house – rang on and on as if unable to cease; then footsteps came along the floor within, and the door was slowly and reluctantly unbarred.

There stood before me a little pale woman with a timid, downcast air. 'Does Mr Netherby live here?' I said.

'Yes; he lodges here, sir.'

'Can I see him?' I said.

'Well, sir, he is not up yet. Does he expect you?'

'Well, not exactly,' I said, faltering; 'but he will know my name – and I have come a long way to see him.'

The woman raised her eyes and looked at me, and I was aware, by some swift intuition, that I was in the presence of a distressed spirit, labouring under some melancholy prepossession.

'Will you be here long?' she asked suddenly.

'No,' I said; 'but I shall have to stay the night, I think. I travelled all last night, and I am very tired; in fact I shall ask to sit down and wait till I can see Mr Netherby.'

She seemed to consider a moment, and then led me into the house. We entered a fine hall, with stone flags and pillars on each side. There hung, so far as I could see in the half-light, grim and faded portraits on the walls, and there were some indistinct pieces of furniture, like couched beasts, in the corners. We went through a door and down a passage and turned into a large rather bare room, which showed, however, some signs of human habitation. There was a table laid for a meal.

An old piano stood in a corner, and there were a few books lying about; on the walls hung large pictures in tarnished frames. I put down my bag, and sat down by the fire in an old armchair, and almost instantly fell into a drowse. I have an indistinct idea of the woman returning to ask if I would like some breakfast, or wait for Mr Netherby. I said hastily that I would wait, being in the oppressed condition of drowsiness when one's only idea is to get a respite from the presence of any person, and fell again into a heavy sleep.

I woke suddenly with a start, conscious of a movement in the room. Basil Netherby was standing close beside me, with his back to the fire, looking down at me with a look which I can only say seemed to me to betoken a deep annoyance of spirit. But seeing me awake, there came on to his face a smile of a reluctant and diplomatic kind. I started to my feet, giddy and bewildered, and shook hands.

'My word,' he said, 'you sleep sound, Ward. So you've found me out? Well, I'm very glad to see you; but what made you think of coming? and why didn't you let me know? I would have sent something to meet you.'

I was a good deal nettled at this ungenial address, after the trouble to which I had put myself. I said, 'Well, really, Basil, I think that is rather strong. Mr Vyvyan called on me yesterday with a letter from you, and some music; and of course I came away at once.'

'Of course,' he said, looking on the ground – and then added rather hastily, 'Now, how did the stuff strike you? I have improved, I think. And it is really very good of you to come off at once to criticise the music – *very* good of you,' he said with some emphasis; 'and, man, you look wretchedly tired – let us have breakfast.'

I was just about to remonstrate, and to speak about the postscript, when he looked at me suddenly with so peculiar and disagreeable a glance that the words literally stuck in my throat. I thought to myself that perhaps the subject was too painful to enter upon at once, and that he probably wished to tell me at his own time what was in the background.

We breakfasted; and now that I had leisure to look at Basil, I was surprised beyond measure at the change in him. I had seen him last a pale, rather haggard youth, loose-limbed and untidy. I saw before me a strongly-built and firmly-knit man, with a ruddy colour and bronzed cheek. He looked the embodiment of health and well-being. His talk, too, after the first impression of surprise wore off, was extraordinarily cheerful and amusing. Again and again he broke out into loud laughter – not the laughter of an excited or hectic person, but the firm, brisk laugh of a man full to the brim of good spirits and health.

He talked of his work, of the country-people that surrounded him, whose peculiarities he seemed to have observed with much relish; he asked me, but without any appearance of interest, what I thought about his work. I tried to tell him what Dr Grierson had said and what I had felt; but I was conscious of being at a strange disadvantage before this genial personality. He laughed loudly at our criticisms. 'Old Grierson,' he said, 'why, he is no better than a clergyman's widow: he would stop his ears if you read Shakespeare to him. My dear man, I have travelled a long way since I saw you last; I have found my tongue – and what is more, I can say what I mean, and as I mean it. Grierson indeed! I can see him looking shocked, like a pelican with a stomach-ache.'

This was a felicitous though not a courteous description of our friend, but I could find no words to combat it; indeed, Basil's talk and whole bearing seemed to carry me away like a swift stream and in my wearied condition I found that I could not stand up to this radiant personality.

After breakfast he advised me to have a good sleep and he took me, with some show of solicitude, to a little bedroom which had been got ready for me. He unpacked my things and told me to undress and go to bed, that he had some work to do that he was anxious to finish, and that after luncheon we would have a stroll together.

I was too tired to resist, and fell at once into a deep sleep. I rose a new man; and finding no-one in Basil's room, I strolled out for a moment on to the drive, and presently saw the odd and timid figure of Mrs Hall coming along, in a big white flapping sort of sun-bonnet, with a basket in her hand. She came straight up to me in a curious, resolute sort of way, and it came into my mind that she had come out for the very purpose of meeting me.

I praised the beauty of the place, and said that I supposed she knew it well. 'Yes,' she said; adding that she was born in the village and her mother had been as a girl a servant at Treheale. But she went on to tell me that she and her husband had lived till recently at a farm down in the valley, and had only been a year or so in the house itself. Old Mr Heale, the last owner, had died three or four years before, and it had proved impossible to let the house. It seemed that when the trustees gave up all idea of being able to get a tenant, they had offered it to the Halls at a nominal rent, to act as caretakers. She spoke in a cheerless way, with her eyes cast down and with the same strained look as of one carrying a heavy burden. 'You will have heard of Mr Heale, perhaps?' she said with a sudden look at me.

'The old Squire, sir,' she said; 'but I think people here are unfair to him. He lived a wild life enough, but he was a kind gentleman in his way – and I have often thought it was not his fault altogether. He married soon after he came into the estate – a Miss Tregaskis from down to St Erne – and they were very happy for a little; but she died after they had been married a couple of years, and they had no child; and then I think Mr Heale went nearly mad – nothing went right after that. Mr Heale shut himself up a good deal among his books – he was a very clever gentleman – and then he got into bad ways; but it was the sorrow in his heart that made him bad – and we must not blame people too much, must we?' She looked at me with rather a pitiful look.

'You mean,' I said, 'that he tried to forget his grief, and did not choose the best way to do it.'

'Yes, sir,' said Mrs Hall simply. 'I think he blamed God for taking away what he loved, instead of trusting Him; and no good comes of that. The people here got to hate him – he used to spoil the young people, sir – you know what I mean – and they were afraid of seeing him about their houses. I remember, sir, as if it were yesterday, seeing him in the lane to St Sibby. He was marching along, very upright, with his white hair – it went white early – and he passed old Mr Miles, the church-warden, who had been a wild young man too, but he found religion with the Wesleyans, and after that was very hard on everyone.

'It was the first time they had met since Mr Miles had become serious; and Mr Heale stopped in his pleasant way, and held out his hand to Mr Miles; who put his hands behind him and said some-thing – I was close to them – which I could not quite catch, but it was about fellowship with the works of darkness; and then Mr Miles turned and went on his way; and Mr Heale stood looking after him with a curious smile on his face – and I have pitied him ever since. Then he turned and saw me; he always took notice of me – I was a girl then; and he said to me, "There, Mary, you see that. I am not good enough, it seems, for Mr Miles. Well, I don't blame him; but remember, child, that the religion which makes a man turn his back on an old friend is not a good religion"; but I could see he was distressed, though he spoke quietly – and as I went on he gave a sigh which somehow stays in my mind. Perhaps sir, you would like to look at his picture; he was painted at the same time as Mrs Heale in the first year of their marriage.'

I said I should like to see it, and we turned to the house. She led me to a little room that seemed like a study. There was a big bookcase full of books, mostly of a scientific kind; and there was a large knee-hole table much dotted with inkspots. 'It was here,' she said, 'he used to work, hour after hour.' On the wall hung a pair of pictures – one, that of a young woman, hardly more than a girl, with a delightful expression, both beautiful and good. She was dressed in some white material, and there was a glimpse of sunlit fields beyond.

Then I turned to the portrait of Mr Heale. It represented a young man in a claret-coloured coat, very slim and upright. It showed a face of great power, a big forehead, clearcut features, and a determined chin, with extraordinarily bright large eyes; evidently the portrait of a man of great physical and mental force, who would do whatever he took in hand with all his might. It was very finely painted, with a dark background of woods against a stormy sky.

I was immensely struck by the picture; and not less by the fact that there was an extraordinary though indefinable likeness to Mrs Hall herself. I felt somehow that she perceived that I had noticed this, for she made as though to leave the room. I could not help the inference that I was compelled to draw. I lingered for a moment looking at the portrait, which was so lifelike as to give an almost painful sense of the presence of a third person in the room. But Mrs Hall went out, and I understood that I was meant to follow her.

She led the way into their own sitting-room, and then with some agitation she turned to me. 'I understand that you are an old friend of Mr Netherby's, sir,' she said.

'Yes,' I said; 'he is my greatest friend.'

'Could you persuade him, sir, to leave this place?' she went on. 'You will think it a strange thing to say – and I am glad enough to have a lodger, and I like Mr Netherby – but do you think it is a good thing for a young gentleman to live so much alone?'

I saw that nothing was to be gained by reticence, so I said, 'Now, Mrs Hall, I think we had better speak plainly. I am, I confess, anxious about Mr Netherby. I don't mean that he is not well, for I have never seen him look better; but I think that there is something going on which I don't wholly understand.'

She looked at me suddenly with a quick look, and then, as if deciding that I was to be trusted, she said in a low voice, 'Yes, sir, that is it; this house is not like other houses. Mr Heale – how shall I say it? – was a very determined gentleman, and he used to say that he never would leave the house – and – you will think it very strange that I should speak thus to a stranger – I don't think he has left it.'

We stood for a moment silent, and I knew that she had spoken the truth. While we thus stood, I can only say what I felt – I became aware that we were not alone; the sun was bright on the woods outside, the clock ticked peacefully in a corner, but there was something unseen all about us which lay very heavily on my mind. Mrs Hall put out her hands in a deprecating way, and then said in a low and hurried voice, 'He would do no harm to me, sir – we are too near for that' – she looked up at me, and I nodded; 'but I can't help it, can I, if he is different with other people? Now, Mr Hall is not like that, sir – he is a plain good man, and would think what I am saying no better than madness; but as sure as there is a God in Heaven, Mr Heale is here – and though he is too fine a gentleman to take advantage of my talk, yet he liked to command other people, and went his own way too much.'

While she spoke, the sense of oppression which I had felt a moment before drew off all of a sudden; and it seemed again as though we were alone.

'Mrs Hall,' I said, 'you are a good woman; these things are very dark to me, and though I have heard of such things in stories, I never expected to meet them in the world. But I will try what I can do to get my friend away, though he is a wilful fellow, and I think he will go his own way too.' While I spoke I heard Basil's voice outside calling me, and I took Mrs Hall's hand in my own. She pressed it, and gave me a very kind, sad look. And so I went out.

We lunched together, Basil and I, off simple fare; he pointed with an air of satisfaction to a score which he had brought into the room, written out with wonderful precision. 'Just finished,' he said, 'and you shall hear it later on; but now we will go and look round the place. Was there ever such luck as to get a harbourage like this? I have been here two months and feel like staying for ever. The place is in Chancery. Old Heale of Treheale, the last of his stock – a rare old blackguard – died here. They tried to let the house, and failed, and put Farmer Hall in at last. The whole place belongs to a girl ten years old. It is a fine house – we will look at that tomorrow; but today we will walk round outside. By the way, how long can you stay?'

'I must get back on Friday at latest,' I said. 'I have a choir practice and a lesson on Saturday.'

Basil looked at me with a good-natured smile. 'A pretty poor business, isn't it?' he said. 'I would rather pick oakum myself. Here I live in a fine house, for next to nothing, and write, write, write – there's a life for a man.'

'Don't you find it lonely?' said I.

'Lonely?' said Basil, laughing loud. 'Not a bit of it. What do I want with a pack of twaddlers all about me? I tread a path among the stars – and I have the best of company, too.' He stopped and broke off suddenly.

'I shouldn't have thought Mrs Hall very enlivening company,' I said. 'By the way, what an odd-looking woman! She seems as if she were frightened.'

At that innocent remark Basil looked at me suddenly with the same expression of indefinable anger that I had seen in his face at our first meeting; but he said nothing for a moment. Then he resumed: 'No, I want no company but myself and my thoughts. I tell you, Ward, if you had done as I have done, opened a door into the very treasure-house of music, and had only just to step in and carry away as much as one can manage at a time, you wouldn't want company.'

I could make no reply to this strange talk; and he presently took me out. I was astonished at the beauty of the place. The ground fell sharply at the back, and there was a terrace with a view over a little valley, with pasture-fields at the bottom, crowned with low woods – beyond, a wide prospect over uplands, which lost themselves in the haze. The day was still and clear; and we could hear the running of the stream below, the cooing of doves and the tinkling of a sheepbell. To the left of the house lay large stables and barns, which were in the possession of the farmer.

We wandered up and down by paths and lanes, sometimes through the yellowing woods, sometimes on open ground, the most perfect views bursting upon us on every side, everything lying in a rich still peace, which came upon my tired and bewildered mind like soft music.

In the course of our walk we suddenly came upon a churchyard surrounded by a low wall; at the farther end, beyond the graves, stood a small church consisting of two aisles, with a high perpendicular tower. 'St Sibby,' said Basil, 'whether he or she I know not, but no doubt a very estimable person. You would like to look at this? The church is generally open.'

We went up a gravel path and entered the porch; the door was open, and there was an odd, close smell in the building. It was a very plain place, with the remains of a rood-loft, and some ancient woodwork; but the walls were mildewed and green and the place looked neglected.

'Vyvyan is a good fellow,' said Basil, looking round, 'but he is single-handed here; the Rector is an invalid and lives at Penzance, and Vyvyan has a wretched stipend. Look here, Leonard; here is the old Heale vault.' He led me into a little chapel near the tower, which opened on to the church by a single arch. The place was very dark; but I could see a monument or two of an ancient type and some brasses. There were a couple of helmets on iron supports and the remains of a mouldering banner. But just opposite to us was a tall modern marble monument on the wall. 'That is old Heale's monument,' said Basil, 'with a long, pious inscription by the old rector. Just look at it – did you ever see such vandalism?'

I drew near – then I saw that the monument had been defaced in a hideous and horrible way. There were deep dints in the marble, like the marks of a hammer; and there were red stains over the inscription, which reminded me in a dreadful way of the stains on the letter given me by Vyvyan.

'Good Heavens!' I said, 'what inconceivable brutality! Who on earth did this?'

'That's just what no-one can find out,' said Basil, smiling. 'But the inscription was rather too much, I confess – look at this: 'WHO DISCHARGED IN AN EXEMPLARY WAY THE DUTIES OF A LAND-OWNER AND A CHRISTIAN.' Old Heale's idea of the duties of a landowner was to screw as much as he could out of his farmers – and he had, moreover, some old ideas, which we may call feudal, about his relations with the more attractive of his tenants: he was a cheerful old boy – and as to the Christian part of it, well, he had about as much of that, I gather, as you take up on a two-pronged fork. Still, they might have left the old man alone. I dare say he sleeps sound enough in spite of it all. He stamped his foot on the pavement as he did so, which returned a hollow sound. 'Are you inside?' said Basil, laughingly; 'perhaps not at home?'

'Don't talk like that,' I said to Basil, whose levity seemed to me disgusting. 'Certainly not, my boy,' he said, 'if you don't like it. I dare say the old man can look after himself.' And so we left the church.

We returned home about four o'clock. Basil left me on the terrace and went into the house to interview Mrs Hall on the subject of dinner. I hung for a time over the balustrade, but, getting chilly and still not feeling inclined to go in, I strolled to the farther end of the terrace, which ran up to the wood. On reaching the end, I found a stone seat; and behind it, between two yews, a little dark sinister path led into the copse.

I do not know exactly what feeling it was which drew me to enter upon the exploration of the place; the path was slippery and over-grown with moss, and the air of the shrubbery into which it led was close and moist, full of the breath of rotting leaves. The path ran with snakelike windings, so that at no point was it possible to see more than a few feet ahead. Above, the close boughs held hands as if to screen the path from the light. Then the path suddenly took a turn to the left and went straight to the house.

Two yews flanked the way and a small flight of granite steps, slimy and mildewed, led up to a little door in the corner of the house – a door which had been painted brown, like the colour of the stone, and which was let into its frame so as to be flush with the wall. The upper part of it was pierced with a couple of apertures like eyes filled with glass to give light to the passage within. The steps had evidently not been trodden for many months, even years; but upon the door, near the keyhole, were odd marks looking as if scratched by the hoofs of some beast – a goat, I thought – as if the door had been impatiently struck by something awaiting entrance there.

I do not know what was the obsession which fell on me at the sight of this place. A cold dismay seemed to spring from the dark and clutch me; there are places which seem so soaked, as it were, in malign memories that they give out a kind of spiritual aroma of evil. I have seen in my life things which might naturally seem to produce in the mind associations of terror and gloom. I have seen men die; I have seen a man writhe in pain on the ground from a mortal injury; but I never experienced anything like the thrill of horror which passed through my shuddering mind at the sight of the little door with its dark eye-holes.

I went in chilly haste down the path and came out upon the terrace, looking out over the peaceful woods. The sun was now setting in the west among cloud-fiords and bays of rosy light. But the thought of the dark path lying like a snake among the thickets dwelt in my mind and poisoned all my senses.

Presently I heard the voice of Basil call me cheerfully from the corner of the house. We went in. A simple meal was spread for us, half tea, half dinner, to which we did full justice. But afterwards, though Basil was fuller than ever, so it seemed to me, of talk and laughter, I was seized with so extreme a fatigue that I drowsed off several times in the course of our talk, till at last he laughingly ordered me to bed.

I slept profoundly. When I awoke, it was bright day. My curtains had been drawn, and the materials for my toilette arranged while I still slept. I dressed hastily and hurried down, to find Basil awaiting me.

That morning we gave up to exploring the house. It was a fine old place, full from end to end of the evidences of long and ancestral habitation. The place was full of portraits. There was a great old dining-room – Basil had had the whole house unshuttered for my inspection – a couple of large drawing-rooms, long passages, bed-rooms, all full of ancient furniture and pictures, as if the family life had been suddenly suspended. I noticed that he did not take me to the study, but led me upstairs.

'This is my room,' said Basil suddenly; and we turned into a big room in the left-hand corner of the garden-front. There was a big four-post bedroom here, a large table in the window, a sofa, and some fine chairs. But what at once attracted my observation was a low door in the corner of the room, half hidden by a screen. It seemed to me, as if by a sudden gleam of perception, that this door must communicate with the door I had seen below; and presently, while I stood looking out of the great window upon the valley, I said to Basil, 'And that door in the corner – does that communicate with the little door in the wood?'

When I said this, Basil was standing by the table, bending over some MSS. He suddenly turned to me and gave me a very long, penetrating look; and then, as if suddenly recollecting himself, said, 'My dear Ward, you are a very observant fellow – yes, there is a little staircase there that goes down into the shrubbery and leads to the terrace. You remember that old Mr Heale of whom I told you –

well, he had this room, and he had visitors at times whom I dare say it was not convenient to admit to the house; they came and went this way; and he too, no doubt, used the stairs to leave the house and return unseen.'

'How curious!' I said. 'I confess I should not care to have this room – I did not like the look of the shrubbery door.'

'Well,' said Basil, 'I do not feel with you; to me it is rather agreeable to have the association of the room. He was a loose old fish, no doubt, but he lived his life, and I expect enjoyed it, and that is more than most of us can claim.'

As he said the words he crossed the room, and opening the little door, he said, 'Come and look down – it is a simple place enough.'

I went across the room, and looking in, saw a small flight of stairs going down into the dark; at the end of which the two square panes of the little shrubbery door were outlined in the shadow.

I cannot account for what happened next: there was a sound in the passage, and something seemed to rush up the stairs and past me; a strange, dull smell came from the passage; I know that there fell on me a sort of giddiness and horror, and I went back into the room with hands outstretched, like Elymas the sorcerer, seeking someone to guide me. Looking up, I saw Basil regarding me with a baleful look and a strange smile on his face.

'What was that?' I said. 'Surely something came up there . . . I don't know what it was.'

There was a silence; then, 'My dear Ward,' said Basil, 'you are behaving very oddly – one would think you had seen a ghost.' He looked at me with a sort of gleeful triumph, like a man showing the advantages of a house or the beauties of a view to an astonished friend. But again I could find no words to express my sense of what I had experienced. Basil went swiftly to the door and shut it, and then said to me with a certain sternness, 'Come, we have been here long enough – let us go on. I am afraid I am boring you.'

We went downstairs; and the rest of the morning passed, so far as I can remember, in a species of fitful talk. I was endeavouring to recover from the events of the morning; and Basil – well, he seemed to me like a man who was fencing with some difficult question. Though his talk seemed spontaneous, I felt somehow that it was that of a weak antagonist endeavouring to parry the strokes of a persistent assailant.

After luncheon Basil proposed a walk again. We went out on a long ramble, as we had done the previous day; but I remember little of what passed. He directed upon me a stream of indifferent talk, but I laboured, I think, under a heavy depression of spirit, and my conversation was held up merely as it might have been as a shield against the insistent demands of my companion. Anyone who has been through a similar experience in which he wrestles with some tragic fact, and endeavours merely to meet and answer the sprightly suggestions of some cheerful companion, can imagine what I felt. At last the evening began to close in; we retraced our steps: Basil told me that we should dine at an early hour, and I was left alone in my own room.

I became the prey of the most distressing and poignant reflections. What I had experienced convinced me that there was something about the whole place that was uncanny and abnormal. The attitude of my companion, his very geniality, seemed to me to be forced and unnatural; and my only idea was to gain, if I could, some notion of how I should proceed. I felt that questions were useless, and I committed myself to the hands of Providence. I felt that here was a situation that I could not deal with and that I must leave it in stronger hands than my own. This reflection brought me some transitory comfort, and when I heard Basil's voice calling me to dinner, I felt that sooner or later the conflict would have to be fought out, and that I could not myself precipitate matters.

After dinner Basil for the first time showed some signs of fatigue, and after a little conversation he sank back in a chair, lit a cigar, and presently asked me to play something.

I went to the piano, still, I must confess, seeking for some possible opportunity of speech, and let my fingers stray as they moved along the keys. For a time I extemporised and then fell into some familiar music. I do not know whether the instinctive thought of what he had scrawled upon his note to me influenced me but I began to play Mendelssohn's anthem *Hear my prayer*. While I played the initial phrase, I became aware that some change was making itself felt in my companion; and I had hardly come to the end of the second phrase when a sound from Basil made me turn round.

I do not think that I ever received so painful a shock in my life as that which I experienced at the sight that met my eyes. Basil was still in the chair where he had seated himself, but instead of the robust personality which he had presented to me during our early inter-views, I saw in a sudden flash the Basil that I knew, only infinitely more tired and haggard than I had known him in life. He was like a man who had cast aside a mask, and had suddenly appeared in his own part. He sat before me as I had often seen him sit, leaning forward in an intensity of emotion. I stopped suddenly, wheeled round in my chair, and said, 'Basil, tell me what has happened.'

He looked at me, cast an agitated glance round the room – and then all on a sudden began to speak in a voice that was familiar to me of old.

What he said is hardly for me to recount. But he led me step by step through a story so dark in horrors that I can hardly bring myself to reproduce it here. Imagine an untainted spirit, entering cheerfully upon some simple entourage, finding himself little by little within the net of some overpowering influence of evil.

He told me that he had settled at Treheale in his normal frame of mind. That he had intended to tell me of his whereabouts, but that there had gradually stolen into his mind a sort of unholy influence. 'At first,' he said, 'I resisted it,' but it was accompanied by so extra-ordinary an access of mental power and vigour that he had accepted the conditions under which he found himself. I had better perhaps try to recount his own experience.

He had come to Grampound in the course of his wanderings and had enquired about lodgings. He had been referred to the farmer at Treheale. He had settled himself there, only congratulating himself upon the mixture of quiet and dignity which surrounded him. He had arranged his life for tranquil study, had chosen his rooms, and had made the best disposition he could of his affairs.

'The second night,' he said, 'that I was here, I had gone to bed thinking of nothing but my music. I had extinguished my light and was lying quietly in bed watching the expiring glimmer of the embers on my hearth. I was wondering, as one does, weaving all kinds of fancies about the house and the room in which I found myself, lying with my head on my hand, when I saw, to my intense astonishment, the little door in the corner of the bedroom half open and close again.

'I thought to myself that it was probably Mrs Hall coming to see whether I was comfortable, and I thereupon said, 'Who is there?' There was no sound in answer, but presently, a moment or two after, there followed a disagreeable laughter, I thought from the lower regions of the house in the direction of the corner. 'Come in, who-ever you are,' I said; and in a moment the door opened and closed, and I became aware that there was someone in the room

'Further than that,' said Basil to me in that dreadful hour, 'it is impossible to go. I can only say that I became aware in a moment of the existence of a world outside of and intertwined with our own; a world of far stronger influences and powers – how far-reaching I know not – but I know this, that all the mortal difficulties and dilemmas that I had hitherto been obliged to meet melted away in the face of a force to which I had hitherto been a stranger.'

The dreadful recital ended about midnight; and the strange part was to me that our positions seemed in some fearful manner to have been now reversed. Basil was now the shrinking, timorous creature, who only could implore me not to leave him. It was in such a mood as this that he had written the letter. I asked him what there was to fear. 'Everything,' he said with a shocking look. He would not go to bed; he would not allow me to leave the room.

Step by step I unravelled the story, which his incoherent statement had only hinted at. His first emotion had been that of intense fright; but he became aware almost at once that the spirit who thus so unmistakably came to him was not inimical to him; the very features of the being – if such a word can be used about so shadowy a thing – appeared to wear a smile. Little by little the presence of the visitant had become habitual to Basil: there was a certain pride in his own fearlessness, which helped him.

Then there was intense and eager curiosity; 'and then, too,' said the unhappy man, 'the influence began to affect me in other ways. I will not tell you how, but the very necessaries of life were provided for me in a manner which I should formerly have condemned with the utmost scorn, but which now I was given confidence to disregard. The dejection, the languorous reflections which used to hang about me, gradually drew off and left me cheerful, vigorous, and, I must say it, delighting in evil imaginations; but so subtle was the evil influence, that it was not into any gross corruption or flagrant deeds that I flung myself; it was into my music that the poison flowed.

'I do not, of course, mean that evil then appeared to me, as I can humbly say it does now, *as* evil, but rather as a vision of perfect beauty, glorifying every natural function and every corporeal desire. The springs of music rose clear and strong within me and with the fountain I mingled from my own stores the subtle venom of the corrupted mind. How glorious, I thought, to sway as with a magic wand the souls of men; to interpret for each all the eager and leaping desires which maybe he had dully and dutifully controlled. To make all things fair – for so potent were the whispers of the spirit that talked at my ear that I believed in my heart that all that was natural in man was also permissible and even beautiful, and that it was nothing but a fantastic asceticism that forbids it; though now I see, as I saw before, that the evil that thwarts mankind is but the slime of the pit out of which he is but gradually extricating himself.'

'But what *is* the thing,' I said, 'of which you speak? Is it a spirit of evil, or a human spirit, or what?'

'Good God!' he said, 'how can I tell?' and then with lifted hand he sang in a strange voice a bar or two from Stanford's *Revenge*.

'Was he devil or man? He was devil for aught they knew.'

This dreadful interlude, the very flippancy of it, that might have moved my laughter at any other time, had upon me an indescribably sickening effect. I stared at Basil. He relapsed into a moody silence with clasped hands and knotted brow. To draw him away from the nether darkness of his thoughts, I asked him how and in what shape the spirit had made itself plain to him.

'Oh, no shape at all,' said he; 'he is *there*, that is enough. I seem sometimes to see a face, to catch the glance of an eye, to see a hand raised to warn or to encourage; but it is all impossibly remote; I could never explain to you *how* I see him.'

'Do you see him now?' I asked.

'Yes,' said Basil, 'a long way off – and he is running swiftly to me, but he has far to go yet. He is angry; he threatens me; he beats the air with his hands.'

'But *where* is this?' I asked, for Basil's eyes were upon the ground.

'Oh, for God's sake, man, be silent,' said Basil. 'It is in the region of which you and others know little; but it has been revealed to me. It lies all about us – it has its capes and shadowy peaks, and a leaden sea, full of sound; it is there that I ramble with him.'

There fell a silence between us. Then I said, 'But, dear Basil, I must ask you this – how was it that you wrote as you did to me?'

'Oh! he made me write,' he said, 'and I think he overreached himself – or my angel, that beholds the Father's face, smote him down. I was myself again on a sudden, the miserable and abject wretch whom you see before you, and knowing that I had been as a man in a dream. Then I wrote the despairing words, and guarded the letter so that he could not come near me; and then Mr Vyvyan's visit to me – that was not by chance. I gave him the letter and he promised to bear it faithfully – and what attempts were made to tear it from him I do not know; but that my adversary tried his best I do not doubt. But Vyvyan is a good man and could not be harmed.

'And then I fell back into the old spell; and worked still more abundantly and diligently and produced this – this accursed thing which shall not live to scatter evil abroad.' As he said these words he rose, and tore the score that lay on the table into shreds and crammed the pieces in the fire. As he thrust the last pieces down, the poker he was holding fell from his hands.

I saw him white as a sheet, and trembling. 'What is the matter?' I said.

He turned a terrible look on me, and said, 'He is here – he has arrived.'

Then all at once I was aware that there was a sort of darkness in the room; and then with a growing horror I gradually perceived that in and through the room there ran a thing like the front of a precipice, with some dark strand at its foot on which beat a surge of phantom waves. The two scenes struggled together. At one time I could plainly see the cliff-front, close beside me – and then the lamp and the firelit room was all dimmed even to vanishing; and then suddenly the room would come back and the cliff die into a steep shadow.

But in either of the scenes Basil and I were there – he standing irresolute and despairing, glancing from side to side like a hare when the hounds close in. And once he said – this was when the cliff loomed up suddenly – 'There are others with him.' Then in a moment it seemed as if the room in which we sat died away altogether and I was in that other place; there was a faint light as from under a stormy sky; and a little farther up the strand there stood a group of dark figures, which seemed to consult together.

All at once the group broke and came suddenly towards us. I do not know what to call them; they were human in a sense – that is, they walked upright and had heads and hands. But the faces were all blurred and fretted, like half-rotted skulls – but there was no sense of comparison in me. I only knew that I had seen ugliness and corruption at the very source, and looked into the darkness of the pit itself.

The forms eluded me and rushed upon Basil, who made a motion as though to seize hold of me, and then turned and fled, his arms outstretched, glancing behind him as he ran – and in a moment he was lost to view, though I could see along the shore of that formless sea something like a pursuit.

I do not know what happened after that. I think I tried to pray; but I presently became aware that I was myself menaced by danger.

It seemed – but I speak in parables – as though one had separated himself from the rest and had returned to seek me. But all was over, I knew; and the figure indeed carried something which he swung and shook in his hand, which I thought was a token to be shown to me. And then I found my voice and cried out with all my strength to God to save me; and in a moment there was the fire-lit room again, and the lamp – the most peaceful-looking room in England.

But Basil had left me; the door was wide open; and in a moment the farmer and his wife came hurrying along with blanched faces to ask who it was that had cried out, and what had happened.

I made some pitiful excuse that I had dozed in my chair and had awoke crying out some unintelligible words. For in the quest I was about to engage in I did not wish that any mortal should be with me.

They left me, asking for Mr Netherby and still not satisfied. Indeed, Mrs Hall looked at me with so penetrating a look that I felt that she understood something of what had happened. And then at once I went up to Basil's room. I do not know where I found the courage to do it; but the courage came.

The room was dark, and a strong wind was blowing through it from the little door. I stepped across the room, feeling my way; went down the stairs, and finding the door open at the bottom, I went out into the snake-like path.

I went some yards along it; the moon had risen now. There came a sudden gap in the trees to the left, through which I could see the pale fields and the corner of the wood casting its black shadow on the ground.

The shrubs were torn, broken, and trampled, as though some heavy thing had crashed through. I made my way cautiously down, endowed with a more than human strength – it was a steep bank covered with trees – and then in a moment I saw Basil.

He lay some distance out in the field on his face. I knew at a glance that all was over; and when I lifted him I became aware that he was in some way strangely mangled, and indeed it was found afterwards that though the skin of his body was hardly contused, yet that almost every bone of the body was broken in fragments.

I managed to carry him to the house. I closed the doors of the staircase; and then I managed to tell Farmer Hall that Basil had had, I thought, a fall and was dead. And then my own strength failed me, and for three days and nights I lay in a kind of stupor.

When I recovered my consciousness, I found myself in bed in my own room. Mrs Hall nursed me with a motherly care and tenderness which moved me very greatly; but I could not speak of the matter to her, until, just before my departure, she came in, as she did twenty times a day, to see if I wanted anything. I made a great effort and said, 'Mrs Hall, I am very sorry for you. This has been a terrible business, and I am afraid you won't easily forget it. You ought to leave the house, I think.'

Mrs Hall turned her frozen gaze upon me, and said, 'Yes, sir, indeed, I can't speak about it or think of it. I feel as if I might have prevented it; and yet I have been over and over it in my mind and I can't see where I was wrong. But my duty is to the house now, and I shall never leave it; but I will ask you, sir, to try and find a thought of pity in your heart for *him*' – I knew she did not mean Basil – 'I don't think he clearly knows what he has done; he must have his will, as he always did. He stopped at nothing if it was for his pleasure; and he did not know what harm he did. But he is in God's hands; and though I cannot understand why, yet there are things in this life which He allows to be; and we must not try to be judges – we must try to be merciful. But I have not done what I could have done; and if God gives me strength, there shall be an end of this.'

A few hours later Mr Vyvyan called to see me; he was a very different person to the Vyvyan that had showed himself to me in Holborn.

I could not talk much with him but I could see that he had some understanding of the case. He asked me no questions, but he told me a few details. He said that they had decided at the inquest that he had fallen from the terrace. But the doctor, who was attending me, seems to have said to Mr Vyvyan that a fall it must have been, but a fall of an almost inconceivable character. 'And what is more,' the old octor had added, 'the man was neither in pain nor agitation of mind when he died.' The face was absolutely peaceful and tranquil; and the doctor's theory was that he had died from some sudden seizure before the fall.

And so I held my tongue. One thing I did: it was to have a little slab put over the body of my friend – a simple slab with name and date – and I ventured to add one line, because I have no doubt in my own mind that Basil was suddenly delivered, though not from death. He had, I supposed, gone too far upon the dark path, and he could not, I think, have freed himself from the spell; and so the cord was loosed, but loosed in mercy – and so I made them add the words:

And in their hands they shall bear thee up.

I must add one further word. About a year after the events above recorded I received a letter from Mr Vyvyan, which I give without further comment.

St Sibby, Dec 18, 189—
DEAR MR WARD
I wish to tell you that our friend Mrs Hall died a few days ago. She was a very good woman, one of the few that are chosen. I was much with her in her last days, and she told me a strange thing, which I cannot bring myself to repeat to you. But she sent you a message which she repeated several times, which she said you would understand. It is simply this: 'Tell Mr Ward I have prevailed.' I may add that I have no doubt of the truth of her words, and you will know to what I am alluding.

The day after she died there was a fire at Treheale: Mr Hall was absolutely distracted with grief at the loss of his wife, and I do not know quite what happened. But it was impossible to save the house; all that is left of it is a mass of charred ruins, with a few walls standing up. Nothing was saved, not even a picture. There is a wholly inadequate insurance, and I believe it is not intended to rebuild the house.

I hope you will bear us in mind; though I know you so little, I shall always feel that we have a common experience which will hold us together. You will try and visit us some day when the memory of what took place is less painful to you. The grass is now green on your poor friend's grave; and I will only add that you will have a warm welcome here. I am just moving into the Rectory, as my old Rector died a fortnight ago, and I have accepted the living. God bless you, dear Mr Ward.

Yours very sincerely,
JAMES VYVYAN

The Uttermost Farthing

A. C. BENSON

I

Yes, Hebden Hill was the next station, the porter told me, and as the dowdy little train puffed sturdily across the wide green flat, intersected by dykes, which had once been a great bay of the sea, I watched with pleasure the low shapely bluffs, like miniature sea-cliffs, but now covered with thickets and copses, which bounded the plain to the west half a mile away, and thought how like it was to the background of an old Italian picture. It was a warm summer evening, not oppressive, as there was a fresh breeze from the sea, along which white clouds sailed lazily landward. I could see far out in the plain hamlets and solitary farms nestling among trees; and it was pleasant to see the birds, crested plovers and pearly-grey gulls, that stood motionless, all facing up the wind in the pastures; and a lean grey heron by the old sluice-gate, poring upon the water.

And then I began to wonder how it was that I was going on so vaguely defined a visit to Hector Bendyshe, whom I knew so slightly. What exactly *did* I know about him? He was just an agreeable man, whom one was never surprised to meet at dinner, and whose talk, mildly interesting, seldom flagged. He had been at Winchester and at Oxford; he had been perhaps in the diplomatic service, and had certainly travelled a good deal. He was clearly wealthy, for he had a flat in town, and a house understood to be of an attractive kind in Sussex, at Hebden Hill. But he had done nothing particular for twenty years – he was a man of fifty – he read a good many books, he was fond of music, he was something of a connoisseur. But the more I reflected the less I seemed to know. He had no relations that I had ever heard of, and no intimate friends, though a host of acquaintances; he went everywhere and got on with everybody. He did not seem mysterious or secretive in any way; he talked easily and frankly about his own concerns and pursuits, and indeed on most topics of general interest.

How then had my visit come about? I was myself a so-called literary man, who lived, not very prosperously, in rooms in town, reviewing, writing literary articles, putting together an occasional book, and enabled by my small earnings and a little private income to exist in tolerable comfort. I was just over forty, and the artistic ambitions I had once had, had long vanished; but I was more than content with my life, and my interest in other people was stronger than ever. The unexpected things that happened, the strange contrasts and contradictions of character, the amazing inconsistency of human beings and their intricate relations, so utterly different from and so much richer than the helpless conventional traditions of fiction – all this had kept alive in me a sense of romance in life which amply atoned for a career which had been disappointing and even humiliating.

I had met Bendyshe at a dinner-party some time in May. I had walked away with him, and he had asked me to his rooms. They were well furnished and comfortable, but with a certain austerity that took my fancy. Our talk had turned somehow on psychical things, in which I was a good deal interested; and before we had talked ten minutes I became aware that Bendyshe had dropped the mask of amiable levity which characterised his habitual conversation, and was speaking seriously and drily, but with a profound sense of conviction, which was quite unlike anything I had ever heard from him.

Suddenly he turned to me, a little sternly, I thought, and said, 'But perhaps you are not interested in these things?'

'Yes and no,' I said, 'but to tell the truth, I am a little surprised to find that *you* are.'

'Well,' he said, 'I don't wonder at that. You see, it has become of late rather a hobby of mine. I will tell you why some day, if you care to know. But tell me one thing: why do you say "Yes and no"?'

'Because,' I said, 'in the first place I think that ordinary talk about psychical things is such fearful twaddle. It seems to me a scientific affair; but when foolish people talk about it, it's all a mixture of feeble sentiment and weak imagination.'

'That's so,' he said; 'but if you feel about it like that, why don't you look into it?'

'Because the sort of experiments people try,' I said, 'such as séances and trances and automatic writing, seem to me more sickening still, like drug-taking; it's like deliberately playing with the ugliest part of one's mind, the part that deals in fear. I don't want to wake that up – I want to think it is not there; and, moreover, I am so much interested in people as I see and know them that I don't want to explore the unknown.'

'You want to live in a fool's paradise, in fact,' said Bendyshe; and I could see from the pallor of his face and his distended nostrils that I had angered him; but he controlled himself. 'No,' he added, 'I ought not to say that – it was rude and stupid! I apologise.'

'No, please don't do that,' I said; 'it was my fault. What I said was very crude; it was like talking to a man of science about 'stinks' or to an actor about his 'patter' – the insolence of the amateur; that's unpardonable.'

'Well, but I *really* want to know,' he said rather gravely. 'I agreed with you up to a certain point; but what you said amounted to this, that you are so much interested in people when they are alive that you don't take any interest in what happens to them after they are dead?'

'Yes,' I said, 'that is quite fair. I am immensely interested in what I can see and observe and infer in people. It seems to me dramatic, exciting, sometimes very beautiful. But I'm a homeless man and a bachelor, and I don't get very near to them. I only see the polite side of life; and when people disappear, as they unhappily do, and I can't follow them further, why, I turn back to what I can see and know.'

'I understand perfectly,' he said; 'but it's just the other way with me. People seem to me so amazing, so incredibly fine at times and so unutterably low at others, that I can't believe it all begins and ends here, and I find myself consumed by the most intense curiosity, to use rather a feeble word, to know what the next act is. It seems to me all like a big rehearsal for something, full of trivial, grotesque, and annoying things – two people playing nap, a girl eating a sandwich as she waits for her cue – but the play is going on all the time, and everybody has his part. I feel that I *must* know what is behind it all, if it can be known. I'm not exaggerating when I say that I have thought many times of putting a pistol to my head in order to find out what does happen; but I doubt if it can be found out that way.'

He was silent for a little, musing inwardly. I watched him as he sat. He was a tall lean man, finely formed and modelled. He had close, crisply curling black hair, a little grizzled. His forehead was high, his eyebrows black, and he had large dark eyes which it seemed to me I had never seen fully opened before. He was clean-shaven, and his nose, straight and clean-cut, came down on a short upper lip; but the under-lip was full, and the chin perhaps a little large for symmetry. He had a slightly worn air, but his face, which was hardly marked by wrinkles, had a fresh colour like that of a man who lived much in the open air. If anything his expression was a little judicial; but when I had seen him on previous occasions, his prevailing expression was one of tolerant good-humour and friendliness. It had never occurred to me that he could be formidable, and indeed my impression had been that, if anything, he over-valued serenity and equanimity. There was nothing ascetic or scholarly about him. His hands were large and mobile, and had, I thought, more expression than his face; and his dress had a touch of negligence about it which became him well.

I had never thought him a particularly interesting man, because he never gave himself away or appeared to have any preferences. But now I had seen something very different, something alert, passionate, even terrifying.

But when he began to talk again, his mood had changed, and he was his old wary and kindly self.

'By the way,' he said, 'what do you generally do in the summer?'

'Oh, I stay about a little,' I said; 'but I have to stick pretty close to my work, you know. I'm a literary hack, and I have to be waiting on the stand in case of a call. If I happen to be in funds, I go to a quiet hotel somewhere – I rather like exploring the country; old houses and churches are the next most interesting things to people. But I generally end by being a little bored.'

'I wish you would come down and stay with me for a week or two,' he said. 'I have got rather a nice old house in Sussex, and it is a pleasant country. It is very quiet, and you could work if you wanted to, or wander about. I should like to talk this matter over with you.'

'Thank you very much,' I said; 'I should enjoy it immensely. Where did you say it was?'

'Hebden Hill,' he said. 'Not very far from Ashford – it's a biggish village. I'll drop you a line.'

2

That was at the end of May. I heard nothing more for a month and began to think he had forgotten all about it, or that he was perhaps sorry that he had shown me the inner side of himself. But at the end of June I had a note asking me to go down on July the 7th, and an hour or two later a wire.

AM UNEXPECTEDLY ALONE, AND SHOULD BE GLAD TO SEE YOU
TOMORROW THURSDAY IF YOU CAN MANAGE IT BUT DON'T
ALTER ARRANGEMENTS. WOULD MEET THE TRAIN ARRIVING
6.30. HOPE YOU CAN STAY A FORTNIGHT.

It seemed to me a little peremptory perhaps? No, I had no engagements, and I was glad to get out of the heat of London, so I wired an acceptance, packed my books and papers, and went; and now that I was embarked I began to have a curious feeling that I was in for an adventure of some kind, not very pleasant.

However, I arrived in the summer twilight. Bendyshe was on the platform to meet me, and I could see from the civility of the officials that he was not only an important personage, but a highly popular one. He had a pleasant word for everybody, and he introduced me formally to the station-master, saying gravely, 'It's very important that my friend Mr Hartley should form a good impression of the place; you know, he writes in all the papers, and could make our fortunes by a paragraph.'

'Indeed, sir?' said the delighted station-master. 'I'm sure you're very welcome to Hebden Hill, sir. We're old-fashioned, but going ahead a bit nowadays.'

Bendyshe had a good car waiting. The station was at the bottom of the hill; and he motored me swiftly up a steep irregular street of red-brick and timbered houses with pleasant gardens – a most comfortable and homely place. At the top of the hill we turned into a small square or piazza, with five or six substantial eighteenth-century houses. Fronting the west end of the church was a long mellow brick wall with big gateposts and a gate of fine ironwork. Behind this there appeared a handsome façade; a brick Georgian mansion with a pediment, a solid pillared doorway, seven windows above and three on each side of the door, and a round window in the pediment. It was evidently the chief mansion of the village. The windows had old heavy casements painted white, and the house was flanked at each end by fine old sycamores.

'Here we are,' said Bendyshe. 'It's called the Manor-house, but it's not my idea of a manor-house at all!'

Inside appeared a white-painted, marble-flagged hall, heavily panelled and pillared, with two mahogany doors on each side and a broad balustraded staircase ascending under an arch at the end. It was all a little bare. There were a few portraits and some solid Chippendale chairs. A venerable and portly butler met us.

'Perhaps you would like to stroll round before you go and dress?' said Bendyshe. 'It's a good thing to get one's bearings clear at once.'

He showed me first a room to the left of the front door, a small dining-room panelled with dark oak. Here there were more portraits, and a fine Italian bust of a young man in red porphyry, evidently a masterpiece. The next room was a little library almost lined with books, with a big french window which opened on to the garden. 'This is *your* room,' said Bendyshe, 'and you can have it entirely to yourself to work in. My own study is upstairs.'

The door to the right of the front door led to a smoking-room, a comfortable place with a few red leather armchairs and some old dark landscape pictures in oil. 'This is everybody's room,' said Bendyshe. 'That other door leads to the back regions; but now we'll have a look at the garden.'

We went out through a door under the stairs. I could not restrain an exclamation of delight. We came out into a portico supported by pillars extending along the whole centre of the house, between two flanking shallow wings; it was paved with black-and-white marble, and furnished with some comfortable oak seats and tables.

The garden was not large, but beautifully designed. On each side it was walled, and shielded from intrusive eyes by a row on either hand of sycamores, fine old trees. The lawn was perfectly plain, but for a fine leaden statue of a youth with clasped hands looking upwards towards the house – a most enchanting piece of work. At the far end, sheltered by a low wall, was a great flower-border, blazing with colour; and as we drew near, I could see that the ground fell rapidly – to a tiny park with clumps of trees on either hand, and beyond, a magnificent view of a great green plain with low wooded ridges and blue shadowy hills to the right, while a mile or two to the left we could see a wide expanse of sea.

I said something feeble about the wonderful beauty of the place, and its magnificence.

'Well, that's rather a tall word,' said Bendyshe. 'It isn't a big house really, and the domain extends to about fifty acres. But it is cleverly designed, and makes the best use of every inch of earth and sky.'

'Has it been long in your family?' I said.

'No, indeed,' said Bendyshe; 'I bought it just as it stands, furniture and all, from the last member of an old family – the Faulkners – that had come to hopeless grief. It was in an awful state – the house almost ruinous, the park full of weeds and thorn bushes. No-one would look at it. But I heard of it by what we call accident, just when

I wanted a house, about fifteen years ago, and saw its possibilities. I got it very cheap, and I really have not spent much money upon it. But I have got uncommonly fond of it, and feel as if I had lived here all my life, and a little more.'

The light was beginning to fade as we went back to the house, which I found was all lit by electric light, carefully subdued and shaded. We went upstairs. There was a corridor above the hall, only not so wide, with three doors on either side, and one to the right, close to the head of the stairs; and these I must describe with some particularity.

The first door on the left as we came up – the staircase had turned round to the right, so that we were facing in the direction of the front door – led to two staircases, one going up to the attics and one descending to the offices. The second door on the left led to Bendyshe's bedroom, a very bare place, with a press or two and a few books; then came a bathroom with a door from the bedroom, and opposite the door, another door led into Bendyshe's study, which communicated with the corridor by what was the third door on the left. The study was entirely filled with books, had a big table covered with papers, and two very uncompromising oak writing-chairs. A room less luxurious I have seldom seen. It had no ornament but a single picture, a very beautiful portrait of a girl, fair-haired and blue-eyed, with an expression of the most perfect naturalness and simplicity, and full of animation and delight. The room had two windows, one looking out to the church, the other down towards the village.

We went out again into the corridor. The door opposite Bendyshe's study was my bedroom, one window of which looked towards the church, and the other on the great sycamore by the corner of the house. A little bathroom was attached. The room was furnished with great comfort, and had some fine water-colours. Returning down the corridor, the two other doors opened into bedrooms similar to mine, each with a bathroom, and at the end, close to the head of the stairs, the remaining door led into another bedroom, which looked out on to the garden. But this room was wholly unfurnished, just a bare-boarded, white-panelled place, with that peculiar and unpleasant staleness that develops in an unventilated sun-baked room.

'I don't like this room,' said Bendyshe. 'It was the room, to tell you the truth, in which the scoundrel from whose heirs I bought the property came to his miserable end. It's a squalid story; and as for the room, well, I think there is something sinister about it. What do you feel? Yet it's a pity not to use it, because it has the finest view in the house!

'I don't know,' said I; 'I think that the best way to exorcise disagreeable associations is not to fasten things up, but to let in a new current of pleasant usage.'

'Yes,' said Bendyshe; 'if I had children, I should make this their schoolroom – then it would be all right!'

An hour later we dined – a well-appointed meal, though a simple one, very promptly served.

'I don't know what you feel,' he said to me, 'but it always seems to me rather uncivilised to dawdle over food.' He himself ate rapidly, but with appetite, and drank a glass or two of wine. After dinner we withdrew to the smoking-room. Bendyshe was in his familiar mood, full of little anecdotes and reminiscences. When we had established ourselves with coffee and cigars, he said, 'Now let me first say how glad I am to see you here. I have a notion that we agree, more than perhaps appeared the other night, about that matter we spoke of; and I think you can help me very much, if you are disposed to do so. I think you are a fair-minded man and impartial. Would you mind telling me exactly where you stand? Or perhaps you are tired and would like to defer it? Tomorrow night, I ought to say, the parson, Fortescue by name, is coming to dine, a very interesting and remarkable man, so that if you would like to leave it alone, we must wait till the day after tomorrow – the evening is the only time to talk seriously about things.'

'I should like to start at once,' I said. 'But tell me, what did you mean by saying I could be of use to you?'

'Why,' said Bendyshe, 'living alone, as I do, and with but few people to talk things over with, one gets into a tangle. I generally have a visitor or two here, because solitude unadulterated is not a wholesome thing. But they are not the sort of people I can really talk to; and just now I have got hold of some new material – I am always collecting materials – and it doesn't seem to fit in with my ideas. But the point is this – how much and how little do you believe?'

'Oh,' I said, 'my position is a simple one. It's all just a question of evidence. Any materials ought to be rigidly scrutinised – one mustn't either accept or dismiss evidence summarily – and then one may begin to draw conclusions.'

'Yes,' said Bendyshe; 'that's very much what I believe. But it's uncommonly hard to trace these psychical stories to their source. I have tried to unravel a good many, and it gives one a deplorable opinion of the value of human evidence. But,' he went on, 'before we begin, I must tell you in as few words as I can how I came to set to work. I don't like to talk about it – it's like tearing open an old wound – but I must make this plain. Some twenty-five years ago I became engaged to a girl, the daughter of a parson; you saw her picture, perhaps, in my room. You must take it on trust from me that she was a wonderful creature, and gave me not only a new view of life, but something to live for.

'We arranged everything. We were to have lived in London, and I was actually thinking of standing for Parliament, when just a month before our marriage she caught diphtheria and died within the week. I can't tell you what an appalling catastrophe it was for me. It had seemed to me that her love was the one thing I had been waiting for all my life, the one thing that had given me a reason for living. You see, I was an only son, entirely trusted and indulged by my parents, and with plenty of money about and no motive for exerting myself.

'The thing very nearly drove me mad. A week before she had been with me, answering every question I had asked of life, and giving me the very water of life to drink. And now she was gone without a word. The last time I saw her she didn't even know me. She was in torture and half-unconscious. And there was nothing left, not a glance or a sign or the faintest message to me whom she loved best, or to any other human being – and there were many that loved her. It was so utterly unlike her, and yet there it was. Her parents were what is called 'wonderful'. They had a strong religious faith, and it helped them through.'

Bendyshe stopped with a kind of gasp, gripped the arms of his chair, and abandoned himself for a minute to a paroxysm of misery. 'It all comes over me again,' he said. 'Don't look at me – I shall be all right in a minute.'

Presently he went on in a low voice: 'I hardly know what I did. I travelled, I did some exploration, I courted death, but it never came near me. But I never had the smallest sense of contact with her, or even of any thought coming from beyond.'

'Then I came back and tried to occupy myself in many ways – what is called social service. But I'm a hopeless individualist, and I don't care about my fellow-men simply as such, and I was taken in many times.

'Then I started this work, and it began to seem to me the one thing worth doing – to find out, if I could, whether there was any possible contact with the spirits of the dead, whether they existed at all. I had all kinds of sickening experiences, but could find nothing definite.

'And I never could cross the threshold, though I came to believe that, under certain obscure conditions, living minds could communicate direct with each other, apart from material agencies. And then the case seemed worse to me than ever, because it all seemed to depend upon material existence as a necessary condition.'

Then after a moment's pause, he went on slowly and rather wearily: 'And what makes things even worse is this. There are a good many stories of appearances which seem to have some element of truth about them. But most of these are connected with horrible and tragic occurrences – crimes, murders, solitary imprisonments, as if (supposing for a moment the things to be true) it were a punishment of some kind to have to return to the earth and to re-enact the scenes of desperation and wickedness. And even the unhappy victims of such outrages seem condemned to the same fate; as if the only motive force that could bring one back were fear and indelible horror, reconstructing incidents which one would give anything to forget, but cannot.

'If there were stories of spirits returning to earth to revive gratefully scenes of happiness and love, delightful experiences of youth and friendship and ingenuous aspiration, when the heart was full of hope and joy, it would be different; but no spirits ever seem to think of this. Are they ungrateful? Have they forgotten?'

'Religious people would perhaps say,' I said, 'that the happiness of the farther world was so great, that a blest spirit would never care to return to these half-lit skies, and to the memory of joys that were always shadowed by some fear of loss and separation.'

'But this is an utterly selfish and indifferent business,' said Bendyshe. 'We should despise it in a living human being. And even if it were so, have they no wish to comfort the hearts that ache with the memories of perished happiness? No; if the spirits of even the blest are so drugged and intoxicated with delight that they have no room for remembrance or tenderness, it is a more ghastly business still.'

We sat for a little while in silence. 'I expect it's about time to go to bed?' he said. 'I ought not to go on soliloquising like this.' He escorted me to my room, and said another friendly word about my visit, adding, 'Breakfast at nine – please ask for anything you want. Hope you'll sleep well; and you will find some good bedside-books there if you want them.'

I was soon in bed, and I fell asleep in a mood of pleasurable anticipation. This was going to be a novel experience, I felt sure, and

Bendyshe's theories interested me; and almost immediately, so it seemed, I woke from a dreamless sleep, with old Bartlett the butler in my room, coughing deferentially, and asking if I would have a cup of tea, and whether I would have a hot or cold bath, and if there was anything else I required.

3

That morning at breakfast I found Bendyshe in a cheerful and eminently commonplace mood. He told me stories about the village and the people and the countryside. I asked some questions about one of the portraits, an old, rugged-looking man with prominent eyes and upstanding hair.

'"*What the dickens!*" I call him,' said Bendyshe, smiling. 'But we'll leave all that to the Vicar, who is coming to dinner this evening – he knows far more about the house and the family than I do. He has been here thirty years – in fact his wife, now dead, was connected in some way with the Faulkners.'

After breakfast I went off to do some writing, but I did very little, and my mind ran with curious persistency on what Bendyshe had told me on the previous night. He did not look like a man who had ever had a great shock or passed through tragic experiences; indeed, his preoccupation with psychical matters seemed to me still a little unaccountable, and inconsistent with the fact that he evidently lived a busy and active life, and took a considerable share in local business.

He came and fetched me out about noon, and we strolled to the church and village. He had a word for all the people he met; he called the boys and girls by their Christian names; his hat went off to any woman. We met an old man hobbling along with two sticks.

'Why, Mr Barry,' said Bendyshe, 'I'm glad to see you about again. Feeling better? You look quite your old self again.'

'Thank you kindly, sir – yes, I'm better, Mr Bendyshe, but feeling powerful giddy at times!'

'Ah, that'll soon pass off in the open air,' said Bendyshe. 'Now, shall I step in this evening for a bit of a gossip, Mr Barry? I always get the news of the place from you. Hartley, this is Mr Barry; I call him the father of the place. He will be a hundred and one years old in January next – isn't that so?'

Mr Barry chuckled. 'Don't you believe Mr Bendyshe, sir,' he said to me with a smile. 'He will have his joke; 'tis only eighty-eight I am, last Febbery!'

So Bendyshe went on – but not for a moment did it seem an assumed heartiness, rather the natural overflowing of a neighbourly geniality; while a word of sympathy which he said to an old lady in rusty black was both tender and straightforward. With the children he was entirely delightful, with mysterious jests and allusions.

I said something about this. 'Oh, yes,' he said, 'a child likes to share a secret with a grown-up person, a secret which no-one else knows. I'm not sure we don't all like it,' he added with a smile; 'a secret's rather an explosive thing.' We went to the church, a fine, ancient place which had evidently been carefully restored; one aisle was full of monuments to the Faulkner family, from a knight in armour in a canopied niche to a weeping nymph by Chantrey. 'Fancy throwing away an inheritance like that,' he said, as we looked at the old tombs; 'but the whole history of the family is a steady process of climbing down. I'll show you the remains of their old mansion, about half a mile away, one of these days. The Vicar thinks it is the doom of sacrilege, but that's rather too businesslike a view for me!'

I grew more astonished as the day went on to find the polite and solitary diner-out transformed here into so bustling and genial a squire. I could not fit the puzzle together; and still less did he seem to me a man who carried about, hidden in his mind, so strange and haunting an aspiration.

In the afternoon it was very hot; we went round the house and looked at the portraits. They were not particularly good, but the family likeness was strong; and the picture of the last of the Faulkner race, as a boy of sixteen, was a graceful and beautiful thing. It represented him in riding-dress standing beside a pony, slender, blue-eyed and light-haired, with a gentle, rather wistful expression. Next to the picture was one of his mother – a woman of rare beauty and charm – and a rather commonplace portrait on the other side of his father, a burly country squire.

'It's all rather an enigma,' said Bendyshe, looking thoughtfully at the portraits. 'Up till that time, you see, they had been very ordinary people, moderately prosperous but not very successful, and quite unadventurous. There doesn't seem to have been a single instance of a man of any eminence among them, not even a soldier or a bishop. One of them was an M.P., but unseated for bribery. And then just when a strain of beauty comes into the family and a touch of romance, that minute the devil comes too. It looks as if there were something in the old idea of Nemesis, as if the way to be happy was not to attract the attention of the powers above. That pretty woman was an heiress, and the boy was born wealthy; and he was certainly charming, and I believe clever too – the Vicar shall tell us all about him this evening.'

I was somewhat struck by the interest which Bendyshe seemed to take in the old family. As a rule, the last thing that a new proprietor is interested in is the history of the family he has ousted. But Bendyshe seemed to wish to bring me into touch with the personalities of his predecessors, as though he desired me to draw some inference or to solve some problem. Indeed, when later in the afternoon he took me out and showed me the relics of the old Faulkner mansion, an octagonal turret and a crow-stepped gable, with a fine chimney-stack of moulded bricks, and a great dovecote, all forming part of a rather ramshackle farm, I became even more sure of this, and commented on it. Bendyshe laughed a short laugh, as though partly pleased and partly disconcerted, and said, 'Yes, don't you think it would all make rather a picturesque article?' adding with a smile, 'You see, if I take you away from your work, I ought to give you some copy in exchange. But don't let me bore you. I am afraid it is rather a tiresome fancy of mine, to speculate about my predecessors.'

'Oh, I'm not bored,' I said – 'quite the reverse. What I feel is rather that you have some idea in your mind, which you want me to perceive for myself, and that you were, so to speak, inoculating me!' Bendyshe looked at me sharply, but I somehow saw that he was not displeased.

After tea I read and wrote a little in the library. I felt rather drowsy after a day in the open air, and fell asleep in my chair, but awakened suddenly with a start, and with a strong impression that someone had entered the room softly, and as softly withdrawn. I had, too, a sensation of something chilly in the air, and a faint earthy odour such as one connects with stone-built, underground, airless places. But it was all a momentary fancy; the flower-scented air was blowing in from the garden, and the bell of the church was ringing for Vespers. I got up and went out into the hall, and found Bendyshe with his hat on just going out of the front-door. 'Was it you who caught me napping just now?' I said.

Bendyshe gave me one of his quick glances, and said, 'Well, I thought you might be having forty winks' – and then added, a little shamefacedly, 'The fact is, I'm going to church – the Vicar is very good about services and doesn't get much of a congregation; besides, it makes me feel cosy, as Mrs Carlyle said of the glass of port. Do you care to come?'

'It isn't very much in my line,' I said lightly, 'but I'll come with pleasure – it's all part of the atmosphere; and besides, I shall get into the Vicar's good graces.'

We sat in the chancel. There were only two other people present, both women. The Vicar, a big, sanguine-faced man with a fine head of silky white hair, read evening prayer with great rapidity but with extreme reverence; and I was pleased to see never once looked in our direction. His reading of the lessons was strangely impressive; the second lesson was a chapter from the Gospel. 'When the evil spirit is gone out of a man, he walketh through dry places, seeking rest, and finding none . . .' He had lowered his voice, and read as though it was a thing almost too terrible to be mentioned, except from a sense of duty. Just before the end of the passage he shut his book and made a slight pause; and then, as though it was his own comment, looking round at us, he added, 'So the last state of that man is worse than the first.' And then he began the *Nunc Dimittis* in a tone of unmistakable relief.

When I got down before dinner, the Vicar and Bendyshe were sitting in the hall, talking in low tones. The Vicar got briskly up, and shook hands with me with great cordiality. His face was full of animation and benevolence. Bendyshe had said something to me about his being much of a mystic; but anything less mystical I had never seen. He was alive to the finger-tips. We had an amusing evening. The Vicar made a remarkably good meal, and told a few excellent stories of a local kind, crisply and shortly, in response to a direct request from Bendyshe. I indulged in some literary gossip, and the Vicar listened to stories about some of the well-known writers of the day with childish avidity and hearty laughter. 'Excellent, excellent!' I remember his saying. 'I have never been able to get on with his books – rather precious, I think? – but I'll give them another try; I didn't know the old man had so much blood in him!'

4

We settled ourselves after dinner in the smoking-room, and as soon as we were alone, Bendyshe said to the Vicar, 'Now I want you to tell Hartley something about Hugh Faulkner' – adding to me, 'that is the man whose portrait as a boy I showed you – and what happened when you came here. I always think it is an extraordinary story. Hartley won't make capital out of it, you know – he is quite discreet!'

'Well, then,' said the Vicar, 'I'll tell you. It was over thirty years ago that Hugh Faulkner – he was a distant cousin of my dear wife – offered me the living through his lawyer. I came down and looked round, but Mr Faulkner was ill, and I could not see him. I was just thirty then, and working in a quiet country curacy; and this gave me exactly what I wanted: more work, and a chance of really getting a hold on a place – and a beautiful church too – and I won't pretend that a larger income wasn't some inducement.

'Well, we settled here; and then bit by bit became aware that things were very wrong indeed in this house. Hugh Faulkner was about forty. His father and mother were both dead. He had been in the Guards, and he had done a good many wild things, and when at last he did something so outrageous that he was summarily told to send in his papers, he came down here. A less courageous man – he had plenty of courage – would have gone abroad for a bit, and waited for the thing to blow over. But he wasn't that sort. He came down here, and tried to brazen it out. But everyone knew about the scandal, and it was no use. People simply would not meet him, and were out when he called. He was cut and cold-shouldered every-where. A few of the village people were civil to him; but he couldn't get servants, no-one would accept his invitations. I've seen people in the street turn back rather than meet him. He stuck to it for weeks and months; and I tell you, Mr Hartley, my heart bled for that man, though one could neither like him nor trust him: but I couldn't help admiring him. He generally took no notice, but once or twice he lost his temper. I saw him with my own eyes stop and say something civil to a farmer – Pratt, by name – in the street, and the man pushed by: Faulkner went after him and screamed something into his ear – Pratt wasn't a very exemplary person, either – and the man went on white and shaking.

'One day he came to the Vicarage. I should say that I and my wife did see something of him; we went to dine there occasionally, but it was quite intolerable. He used to tell unpleasant stories, not any-thing to which you could take open exception, but one saw what he meant; and he had an old soldier-servant, a real ruffian, who used to giggle at the sideboard. One day he had come in to tea at the Vicarage, and he looked tired to death. While we were at tea, a neighbouring parson and his wife called. I mentioned Faulkner's name; they made hasty excuses – they couldn't stay for tea – they had only looked in. They didn't say a word to Faulkner, who stood there with his tea-cup looking as if he was on fire within. Then he went up to the parson as he was leaving the room, and said to him in a low voice, "So this is what you do for sinners, Mr Hale? What is your tone with the publicans?" What made it worse was that old Hale had the reputation of being rather too good a judge of wine.

'Then he said goodbye to us and marched out. I went back with him afterwards and did my best to talk to him. We parsons see some bad things, Mr Hartley, but I never had a worse hour. The man was possessed by devils, not by one only. He was not violent or obscene, he was simply desperate. And he told me, sitting in this very room, what some of his performances had been, and such a catalogue I never heard. However, that is all *sub sigillo*, you know. He said, I remember, that he had carefully considered whether he could have helped behaving so, and he had decided that he could not help it, and would do just the same again under the same conditions. "You see, I didn't make myself," he said.

'Then he went on to say that once he had left the army he had kept clear of it all, except in one respect; but that the more he put the pillow on his desires, the more they peeped round the corner of it. He was quoting *Martin Chuzzlewit*, I believe? – he was a great reader, I should say – and then he asked me to tell him plainly if I thought he had a chance of putting things straight – 'I'm really rather a good-natured man,' he said, with a sort of pathos. "I hardly expect to be liked – but I want to live on decent terms with my neighbours." I said that it would take time, and it would depend on how he behaved – but that if he spoke to people as he had spoken to Hale at the Vicarage it was of no use expecting things to go better. "But the man was damnably insolent!" he said, "and I won't take that from anyone."

'Well, we argued on, and then I tried to go a step farther – that's my trade, you know – and I wanted to see if the man felt any kind of regret for any of the things he had done. He was quieter by that time, but he told me plainly to remember that I was not in my Sunday school. I nearly lost my temper at that, but I saw that it wouldn't do to back out. So I said that I was there to help him if I could, but that I could do nothing unless I knew more or less what his feeling was. "It's like calling in a doctor," I said, "and then keeping back some of your symptoms."

'And then, Mr Hartley, I had a look for the first and last time of my life into the soul of a very bad man. He told me that he regretted it, in a way, because he didn't like the consequences. But that if there were no consequences, he would not even regret it. One phrase of his I remember, "Why, I think no more of doing this and that than you think about taking a cup of tea!" He went on to say that when certain temptations came to him, he had no choice – 'I really don't think I am quite responsible,' he said; "there is nothing in my mind that even wishes to resist." And as to feeling the need of forgiveness either from the people he had wronged or Almighty God, the idea seemed simply laughable to him; and I will only say this, that for the first and only time in my life I felt like doubting the power of God. And then at last I got away. I may add that for a month or two afterwards I was really ill. I could not sleep; I could not get the man's face out of my mind.

'And then there came a worse complication. Pratt, the farmer to whom Faulkner had spoken in the street, had an accident and was thrown out of his dog-cart; and Hale had a sort of stroke and was ill for some time. And this I think made matters hopeless. You know what sort of things people say, and underneath all our civilisation there's a great deal of the ugliest old superstition left.

'After that Faulkner shut himself up altogether, except that he would ride or walk in the early summer mornings before people were about. In winter he hardly ever left the house; and what went on here I don't know – I don't like to think. He read a great deal, he did some gardening. I went to see him from time to time, but he would never talk freely again. He used to ask a few questions, and sometimes told me stories about his boyhood, things his mother had said to him – he had a curious kind of affection for her – the tricks he had played on his father; he seemed to me like a man in a dream. He also took to speculating on the Stock Exchange, and lost a lot of money. The only person who stuck to him was the old soldier-servant. They lived in three or four rooms, did their own cooking, smoked and drank together, and the house got into a filthy state. But nothing happened: he didn't die, he was never ill, he simply lived on. Once or twice old friends came to see him; and I remember one man – a retired Colonel, I believe – whom I met, leaving the house in haste, looking very much perturbed. He came up and spoke to me, said he had been to see his old friend Faulkner – they had been subalterns together – and he had been very much shocked, "though I'm not very particular," he added. Then he suddenly said, "Tell me, is he mad?" "Not in the least," I said. "Then, good God," said the Colonel, "why doesn't the man shoot himself?" – and he went off straight to the station.

'Now, for more than ten years things went on – think what that means – the garden was all overgrown with bushes and brambles, with a path through to a plot where they grew vegetables; and in front the shrubs grew over the lower windows, and most of the upper windows were broken. But it shows what a strange thing human nature is, Mr Hartley, for I believe the people here were rather proud of it than otherwise, though there was once an ugly demonstration. The old soldier-servant used to be seen about – he did the shopping, and he was rather a feature of the place. And strange to say, I got rather to like the man. He had been a real ruffian, I expect, but the way that man stuck to poor Hugh – it was heroic. There was nothing he wouldn't have done for him, and he simply worshipped him. I used to wonder what would happen to Hugh if he died.

'I still went in at times to see Hugh, and I believe he was glad to see me, though when he was in a bad mood he used to ask me all kinds of ingenious and bewildering questions about religious matters which I could not answer; but as a rule I don't think he was even very consciously unhappy. They lived by a routine, and Hugh used to talk mysteriously of his experiments – I never quite knew what he meant, but nothing very good, I fear. And then there were stories – at one time the garden was thought to be full of great black birds; and at another there were supposed to be creatures which grunted and snorted about among the bushes, and screamed out sharply at night. There were said to be curious mounds in the garden, like earth thrown out from burrows. Sometimes the windows were lighted up, and music was heard; and a man was said to have been seen going up the wall at the back like a fly. But I never saw anything myself, except for the fact that the house seemed to me sometimes to be full of smells – bitter, suffocating smells, like nothing on earth; and at times appeared full of shadows, gliding blacknesses, like mist or smoke. But I dare say all these things had some explanation.'

'But I must bring my story to an end – and I must add that though I never quite gave up trying to get hold of something in Hugh's mind and heart that I could pull on, and though I said many prayers for him, it all was a total failure; but I somehow became aware of a change of atmosphere about the house, about Hugh himself. I had generally had the feeling as if some struggle was going on somewhere out of sight, or even as though one were watched by something that would like to make a spring if it dared. Hugh himself was less violent and quieter; it seemed like exhaustion.

'One night, about the end of April (I was alone then, for my dear wife had died the year before; and I must tell you that in one of the last talks we had, she said to me, 'Don't give Hugh up – I think there is something coming to him,' but she could not explain), I was working late when I heard someone tapping at the door, quietly and insistently; and I found it was Hugh's servant. He wanted me to come and see Hugh at once. "Did he send for me?" I said. "No, sir – but I'm frightened about him. He doesn't eat, he doesn't sleep – he sits watching something." The man kept moistening his lips as he spoke and then broke out, "Come and see if you can help him."

'I went off at once; and when we got into the house I knew that there was something very wrong indeed. There was a silence that appalled me – I have never experienced such a silence; and though it was a warm night, the house was deadly cold. But worse still, there seemed something holding us back which required pushing into. I fought my way upstairs; but the old servant gave up, sat down on the bottom step and watched me. There was one solitary candle in the hall, which flickered and cast hideous shadows.

'I went straight into Hugh's room – the room at the top of the stairs. I found him stretched fully dressed upon his bed, his eyes closed, and making motions with his hands as if he were trying to thrust something away. His brow was horribly puckered and his face seemed swollen and congested. I went up and took his hand, and he gave a kind of moan or wail – the sort of cry a hare gives when a keeper takes hold of it. "Don't be afraid," I said; "it's only me. John, you know!" At this he sat up and opened his eyes. "The dream," he said, "the dream – it's closing in on me!" Then he said to me in a faint voice, "Surely it's enough? – it's all empty and dark – it's draining my life away!" Then he turned to me and said, "Where have I been?" I knew well enough. It isn't only a name, Mr Hartley, it's a very real thing – the most real thing but one in the world. Then he said to me, "Fifteen years of hell, John – does anything deserve that?" I hardly knew what I was saying then, for the cold that I had felt on the stairs was gathering in, thicker than ever. But I said – the words were given me somehow, "Perhaps you have done your punishment, Hugh; it's over and done." He shook his head and lay down again; and I just knelt down and said the last prayers, and in the middle he gave one shudder, which went through him from head to foot, and I knew he was gone.

'Yes, I know what you would like to ask me, Mr Hartley, and my answer is that I don't know.' He was gone, but something else was gone too. The servant came running up the stairs, and looked in. I beckoned to him. He came and knelt down by me, and I finished the prayers; and when I had finished, he took my hand and pressed it;

and then he took Hugh in his arms and stroked his face. I left them there, and went away a wiser man, I hope.

'The family lawyer came down, and he and I made a search for documents to no purpose. He had kept some papers in a despatch-box that was always near him; but this was missing, and could not be found. There was nothing to throw light on the matter, except that the servant said that he had lately been strange in manner and apathetic, and that he had lost his appetite; and I will only add that there was an inquest. I told my tale with reservations, and they called it natural death. I didn't hesitate to bury him in the church-yard, and there he lies; but no-one came to the funeral. And the Bishop sent for me to enquire into the circumstances; but when I had finished the story, as much as it was fit for a Bishop to hear, he told me frankly that he had meant to suggest to me to resign my living, but that now he had altered his mind, and that I must on no account leave the place. I never saw a man in such a state of what we will call godly embarrassment. And the next Sunday I made my flock a little sermon on "Judge not, that ye be not judged", and gave them a bit of my mind. And, strange to say, I have never had any trouble to speak of since.'

The Vicar made a long pause, and shook his head. I could see that there was something further in his mind which he had decided not to mention. I confess that this strange and tragic story produced an extraordinary effect upon me. For one thing, it was all so darkly mysterious, so full of unexplained hints and suggestions of evil, that it aroused in me a vague terror which made me wish that I had never listened to it. Not so Bendyshe; he was sitting back in his chair, his hands clasped together, looking at the Vicar with gleaming eyes, like a man on the brink of a great discovery.

Then the Vicar turned to me, and said, 'There, Mr Hartley, I have told you the story at Mr Bendyshe's request. You may be thinking that it is the sort of tale that had better not be told, and that such a collection of shocking incidents is better forgotten and buried in oblivion. But I have two reasons for telling you. In the first place, the outline of the story, only greatly exaggerated, is known to and repeated by a good many people in this place, and I should wish you to have a more accurate version of what happened – anything is better than secrecy about such things; and Mr Bendyshe tells me he has a special reason for asking me to relate it to you, which you no doubt know, and of which I approve. I think it ought to be seriously investigated.'

'And then, too, I have a further reason. There are very dark corners in this world of ours, and facts of our existence, which seem inconsistent with any faith in a beneficent and Almighty Creator; and I don't think it right to ignore them. My own belief – I will speak frankly – is that God is slowly and patiently making a conquest of a world in which there exists – how originated I cannot even guess – a strong element of something atrocious and horrible, which defies Him, and seizes every opportunity of undoing His work. And to my mind, the horror of this story is that it seems like a deliberate attempt to focus this evil power, an attempt which failed, because this malignant influence, as I interpret it, is essentially what is called stupid. It has no principle; it works at details with a laborious persistency – that is where its essential weakness lies; but it ought not to be ignored; it must be met by anyone who comes across it with courage and intelligence. I don't think that Hugh Faulkner did any very serious or deep-seated harm here, and he certainly did not succeed in making evil attractive. He may have struck a blow at individuals, and I believe that he certainly did – but that is all.'

'And now I must ask you to excuse me, if I say good night. May I have the pleasure of seeing you at the Vicarage, Mr Hartley? You may have some questions to ask about what I have told you. But I have nothing to add, and I may not be in a position to give you an answer.'

The Vicar took his leave, and left on my mind the impression of great simplicity and goodness. He and Bendyshe went to the door together, and stood talking for some little time in low tones.

When Bendyshe came back, he said to me with a curious look, 'Now what do you think of all that?'

'I don't know what to make of it,' I said – 'at present I'm simply rather stupefied. One goes along making the best of life and thinking the world on the whole a satisfactory and wholesome place; and then comes a tale like this, and one wonders if one has any real idea of what is going on, or of what may be hidden away in the minds of men and women. I wish I had never heard the story.'

'Oh, come,' said Bendyshe, 'don't say that – it seems to me to have all the elements of a big adventure. I would give anything to get a little more information; but here one only gets the wildest and silliest gossip. I may tell you that I have tried to get on the track of Faulkner's servant, but I can't find a trace of him.'

'I expect he is dead by this time,' I said.

'No,' said Bendyshe; 'he is not dead. I can say that quite confidently – I have my reasons.'

We sat for some little time together, and I asked Bendyshe one or two disjointed questions. I said, 'There was one point in what the Vicar said which I did not quite understand. He spoke of Faulkner doing harm to individuals. What did he mean by that?'

'Well,' said Bendyshe, 'he meant Hale and Farmer Pratt in the first place; and there are some other cases too, if you care to hear them.'

'No, I don't want to hear them,' I said; 'but tell me this. Do you, and does the Vicar, really believe that Faulkner had the power of inflicting bodily damage upon these unfortunate men, without using some known human agency? Of course it might be that some mental shock and physical deterioration followed from a fright which – '

But Bendyshe interrupted me. 'Do I believe it?' he said. 'Why, I *know* it. Faulkner was just as much responsible for their illness as if he had fired a gun at them.'

'But how is it possible?' I said.

'Ah, I don't know that,' said Bendyshe; 'but that he had the power of doing that sort of thing – at all events in the case, let us say, of people whose moral force was weakened by some indulgence – is incontestable. He didn't use it often, I admit; he was afraid to do so; but in both of these cases, and in others which I could tell, he lost all control of himself, and I believe that he let loose against them an undiluted current of evil; and the Vicar believes it too.'

'But it isn't rational,' I said; 'we don't believe in witchcraft in the twentieth century.'

'Perhaps it would be better if we did,' said Bendyshe grimly. 'We can't get rid of facts by calling them irrational.'

I saw that he was getting nettled by the discussion, so I said, 'Well, I must have time to let all this settle down.'

In a moment the other Bendyshe appeared. 'Yes,' he said; 'we mustn't let this visit of yours degenerate into a series of shocks and explosions. I've no right to do that, and if you give me a hint, I will drop my theory for a bit. But I very much hope you will help me to look into the matter. We'll have an easy day tomorrow.'

He accompanied me to my room and said, 'I hope the story tonight hasn't made you nervous? Perhaps this will reassure you.' He showed me, let in beneath the dado-cornice, in the corner by my bed, a little circle looking like the top of a wooden peg, and painted white like the rest of the room. 'That's a fancy of mine. My butler, Bartlett, doesn't sleep in the house – he has a house in the village. And this bell rings in my room – both the other spare bedrooms have it. I put it up when old Ford was staying here, and was taken ill in the night and couldn't make anyone hear. If you press on that, I'll be with you in a minute. I'm a very light sleeper!'

'Oh, I'm not nervous,' I said. 'I'm a sound sleeper, and then I'm a rational man.'

Bendyshe smiled at this and said, 'Yes; that's just why I want your help. Good night, old man.'

5

Left to myself that night, I went slowly and deliberately to bed. I felt curiously tired and drowsy after the cataract of varied impressions which I had received during the day; and I was conscious, too, of a growing excitement. The Vicar's story had done more to arouse this than any of Bendyshe's semi-scientific theories. The Vicar, I felt, was a man without an axe to grind, and with a certain duty to perform in the world, a desire to illumine the darkness, to extinguish evil. He did not turn his back upon it or ignore it, and his aim was a practical one. Bendyshe, on the other hand, was like a man engaged in research; he simply wanted to arrive at facts. Indeed, there had been moments in the day when I had suspected him of being something very monomaniac; but his friendliness was engaging, and the appeal he had made to me for help had touched me. But help in what? That I could not say.

Just, I imagine, before I slept, I had a curious sensation of something vague and restless in the house, something that faintly jarred my drowsy nerves; it was all a fancy, but I thought dimly that someone, sleeplessly and wearily, was engaged in pacing about, and searching for a thing both secret and momentous, which had been mislaid or hidden. I wondered vaguely if the inquisitive brain of Bendyshe, weighing, considering, discriminating, was having a sort of telepathic effect on my own. The house was absolutely still; the church clock struck two with a murmur sweet as honey; and then, curiously enough, I had a sensation of great mental ease. If anything was going forward, I was at least in no way concerned in it; the searcher did not wish me ill – my presence there was nothing to him. And then, I suppose, I passed into sleep.

While I dressed in the morning, I could see Bendyshe pacing in the narrow strip of garden that lay beneath my windows, lost in thought. He greeted me when I came downstairs with much effusion. 'Slept well?' he said. 'That's right. You look very fit and spry. We'll have a good spin today – we might go to Canterbury perhaps?' And yet, strange to say, I had an indefinable sense that Bendyshe was in some way disappointed.

Our run was uneventful enough. Bendyshe made no allusion to the narrative of the previous evening. I thought, indeed, that he was a little conscience-stricken for having plunged me, so to speak, up to the neck in these dark matters. In fact I do not think he had intended to do so, but his own overpowering interest, in the company of someone whom he thought sympathetic, had run away with him. I felt in a singularly placid mood, and the summer fields, the woodland corners, the hop-gardens, the hamlets through which we went, worked upon me like some gentle anodyne. We ate our luncheon on the shoulder of a high, upstanding ridge along which the road passed; and I was amazed at Bendyshe's knowledge of the country. There was hardly a church-tower visible that he could not name, and he was full of local and personal anecdotes which beguiled the time very pleasantly.

We got back for tea, and I then experienced something of a reaction. In spite of the beauty and comfort of the house, there came on me a sense of lurking dreariness which I could not analyse; something was going on there, in the cool rooms, the panelled corridors, which I could not penetrate. I tried to work, I tried to read – Bendyshe had gone off to the village on some friendly errand – and I became aware that I did not wish to be alone. When the dressing-gong sounded, I felt a strong disinclination to leave the room.

Ten minutes later I heard the front door open. Bendyshe's brisk stride was audible in the hall. This was a relief to me; but instead of coming, as I had expected, to the library, he went quickly upstairs. I decided that I must go too; but just as I got to the head of the stairs, I became aware that someone was coming down the corridor as if from Bendyshe's room. It was beginning to be dusk, and I could not see the figure very plainly. It was a man, carelessly dressed in an old grey suit of clothes, shuffling along very noiselessly, his head hanging down, with a markedly sullen and dejected air. The face looked healthy but careworn, and it came into my mind that it was some petitioner who had come to make a request of Bendyshe, but who had been decisively and perhaps unceremoniously refused. I said 'Good evening' to the man as he passed me, and then I had a real surprise of rather an unpleasant kind, for he took not the slightest notice of me or my salutation, as if he neither heard nor saw me; he shuffled on down the corridor and was swallowed up in the shadow at the head of the stairs. Yet it did not seem to me an intentional rudeness, but rather as if the stranger's preoccupation was so intense that there was no room in his mind for any other impression.

I went and dressed and was downstairs in the smoking-room when Bendyshe appeared. 'You've had a busy evening,' I said. 'And I saw you got caught by a caller on coming in.'

Bendyshe looked at me quickly and interrogatively. 'Oh, yes,' he said, 'I have endless visitors – there's nothing I'm not asked to do.'

'But I expect you can't always do it,' I said. 'I passed your friend in the corridor, and I never saw disappointment so legibly written on anyone's face as on his – he hadn't even time to exchange civilities!'

'You spoke to him?' said Bendyshe, adding, 'Poor chap, yes, he has no end of troubles. But what the real trouble is I don't quite know. So he struck you as disappointed, did he?'

'Yes, indeed,' I said. 'I almost wonder that you had the heart to refuse him. He looked quite worn out, and took no notice whatever of me. I should like to know his history.'

Bendyshe stared at me in silence, and it struck me that I had been impertinent. 'I'm sorry,' I said, 'if I have been too inquisitive.'

'Good Lord, it isn't that,' said Bendyshe; 'but the man doesn't know what he wants, or at least I don't know what he wants – I can't make out, and that's just the difficulty. And when I find out, then – well, then I shall know what to do.'

Bendyshe was in a very strange mood that evening – so strange that I more than once thought that my half-formed conjecture of the previous night was true. He seemed to be wrestling against the approach of a secret and triumphant mirth. Our talk turned on the ailments of middle-age, and I confessed to being conscious of the necessity of a régime. 'I don't believe in taking care of oneself,' he said – 'plenty of air, enough exercise, variety, work, plenty of other people's business, not too much eating and drinking and smoking; and most of all, if you think you can't do a particular thing or don't want to, go and do it!'

'That's rather Spartan,' I said.

'No,' said Bendyshe; 'it's simply this – we have all of us got three at least, or even more, people inside us. There's the one that admires and enjoys – he's all right. Then there's the one that criticises and reflects. Then there's the animal, which needs to be sensibly and good-humouredly drilled, like a dog or horse, and he's a patient and serviceable fellow enough. But behind them all, in the little inner-most room, there's the one that fears, and he mustn't be listened to for a single instant, or he will run the whole show.'

'I never thought of it like that,' said I; 'yet I'm sure you are right. But which is the one that *wills?*'

'Oh, they all do that,' said Bendyshe, laughing; 'it's a kind of board. The point is that the right man should have the casting vote.' And then he was again overtaken by his tendency to laughter, and laughed unreservedly. I suppose that he detected some annoyance in my face, for he suddenly stopped. 'Forgive me,' he said; 'I have a fit of the giggles sometimes, and it is bad manners. But I have been lucky today. I have made some progress – more than I expected.'

After dinner we had a game of piquet, and went up to bed about midnight. As we came out at the head of the stairs, Bendyshe said, 'Was it here you met my poor friend? Which way did he go?'

'Down the stairs,' said I; 'but I lost sight of him.'

'Ah, he ought to have gone down the backstairs,' said Bendyshe, 'but I suppose he forgot. Hullo, what's this?' He turned sharply round. The door leading into the unfurnished bedroom was open, and the moon shone in, showing the boarded floor and the clean-cut panelling. 'Who the devil did that?' said Bendyshe very irritably 'Here, come in – let's have a look. Has there been someone prowling about, I wonder?' He led the way into the room, but I felt an insupportable reluctance to enter it. 'I must have this place locked up,' said Bendyshe, half to himself, 'Hullo, this is all quite new.'

I followed him into the room, suddenly feeling the need of company. He was bending down, looking at something on the floor. 'The wet must have got through,' said Bendyshe to himself. I drew nearer, and saw that a quantity of plaster had fallen from the ceiling; up above an irregular square opening appeared; but what, I confess, gave me a shudder of dismay was that the plaster on the floor had a strange resemblance to the shape of a prostrate figure. I saw at once that it was a merely accidental likeness, and even as I looked Bendyshe with his foot swept the debris together.

He took me to my room and said a few friendly words. I saw that he wished to obliterate the impression caused by his merriment. I went to bed, and, contrary to all my expectations, for the evening had been an agitating one, I slept profoundly. But before I slept, I half determined that I would not prolong my stay. Bendyshe was behaving very oddly; but then I thought of the Vicar, and I decided that as he had asked me to his house, I would go and consult him; and this brought me a sense of relief.

6

The morning turned out insufferably hot. Bendyshe was very cheerful and pleasant at breakfast. He said he had directed that some chairs should be taken out into the shade of the sycamores. 'The verandah is a bit stuffy,' he said, 'when the wind is in the north.' He had got down a parcel of books from town, new books which he thought might interest me. And when we went out there was a table, and two chairs, and an irresistible heap of neat volumes of all shapes and sizes. We sat mostly in silence; occasionally Bendyshe went off to the house, and twice at least he was summoned by the butler to see a caller. 'I lead a dog's life,' he said, laughing – 'plenty of fleas!'

I had again become immersed in my book, when a sudden exclamation from Bendyshe, betraying a poignant and acute emotion, made me look up. He was leaning forwards, his gaze bent on the front of the house. At the closed window of the unfurnished bedroom, plainly visible, and indeed made curiously luminous by the sunlight, a man was standing looking out into the garden. He was, so far as I could judge, an elderly man, with a shock of grey hair, and a curiously blurred and puffy face, red and bloated. He was dressed in a sort of apron, dirty white, showing arms bare to the elbow. 'Who's that? What's that?' said Bendyshe in indescribable agitation. It seemed to me so unnecessary and unaccountable an excitement, that I said, 'Well, if you ask me, I should say it was the plasterer come to repair the ceiling.'

'You're right – you're right,' said Bendyshe, with a gesture of intense relief. 'Of course, I forgot – I mentioned it to Bartlett – but I didn't expect him today. I imagined – well, I don't know what I did imagine.' He got up from his chair and went hurriedly to the house.

I was by this time very seriously perturbed indeed about Bendyshe, and began to believe that he was on the brink of insanity. It rushed into my mind that I would go to the Vicarage at once. I went back to the house, where all was silent. Old Bartlett was laying the table in the dining room. I said to him, 'If Mr Bendyshe asks for me, will you tell him I have just gone into the village, but shall be back in a few minutes?'

He was a comfortable and amiable old fellow. 'Certainly, sir,' he said; 'but it's a terrible hot day for the street – you'll wear your straw, no doubt, sir,' and he bustled out to open the door for me.

I arrived at the Vicarage – an old substantial house, behind the church – and was shown straight into the study. The Vicar greeted me very warmly. 'Yes, I had hoped I might see you, Mr Hartley,' he said. 'I'm afraid you think you have got into a very strange place here, and I'm not surprised at your coming.'

I sat down and told him the incidents of the morning and the previous day. He listened to me very gravely. Then he said: 'I can't cast any light, I fear, on what has been happening – indeed, I am under a promise to Mr Bendyshe not to do so. But the important point is this. You may be absolutely and entirely reassured about his sanity. He is as sane as you are, and a great deal more sane than I am. He is the hardest-headed man I know. Mr Hartley, I can tell you that that man has gone through experiences which would have sent nine out of ten men crazy. And he is a man of great emotional sensibility too, but he has got infinite courage and inflexible purpose. I cannot tell you how I admire and reverence him. But I must add this: Bendyshe wants your help very much. It is worth your while to give it to him, and I think that, so far as I can judge from our short acquaintance, he has made a remarkably shrewd choice. But if, on the other hand, you feel in any way alarmed or repelled by the claim, I will go over to the Manor-house with you, and insist on your being released from any obligation – and he will take my advice.'

'No,' I said; 'once really assured of Bendyshe's sanity, I have no wish to be released. He shall have whatever help I can give him, for as long as I can give it – but I confess I do not quite trust myself.'

'Mr Hartley,' said the Vicar, 'you have chosen the right course, and I am infinitely relieved; and I may add this, that the results may turn out to be of the utmost importance. Please consult me at any time.'

Just as I was going, the Vicar said, 'Would it be troublesome if I asked you to take a note for me to Bendyshe? I will come round at 2.30 to speak to him about it; but I think he ought to have this news at once.'

The Vicar scribbled a few words on a sheet of writing-paper, enclosed in it an open telegram which was lying on the table, sealed and addressed an envelope, and handed it to me.

I returned to find luncheon ready and Bendyshe pacing in the hall, evidently in a state of great suppressed excitement. I handed him the note and gave him the Vicar's message. He tore the envelope open, read the enclosure, and a cry of surprise not unmixed with a deep satisfaction escaped from his lips. I thought for a moment that he was going to hand it to me; but he did not, and presently replaced it carefully in the envelope. Then he looked at me, rather a grim and searching look. 'So you went round to see the Vicar?' he said. 'May I ask what you went to talk about?'

'Yes, certainly,' I replied. 'I was beginning to feel this morning that I was getting too deep into a rather mysterious business; and I don't feel very sure of myself. You must remember how new and unfamiliar this all is to me – how little, in fact, I know of you beyond a mere acquaintanceship, to speak plainly; and I felt the other night that the Vicar was a man I could trust, so I went round to ask him a few questions.'

Bendyshe put down his knife and fork and drummed with his fingers on the table. 'Well,' he said in rather a grim tone, 'what's the result?'

'He seemed to think,' I said, 'that you needed my assistance, and he was very insistent that I should give it, if I felt able to do so. And the long and short of it is that I decided to do so.'

Bendyshe's face lit up with a smile; he held out his hand to me, and I grasped it, feeling that some compact of a momentous kind was being made. 'Well, old man,' he added in a tone which showed that he was deeply moved, 'I can only say that I am truly grateful and thankful. It's a big business, and I want someone at hand whom I can trust, very badly indeed. Mind,' he added, 'I'm not afraid of anything that may happen – but I want a perfectly fair-minded man, who isn't afraid either, and that's what I feel you are. Now,' he went on, 'I'll have no secrets from you. Ask me any questions, and I'll answer them.'

'No,' I said, 'I won't ask for that. I know that you want an impartial observer. I can see that something very queer is going on in this house, but I won't ask questions; I'll draw my own conclusions, and then when you think it best you shall tell me.'

'That's right,' said Bendyshe, 'just what I want, and that's a bargain. If you will keep your ears and eyes open, it's all I ask. You may be surprised – you may even be shocked; but I can assure you that there is nothing to be afraid of – nothing whatever. We will just go our own way for a bit, and see how things turns out. Now, this letter,' he went on, slapping his pocket, 'is the most important thing that has happened yet. Perhaps you will see the Vicar when he comes up, and tell him anything you have noticed, anything in the smallest degree unusual; and then leave us to discuss it – and thank you once again.'

While we were smoking, the Vicar arrived, and I saw that he looked perturbed. I left the two alone together, and half an hour later Bendyshe came to the library, and said that the Vicar and himself were obliged, owing to the news received, to go away on the following day.

'We shall leave immediately after breakfast in my car,' he said, 'and we shall be back for dinner, unless anything unforeseen occurs. It's very inhospitable, I know,' he added, 'and I don't feel sure if you will care to be so long alone. Have you anything in town that you want to do? Or you could easily spend the day at the Vicarage – that could be arranged. I'm afraid it is absolutely imperative for us to go.'

'Oh, don't bother about me,' I said. 'I will do what I am very fond of doing – go out for a long vague walk, get some food at a village inn, and be back in good time in the evening. It will do me good; and I can think over things a bit.'

'It's very good of you,' said Bendyshe, looking decidedly relieved.

The rest of the day passed quietly enough. We sat in the garden, and the only event that struck me was that one of the gardeners and the chauffeur, in the course of the afternoon, brought a ladder across the lawn and got it into the house with some difficulty.

Bendyshe was thoughtful and cheerful. We played a game after dinner, and he proposed an early adjournment.

I was glad to go to bed – the day had been one of some agitation. But when I had got to bed I could not sleep. I was seized with a kind of detective fever, and found myself speculating as to what the whole mystery could be. I did not believe very firmly in its supernatural character, and as for the occult side of it all, I may say I was frankly sceptical. It seemed to me that the Vicar and Bendyshe were probably affected by the tragic fate of Faulkner, and were perhaps inclined to attribute significance to circumstances of no great importance, but there were evidently things which had yet to be told me. While I was pursuing this train of thought – it was now nearly one – I distinctly heard soft footsteps in the corridor. I went to the door, opened it very quietly, and looked out. I saw Bendyshe, in his shirt and trousers, carrying in his hand a lantern, walking very gently, his back to me, towards the staircase. He came to the door of the unfurnished room, drew a key from his pocket, unlocked the door, and went in, closing it with great precaution. I had a strong impulse to follow him, but thought that he might be annoyed at my intrusion; so I left my door half-open, and feeling restless and anxious, I put on some clothes, sat down in an armchair near the door, prepared to rise and close it the moment I heard the door of the unfurnished room open. I will admit that I was far from easy in my mind about this solitary exploration, but I had by this time a robust confidence in Bendyshe's strength of will.

For a time I heard nothing; but then I began to perceive very faint muffled sounds overhead, as though Bendyshe (I supposed) was moving about slowly and cautiously, and perhaps searching for something that was not easily to be discovered – for there were long pauses between the sounds, as if the searcher were standing still.

I suddenly perceived what was happening. The ladder had no doubt been brought upstairs and put in the unfurnished room. Bendyshe was certainly using it to obtain access through the hole in the ceiling to some room or loft overhead, and was quietly investigating it at night, so as to be secure against interruption. I confess that the nerve which would be required for such a proceeding fairly amazed me, particularly when I thought of the supernatural influences Bendyshe clearly believed to be at work in the house.

I suppose that half an hour had passed thus, when suddenly I became aware that a very alarming interruption had happened overhead. Heavy footsteps stamped and rushed in the loft above me, then grew fainter, and then I heard the sound of a fall and a half-stifled cry from the direction of the unfurnished room. I rose and hurried down the corridor, flung open the door of the room and saw a sight which horrified me. The moonlight streamed in at the open window. Bendyshe was sitting on the ground with his hands clasped on his forehead; beside him lay the extinguished lantern.

'What has happened, Bendyshe?' I said, hastening to his side. He unclasped his hands and looked at me, and I could see that blood was flowing on to his shirt.

'I have had an accident, old man,' said Bendyshe in rather a husky tone, 'but I'm not much the worse, I think. No, don't ask questions – just help me up.' I held out a hand and lifted him to his feet. He looked dizzily round. 'Good God, what a fool I was!' he said. 'I might have known it wouldn't do – here, Hartley, pick up that lantern, there's a good fellow, and come to my room with me. I don't think I'm much amiss, after all. I only hope to God that no-one else heard. How did you know I was here? You came like lightning.'

'I saw you go in here,' I said, 'and I heard you overhead – and I had a feeling that I might be wanted.'

We went into the passage; I passed my arm through his, and he seemed glad of the support. He turned on the electric light in his room and I followed him into the bathroom. He was very pale, his hair disordered; the wound turned out to be at the base of his throat, a scratch or cut, torn and lacerated. He bathed it, and it proved not to be very deep. 'I must have caught my neck on the broken edges of some of the laths,' he said. 'Well, I'm thankful it's no worse.' He came back into his bedroom, and opened a small case which I saw contained some surgical appliances. He soaked a bit of cotton-wool in some disinfectant; and very deftly wrapped a bandage round his neck and under his arms, only asking me to fasten it for him. Then he dropped some liquid into a glass and swallowed it. 'Now, old man,' he said, 'you get to bed and let me have a sleep. I have got a long day tomorrow.'

'But you won't go in this condition?' I said.

'Yes, I must go,' he said, 'but Elton will drive. I shall be all right. I have just had a bit of a shock – I slipped on the ladder, you see, and I'm only thankful I didn't break a limb. Now go and get some sleep yourself,' he added – 'you look as if you wanted it; and mind, don't be *excited*! Nothing more will happen tonight, you may be sure of that – I've had a lesson, anyhow!'

And so I left him, but lay long awake, pondering and speculating what had Bendyshe expected to find in the loft; and what had he found or seen that caused him to beat so hasty a retreat. For I knew enough of Bendyshe by this time to know that it must have been something of a very alarming or startling kind to upset him so.

7

I was relieved to find in the morning that Bendyshe showed few signs of the adventure of the previous day. The man was as tough as steel! He limped a little, and the wound in his neck was stiff and uncomfortable; but he was cheerful, not with any assumed cheerfulness, but with the tranquil assurance of the soldier who has come out unexpectedly well from a dangerous affray. I saw that the element of danger, whatever it was, about the whole investigation was a stimulus to him rather than the reverse.

It was a fine cool day, and the Vicar and he started about ten o'clock. It was a four-hour drive, Bendyshe told me, and they hoped to be back at seven. 'If we are delayed,' he said, 'we will wire at once; and if you then don't care about staying here alone, the Vicar has arranged for his housekeeper to give you a cold supper at the Vicarage.' I wrote a letter or two, and telling Bartlett that I should be out for luncheon and probably for tea as well, I went off soon after eleven.

It was astonishing to find how much more cheerful and lighthearted I became on getting clear of the house. I had hardly realised how much the atmosphere of the place was weighing on my spirits. It was not what had actually occurred, for that was trivial enough. It was a feeling of suspense, of hardly knowing from hour to hour what might not happen.

I walked off into the country, delighting in the freshness of the green lanes, the views from higher ground, the pleasant villages and farms I passed through. I got some bread and cheese at an inn. The landlord was a chatty old man, amiably inquisitive. He asked where I had come from, and when I said from Hebden Hill, he brightened up. He knew Hebden well, it seemed, and had some relations living there. Then he asked me if I knew the Manor-house. 'You mean the big house opposite the west end of the church?' I said.

'That's it, sir,' he said. 'Did you ever hear tell of Squire Faulkner?' he went on.

'Yes,' I said, 'I have heard the name – I think the Vicar mentioned it.'

'Ah! that would be Mr Fortescue,' he said. 'I knew him when I was a young man.' Then he went on in a rambling way, telling me about the Squire. 'They did say he done a murder, or next door to it, and he come out of the army, and he lived all alone at the Manor with an old soldier as had been in his regiment for his servant, and they carried on dreadful. People used to say that they cooked the mice and rats and ate them, and the drink going from morning to night. But there were worse stories than that, sir,' the old man went on, dropping his voice. 'Folk said the Squire had sold himself to you know who, sir, that ain't the one above – and that don't seem hardly worth while, do it? And if the Squire had an ill-will to anyone, he could bring all sorts of mischief to pass. I don't know rightly about it, sir, but it wasn't thought hardly safe to cross the Squire, and they used to say that the two would catch a cat, as it might be, and burn it alive, and then it would be like poison to the man the Squire had an ill-will to.'

'And there was one bad story about a poor girl – a pretty girl she was, Annie Rogers by name, who lived with her mother that was a widow, and had a little money of her own. The old sergeant, it seems, took a fancy to her, and wanted her to marry him, but she couldn't abide the sight of him. That was hard enough, but then the Squire got wind of it, and thought that if the sergeant married her, he would lose his servant. And they had very high words about it, it was said. But the Squire went secret to work, and first old Mrs Rogers lost her bit of money and had to go out for jobs; and then she died; and Mr Fortescue was very good to Annie, and took her as a servant – but she was afraid of meeting the sergeant about the place; and one day the Vicar found him at the back door, speaking to Annie and frightening the girl with some nonsense; and the Vicar ordered him off, and the sergeant swore and that, and the Vicar went after him to the gate. There were some people passing by who stopped to look on; and the Vicar kept quite cool, and said to the sergeant in a loud voice that he was going to say before them all what he thought of him; and he said he was a dangerous and drunken ruffian – those were his words – and that if he ever annoyed the girl again, he would have him up before the magistrates and they would put him where he would have to hold his tongue.'

'The sergeant kept quiet after that for a long time; some of the Hebden men liked him well enough, for he could be very friendly when he chose, and could tell a good story. But poor Annie fell ill after that, and the Vicar sent her to the seaside, but she died for all that – they said it was a decline.'

The old man stopped for breath. 'But if the Squire was like that,' I said, 'and if the people believed all this about him, did they never show him what they thought of him?'

'Well, not for a long time, sir,' said the old man. 'You see, he was a cousin of the Vicar's, and the Vicar used to stand up for him. Some of the men in the place went one day to the Vicar and complained about the Squire; and the Vicar said to them, "It isn't the Squire," he said, "as does the harm – it's your fear of him. The worst harm he can do is to make you afraid of him – it's the fear does the rest." That was a true word, sir. But a little while after that, some of the same men, who had been having a bit of a drink, went up to the Manor, and began shouting under the windows, and beating on cans, and carrying on. And some of them threw stones and broke some of the windows – the Squire would never have them mended afterwards, but boarded them up. Someone saw and told the Vicar, and he ran down, but before he got there, the big door flung open, and the Squire, he marched out, and stood on the steps between the gate-posts. "Here I am," he says, without turning a hair, and they say his face was dreadful to look upon, all white, with his eyes flaming; and then he called them cowards, brute beasts, and a lot of things that it wouldn't be hardly proper for me to repeat nor for you to hear. And he invited them to do what they liked to him. But no-one dare lift a finger. "There," he said, "you daren't so much as speak." And someone in the crowd piped up at that and called him a hard name. "Oh, so that's what you think," said the Squire; "and if you weren't such a little cur, I'd ask you to step out here, and do you the honour of knocking you down." And then he stopped short, and said, "But there's a better way than that!" and he looked about him, they say, like a devil, and then they began to slink away, one by one; and some of them began to run. And that was the end of that evening's work. But would you believe it, sir, Billy Dale – that's the one that spoke – within a week went clean crazy, and was took away; and after that they left the Squire alone."

I felt that I had perhaps better not listen to more of these tales. I did not know how much was fact and how much fiction. But it was clear that the Squire was a man suspected of unspeakable things, and not without some reason. I began to feel that the best course would be to forget all about them. But then, why was Bendyshe so hot on the scent; and suddenly, like a flash of lightning, the truth, or what seemed the truth, dawned upon me. The evil was not dead; it was alive and active; and Bendyshe was trying to drag it to the light. Evil, of course, was anywhere and everywhere. But had something been done, did something remain in the house, that formed as it were a guarded stronghold of evil? Was there a core of malignant influence which needed to be extirpated? And if so, by what hideous personal agency, what bodiless ministers of fear was it perpetuated?

And then it dawned upon me that if there was any truth in my thoughts, Bendyshe must be exposed to dangers of a kind that defied precaution, and the more courageous he was, the nearer he got to the goal, the more appalling was the danger. I could not quite understand what part the Vicar was playing in all this. He was standing by Bendyshe – that was clear; but I thought that his kindly and generous nature might perhaps blind him to the danger, by leading him to believe that things had never been so bad as were supposed. In any case my duty was clear: I must stand by Bendyshe at any risk, and share the danger with him. It was a contest of wills, perhaps; and I could possibly, by throwing my own will into the scale, turn the current against our adversaries. And in any case I felt that I must not be left any longer in the dark, but must know exactly what had happened, and what had induced Bendyshe to embark on the quest.

I wandered on in the grip of these thoughts, hardly knowing where I went; I felt for a moment that I ought to return at once to the house – that I was like a sentinel deserting his post; but, on the other hand, I felt that it might be simply foolhardy and reckless to go back and wait in solitude until Bendyshe and the Vicar returned, and that some experience might befall me which would mar or damage such effectiveness as I might possess.

I got a cup of tea at an inn which proved to be about five miles from Hebden; and then I strolled quietly back, arriving about seven. To my relief the car caught me up about half a mile out of the village. Both Bendyshe and the Vicar looked tired, and were very grave. I talked vaguely about my wanderings, and they gave me but scanty attention.

When we got to the house, I said to Bendyshe, 'If the Vicar is not too tired, would he come back to dinner? – I have a special reason for asking this. I have something to tell you and some further questions to ask.' The Vicar assented, and Bendyshe and I entered the house together, while the Vicar pledged himself to return at eight.

Bendyshe went to the smoking-room, and flung himself down in a deep chair. 'Any the worse for yesterday?' I said.

'Oh, I'm stiff as a board, and dog-tired,' he said rather impatiently, 'and just when I had need of all my strength; but we have found what we wanted to know, and it is all as I expected, only worse; and now the whole business is in such a tangle that I hardly know what to do!' Then he added, 'Why were you so keen that the Vicar should come back? He has had a shock, and seems to me done up.'

'I couldn't help it,' I said; 'today I have thought it all out, and I'll stick to you through thick and thin; but I feel that I must know all, and know at once. If I am to share a danger, I must know what the danger is; I can't be of any use if I am still groping in the dark.'

'Yes, you're right,' said Bendyshe wearily. 'I have been feeling that too – but I wanted you to form your own opinion.'

When we went up to dress, Bendyshe said, looking round, 'I don't like the feel of the house tonight, old man. There's mischief brewing of a bad kind – but we'll weather it out!' I was conscious too myself of a sort of heavy and brooding stillness everywhere; but I saw and heard nothing.

8

At dinner, while the servants were in the room, we did our best to talk of indifferent matters. It was like a bad play, I thought. When we adjourned to the smoking-room, Bendyshe said to the Vicar, "Here, Vicar, Hartley says that he thinks he had better have the whole story, and I agree with him. He won't be taken by surprise; and it's no use pretending now that it is a mild sort of investigation; it's a battle of a bad kind, and we must be forearmed, if we can. I made a mistake last night by taking the offensive – and now hell's loose – But I'll go ahead.

'It was about three years ago that the thing began,' said Bendyshe. 'I don't know why it didn't begin before – perhaps it *had* begun; but I had been getting more and more interested in my problem, and I had been, I suppose, training my perceptions without knowing it; and the curtain went up with a run. I ought to say that when I first settled in here, I had taken the unfurnished room for my study. But I could never work there in any peace. There seemed to be something on the move there, and if I sat at the table, I used to feel there was someone behind me; and there were odd noises overhead too. I had the roof examined – the only way in was through a little trap-door in the ceiling, in the corner where the plaster came down – but above, there was only a long, low loft, lit by a window looking out on the tiles and gutters, with a cistern in it and water-pipes, and the builder said that the noises came from the pipes.

'However, one day I was coming down the corridor, I saw a man standing by the door of the room – the same man, Hartley, I will tell you at once, that you saw up there, the same dress, the same sort of expression. I thought it must be a plumber for a moment; when it suddenly came upon me with a rush that the wall, so to speak, was broken down, and I had seen something that a normal healthy man has no business to see. I said out loud, 'What are you doing there? – Who are you?' but he took no notice of me whatever, and continued to stand by the door, like a man who wanted something badly, and had been trying for a long time to get it, but all in vain. I didn't think of it as being in any definite and actual way connected with the place – I thought it was an hallucination produced by overtasking my nerves in one direction. I went along to the door, my eyes fixed on the man, and suddenly he was gone. I wasn't exactly frightened, but I felt uneasy about myself. I went up to town and saw a doctor, a friend of mine. He sounded me and questioned me up and down; then he declared me perfectly well in every way. I told him about my studies, and he asked me if I had ever seen any such figure in real life, in childhood, or had any fright or shock connected with such a figure. But I couldn't think of anything. He told me at last that he was frankly puzzled, but that he had little doubt that it was an hallucination, and did in some way result from my thinking so much about such phenomena. He gave me the advice to turn to other occupations for a bit, limit my work, have more company in the house – all very sensible.

'I did just what he advised, and had a succession of guests here, who bored me to death; and I took up constitutional history, as the least exciting subject I could find. But a fortnight later I saw the thing again, this time in my study, looking up at the trap-door. I got up, and walked straight up to him – and the same thing happened; he took no notice of me whatever, and when I was within a foot of him, disappeared.

'Then I did what I ought to have done before; I went to the Vicar and told him the whole story – and then it came out. The Vicar told me, with a good deal of hesitation, that the figure I described was beyond all doubt the figure of Hugh Faulkner himself, just as he looked in his later years. Wasn't that so?'

The Vicar nodded. 'It was unmistakable, your description! And it gave me a dreadful shock, though I can't say I was exactly surprised.' Then the Vicar turned to me and said, 'Of course, Mr Hartley, I am a firm believer in the immortality of the spirit; and I believe that we preserve identity and intelligence, and are not much affected or altered by death; but the spirit is, of course, a bodiless thing – a conscious and intelligent influence. I want to make this clear. There was nothing *material* there to see; but I realised that Bendyshe had somehow or other got within the range of Faulkner's thought, and that the figure was evolved out of this thought acting on Bendyshe's mind, just as we evolve figures in our dreams.'

'Yes,' said Bendyshe, 'but I was also aware that Faulkner was not consciously influencing me – in fact, I think he was wholly unaware of my existence then; and this was a great relief to me – I was simply a spectator of what was going on, just as you were when you saw him. In fact, if I may say so, I doubt if it was *his* mind acting on yours which made you see him. I think it was *my* mind. And then,' he went on, 'I saw the figure pretty often. But never in the presence of anyone else – that seemed an absolute bar, I don't know why. I lost all fear of it, and just accepted it as a fact. Once or twice I saw it in the garden, and once or twice downstairs, but almost always in the corridor upstairs, or in the empty room. But I didn't want to run any risks. So I had the trap-door plastered up, moved the furniture out, and locked the place up.'

'Meanwhile I speculated about it, and discussed it with the Vicar; and we came to the conclusion that there was some particular thing that Faulkner was – I won't say looking for exactly, but trying to trace, some book, perhaps, or manuscript – I couldn't make it out – but we decided at last that it was something which someone else had hidden; but was it in the house at all? Or if so, why couldn't he see it? Or if he could see it, what could he do with it? I don't believe that these spirits have any material powers at all – they can only act through living brains.'

I turned to the Vicar. 'Did you ever see the figure?' I said.

'No,' he said, 'I did not – I don't know why. I was nearer to Faulkner than anyone living, except his servant. But I have thought that perhaps Faulkner wished to conceal the very existence of the thing, whatever it is, from me, and was careful not to bring me in.'

'But why then did Bendyshe see him?' I asked.

'Oh,' said Bendyshe, 'I stumbled into it by accident, I believe – it was just a question of my power of perception being heightened.'

'But let me ask one other thing,' I said: 'How do you account for your seeing it only occasionally? If the thing is always in Faulkner's mind, you ought to see it constantly.'

'Well,' said Bendyshe, 'we don't know what his mental occupations may be – I dare say he has other things to think of.'

'Yes, indeed,' said the Vicar, shaking his head; 'he was a very self-willed and perverse man – he has much to learn.'

Bendyshe gave a grim smile, and went on, 'What I believe is this – that at times the spirit of Faulkner remembers this thing, whatever it is, and believes it to be still in this house. The result is that for a time his thought is occupied with the house and the familiar rooms; and being an abstract essence, it ranges about the well-known scene; and if one comes within the reach of it, one sees the figure automatically.'

'But why, then, does the figure disappear when you come close to it?'

'Ah, I don't know everything,' said Bendyshe; 'indeed, there is much that quite baffles me. But I have thought that it may be in some way obliterated by the proximity of my own consciousness, as the moon obliterates the light of the surrounding stars – but that is only my idea.'

'And now,' he went on, 'we come to the more serious part of the story. Some weeks ago I became suddenly aware that the spirit of Faulkner had become aware of mine. I suppose I had begun to speculate more closely as to where the lost thing was, and what it might be. And then, too, it had occurred to me that the old sergeant might be still alive – the Vicar had told me that he thought he was dead – and I had begun to make some enquiries, and had employed a detective to try to trace the man. We now know that he was alive all the time. Faulkner had given him some money at various times, and after Faulkner's death the sergeant had rented a farm in Hampshire, a little bit of a place; but he had taken to drink, and was in a bad way, nearly at the end of his resources. He became aware that he was being tracked, and I dare say there were plenty of other things about which he might have got into trouble. Anyhow, he was frightened. He sold his farm, which was mortgaged, so he only got a few pounds out of it; and he went off on the tramp. The money was spent at last, and he took cold by sleeping in the open air; he was taken to the workhouse at Pentlow, near Horsham, and went to the infirmary with rheumatic fever.'

'But I must go back for a moment. While all this was going on, I became aware, as I told you, that I had for some reason or other come within Faulkner's consciousness, and that he realised that someone was on the same scent as himself. His expression seemed to me to change when I saw him, he looked angry and defiant, and as though he was guarding the approach to something. But even so he was not apparently at first conscious of my physical presence. Then he assumed a menacing air, and made gestures of anger and rage. It was at this time that I asked you to join me here, because I began to feel that I *must* have someone with me – that I could not be sure of my nerves not failing me; moreover, his appearances became much more frequent.'

'And then you came, but instead of telling you everything at once, which would have been by far the best course, I waited, in order to see whether you had any perception of his presence; and when you began to notice certain phenomena, I made excuses and gave explanations – it was all very stupid – in order that you might have your own experiences and draw your own conclusions.'

'And then a quite new development occurred. The old sergeant died in the workhouse, and the first intimation of it that I got was the appearance of a new figure at the window, which you also saw. I did not know what to make of this, though I had a strong suspicion; but it happened that they found on the man a letter from someone in the village – one of his old acquaintances – which seemed to show that he had lived here; and then they wired to the Vicar to say that an unknown man had died in the workhouse – they gave a brief description of him – who seemed to have once lived at Hebden. The Vicar sent the wire on to me, as you know, and I was sure who it was; we went off together to identify him, and the Vicar recognised him at once. That is the position of affairs.'

'But,' I said, 'in what way is he connected with these papers, or whatever they are?'

'Do you remember,' said Bendyshe, 'that the Vicar said something about a despatch-box that was missing after Faulkner's death?'

The Vicar turned to me. 'I ought to have been more explicit,' he said. 'For some time before his death, I noticed that Faulkner was always writing when I saw him, and that when I came in, he always slipped the papers into an old despatch-box on the table, and locked them up. I remember once asking him what he was writing. 'My memoirs,' he said with an ugly kind of smile – 'an interesting book, don't you think?' When he died, I am nearly certain that the box was by his bedside, though I could not swear to it; and we thought – the lawyer who came down to see about the property and I – that there might be papers of importance in it; but when we questioned the sergeant, who knew the box perfectly well, he stuck to it that he hadn't seen the box for the day or two preceding Faulkner's death, and that he was quite certain that Faulkner had hidden it some-where – and I couldn't be sure that he was not right.'

'Yes,' said Bendyshe, 'and what I conjecture happened was that the sergeant, thinking that the contents of the box might be valuable, or indeed might incriminate himself in some way, had secured it him-self, meaning later to remove it. That would explain everything – it would explain why Faulkner did not seem to know where it was, and further it would explain what happened to me there last night.'

'What exactly did happen?' I asked.

'I'll tell you,' said Bendyshe, looking up at me, 'just how it was. I had had a ladder brought up here. Whether the fall of the plaster was purely accidental, I don't know, but anyhow it gave me the idea that the papers had been hidden up in the loft. I didn't like to ask you to join me, Hartley, but I did a very rash and idiotic thing. In the afternoon, I took the ladder into the room, and when the house was all quiet, I went in with a lantern and up into the loft. At first all was quiet, and I hunted about everywhere, but found nothing. Then suddenly I became aware that I was not alone, and I saw two figures standing together in the far corner of the loft looking down at the boarded floor. And then I felt no doubt at all that I had got near the hiding-place. I had better have gone away at once, and bided my time; but instead, I was fool enough to go to the place. I don't quite know what happened. They flew at me like two wild beasts. It was not a case of any physical violence – it was just a contest of will and brain; but I had all the terror of being attacked, without the possibility of offering any physical resistance. I simply felt that my mind would give way. I ran down the loft, and tried to get on to the ladder; but I slipped when I was half through the hole, cut my neck, I suppose, on the jagged edges of the broken laths; and you heard my fall!'

'What an appalling business!' I said – and there was a silence for a moment. Then I said, 'But why did the sergeant not remove the box after Faulkner's death?'

'Ah! I can explain that,' said the Vicar. 'He had not the time. We had moved Faulkner's body into another room, and we had some talk with the sergeant, Mr Hartley, and I suppose he was frightened. He had got hold of a certain amount of money, as it was; and I imagine he never dared to come back.'

'There are just two things more,' I said: 'what *are* these papers, after all?'

'Ah! that I don't know,' said Bendyshe; 'but I imagine that they are what Faulkner called his experiments – an account of what he did, or tried to do, and the devices by which he carried them out. The force he used was fear, and the question is, how can you frighten people purely through the agency of the mind? We must remember that Faulkner was a very able man, and that the sergeant was clever enough in his way too – and that they were both men of remarkable courage and force of character.'

'And if we grant that,' I said, 'what do they want to do with the papers?'

'My belief,' said Bendyshe, 'is that they just want to guard them – to preserve them somehow. I don't think they have a very clear idea about them. They don't want them to be made public, and yet they want to hand on their secrets to someone who will use them. If any of us three, for instance, were a man inclined to make use of these evil agencies, we should encounter no opposition; but at present they simply know that we are hostile, that we want to find the papers, and perhaps to put an end to them; and this they mean to prevent as well as they can.'

'What are we going to do?' I said.

'I am afraid that the question rather is,' said Bendyshe, 'what are *they* going to do?'

The words were hardly out of his lips when an answer came – a thin high mocking laugh was heard in the air, in the middle of us. I can't say how inexpressibly horrible it was, to feel in the presence of something hostile and derisive, and yet not to know what it could do or might do. The horror was that it was *there*. The silent auditor knew what we had said and what was in our minds; and we could do nothing. It seemed to me for a moment as if I should lose control of myself, and that my brain would give way under the consciousness of this unseen and intangible presence. I looked at Bendyshe, and he was sitting clasping the arms of his chair, looking down and frowning.

The Vicar rose unsteadily to his feet, his face very pale. 'Merciful God,' he said, 'here have I been fighting with evil all my days, and trying to think it was weaker than good – and now that I am confronted with it, I can do nothing – nothing.'

'No,' said Bendyshe, looking up; 'that isn't so, Vicar! You have a far stronger hold of this business than either Hartley or myself. We are just fighting for ourselves and our sanity, but you have got bigger forces with you. I want to ask you one thing: Hartley and I – or I – must go and find this thing, whatever it is – *and there's no time to be lost*! The longer we put it off, the worse it will be. But will you stay with us, and see the end? Whatever happens, you must not lose faith.'

When Bendyshe spoke of the necessity of our going straight to our goal and without delay, I confess that I had an access of fear more terrible than anything I had ever experienced. The blood seemed to stand still in my brain – my strength seemed to ebb from me; but I felt too that the idea of giving up, of turning tail now, would leave even a worse legacy of terror behind. It was not a question of moral courage – there simply was no way out.

The Vicar said nothing in reply, but he put up his hand – clasped first Bendyshe's and then mine. And the next minute we were out in the hall. Then Bendyshe took command.

9

We had risen, and stood looking at each other in silence.

'Now, don't hurry,' Bendyshe said. 'Try just to think of what we are going to do. I shall want something to prise up the boards with. I know!' He went back to the smoking-room, and returned in a moment with an old ice-axe. Its blade was protected by a leathern cover, and Bendyshe slipped it off. Then he strode to the foot of the stairs and went deliberately up; I followed him, and the Vicar followed me. In a moment we were on the landing. The house was deathly still, with a brooding stillness like that of a thunder-cloud. Bendyshe drew out his key, and produced two electric torches from his pocket, and then said, 'Now, I go first, because I know where the thing is; and when I am up the ladder – in the loft, Hartley – you come up; and, Vicar, will you stay in the room, and lend a hand? And mind this – they can do *nothing* so long as we don't fear them; or if we do, we must behave as if we did not.'

Then he unlocked the door, and we went into the room. Bendyshe clicked on both the electric torches, and gave one to the Vicar. The moon was shining bright, and the shadow of the casements lay dark on the floor.

Then I suddenly became aware of a strange shadow, of an impenetrable blackness, in the corner of the room under the trapdoor. But Bendyshe strode out straight to the foot of the ladder, and seemed to me for a moment engulfed in darkness. I followed close behind; and there was nothing there. 'You see,' said Bendyshe to me in a low tone – 'it will all be like that.'

But as we stood together at the foot of the ladder, a stream of ice-cold air came gushing down from the hole in the ceiling, as if coming out of some frozen cave, so cold that I felt my very bones shivering under their covering of flesh. But Bendyshe slipped his hand through the loop of the axe, and then very slowly and deliberately began to ascend the ladder. 'Come when I call,' he said, 'and not before.' I looked round; the Vicar was on his knees in prayer; but neither that nor Bendyshe's courage gave me any relief. I just thought of the next thing I had to do. Bendyshe disappeared through the hole, and I heard him step out on the floor of the loft. Then he said, 'Now come!' The Vicar held his torch up to illuminate the steps of the ladder, and step by step I went slowly up in the icy air.

As soon as my head and shoulders were in the loft, I felt Bendyshe grasp my arm. 'Steady,' he said, 'step carefully.' Bendyshe raised his torch, which sent a long stream of light down the loft, and then in the silence came a strange tremor and agitation of the empty air. 'Now,' said Bendyshe, 'it will be all over in a moment! Hold on to the top of the ladder, and keep your eye on me.' He walked slowly along the loft, to a place about twenty feet away, looking carefully at the boards and turning the torch down on them. 'Now,' he said, 'come up here slowly and hold the torch for me – this is the place!'

Bendyshe bent his head down, and examined the boards. Then he raised his axe and delivered a tremendous blow at the chink between the boards, and then another. The chips of the broken board flew out on the floor; suddenly from the hole he had made there was protruded a dusky thing. It was the head of a great snake; I could see its dull blinking eyes, the black spots that ran in a chain down its forehead, its flickering tongue, and the greenish pallor of its throat. Bendyshe struck another blow, and the creature came out, reared itself up as though to strike at us, and then as suddenly darted back into the hole again. Bendyshe again raised the axe, and struck fearlessly again. There was now a considerable hole between the boards, and he reversed the axe, inserted the point under the loose board, and putting his foot on the head of the axe brought it down like a lever; the board cracked and split; Bendyshe dropped the axe, and bending down seized the board and tore it up.

A dreadful sight met my eyes. The whole cavity was filled with snakes, entwining, interlocked, writhing; sometimes a head was put up from the mass, and sometimes half a dozen would detach themselves and wriggle over the floor. I must confess that I was now half frantic with horror. But Bendyshe plunged his hands into the mass of snakes, and drew out an old leather despatch-box covered with dust. 'This is it,' he said; and I was bending down to look at it, when a thing more dreadful than any of our previous experiences occurred. The icy air beat upon us, and turning my head, I saw standing behind us, stiff and upright, a corpse, swathed in grave-clothes, with pale leaden-coloured hands hanging down; the face was of the same hue, with a fringe of ragged-looking grey hair straggling over the forehead. It had a faint smile, it seemed, on its lips, and its dull eyes, grey like chalcedony, looked fixedly at the opening in the floor; and then a heavy odour of corruption began to spread around us. And then for a moment I wished that I had died rather than have come into this place of horrors. Bendyshe himself turned, and confronted the gaze of the figure. Then he signed to me to pick up the torch and axe, and walked firmly down the loft to the ladder's head.

'Go down first,' he said, 'and I will lower the box to you – don't leave go of it, whatever happens.' And so I pushed on. It was no time to hesitate. I climbed hastily down the ladder, and on reaching the floor, saw the Vicar standing with his back to me, looking out of the window. But I had no time to attend to anything else, and cried out in a cautious tone, 'Now, the box' – and it appeared from the orifice. I seized hold of it, and a moment later Bendyshe began to descend the ladder. But when he reached me, I saw that his strength was failing. At that moment the Vicar turned round, and came up to me with outstretched hands as if to receive the box. I was about to hand it to him, when Bendyshe cried out in an unsteady voice, 'No, no – keep hold of it, I say – don't you see?'

And then I hardly knew for a moment what happened. Something seemed to rush towards me in a passion half of rage, half of entreaty. I was fighting with shadows. The figure that I had thought to be the Vicar came nearer and looked me in the face – and it was Faulkner himself, in a fury of baffled rage and despair, such as a human mind can hardly conceive; and while I gazed fascinated, I heard Bendyshe come close beside me; and the Vicar himself came forward out of the dark corner of the room, and after that I knew no more.

I awoke not long after from a kind of stupor. I was conscious of having been led and propelled down the corridor. I was in my bedroom, lying on my bed, and the Vicar was sitting beside me with a very anxious face. 'How do you feel?' he said in a gentle voice.

'Oh,' I said, 'I'm all right – in mind, that is; I feel very tired and battered, but not damaged, at least not irretrievably. What I most want is sleep, I think. I suppose I fainted?'

'Yes,' said the Vicar, 'and I was afraid it was worse; but don't let us talk about that now.'

'Where is Bendyshe?' I said.

'Oh, he is all right,' said the Vicar; 'he has just gone to get something for you. He will be here in a moment. He is very anxious, and so am I, that we should settle at once, without any delay, about these papers, whatever they are. But he and I disagree; and if you feel up to it, he would like to have your opinion.'

'I don't know that my opinion is worth much just now,' I said.

But at that moment Bendyshe entered the room with a little cut-glass flask in his hand. He showed few traces of an ordeal – indeed he looked more self-possessed and determined than ever. He carried the box with him, I noticed. He came to my bedside and took my hand. 'Well, old man,' he said, 'this is a good sight! I was afraid . . . well, I won't say what I feared, but I felt that if things had gone wrong, I should never have forgiven myself for bringing you in. How are you feeling – only a faint, you think? Well, I am sure of it – heart, not brain, gave way.' He poured something out of the flask, a clear aromatic liquid, and asked me to drink it off. 'It is quite harmless,' he said. 'It will give you an extreme lucidity of mind for about half an hour, and then the best sleep you have ever had in your life.'

I drank it, and the other two sat in silence. A few minutes later I sat up and said, 'It is very strange – I could not have believed I could have felt like this. I can remember and see quite clearly all that happened yesterday – was it yesterday? But there's no horror about it. I feel extraordinarily happy – something poisonous seems to have cleared away, and I don't think it will come back.'

'Yes,' said Bendyshe, 'I think we have cleared the air somewhat – blown up the wasps' nest, perhaps! But now – do you feel fit to hear two sides of a question? These horrible papers – what is to be done with them? My own view is that I should go through them carefully. They may have immense evidential value. Here is the packet.' He opened the despatch-box – I noticed that he had forced the lid – and took out a small packet of papers, not more than a hundred sheets, I guessed, carefully tied up with black ribbon, and sealed with two large seals. He put the packet in my hands. On the first page was written in a bold handwriting,

A record of experiments made at Hebden Manor-house between the years 1890 and 1903, with the results obtained by Hugh Faulkner and Harry M'Gee. It is earnestly desired that anyone into whose hands they may come will have them examined by someone of scientific eminence, as they deal with the surprising development of a comparatively unknown psychical force, the results of which have been of an extraordinary character.'

It was signed 'HUGH FAULKNER'.

'Mind,' said Bendyshe, 'I will take the entire and sole responsibility for examining the packet; and I will add that if I had been able to find the packet unaided – as I think I should have done – I should have gone through the whole thing with the utmost care.'

'Bendyshe,' said the Vicar, very gravely – and I saw that he was in a state of great depression and exhaustion – 'I implore you not to speak like this! If you had attempted to take possession of the packet single-handed, it would have cost you your reason, and perhaps your life. It may be that you would have lost something even more precious than life. And I must say something more, painful though it may be. You are not as strong as you think! You are in greater danger at the moment than you were in either of your two visits to that unholy place up there. My feeling is that the papers should be instantly destroyed. I regard them as I would regard a case which I knew to contain the living germs of all the deadliest diseases known to humanity. For you to read them would be deliberately to introduce into your own spirit the most satanical of all infections.'

Bendyshe listened to the Vicar's words with a look of ill-concealed impatience, and then turning to me, he said, 'Now, Hartley, it is for you to decide. The quest was mine, and it was the Vicar's duty to help me; but you are the volunteer, who might have been a martyr, who made the search successful. I leave it in your hands.'

'Bendyshe,' I said, 'you have given me a dreadful task. I see what you feel about it, but I have no sort of doubt that the Vicar is right. We have torn the evil out by the roots, with terrible risks, and you would propose to plant it again for the sake of scientific curiosity?'

Bendyshe stood holding the packet in his hands.

'You would destroy knowledge which has been paid for by a man's soul,' he said.

'Yes,' said the Vicar, 'because it is the price of blood – and you dare not traffic with that!'

I looked up; and in a flash I saw, a little way from the group, the figure of Faulkner kneeling, his hands clasped and a look of agonised entreaty on his face. I lost control of myself. 'It must be destroyed at once,' I said, 'now and here!'

'Very well,' said Bendyshe, 'I yield – but I shall regret it all my life!' He said no more, but drew a knife from his pocket, cut the ribbon, drew out a mass of closely-written sheets, stuffed them loosely into the empty hearth, and set fire to the heap. The little pile flared up, and in five minutes was a glowing lump, the writing standing out in lines of fire; and a moment later it was nothing but ashes. And at that moment Bendyshe and the Vicar, who had been gazing at the fire, looked up; and they too saw the figure of Faulkner. But then a strange thing happened, and so swiftly that I can hardly say what it was – a figure in white, young, radiant, smiling, seemed to step up to Faulkner from behind, like a bringer of good tidings.

Bendyshe put his hand before his eyes. The Vicar clasped his hands together. 'The uttermost farthing!' he said in a tone of intense joy, 'and he departs thence – that is the mercy of God.'

The Watcher

R. H. BENSON

On the following day we went out soon after breakfast and walked up and down a grass path between two yew hedges; the dew was not yet off the grass that lay in shadow; and thin patches of gossamer still hung like torn cambric on the yew shoots on either side. As we passed for the second time up the path, the old man suddenly stooped and pushing aside a dock-leaf at the foot of the hedge lifted a dead mouse, and looked at it as it lay stiffly on the palm of his hand, and I saw that his eyes filled slowly with the ready tears of old age.

'He has chosen his own resting-place,' he said. 'Let him lie there. Why did I disturb him?' – and he laid him gently down again; and then gathering a fragment of wet earth he sprinkled it over the mouse. 'Earth to earth, ashes to ashes,' he said, 'in sure and certain hope' – and then he stopped; and straightening himself with difficulty walked on, and I followed him.

'You seemed interested,' he said, 'in my story yesterday. Shall I tell you how I saw a very different sight when I was a little older.' And when I had told him how strange and attractive his story had been, he began.

'I told you how I found it impossible to see again what I had seen in the glade. For a few weeks, perhaps months, I tried now and then to force myself to feel that Presence, or at least to see that robe, but I could not, because it is the gift of God, and can no more be gained by effort than ordinary sight can be won by a sightless man; but I soon ceased to try.

'I reached eighteen years at last, that terrible age when the soul seems to have dwindled to a spark overlaid by a mountain of ashes – when blood and fire and death and loud noises seem the only things of interest, and all tender things shrink back and hide from the dreadful noonday of manhood. Someone gave me one of those shot-pistols that you may have seen, and I loved the sense of power that it gave me, for I had never had a gun. For a week or two in the summer holidays I was content with shooting at a mark, or at the level surface of water, and delighted to see the cardboard shattered, or the quiet pool torn to shreds along its mirror where the sky and green lay sleeping. Then that ceased to interest me, and I longed to see a living thing suddenly stop living at my will. Now,' and he held up a deprecating hand, 'I think sport is necessary for some natures. After all, the killing of creatures is necessary for man's food, and sport as you will tell me is a survival of man's delight in obtaining food, and it requires certain noble qualities of endurance and skill. I know all that, and I know further that for some natures it is a relief – an escape for humours that will otherwise find an evil vent. But I do know this – that for me it was not necessary.

'However, there was every excuse, and I went out in good faith one summer evening intending to shoot some rabbit as he ran to cover from the open field. I walked along the inside of a fence with a wood above me and on my left, and the green meadow on my right. Well, owing probably to my own lack of skill, though I could hear the patter and rush of the rabbits all round me, and could see them in the distance sitting up listening with cocked ears, as I stole along the fence, I could not get close enough to fire at them with any hope of what I fancied was success; and by the time that I had arrived at the end of the wood I was in an impatient mood.

'I stood for a moment or two leaning on the fence looking out of that pleasant coolness into the open meadow beyond; the sun had at that moment dipped behind the hill before me and all was in shadow except where there hung a glory about the topmost leaves of a beech that still caught the sun. The birds were beginning to come in from the fields, and were settling one by one in the wood behind me, staying here and there to sing one last line of melody. I could hear the quiet rush and then the sudden clap of a pigeon's wings as he came home, and as I listened I heard pealing out above all other sounds the long liquid song of a thrush somewhere above me. I looked up idly and tried to see the bird, and after a moment or two caught sight of him as the leaves of the beech parted in the breeze, his head lifted and his whole body vibrating with the joy of life and music. As someone has said, his body was one beating heart. The last radiance of the sun over the hill reached him and bathed him in golden warmth. Then the leaves closed again as the breeze dropped but still his song rang out.

'Then there came on me a blinding desire to kill him. All the other creatures had mocked me and run home. Here at least was a victim, and I would pour out the sullen anger that had been gathering during my walk, and at least demand this one life as a substitute. Side by side with this I remembered clearly that I had come out to kill for food: that was my one justification. Side by side I saw both these things, and I had no excuse – no excuse.

'I turned my head every way and moved a step or two back to catch sight of him again, and, although this may sound fantastic and overwrought, in my whole being was a struggle between light and darkness. Every fibre of my life told me that the thrush had a right to live. Ah! he had earned it, if labour were wanting, by this very song that was guiding death towards him; but black sullen anger had thrown my conscience, and was now struggling to hold it down till the shot had been fired. Still I waited for the breeze, and then it came, cool and sweet-smelling like the breath of a garden, and the leaves parted. There he sang in the sunshine, and in a moment I lifted the pistol and drew the trigger.

'With the crack of the cap came silence overhead, and after what seemed an interminable moment came the soft rush of something falling and the faint thud among last year's leaves. Then I stood half terrified, and stared among the dead leaves. All seemed dim and misty. My eyes were still a little dazzled by the bright background of sunlit air and rosy clouds on which I had looked with such intensity, and the space beneath the branches was a world of shadows. Still I looked a few yards away, trying to make out the body of the thrush, and fearing to hear a struggle of beating wings among the dry leaves.

'And then I lifted my eyes a little, vaguely. A yard or two beyond where the thrush lay was a rhododendron bush. The blossoms had fallen and the outline of dark, heavy leaves was unrelieved by the slightest touch of colour. As I looked at it, I saw a face looking down from the higher branches.

'It was a perfectly hairless head and face, the thin lips were parted in a wide smile of laughter, there were innumerable lines about the corners of the mouth, and the eyes were surrounded by creases of merriment. What was perhaps most terrible about it all was that the eyes were not looking at me, but down among the leaves; the heavy eyelids lay drooping, and the long, narrow, shining slits showed how the eyes laughed beneath them. The forehead sloped quickly back, like a cat's head. The face was the colour of earth, and the outlines of the head faded below the ears and chin into the gloom of the dark bush. There was no throat, or body or limbs so far as I could see. The face just hung there like a down-turned Eastern mask in an old curiosity shop. And it smiled with sheer delight, not at me, but at the thrush's body. There was no change of expression so long as I watched it, just a silent smile of pleasure petrified on the face. I could not move my eyes from it.

'After what I suppose was a minute or so, the face had gone. I did not see it go, but I became aware that I was looking only at leaves.

'No; there was no outline of leaf, or play of shadows that could possibly have taken the form of a face. You can guess how I tried to force myself to believe that that was all; how I turned my head this way and that to catch it again; but there was no hint of a face.

'Now, I cannot tell you how I did it; but although I was half beside myself with fright, I went forward towards the bush and searched furiously among the leaves for the body of the thrush; and at last I found it, and lifted it. It was still limp and warm to the touch. Its breast was a little ruffled, and one tiny drop of blood lay at the root of the beak below the eyes, like a tear of dismay and sorrow at such an unmerited, unexpected death.

'I carried it to the fence and climbed over, and then began to run in great steps, looking now and then awfully at the gathering gloom of the wood behind, where the laughing face had mocked the dead. I think, looking back as I do now, that my chief instinct was that I could not leave the thrush there to be laughed at, and that I must get it out into the clean, airy meadow. When I reached the middle of the meadow I came to a pond which never ran quite dry even in the hottest summer. On the bank I laid the thrush down, and then deliberately but with all my force dashed the pistol into the water; then emptied my pockets of the cartridges and threw them in too.

'Then I turned again to the piteous little body, feeling that at least I had tried to make amends. There was an old rabbit hole near, the grass growing down in its mouth, and a tangle of web and dead leaves behind. I scooped a little space out among the leaves, and then laid the thrush there; gathered a little of the sandy soil and poured it over the body, saying, I remember, half-unconsciously, "Earth to earth, ashes to ashes, in sure and certain hope" – and then I stopped, feeling I had been a little profane, though I do not think so now. And then I went home.

'As I dressed for dinner, looking out over the darkening meadow where the thrush lay, I remember feeling happy that no evil thing could mock the defenceless dead out there in the clean meadow where the wind blew and the stars shone down.'

We reached in our going to and fro up the yew path a little seat at the end standing back from the path. Opposite us hung a crucifix, with a pent-house over it, that the old man had put up years before. As he did not speak I turned to him, and saw that he was looking steadily at the Figure on the Cross; and I thought how He who bore our griefs and carried our sorrows was one with the heavenly Father, without whom not even a sparrow falls to the ground.

The Blood-Eagle

R. H. BENSON

One night when I went to my room I found in a little shelf near the window a book, whose title I now forget, describing the far-off days when the religion of Christ and of the gods of the north strove together in England. I read this for an hour or two before I went to sleep, and again as I was dressing on the following morning, and spoke of it at breakfast.

'Yes,' said the old man, 'that was one of my father's books. I remember reading it when I was a boy. I believe it is said to be very ill-informed and unscientific in these days. My parents used to think that all religions except Christianity were of the devil. But I think St Paul teaches us a larger hope than that.'

He said nothing more at the time; but in the course of the morning, as I was walking up and down the raised terrace that runs under the pines beside the drive, I saw the priest coming towards me with a book in his hand. He was a little dusty and flushed.

'I went to look for something that I thought might interest you, after what you said at breakfast,' he began, 'and I have found it at last in the loft.'

We began to walk together up and down.

'A very curious thing happened to me,' he said, 'when I was a boy. I remember telling my father of it when I came home, and it remained in my mind. A few years afterwards an old professor was staying with us; and after dinner one night, when we had been talking about what you were speaking of at breakfast, my father made me tell it again, and when I had finished the professor asked me to write it down for him. So I wrote it in this book first; and then made a copy and sent it to him. The book itself is a kind of irregular diary in which I used to write sometimes. Would you care to hear it?'

When I had told him I should like to hear the story, he began again.

'I must first tell you the circumstances. I was about sixteen years old. My parents had gone abroad for the holidays, and I went to stay with a school friend of mine at his home not far from Ascot. We used to take our lunch with us sometimes on bright days – for it was at Christmas time – and go off for the day over the heather. You must remember that I was only a schoolboy at the time, so I dare say I exaggerated or elaborated some of the details a little, but the main facts of the story you can rely upon. Shall we sit down while I read it?'

Then, when we had seated ourselves on a bench that stood at the end of the terrace, with the old house basking before us in the hot sunshine, he began to read.

'About six o'clock in the evening of one of the days towards the end of January, Jack and I were still wandering on high, heathy ground near Ascot. We had walked all day and had lost ourselves; but we kept going in as straight a line as we could, knowing that in time we should strike across a road. We were rather tired and silent; but suddenly Jack uttered an exclamation, and then pointed out a light across the heath. We stood a moment to see if it moved, but it remained still.

'"What is it?" I asked. "There can be no house near here."

'"It's a broomsquire's cottage, I expect," said Jack.

'I asked what that meant.

'"Oh! I don't know exactly," said Jack; "they're a kind of gipsies."

'We stumbled on across the heather, while the light grew steadily nearer. The moon was beginning to rise, and it was a clear night, one of those windless, frosty nights that sometimes come after a wet autumn. Jack plunged at one place into a hidden ditch, and I heard the crackling of ice as he scrambled out.

'"Skating tomorrow, by Jove," he said.

'As we got closer I began to see that we were approaching a copse of firs; the heather began to get shorter. Then, as I looked at the light, I saw there was a fixed outline of a kind of house out of which it shone. The window apparently was an irregular shape, and the house seemed to be leaning against a tall fir on the outskirts of the copse. As we got quite close, our feet noiseless on the soft heather, I saw that the house was built altogether round the fir, which served as a kind of central prop. The house was made of wattled boughs, and thatched heavily with heather.

'I felt more and more anxious about it, for I had never heard of "broomsquires", and also, I confess, a little timid; for the place was lonely, and we were only two boys. I was leading now, and presently reached the window and looked in.

'The walls inside were hung with blankets and clothes to keep the wind out; there was a long old settle in one corner, the floor was carpeted with branches and blankets apparently, and there was an opening opposite, partly closed by a wattled hurdle that leaned against it. Half sitting and half lying on the settle, was an old woman with her face hidden. An oil-lamp hung from one of the branches of the fir that helped to form the roof. There was no sign of any other living thing in the place. As I looked Jack came up behind and spoke over my shoulder.

' "Can you tell us the way to the nearest high-road?" he asked.

'The old woman sat up suddenly, with a look of fright on her face. She was extraordinarily dirty and ill-kempt. I could see in the dim light of the lamp that she had a wrinkled old face, with sunken dark eyes, white eyebrows, and white hair; and her mouth began to mumble as she looked at us. Presently she made a violent gesture to wave us from the window.

'Jack repeated the question, and the old woman got up and hobbled quietly and crookedly to the door, and in a moment she had come round close to us. I then saw how very small she was. She could not have been five feet tall, and was very much bent. I must say again that I felt very uneasy and startled with this terrifying old creature close to me and peering up into my face. She took me by the coat and with her other hand beckoned quickly away in every direction. She seemed to be warning us away from the copse, but still she said nothing.

'Jack grew impatient.

' "Deaf old fool!" he said in an undertone, and then loudly and slowly, "Can you tell us the way to the nearest high-road?"

'Then she seemed to understand, and pointed vigorously in the direction from which we had come.

' "Oh! nonsense," said Jack, "we've come from there. Come on this way," he said, "we can't spend all night here." And then he turned the side of the little house and disappeared into the copse.

'The old woman dropped my coat in a moment, and began to run after Jack, and I went round the other side of the house and saw Jack moving in front, for the firs were sparse at the edge of the wood, and the moonlight filtered through them. The old woman, I saw as I turned into the wood, had stopped, knowing she could not catch us, and was standing with her hands stretched out, and a curious sound, half cry and half sob, came from her. I was a little uneasy, because we had not treated her with courtesy, and stopped, but at that moment Jack called.

'"Come on," he said, "we're sure to find a road at the end of this."

'So I went on.

'Once I turned and saw the little old woman standing as before; and as I looked between the trees she lifted one hand to her mouth and sent a curious whistling cry after us, that somehow frightened me. It seemed too loud for one so small.

'As we went on the wood grew darker. Here and there in an open patch there lay a white splash of moonlight on the fir needles, and great dim spaces lay round us. Although the wood stood on high ground, the trees grew so thickly about us that we could see nothing of the country round. Now and then we tripped on a root, or else caught in a bramble, but it seemed to me that we were following a narrow path that led deeper and deeper into the heart of the wood. Suddenly Jack stopped and lifted his hand.

'"Hush!" he said.

'I stopped too, and we listened breathlessly. Then in a moment more – "Hush!" he said, "something's coming," and he jumped out of the path behind a tree, and I followed him.

'Then we heard a scuffling in front of us and a grunting, and some big creature came hurrying down the path. As it passed us I looked, almost terrified out of my mind, and saw that it was a huge pig; but the thing that held me breathless and sick was that there ran nearly the whole length of its back a deep wound, from which the blood dripped. The creature, grunting heavily, tore down the path towards the cottage, and presently the sound of it died away. As I leaned against Jack, I could feel his arm trembling as it held the tree.

'"Oh!" he said in a moment, "we must get out of this. Which way, which way?"

'But I had been still listening, and held him quiet.

'"Wait," I said, "there is something else."

'Out of the wood in front of us there came a panting, and the soft sounds of hobbling steps along the path. We crouched lower and watched. Presently the figure of a bent old man came in sight, making his way quickly along the path. He seemed startled and out of breath. His mouth was moving, and he was talking to himself in a low voice in a complaining tone, but his eyes searched the wood from side to side.

'As he came quite close to us, as we lay hardly daring to breathe, I saw one of his hands that hung in front of him, opening and shutting; and that it was stained with what looked black in the moonlight. He did not see us, as by now we were hidden by a great bramble bush, and he passed on down the path; and then all was silent again.

'When a few minutes had passed in perfect stillness, we got up and went on, but neither of us cared to walk in the path down which those two terrible dripping things had come; and we went stumbling over the broken ground, keeping a parallel course to the path for about another two hundred yards. Jack had begun to recover himself, and even began to talk and laugh at being frightened at a pig and an old man. He told me afterwards that he had not seen the old man's hand.

'Then the path began to lead uphill. At this point I suddenly stopped Jack.

'"Do you see nothing?" I asked.

'Now I scarcely remember what I said or did. But this is what my friend told me afterwards. Jack said there was nothing but a little rising ground in front, from which the trees stood back.

'"Do you see nothing on the top of the mound? Out in the open, where the moonlight falls on her?"

'Jack told me afterwards that he thought I had gone suddenly mad, and grew frightened himself.

'"Do you not see a woman standing there? She has long yellow hair in two braids; she has thick gold bracelets on her bare arms. She has a tunic, bound by a girdle, and it comes below her knees: and she has red jewels in her hair, on her belt, on her bracelets; and her eyes shine in the moonlight: and she is waiting – waiting for that which has escaped."

'Now Jack tells me that when I said this I fell flat on my face, with my hands stretched out, and began to talk: but he said he could not understand a word I said. He himself looked steadily at the rising ground, but there was nothing to be seen there: there were the fir-trees standing in a circle round it, and a bare space in the middle, from which the heather was gone, and that was all. This mound would be about fifteen yards from us.

'I lay there, said Jack, a few minutes, and then sat up and looked about me. Then I remembered for myself that I had seen the pig and the old man, but nothing more: but I was terrified at the remembrance, and insisted upon our striking out a new course through the wood, and leaving the mound to our left. I did not know myself why the mound frightened me, but I dared not go near it. Jack wisely did not say anything more about it until afterwards. We presently found our way out of the copse, struck across the heath for another half-mile or so, and then came across a road which Jack knew, and so we came home.

'When we told our story, and Jack, to my astonishment, had added the part of which I myself had no remembrance, Jack's father did not say very much; but he took us next day to identify the place. To our intense surprise the house of the broomsquire was gone; there were the trampled branches round the tree, and the smoked branch from which the oil lamp had hung, and the ashes of a wood-fire outside the house, but no sign of the old man or his wife. As we went along the path, now in the cheerful frosty sunshine, we found dark splashes here and there on the brambles, but they were dry and colourless. Then we came to the mound.

'I grew uneasy again as we came to it, but was ashamed to show my fear in the broad daylight.

'On the top we found a curious thing, which Jack's father told us was one of the old customs of the broomsquires, that no-one was altogether able to explain. The ground was shovelled away, so as to form a kind of sloping passage downwards into the earth. The passage was not more than five yards long; and at the end of it, just where it was covered by the ground overhead, was a sort of altar, made of earth and stones beaten flat; and plastered into its surface were bits of old china and glass. But what startled us was to find a dark patch of something which had soaked deep into the ground before the altar. It was still damp.'

When the old man had read so far, he laid down the book.

'When I told all this to the Professor,' he said, 'he seemed very deeply interested. He told us, I remember, that the wound on the pig identified the nature of the sacrifice that the old man had begun to offer. He called it a "blood-eagle", and added some details which I will not disgust you with. He said too that the broomsquire had confused two rites – that only human sacrifices should be offered as "blood-eagles". In fact it all seemed perfectly familiar to him: and he said more than I can either remember or verify.'

'And the woman on the rising ground?' I asked.

'Well,' said the old man, smiling, 'the Professor would not listen to my evidence about that. He accepted the early part of the story, and simply declined to pay any attention to the woman. He said I had been reading Norse tales, or was dreaming. He even hinted that I was romancing. Under other circumstances this method of treating evidence would be called "Higher Criticism", I believe.'

'But it's all a brutal and disgusting worship,' I said.

'Yes, yes,' said the old man, 'very brutal and disgusting; but is it not very much higher and better than the Professor's faith ? He was only a skilled Ritualist after all, you see.'

'Consolatrix Afflictorum'

R. H. BENSON

The following letter will explain itself. The original was read to me by my friend on one of those days during my stay with him; and he allowed me, at my request, to make a copy. The sermon referred to in the first sentence of the letter was preached in a foreign watering-place on Christmas Day.

Villa —
December 29, 18—

REVEREND AND DEAR SIR,
I listened with great attention to sermon on Christmas Day; I am getting on in years, and I am an invalid; so you will understand that I have few friends – and I think none who would not think me mad if I told them the story that I am proposing to tell you. For many years I have been silent on this subject, since it always used to be received with incredulity. But I fancy that you will not be incredulous. As I watched you and listened to you on Christmas Day, I thought I saw in you one to whom the supernatural was more than a beautiful and symbolical fairy-story, and one who held it not impossible that this unseen should sometimes manifest itself. As you reminded us, the Religion of the Incarnation rests on the fact that the Infinite and the Eternal expresses Himself in terms of space and time; and that it is in this that the greatness of the Love of God consists. Since then, as you said, the Creation, the Incarnation, and the Sacramental System alike, in various degree, are the manifestation of God under these conditions, surely it cannot be "materialistic" (whatever that exactly means) to believe that the "spiritual" world and the personages that inhabit it sometimes express themselves in the same manner as their Maker. However, will you have patience with me while I tell you this story? I cannot believe that such a grace should kept in darkness.

I was about seven years old when my mother died, and my father left me chiefly to the care of servants. Either I must have been a difficult child, or my nurse must have been a hard woman: but I never gave her my confidence. I had clung to my mother as a saint clings to God: and when I lost her it nearly broke my heart. Night after night I used to lie awake, with the firelight in the room, remembering how she would look in on her way to bed; when at last I slept it seems to me now as if I never did anything but dream of her; and it was only to wake again to that desolate emptiness. I would torture myself by closing my eyes, and fancying she was there; and then opening them and seeing the room empty. I would turn and toss and sob without a sound. I suppose that I was as near the limit that divides sanity from madness as it is possible to be. During the day I would sit on the stairs when I could get away from my nurse, and pretend that my mother's footsteps were moving overhead, that her door opened, that I heard her dress on the carpet: again I would open my eyes, and in self-cruelty compel myself to understand that she was gone. Then again I would tell myself that it was all right: that she was away for the day, but would come back at night. In the evenings I would be happier, as the time for her return drew nearer; even when I said my prayers I would look forward to the moment, into which I had cheated myself in believing, when the door would open, after I was in bed, and my mother look in. Then as the time passed, my false faith would break down, and I would sob myself to sleep, dream of her, and sob myself awake again. As I look back it appears to me as if this went on for months: I suppose, however, in reality, it could not been more than a very few weeks, or my reason would have given way. And at last I was caught on the edge of the precipice, and drawn lovingly back to safety and peace.

I used to sleep alone in the night-nursery at this time, and my nurse occupied a room opening out of it. The night-nursery had two doors, one at the foot of my bed, one at the further end of the room, in the corner diagonally opposite to that in which the head of my bed stood. The first opened upon the landing, and the second my nurse's room, and this latter was generally kept a few inches open. There was no light in my room, but a night-light was kept burning in the nurse's room, so that even without the firelight my room was not in total darkness.

I was lying awake one night (I suppose it would be about eleven o'clock), having gone through a dreadful hour or two of misery, half-waking and half-sleeping. I had been crying quietly, for fear my nurse should hear through the partly opened door, burying my hot face in the pillow. I was feeling really exhausted, listening to my own heart, and cheating myself into the half-faith that its throbs were the footsteps of my mother coming towards my room; I had raised my face and was staring at the door at the foot of my bed, when it opened suddenly without a sound; and there, as I thought, my mother stood, with the light from the oil-lamp outside shining upon her. She was dressed, it seemed, as once before I had seen her in London, when she came into my room to bid me good-night before she went out to an evening party. Her head shone with jewels that flashed as the firelight rose and sank in the room, a dark cloak shrouded her neck and shoulders, one hand held the edge of the door, and a great jewel gleamed on one of her fingers. She seemed to be looking at me.

I sat up in bed in a moment, amazed but not frightened, for was it not what I had so often fancied? and I called out to her: 'Mother, mother!'

At the word she turned and looked on to the landing, and gave a slight movement with her head, as if to someone waiting there, either of assent or dismissal, and then turned to me again. The door closed silently, and I could see in the firelight, and in the faint glimmer that came through the other door, that she held out her arms to me. I threw off the bedclothes in a moment, and scrambled down to the end of the bed, and she lifted me gently in her arms, but said no word. I, too, said nothing, but she raised the cloak a little and wrapped it round me, and I lay there in bliss, my head on her shoulder, and my arm round her neck. She walked smoothly and noiselessly to a rocking chair that stood beside the fire and sat down, and then began to rock gently to and fro. Now it may be difficult to believe, but I tell you that I neither said anything, nor desired to say anything. It was enough that she was there. After a little while I suppose I fell asleep, for I found myself in an agony of tears and trembling again, but those arms held me firmly, and I was soon at peace; still she spoke no word, and I did not see her face.

When I woke again she was gone, and it was morning, and I was in bed, and the nurse was drawing up the blind, and the winter sunshine lay on the wall. That day was the happiest I had known since my mother's death; for I knew she would come again.

After I was in bed that evening I lay awake waiting, so full of happy content and certainty that I fell asleep. When I awoke the fire was out, and there was no light but a narrow streak that came through the door from my nurse's room. I lay there a minute or two waiting, expecting every moment to see the door open at the foot of my bed; but the minutes passed, and then the clock in the hall below beat three. Then I fell into a passion of tears; the night was nearly gone, and she had not come to me. Then, as I tossed to and fro, trying to stifle my crying, through my tears there came the misty flash of light as the door opened, and there she stood again. Once again I was in her arms, and my face on her shoulder. And again I fell asleep there.

Now this went on night after night, but not every night, and never unless I awoke and cried. It seemed that if I needed her desperately she came, but only then.

But there were two curious incidents that occurred in the order in which I will write them down. The second I understand now, at any rate; the first I have never altogether understood, or rather there are several possible explanations.

One night as I lay in her arms by the fire, a large coal suddenly slipped from the grate and fell with a crash, awaking the nurse in the other room. I suppose she thought something was wrong, for she appeared at the door with a shawl over her shoulders, holding the night-light in one hand and shading it with the other. I was going to speak, when my mother laid her hand across my mouth. The nurse advanced into the room, passed close beside us, apparently without seeing us, went straight to the empty bed, looked down on the tumbled clothes, and then turned away as if satisfied, and went back to her room. The next day I managed to elicit from her, by questioning, the fact that she had been disturbed in the night, and had come into my room, but had seen me sleeping quietly in bed.

The other incident was as follows. One night I was lying half dozing against my mother's breast, my head against her heart, and not, as I usually lay, with my head on her shoulder. As I lay there it seemed to me as if I heard a strange sound like the noise of the sea in a shell, but more melodious. It is difficult to describe it, but it was like the murmuring of a far-off crowd, overlaid with musical pulsations. I nestled closer to her and listened; and then I could distinguish, I thought, innumerable ripples of church bells pealing, as if from another world. Then I listened more intently to the other sound; there were words, but I could not distinguish them. Again and again a voice seemed to rise above the others, but I could hear no intelligible words. The voices cried in every sort of tone – passion, content, despair, monotony. And then as I listened I fell asleep. As I look back now, I have no doubt what voices those were that I heard.

And now comes the end of the story. My health began to improve so remarkably that those about me noticed it. I never gave way, during the day at any rate, to those old piteous imaginings; and at night, when, I suppose, the will partly relaxes its control, whenever my distress reached a certain point, she was there to comfort me.

But her visits grew more and more rare, as I needed her less, and at last ceased. But it is of her last visit, which took place in the spring of the following year, that I wish to speak.

I had slept well all night, but had awakened in the dark just before the dawn from some dream which I forget, but which left my nerves shaken. When in my terror I cried out, again the door opened, and she was there. She stood with the jewels in her hair, and the cloak across her shoulders, and the light from the landing lay partly on her face. I scrambled at once down the bed, and was lifted and carried to the chair, and presently fell asleep. When I awoke the dawn had come, and the birds were stirring and chirping, and a pleasant green light was in the room; and I was still in her arms. It was the first time, except in the instance I have mentioned, that I had awakened except in bed, and it was a great joy to find her there. As I turned a little I saw the cloak which sheltered us both – of deep blue, with an intricate pattern of flowers and leaves and birds among branches. Then I turned still more to see her face, which was so near me, but it was turned away; and even as I moved she rose and carried me towards the bed. Still holding me on her left arm she lifted and smoothed the bedclothes, and then laid me gently in bed, with my head on the pillow. And then for the first time I saw her face plainly.

She bent over me, with one hand on my breast as if to prevent me from rising, and looked straight into my eyes; and it was not my mother.

There was one moment of blinding shock and sorrow, and I gave a great sob, and would have risen in bed, but her hand held me down, and I seized it with both my own, and still looked in her eyes. It was not my mother, and yet was there ever such a mother's face as that? I seemed to be looking into depths of indescribable tenderness and strength, and I leaned on that strength in those moments of misery. I gave another sob or two as I looked, but I was quieter, and at last peace came to me, and I had learnt my lesson.

I did not at the time know who she was, but my little soul dimly saw that my own mother for some reason could not at that time come to me who needed her so sorely, and that another great Mother had taken her place; yet, after the first moment or so, I felt no anger or jealousy, for one who had looked into that kindly face could have no such unworthy thought.

Then I lifted my head a little, I remember, and kissed the hand that I held in my own, reverently and slowly. I do not know why I did it, except that it was the natural thing to do. The hand was strong and white, and delicately fragrant. Then it was withdrawn, and she was standing by the door, and the door was open; and then she was gone, and the door was closed.

I have never seen her since, but I have never needed to see her, for I know who she is; and, please God, I shall see her again; and next time I hope my mother and I will be together; and perhaps it will not be very long; and perhaps she will allow me to kiss her hand again.

Now, my dear Sir, I do not know how all this will appear to you; it may seem to you, though I do not think it will, merely childish. Yet, in a sense, I desire nothing more than that, for our Saviour Himself told us to be like children, and our Saviour too once lay on His Mother's breast. I know that I am getting an old man, and that old men are sometimes very foolish; but it more and more seems to me that experience, as well as His words, tells me the great Kingdom of Heaven has a low and narrow door that only little children can enter, and that we must become little again, and drop all our bundles, if we would go through.

That, dear and Reverend Sir, is my story. And may I ask you to remember me sometimes at the altar and in your prayers? For surely God will ask much from one to whom He has given so much, and as yet I have nothing to show for it; and my time must be nearly at an end, even if His infinite patience is not.

Believe me,

Yours faithfully,

—— ——

Over the Gateway

R. H. BENSON

We were sitting together one morning in the common sitting-room in the centre of the house. There had been a fall during the night, and it was thought that the old man should not sit in the garden until the sun had dried the earth – we sat indoors instead, but with the great door wide open, that looked on to a rectangle of lawn that lay before the house. Once a drive had led to this door through a gate with pedestals and stone balls, that stood exactly opposite, about [fifty] yards away, but the drive had long been grassed over; although even now it showed faintly under two slight ridges in the grass that ran from the gate to the door. Otherwise the lawn was enclosed by a low old brick wall, almost hidden by a wealth of ivy, against which showed in rich masses of colour the heads of purple and yellow irises and tawny wallflowers.

The old man had been silent at breakfast. He had offered the Holy Sacrifice as usual that morning in the little chapel upstairs, and I had noticed at the time even that he seemed preoccupied: and at breakfast he had talked very little, letting every subject drop as I suggested it; and I had understood at last that his thoughts were far away in the past, and I did not wish to trouble him.

We were sitting in two tall carved chairs at the doorway, his feet were wrapped in a rug, and his eyes were looking steadily and mournfully out across towards the ironwork gate in the wall. Tall grasses of the patch of uncut meadow outside leaned against it or pushed their feathery heads through it; and I saw presently that the priest was looking at the gate, letting his eyes rove over every detail of climbing plant, ironwork and the old brickwork – and not, as I had at first thought, merely gazing into the dim distances of the years behind him.

Suddenly he broke the long silence.

'Did I ever tell you,' he asked, 'about what I saw out there in the garden? It looks ordinary enough now: yet I saw there what I suppose

I shall never see again on this side of death, or at least not until I am in the very gate of death itself.'

I too looked out at the gate. The atmosphere was full of that 'clear shining after rain' of which King David sang – it was air made visible and radiant by the union [of fire] and water, those two most joyous creatures of God. A great chestnut tree blotted out all beyond the gate.

'Tell me if you can,' I said. 'You [know] how I love to hear those stories.'

'Years ago, as perhaps you know, not long after my ordination I was working in London. My father lived here then, as his father before him. That coat of arms in the centre of that iron gate was put up by him soon after he succeeded to the property. I used to come down here now and then for a breath of country air. I hardly remember any pleasure so keen as the pleasure of coming into this glorious country air out of the smoke and noise of London – or of lying awake at night with the rustle of the pines outside my window instead of the ceaseless human tumult of the town.

'Well, I came down here once, suddenly, on a summer evening, bearing heavy news. I need not go into details; it would be useless to do that – but it will be enough to say that the news did not personally affect me or my family. It was a curious series of circumstances that led me to be the bearer of such news at all – but it was to a lady who happened by the merest chance to be staying with my family. I scarcely knew her at all – in fact I had only seen her once before. The news had come to my ears in London, and I had heard that the one whom it most concerned did not know it – that they dared not write or telegraph. I volunteered, of course, to take the news

'It was with a very heavy heart that I walked up from the station – the road seemed intolerably short. I may say that I knew that the news would be heartbreaking to her who had to hear it. I came in by gate at the end of the avenue' (he waved his hand round to the right) 'and passed right down to the back of the house behind us. This door at which we are sitting had been the front door, but the drive had just been turfed over, and we used the door at the back instead, and this lawn here was very much as you see it now, only the drive still showed plainly like a long narrow grave across grass.

'As I came in through the door at the back, she was coming out, with a book and a basket-chair to sit in the garden. My heart gave a terrible throb of pain – for I knew that by the time my business was done there would be no thought of a quiet evening in the garden, and that look of serene happiness would be wiped out of her face – and all through what I had to say. For a moment she did not recognise me in the dark entry and stood back as I came in, and then –

'"Why, it is you," she said; "you have come home. I did not know you were expected."

'I breathed a moment steadily to recover myself.

'"I was not expected," I said; and then, after a moment: "May I speak to you?"

'"Speak to me? Why, certainly. In the garden or here?"

'"In here,' I answered, and went past her and pushed open the door into this room.

'She came past me, and stood here by the door still holding the book, with her finger between the leaves.

'Now you are wondering, I expect, why I did not get some other woman to break the news to her. Well, I had debated that ever since I had volunteered to be the bearer of these tidings: and partly because I was afraid of being cowardly – call it pride if you will – and partly for other reasons which I need not mention, I felt I was bound to fulfil my promise literally. It might be, I thought, too, that she would prefer the news to be known by as few people as possible. At least, whether I judged rightly or wrongly, here was my task before me.

'She stood there,' the old man went on, pointing to the doorpost on the right, 'and I here,' and he pointed a yard further back, 'and the door was wide open as it is now, and the fragrant evening air poured past us into the room. Her face would be partly in shadow; but in her eyes there was just a dawning wonder at my abruptness, with perhaps the faintest tinge of anxiety, but no more.

'"I have come," I said slowly, looking out into the garden, "on a very hard errand." I could not go on. I turned and looked at her. Ah! the anxiety had deepened a little. "And – and it concerns you and your happiness." I looked again, and I remember how her face had changed. Her lips were a little open, and her eyes shone wide open, half in shadow and half in light, and there were new and terrible little lines on her forehead. And then I told her.

'It was done in a sentence or two, and when I looked again her lips had closed and her hand had clenched itself into the moulding of the doorpost. I can see her rings now blazing in the light that poured over the chestnut tree (it was lower then) into the room. Then her lips moved once or twice – her hand unclenched itself hesitatingly – and she went steadily across the room. There was a great sofa there then, and when she reached it she threw herself face downwards across the arm and back.

And I waited at the doorway, looking out at the iron gate. Sorrow was new to me then. I had not learnt to understand it then, or to be quiet under it. And as I looked I knew only that there was a terrible struggle going on in the room behind. There in front of me was a garden full of peace and sweetness and the soft glow of sunset light; and there behind me was something very like hell – and I stood between the living and the dead.

'Then I remembered that I was a priest, and ought to be able to say something – just a word of the Divine message that the Saviour brought – but I could not. I felt I was in deep waters. Even God seemed far away, intolerably serene and aloof; and I longed with all my power for a human person to pray and to bear a little of that strife behind me, from which I felt separated by so wide a gulf. And then God gave me the clear vision again.

'You see the iron gate,' the old man went on, pointing. 'Well, right between those posts, but a little above them, outlined clearly against the chestnut tree, beyond, was the figure of a man.

'Now I do not know how to explain myself, but I was conscious that across this material world of light and colour there cut a plane of the spiritual world, and that where the planes crossed I could look through and see what was beyond. It was like smoke cutting across a sunbeam. Each made the other visible.

'Well, this figure of a man, then, was kneeling in the air, that is the only way I can describe it – his face was turned towards me, but upwards. Now the most curious thing that struck me at the time was that he was, as it were, leaning at a sharp angle to one side; but it did not appear to be grotesque. Instead the world seemed tilted; the chestnut tree was out of the perpendicular, the wall out of the horizontal. The true level was that of the man.

'I know this sounds foolish, but it showed me how the world of spirits was the real world, and the world of sense comparatively unreal, just as the sorrow of the woman behind me was more real than the beams overhead.

'And again, compared with the kneeling figure, the chestnut tree and the gate seemed unsubstantial and shadowy. I know that men who see visions tell us that it is usually the other way. All I can say is that it was not so with me. This figure was kneeling, as I have said; his robe streamed away behind him – a great cloak – drawn tightly back from the shoulders, as if he were battling with a strong wind –

the Wind of Grace, I suppose, that always blows from the throne. His arms were stretched out in front of him, but opened sufficiently to let me see his face; and his face will be with me till I die, and please God afterwards. It was beardless, and bore the unmistakable character of a priest's face.

'Now you know how close the intensest pain and the intensest joy lie together. Their lines so nearly meet. In this man's face they did meet. Anguish and ecstasy were one. His eyes were open, his lips parted. I could not tell whether he was old or young. His face was ageless, as the faces of all are who look upon Him who inhabits eternity. He was praying. I can say no more than that. He had opened his heart to this woman's sorrow. He had made it his own: and it met there, in petition if you wish to call it so, or in resignation if you prefer that name for it, or in adoration – you may call it what you will – all that is true, but each is inadequate – but that sorrow met there with his own purified will, which itself had become one with the eternal will of God. I tell you I know it.

'I looked at him, and in my ears was a sobbing from the room behind; but as I looked the glory of anguish deepened on his face and the sobbing behind me slackened and ceased, and I heard a whispering and the name of God and of His Son, and then the sight before me had passed; and there stood the chestnut tree again as real and as beautiful as before; and when I turned the woman was standing up, and the light of conquest was in her eyes.

She held out her hand to me, and I stooped and kissed it, but I dared not take it in my own, for she had been in heavenly places. I had seen her sorrow carried and laid before the throne of God by one greater than either of us, and something of his glory rested upon her.'

The old man's voice ceased. When I turned to look at him he was looking steadily again at the iron gate in the wall, and his eyes were shining like the radiant air outside. 'I do not know,' he said in a moment, 'whether she is alive or dead, but I offered Holy Sacrifice this morning for her peace in either state.'

Father Meuron's Tale

R. H. BENSON

Father Meuron was very voluble at supper on the Saturday. He exclaimed; he threw out his hands; his bright black eyes shone above his rosy cheeks, and his hair appeared to stand more on end than I had ever known it.

He sat at the further side of the horseshoe table from myself, and I was able to remark on his gaiety to the English priest who sat beside me, without fear of being overheard.

Father Brent smiled.

'He is drunk with *la gloire*,' he said. 'He is to tell the story tonight.'

This explained everything.

I did not look forward, however, to his recital. I was confident that it would be full of tinsel and swooning maidens who ended their days in convents under Father Meuron's spiritual direction; and when we came upstairs I found a shadowy corner, a little back from the semi-circle, where I could fall asleep if I wished without provoking remark.

In fact, I was totally unprepared for the character of his narrative. When we had all taken our places, and Monsignor's pipe was properly alight, and himself at full length in his deck chair, the Frenchman began. He told his story in his own language; but I am venturing to render it in English as nearly as I am able.

'My contribution to the histories,' he began, seated in his upright armchair in the centre of the circle, a little turned away from me – 'my contribution to the histories which these good priests are to recite is an affair of exorcism. That is a matter with which we who live in Europe are not familiar in these days. It would seem, I suppose, that grace has a certain power, accumulating through the centuries, of saturating even physical objects with its force. However men may rebel, yet the sacrifices offered and the prayers poured out have a faculty of holding Satan in check and preventing his more formidable manifestations. Even in my own poor country at this hour, in spite of widespread apostasy, in spite even of the deliberate worship of Satan, yet grace is in the air; and it is seldom indeed that a priest has to deal with a case of possession. In your respectable England, too, it is the same; the simple piety of Protestants has kept alive to some extent the force of the Gospel. Here in this country of Italy it is somewhat different. The old powers have survived the Christian assault, and while they cannot live in Holy Rome, there are corners where they do so.'

From my place I saw Padre Bianchi turn a furtive eye upon the speaker, and I thought I read in it an unwilling assent.

'However,' went on the Frenchman with a superb dismissory gesture, 'my recital does not concern this continent, but the little island of La Souffrière. There circumstances are other than here. It was a stronghold of darkness when I was there in 1891. Grace, while laying hold of men's hearts, had not yet penetrated the lower creation. Do you understand me? There were many holy persons whom I knew, who frequented the Sacraments and lived devoutly, but there were many of another manner. The ancient rites survived secretly among the negroes, and darkness – how shall I say it? – dimness made itself visible.

'However, to our history.'

The priest resettled himself in his chair and laid his fingers together like precious instruments. He was enjoying himself vastly, and I could see that he was preparing himself for a revelation.

'It was in 1891,' he repeated, 'that I went there with another of our Fathers to the mission-house. I will not trouble you, gentlemen, with recounting the tale of our arrival, nor of the months that followed it, except perhaps to tell you that I was astonished by much that I saw. Never until that time had I seen the power of the Sacraments so evident. In civilised lands, as I have suggested to you, the air is charged with grace. Each is no more than a wave in the deep sea. He who is without God's favour is not without His grace at each breath he draws. There are churches, religions, pious persons about him; there are centuries of prayers behind him. The very buildings he enters, as M. Huysmans has explained to us, are browned by prayer. Though a wicked child, he is yet in his father's house: and the return from death to life is not such a crossing of the abyss, after all. But there in La Souffrière all is either divine or Satanic, black or white, Christian or devilish. One stands, as it were, on the seashore to watch the breakers of grace, and each is a miracle. I tell you I have seen holy catechumens foam at the mouth and roll their eyes in pain, as the saving water fell on them, and that which was within went out. As the Gospel relates, "*Spiritus conturbavit illum: et elisus in terram, volutabatur spumans.*"

Father Meuron paused again.

I was interested to hear this corroboration of evidence that had come before me on other occasions. More than one missionary had told me the same thing; and I had found in their tales a parallel to those related by the first preachers of the Christian religion in the early days of the Church.

'I was incredulous at first,' continued the priest, 'until I saw these things for myself. An old father of our mission rebuked me for it. "You are an ignorant fellow," he said; "your airs are still of the seminary." And what he said was just, my friends.

'On one Monday morning as we met for our council I could see that this old priest had somewhat to say. M. Lasserre was his name. He kept very silent until the little businesses had been accomplished, and then he turned to the Father Rector.

'"Monseigneur has written," he said, "and given me the necessary permission for the matter you know, my father. And he bids me take another priest with me. I ask that Father Meuron may accompany me. He needs a lesson, this zealous young missionary."

'The Father Rector smiled at me as I sat astonished, and nodded at Father Lasserre to give permission.

'"Father Lasserre will explain all to you," he said as he stood up for the prayer.

'The good priest explained all to me as the Father Rector had directed.'

It appeared that there was a matter of exorcism on hand. A woman who lived with her mother and husband had been affected by the devil, Father Lasserre said. She was a catechumen, and had been devout for several months, and all seemed well until this – this assault had been made on her soul. Father Lasserre had visited the woman and examined her, and had made his report to the Bishop, asking permission to exorcise the creature, and it was this permission that had been sent on that morning.

'I did not venture to tell the priest that he was mistaken and that the affair was one of epilepsy. I had studied a little in books for my medical training, and all that I heard now seemed to confirm me in the diagnosis. There were the symptoms, easy to read. What would you have?' – the priest again made his little gesture – 'I knew more in my youth than all the Fathers of the Church. Their affairs of devils were nothing but an affection of the brain – dreams and fancies! And if the exorcisms had appeared to be of direct service, it was from the effect of the solemnity upon the mind. It was no more.'

He laughed with a fierce irony.

'You know it all, gentlemen!'

I had lost all desire to sleep now. The French priest was more interesting than I had thought. His elaborateness seemed dissipated; his voice trembled a little as he arraigned his own conceit, and I began to wonder how his change of mind had been wrought.

'We set out that afternoon,' he continued. 'The woman lived on the further side of the island, perhaps a couple of hours' travel, for it was rough going; and as we went up over the path Father Lasserre told me more.

'It seemed that the woman blasphemed. (The subconscious self, said I to myself, as M. Charcot has explained. It is her old habit reasserting itself.)

'She foamed and rolled her eyes. (An affection of the brain, said I.)

'She feared holy water; they dared not throw it on her, her struggles were so fierce. (Because she has been taught to fear it, said I.)

'And so the good father talked, eyeing me now and again, and I smiled in my heart, knowing that he was a simple old fellow who had not studied the new books.

'She was quieter after sunset, he told me, and would take a little food then. Her fits came on her for the most part at midday. And I smiled again at that. Why it should be so I knew. The heat affected her. She would be quieter, science would tell us, when evening fell. If it were the power of Satan that held her she would surely rage more in the darkness than in the light. The Scriptures tell us so.

'I said something of this to Father Lasserre, as if it were a question, and he looked at me.

'"Perhaps, brother," he said, "she is more at ease in the darkness and fears the light, and that she is quieter therefore when the sun sets."

'Again I smiled to myself. "What piety," said I, "and what foolishness!"

'The house where the three lived stood apart from any others. It was an old shed into which they had moved a week before, for the neighbours could no longer bear the woman's screaming. And we came to it towards a sunset.

'It was a heavy evening, dull and thick, and as we pushed down the path I saw the smoking mountain high on the left hand between the tangled trees. There was a great silence round us, and no wind, and every leaf against the rosy sky was as if cut of steel.

'We saw the roof below us presently, and a little smoke escaped from a hole, for there was no chimney.

'"We will sit here a little, brother," said my friend. "We will not enter till sunset."

'And he took out his office book and began to say his Matins and Lauds, sitting on a fallen tree-trunk by the side of the path.

'All was very silent about us. I suffered terrible distractions, for I was a young man and excited; and though I knew it was no more than epilepsy that I was to see, yet epilepsy is not a good sight to regard. But I was finishing the first Nocturn when I saw that Father Lasserre was looking off his book.

'We were sitting thirty yards from the roof of the hut, which was built in a scoop of the ground, so that the roof was level with the ground on which we sat. Below it was a little open space, flat, perhaps twenty yards across, and below that yet further was the wood again, and far over that was the smoke of the village against the sea. There was the mouth of a well with a bucket beside it; and by this was standing a man, a negro, very upright, with a vessel in his hand.

'This fellow turned as I looked, and saw us there, and he dropped the vessel, and I could see his white teeth. Father Lasserre stood up and laid his finger on his lips, nodded once or twice, pointed to the west, where the sun was just above the horizon, and the fellow nodded to us again and stooped for his vessel.

'He filled it from the bucket and went back into the house.

'I looked at Father Lasserre and he looked at me.

'"In five minutes," he said; "that is the husband. Did you not see his wounds?"

'I had seen no more than his teeth, I said, and my friend nodded again and proceeded to finish his Nocturn.'

Again Father Meuron paused dramatically. His ruddy face seemed a little pale in the candle-light, and yet he had told us nothing yet that could account for his apparent horror. Plainly, something was coming soon.

The Rector leaned back to me and whispered behind his hand in reference to what the Frenchman had related a few minutes before, that no priest was allowed to use exorcism without the special leave of the Bishop. I nodded and thanked him.

Father Meuron flashed his eyes dreadfully round the circle, clasped his hands and continued: 'When the sun showed only a red rim above the sea we went down to the house. The path ran on high ground to the roof and then dipped down the edge of the cutting past the window to the front of the shed.

'I looked through this window sideways as I went after Father Lasserre, who was carrying his bag with the book and the holy water, but I could see nothing but the light of the fire. And there was no sound. That was terrible to me!

'The door was closed as we came to it, and as Father Lasserre lifted his hand to knock there was a howl of a beast from within.

'He knocked and looked at me.

' "It is but epilepsy!" he said, and his lips wrinkled as he said it.'

The priest stopped again, and smiled ironically at us all. Then he clasped his hands beneath his chin like a man in terror.

'I will not tell you all that I saw,' he went on, 'when the candle was lighted and set on the table, but only a little. You would not dream well, my friends – as I did not that night.

'But the woman sat in a corner by the fireplace, bound with cords by her arms to the back of the chair and her feet to the legs of it.

'Gentlemen, she was like no woman at all ... The howl of a wolf came from her lips, but there were words in the howl. At first I could not understand till she began in French, and then I understood. My God!

'The foam dripped from her mouth like water, and her eyes – but there! I began to shake when I saw them until the holy water was spilled on the floor, and I set it down on the table by the candle. There was a plate of meat on the table, roasted mutton, I think, and a loaf of bread beside it. Remember that, gentlemen – that mutton and bread! And as I stood there I told myself, like making acts of faith, that it was but epilepsy, or at the most madness.

'My friends, it is probable that few of you know the form of exorcism. It is neither in the Ritual or the Pontifical, and I cannot remember it all myself. But it began thus.'

The Frenchman sprang up and stood with his back to the fire, with his face in the shadow.

'Father Lasserre was here where I stand, in his cotta and stole, and I beside him. There where my chair stands was the square table, as near as that, with the bread and meat and the holy water and the candle. Beyond the table was the woman; her husband stood beside her on the left hand, and the old mother was there' – he flung out a hand to the right, 'on the floor telling her beads and weeping – but weeping.

'When the Father was ready and had said a word to the others, he signed to me to lift the holy water again – she was quiet at the moment – and then he sprinkled her.

'As he lifted his hand she raised her eyes, and there was a look in them of terror, as if at a blow, and as the drops fell she leaped forward in the chair, and the chair leaped with her. Her husband was at her [side,] and dragged the chair back. But my God! it was terrible to see him; his teeth shone as if he smiled, but the tears ran down his face.

'Then she moaned like a child in pain. It was as if the holy water burned her; she lifted her face to her man as if she begged him to wipe off the drops.

'And all the while I still told myself that it was the terror of her mind only at the holy water – that it could not be that she was possessed by Satan – it was but madness – madness and epilepsy!

'Father Lasserre went on with the prayers, and I said Amen, and there was a psalm – *Deus in nomine tuo salvum me fac* – and then came the first bidding to the unclean spirit to go out, in the name of the Mysteries of the Incarnation and Passion.

'Gentlemen, I swear to you that something happened then, but I do not know what. A confusion fell on me and a kind of darkness. I saw nothing – it was as if I were dead.'

The priest lifted a shaking hand to wipe off the sweat from his forehead. There was a profound silence in the room. I looked once at Monsignor, and he was holding his pipe an inch off his mouth, and his lips were slack and open as he stared.

'Then when I knew where I was, Father Lasserre was reading out of the Gospels; how Our Lord gave authority to his Church to cast out unclean spirits, and all this while his voice never trembled.'

'And the woman?' said a voice hoarsely from Father Brent's chair. 'Ah! the woman! My God! I do not know. I did not look at her. I stared at the plate on the table; but at least she was not crying out now.

'When the Scripture was finished Father Lasserre gave me the book.

' "Bah, Father!" he said; "it is but epilepsy, is it not?"

'Then he beckoned me, and I went with him, holding the book till we were within a yard of the woman. But I could not hold the book still, it shook, it shook – '

Father Meuron thrust out his hand. 'It shook like that, gentlemen. He took the book from me, sharply and angrily. "Go back, sir," he said, and he thrust the book into the husband's hand.

' "There," he said.

'I went back behind the table and leaned on it.

'Then Father Lasserre – my God! the courage of this man! – he set his hands on the woman's head. She writhed up her teeth to bite, but he was too strong for her, and then he cried out from the book the second bidding to the unclean spirit.

' "*Ecce crucem Domini!* Behold the Cross of the Lord! Flee ye adverse hosts! The lion of the tribe of Judah hath prevailed!"

'Gentlemen' – the Frenchman flung out his hands – 'I who stand here tell you that something happened. God knows what. I only know this, that as the woman cried out and scrambled with her feet on the floor, the flame of the candle became smoke-coloured for one instant. I told myself it was the dust of her struggling and her foul breath . . . Yes, gentlemen, as you tell yourselves now . . . Bah! it is but epilepsy, is it not so, sir?'

The old Rector leaned forward with a deprecating hand, but the Frenchman glared and gesticulated; there was a murmur from the room, and the old priest leaned back again and propped his head on his hand.

'Then there was a prayer. I heard *Oremus*, but I did not dare to look at the woman. I fixed my eyes so on the bread and meat; it was the one clean thing in that terrible room. I whispered to myself, "Bread and mutton, bread and mutton". I thought of the refectory at home – anything. You understand me, gentlemen – anything familiar to quiet myself.

'Then there was the third exorcism . . . '

I saw the Frenchman's hands rise and fall, clenched, and his teeth close on his lip to stay its trembling. He swallowed in his throat once or twice. Then he went on in a very low, hissing voice.

'Gentlemen, I swear to you by God Almighty that this was what I saw. I kept my eyes on the bread and meat. It lay there beneath my eyes, and yet I saw, too, the good Father Lasserre lean forward to the woman again, and heard him begin, "*Exorcizo te . . .* "

'And then this happened – this happened . . .

'The bread and the meat corrupted themselves to worms before my eyes . . . '

Father Meuron dashed forward, turned round and dropped into his chair as the two English priests on either side sprang to their feet.

In a few minutes he was able to tell us that all had ended well; that the woman had been presently found in her right mind, after an incident or two that I will take leave to omit; and that the apparent paroxysm of nature that had accompanied the words of the third exorcism had passed away as suddenly as it had come.

Then we went to night-prayers and fortified ourselves against the dark.

Father Macclesfield's Tale

R. H. BENSON

Monsignor Maxwell announced next day at dinner that he had already arranged for the evening's entertainment. A priest, whose acquaintance he had made on the Palatine, was leaving for England the next morning; and it was our only chance therefore of hearing his story. That he had a story had come to the Canon's knowledge in the course of a conversation on the previous afternoon.

'He told me the outline of it,' he said. 'I think it very remarkable. But I had a great deal of difficulty in persuading him to repeat it to the company this evening. But he promised at last. I trust, gentlemen, you do not think I have presumed in begging him to do so.'

Father Macclesfield arrived at supper.

He was a little unimposing dry man, with a hooked nose and grey hair. He was rather silent at supper; but there was no trace of shyness in his manner as he took his seat upstairs, and without glancing round once, began in an even and dispassionate voice: 'I once knew a Catholic girl that married an old Protestant three times her own age. I entreated her not to do so; but it was useless. And when the disillusionment came she used to write to me piteous letters, telling me that her husband had in reality no religion at all. He was a convinced infidel, and scouted even the idea of the soul's immortality.

'After two years of married life the old man died. He was about sixty years old; but very hale and hearty till the end.

'Well, when he took to his bed, the wife sent for me; and I had half-a-dozen interviews with him; but it was useless. He told me plainly that he wanted to believe – in fact he said that the thought of annihilation was intolerable to him. If he had had a child he would not have hated death so much; if his flesh and blood in any manner survived him, he could have fancied that he had a sort of vicarious life left; but as it was there was no kith or kin of his alive, and he could not bear that.'

'I may say that his deathbed was extremely unpleasant. He was a coarse old fellow, with plenty of strength in him; and he used to make remarks about the churchyard – and – in fact the worms, that used to send his poor child of a wife half fainting out of the room. He had lived an immoral life too, I gathered.

'Just at the last it was – well – disgusting. He had no consideration (God knows why she married him!). The agony was a very long one; he caught at the curtains round the bed, calling out; and all his words were about death, and the dark. It seemed to me that he caught hold of the curtains as if to hold himself into this world. And at the very end he raised himself clean up in bed, and stared horribly out of the window that was open just opposite.

'I must tell you that straight away beneath the window lay a long walk, between sheets of dead leaves with laurels on either side, and the branches meeting overhead, so that it was very dark there even in summer; and at the end of the walk away from the house was the churchyard gate.'

Father Macclesfield paused and blew his nose. Then he went on still without looking at us.

'Well, the old man died; and he was carried along this laurel path, and buried.

'His wife was in such a state that I simply dared not go away. She was frightened to death, and, indeed, the whole affair of her husband's dying was horrible. But she would not leave the house. She had a fancy that it would be cruel to him. She used to go down twice a day to pray at the grave, but she never went along the laurel walk. She would go round by the garden and in at a lower gate, and come back the same way, or by the upper garden.

'This went on for three or four days. The man had died on a Saturday, and was buried on Monday; it was in July; and he had died about eight o'clock.

'I made up my mind to go on the Saturday after the funeral. My curate had managed [to get] along very well for a few days; but I did not like to leave him for a second Sunday.

'Then on the Friday at lunch – her sister had come down, by the way, and was still in the house – on the Friday the widow said something about never daring to sleep in the room where the old man had died. I told her it was nonsense, and so on, but you must remember she was in a dreadful state of nerves, and she persisted. So I said I would sleep in the room myself. I had no patience with such ideas then.

'Of course she said all sorts of things, but I had my way; and my things were moved in on Friday evening.

'I went to my new room about a quarter before eight to put on my cassock for dinner. The room was very much as it had been – rather dark because of the trees at the end of the walk outside. There was the four-poster there with the damask curtains; the table and chairs, the cupboard where his clothes were kept, and so on.

'When I had put my cassock on, I went to the window to look out. To right and left were the gardens, with the sunlight just off them, but still very bright and gay, with the geraniums, and exactly opposite was the laurel walk, like a long green shady tunnel, dividing the upper and lower lawns.

'I could see straight down it to the churchyard gate, which was about a hundred yards away, I suppose. There were limes overhead, and laurels, as I said, on each side.

'Well – I saw someone coming up the walk; but it seemed to me at first that he was drunk. He staggered several times as I watched; I suppose he would be fifty yards away – and once I saw him catch hold of one of the trees and cling against it as if he were afraid of falling. Then he left it, and came on again slowly, going from side to side, with his hands out. He seemed desperately keen to get to the house.

'I could see his dress; and it astonished me that a man dressed so should be drunk; for he was quite plainly a gentleman. He wore a white top hat, and a grey cut-away coat, and grey trousers, and I could make out his white spats.

'Then it struck me he might be ill; and I looked harder than ever, wondering whether I ought to go down.

'When he was about twenty yards away he lifted his face; and it struck me as very odd, but it seemed to me he was extraordinarily like the old man we had buried on Monday; but it was darkish where he was, and the next moment he dropped his face, threw up his hands and fell flat on his back.

'Well, of course, I was startled at that, and I leaned out of the window and called out something. He was moving his hands, I could see, as if he were in convulsions; and I could hear the dry leaves rustling.

'Well, then I turned and ran out and downstairs.'

Father Macclesfield stopped a moment.

'Gentlemen,' he said abruptly, 'when I got there, there was not a sign of the old man. I could see that the leaves had been disturbed, but that was all.'

There was an odd silence in the room as he paused; but before any of us had time to speak he went on.

'Of course I did not say a word of what I had seen. We dined as usual; I smoked for an hour or so by myself after prayers; and then I went up to bed. I cannot say I was perfectly comfortable, for I was not; but neither was I frightened.

'When I got to my room I lit all my candles, and then went to a big cupboard I had noticed, and pulled out some of the drawers. In the bottom of the third drawer I found a grey cut-away coat and grey trousers; I found several pairs of white spats in the top drawer; and white hat on the shelf above. That is the first incident.'

' Did you sleep there, Father?' said a voice softly.

'I did,' said the priest. 'There was no reason why I should not. I did not fall asleep for two or three hours; but I was not disturbed in any way, and came to breakfast as usual.

'Well, I thought about it all a bit; and finally I sent a wire to my curate telling him I was detained. I did not like to leave the house just then.'

Father Macclesfield settled himself again in his chair and went on, in the same dry uninterested voice.

'On Sunday we drove over to the Catholic Church six miles off, and I said Mass. Nothing more happened till the Monday evening.

'That evening I went to the window again about a quarter before eight, as I had done both on the Saturday and Sunday. Everything was perfectly quiet, till I heard the churchyard gate unlatch; and I saw a man come through.

'But I saw almost at once that it was not the same man I had seen before; it looked to me like a keeper, for he had a gun across his arm; then I saw him hold the gate open an instant, and a dog came through and began to trot up the path towards the house with his master following.

'When the dog was about fifty yards away he stopped dead and pointed.

'I saw the keeper throw his gun forward and come up softly; and as he came the dog began to slink backwards. I watched very closely, clean forgetting why I was there; and the next instant something – it was too shadowy under the trees to see exactly what it was – but something about the size of a hare burst out of the laurels and made straight up the path, dodging from side to side, but coming like the wind.

'The beast could not have been more than twenty yards from me when the keeper fired, and the creature went over and over in the dry leaves, and lay struggling and screaming. It was horrible! But what astonished me was that the dog did not come up. I heard the keeper snap out something, and then I saw the dog making off down the avenue in the direction of the churchyard as hard as he could go.

'The keeper was running now towards me; but the screaming of the hare, or of whatever it was, had stopped; and I was astonished to see the man come right up to where the beast was struggling and kicking, and then stop as if he was puzzled.

'I leaned out of the window and called to him. "Right in front of you, man," I said. "For God's sake kill the brute."

'He looked up at me, and then down again. "Where is it, sir?" he said. "I can't see it anywhere."

'And there lay the beast, clear before him all the while, not a yard away, still kicking.

'Well, I went out of the room and downstairs and out to the avenue.

'The man was standing there still, looking terribly puzzled, but the hare was gone. There was not a sign of it. Only the leaves were disturbed, and the wet earth showed beneath.

'The keeper said that it had been a great hare, he could have sworn to it, and that he had orders to kill all hares and rabbits in the garden enclosure. Then he looked rather odd.

'Did you see it plainly, sir?' he asked.

'I told him, not very plainly; but I thought it a hare too.

'Yes, sir,' he said, 'it was a hare, sure enough; but, do you know, sir, I thought it to be a kind of silver-grey with white feet. I never saw one like that before!'

'The odd thing was that not a dog would come near; his own dog was gone, but I fetched the yard dog, a retriever, out of his kennel in the kitchen yard, and if ever I saw a frightened dog it was this one. When we dragged him up at last, all whining and pulling back, he began to snap at us so fiercely that we let go, and he went back like the wind to his kennel. It was the same with the terrier.

'Well, the bell had gone, and I had to go in and explain why I was late; but I didn't say anything about the colour of the hare. That was the second incident.'

Father Macclesfield stopped again, smiling reminiscently to himself. I was very much impressed by his quiet air and composure. I think it helped his story a good deal.

Again, before we had time to comment or question, he went on.

'The third incident was so slight that I should not have mentioned it, or thought anything of it, if it had not been for the others; but it seemed to me there was a kind of diminishing gradation of energy, which explained [it]. Well, now you shall hear.

'On the other nights of that week I was at my window again; but nothing happened till the Friday. I had arranged to go for certain next day; the widow was much better and more reasonable, and even talked of going abroad herself in the following week.

'On that Friday evening I dressed a little earlier, and went down to the avenue this time, instead of staying at my window, at about twenty minutes to eight.

'It was rather a heavy depressing evening, without a breath of wind; and it was darker than it had been for some days.

'I walked slowly down the avenue to the gate and back again; and I suppose it was fancy, but I felt more uncomfortable than I had felt at all up to then. I was rather relieved to see the widow come out of the house and stand looking down the avenue. I came out myself then and went towards her. She started rather when she saw me and then smiled.

' "I thought it was someone else," she said. "Father, I have made up my mind to go. I shall go to town tomorrow, and start on Monday. My sister will come with me."

'I congratulated her; and then we turned and began to walk back to the lime avenue. She stopped at the entrance, and seemed unwilling to come any further.

'Come down to the end,' I said, 'and back again. There will be time before dinner.'

'She said nothing, but came with me; and we went straight down to the gate and then turned to come back.

'I don't think either of us spoke a word; I was very uncomfortable indeed by now; and yet I had to go on.

'We were half-way back, I suppose, when I heard a sound like a gate rattling; and I whisked round in an instant, expecting to see someone at the gate. But there was no-one.

'Then there came a rustling overhead in the leaves; it had been dead still before. Then I don't know why, but I took my friend suddenly by the arm and drew her to one side out of the path, so that we stood on the right hand, not a foot from the laurels.

'She said nothing, and I said nothing; but I think we were both looking this way and that, as if we expected to see something.

'The breeze died, and then sprang up again, but it was only a breath. I could hear the living leaves rustling overhead, and the dead leaves underfoot; and it was blowing gently from the churchyard.

'Then I saw a thing that one often sees; but I could not take my eyes off it, nor could she. It was a little column of leaves, twisting and turning and dropping and picking up again in the wind, coming slowly up the path. It was a capricious sort of draught, for the little scurry of leaves went this way and that, to and fro across the path. It came up to us, and I could feel the breeze on my hands and face. One leaf struck me softly on the cheek, and I can only say that I shuddered as if it had been a toad. Then it passed on.

'You understand, gentlemen, it was pretty dark; but it seemed to me that the breeze died and the column of leaves – it was no more than a little twist of them – sank down at the end of the avenue.

'We stood there perfectly still for a moment or two; and when I turned, she was staring straight at me, but neither of us said one word.

'We did not go up the avenue to the house. We pushed our way through the laurels, and came back by the upper garden.

'Nothing else happened; and the next morning we all went off by the eleven o'clock train.

'That is all, gentlemen.'

The Traveller

R. H. BENSON

I am amazed, not that the Traveller returns from that Bourne, but that he returns so seldom.

The Pilgrim's Way

On one of these evenings as we sat together after dinner in front of the wide open fireplace in the central room of the house, we began to talk on that old subject – the relation of Science to Faith.

'It is no wonder,' said the priest, 'if their conclusions appear to differ, to shallow minds who think that the last words are being said on both sides, because their standpoints are so different. The scientific view is that you are not justified in committing yourself one inch ahead of your intellectual evidence: the religious view is that in order to find out anything worth knowing your faith must always be a little in advance of your evidence; you must advance *en échelon*. There is the principle of our Lord's promises. "Act as if it were true, and light will be given." The scientist on the other hand says, "Do not presume to commit yourself until light is given." The difference between the methods lies, of course, in the fact that Religion admits the heart and the whole man to the witness-box, while Science only admits the head – scarcely even the senses. Yet surely the evidence of experience is on the side of Religion. Every really great achievement is inspired by motives of the heart, and not of the head; by feeling and passion, not by a calculation of probabilities. And so are the mysteries of God unveiled by those who carry them first by assault; 'The Kingdom of Heaven suffereth violence; and the violent take it by force.'

'For example,' he continued after a moment, 'the scientific view of haunted houses is that there is no evidence for them beyond that which may be accounted for by telepathy, a kind of thought-reading. Yet if you can penetrate that veneer of scientific thought that is so common now, you find that by far the larger part of mankind still believes in them. Practically not one of us really accepts the scientific view as an adequate one.'

'Have you ever had an experience of that kind yourself?' I asked.

'Well,' said the priest, smiling, 'you are sure you will not laugh at it? There is nothing commoner than to think such things a subject for humour; and that I cannot bear. Each such story is sacred to one person at the very least, and therefore should be to all reverent people.'

I assured him that I would not treat his story with disrespect.

'Well,' he answered, 'I do not think you will, and I will tell you. It only happened a very few years ago. This was how it began.

'A friend of mine was, and is still, in charge of a church in Kent, which I will not name; but it is within twenty miles of Canterbury. The district fell into Catholic hands a good many years ago. I received a telegram, in this house, a day or two before Christmas, from my friend, saying that he had been suddenly seized with a very bad attack of influenza, which was devastating Kent at that time; and asking me to come down, if possible at once, and take his place over Christmas. I had only lately given up active work owing to growing infirmity, but it was impossible to resist this appeal; so Parker packed my things and we went together by the next train.

'I found my friend really ill, and quite incapable of doing anything; so I assured him that I could manage perfectly, and that he need not be anxious.

'On the next day, a Wednesday and Christmas Eve, I went down to the little church to hear confessions. It was a beautiful old church, though tiny, and full of interesting things: the old altar had been set up again; there was a rood-loft with a staircase leading on to it; and an awmbry on the north of the sanctuary had been fitted up as a receptacle for the Most Holy Sacrament, instead of the old hanging pyx. One of the most interesting discoveries made in the church was that of the old confessional. In the lower half of the rood-screen, on the south side, a square hole had been found, filled up with an insertion of oak; but an antiquarian of the Alcuin Club, whom my friend had asked to examine the church, declared that this without doubt was the place where in the pre-Reformation times confessions were heard. So it had been restored, and put to its ancient use; and now on this Christmas Eve I sat within the chancel in the dim fragrant light, while penitents came and knelt outside the screen on the single step, and made their confessions through the old opening.

'I know this is a great platitude, but I never can look at a piece of old furniture without a curious thrill at a thing that has been so much saturated with human emotion; but, above all that I have ever seen, I think that this old confessional moved me. Through that little opening had come so many thousands of sins, great and little, weighted with sorrow; and back again, in Divine exchange for those burdens, had returned the balm of the Saviour's blood. "Behold! a door opened in heaven", through which that strange commerce of sin and grace may be carried on – grace pressed down and running over, given into the bosom in exchange for sin. *O bonum commercium!*'

The priest was silent for a moment, his eyes glowing. Then he went on.

'Well, Christmas Day and the three following festivals passed away very happily. On the Sunday night after service, as I came out of the vestry, I saw a child waiting. She told me, when I asked her if she wanted me, that her father and others of her family wished to make their confessions on the following evening about six o'clock. They had had influenza in the house, and had not been able to come out before; but the father was going to work next day, as he was so much better, and would come, if it pleased me, and some of his children to make their confessions in the evening and their communions the following morning.

'Monday dawned, and I offered the Holy Sacrifice as usual, and spent the morning chiefly with my friend, who was now able to sit up and talk a good deal, though he was not yet allowed to leave his bed.

'In the afternoon I went for a walk.

'All the morning there had rested a depression on my soul such as I have not often felt; it was of a peculiar quality. Every soul that tries, however poorly, to serve God, knows by experience those heavinesses by which our Lord tests and confirms His own; but it was not like that. An element of terror mingled with it, as of impending evil.

'As I started for my walk along the high road this depression deepened. There seemed no physical reason for it that I could perceive. I was well myself, and the weather was fair; yet air and exercise did not affect it. I turned at last, about half-past three o'clock, at a milestone that marked sixteen miles to Canterbury.

'I rested there for a moment, looking to the south-east, and saw that far on the horizon heavy clouds were gathering; and then I started homewards. As I went I heard a far-away boom, as of distant guns, and I thought at first that there was some sea-fort to the south where artillery practice was being held; but presently I noticed that it was too irregular and prolonged for the report of a gun; and then it was with a sense of relief that I came to the conclusion it was a far-away thunderstorm, for I felt that the state of the atmosphere might explain away this depression that so troubled me. The thunder seemed to come nearer, pealed more loudly three or four times, and ceased.

'But I felt no relief. When I reached home a little after four Parker brought me in some tea, and I fell asleep afterwards in a chair before the fire. I was wakened after a troubled and unhappy dream by Parker bringing in my coat and telling me it was time to keep my appointment at the church. I could not remember what my dream was, but it was sinister and suggestive of evil, and, with the shreds of it still clinging to me, I looked at Parker with something of fear as he stood silently by my chair holding the coat.

'The church stood only a few steps away, for the garden and churchyard adjoined one another. As I went down carrying the lantern that Parker had lighted for me, I remember hearing far away to the south, beyond the village, the beat of a horse's hoofs. The horse seemed to be in a gallop, but presently the noise died away behind a ridge.

'When I entered the church I found that the sacristan had lighted a candle or two as I had asked him, and I could just make out the kneeling figures of three or four people in the north aisle.

'When I was ready I took my seat in the chair set beyond the screen, at the place I have described; and then, one by one, the labourer and his children came up and made their confessions. I remember feeling again, as on Christmas Eve, the strange charm of this old place of penitence, so redolent of God and man, each in his tenderest character of Saviour and penitent; with the red light burning like a luminous flower in the dark before me, to remind me of how God was indeed tabernacling with men, and was their God.

'Now I do not know how long I had been there, when again I heard the beat of a horse's hoofs, but this time in the village just below the churchyard; then again there fell a sudden silence. Then presently a gust of wind flung the door wide, and the candles began to gutter and flare in the draught. One of the girls went and closed the door.

'Presently the boy who was kneeling by me at that time finished his confession, received absolution and went down the church, and I waited for the next, not knowing how many there were.

'After waiting a minute or two I turned in my seat, and was about to get up, thinking there was no-one else, when a voice whispered sharply through the hole a single sentence. I could not catch the words, but I supposed they were the usual formula for asking a blessing, so I gave the blessing and waited, a little astonished at not having heard the penitent come up.

'Then the voice began again.'

The priest stopped a moment and looked round, and I could see that he was trembling a little.

'Would you rather not go on?' I said. 'I think it disturbs you to tell me.'

'No, no,' he said; 'it is all right, but it was very dreadful – very dreadful.

'Well, the voice began again in a loud quick whisper, but the odd thing was that I could hardly understand a word; there were just phrases here and there, like the name of God and of our Lady, that I could catch. Then there were a few old French words that I knew; "*le roy*" came over and over again. Just at first I thought it must be some extreme form of dialect unknown to me; then I thought it must be a very old man who was deaf, because when I tried, after a few sentences, to explain that I could not understand, the penitent paid no attention, but whispered on quickly without a pause. Presently I could perceive that he was in a terrible state of mind; the voice broke and sobbed, and then almost cried out, but still in this loud whisper; then on the other side of the screen I could hear fingers working and moving uneasily, as if entreating admittance at some barred door. Then at last there was silence for a moment, and then plainly some closing formula was repeated, which gradually grew lower and ceased. Then, as I rose, meaning to come round and explain that I had not been able to hear, a loud moan or two came from the penitent. I stood up quickly and looked through the upper part of the screen, and there was no-one there.

'I can give you no idea of what a shock that was to me. I stood there glaring, I suppose, through the screen down at the empty step for a moment or two, and perhaps I said something aloud, for I heard a voice from the end of the church.

'"Did you call, sir?" And there stood the sacristan, with his keys and lantern, ready to lock up.

'I still stood without answering for a moment, and then I spoke; my voice sounded oddly in my ears. "Is there anyone else, Williams? Are they all gone?" or something like that.

'Williams lifted his lantern and looked round the dusky church. "No, sir; there is no-one."

'I crossed the chancel to go to the vestry, but as I was half-way, suddenly again in the quiet village there broke out the desperate gallop of a horse.

'"There! There!" I cried. "Do you hear that?"

'Williams came up the church towards me. "Are you ill, sir?" he said. "Shall I fetch your servant?"

'I made an effort and told him it was nothing; but he insisted on seeing me home: I did not like to ask him whether he had heard the gallop of the horse; for, after all, I thought, perhaps there was no connection between that and the voice that whispered.

'I felt very much shaken and disturbed; and after dinner, which I took alone of course, I thought I would go to bed very soon. On my way up, however, I looked into my friend's room for a few minutes. He seemed very bright and eager to talk, and I stayed very much longer than I had intended. I said nothing of what had happened in the church, but listened to him while he talked about the village and the neighbourhood. Finally, as I was on the point of bidding him good-night, he said something like this: "Well, I mustn't keep you, but I've been thinking while you've been in church of an old story that is told by antiquarians about this place. They say that one of St Thomas à Becket's murderers came here on the very evening of the murder. It is his day today, you know, and that is what put me in mind of it, I suppose."

'While my friend said this, my old heart began to beat furiously; but, with a strong effort of self-control, I told him I should like to hear the story.

'"Oh! there's nothing much to tell," said my friend; "and they don't know who it's supposed to have been; but it is said to have been either one of the four knights, or one of the men-at-arms."

'"But how did he come here?" I asked, "and what for?"

'"Oh! he's supposed to have been in terror for his soul, and that he rushed here to get absolution, which, of course, was impossible.'

'"But tell me," I said. "Did he come here alone, or how?"

'"Well, you know, after the murder they ransacked the Archbishop's house and stables; and it is said that this man got one of the fastest horses and rode like a madman, not knowing where he was going; and that he dashed into the village, and into the church where the priest was: and then afterwards, mounted again and rode off. The priest, too, is buried in the chancel somewhere, I believe. You see it's a very vague and improbable story. At the Gatehouse at Malling, too, you know, they say that one of the knights slept there the night after the murder."

'I said nothing more; but I suppose I looked strange, because my friend began to look at me with some anxiety, and then ordered me off to bed: so I took my candle and went.

'Now,' said the priest, turning to me, 'that is the story. I need not say that I have thought about it a great deal ever since: and there are only two theories which appear to me credible, and two others, which would no doubt be suggested, which appear to me incredible.

'First, you may say that I was obviously unwell: my previous depression and dreaming showed that, and therefore that I dreamt the whole thing. If you wish to think that – well, you must think it.

'Secondly, you may say, with the Psychical Research Society, that the whole thing was transmitted from my friend's brain to mine; that his was in an energetic, and mine in a passive state, or something of the kind.

'These two theories would be called "scientific", which term means that they are not a hair's-breadth in advance of the facts with which the intellect, a poor instrument at the best, is capable of dealing. And these two "scientific" theories create in their own turn a new brood of insoluble difficulties.

'Or you may take your stand upon the spiritual world, and use the faculties which God has given you for dealing with it, and then you will no longer be helplessly puzzled, and your intellect will no longer overstrain itself at a task for which it was never made. And you may say, I think, that you prefer one of two theories.

'First, that human emotion has a power of influencing or saturating inanimate nature. Of course this is only the old familiar sacramental principle of all creation. The expressions of your face, for instance, caused by the shifting of the chemical particles of which it is composed, vary with your varying emotions. Thus we might say that the violent passions of hatred, anger, terror, remorse, of this poor murderer, seven hundred years ago, combined to make a potent spiritual fluid that bit so deep into the very place where it was all poured out, that under certain circumstances it is reproduced. A phonograph, for example, is a very coarse parallel, in which the vibrations of sound translate themselves first into terms of wax, and then re-emerge again as vibrations when certain conditions are fulfilled.

'Or, secondly, you may be old-fashioned and simple, and say that by some law, vast and inexorable, beyond our perception, the personal spirit of the very man is chained to the place, and forced to expiate his sin again and again, year by year, by attempting to express his grief and to seek forgiveness, without the possibility of receiving it. Of course we do not know who he was; whether one of the knights who afterwards did receive absolution, which possibly was not ratified by God; or one of the men-at-arms who assisted, and who, as an anonymous chronicle says, *"sine confessione et viatico subito rapti sunt"*.

'There is nothing materialistic, I think, in believing that spiritual beings may be bound to express themselves within limits of time and space; and that inanimate nature, as well as animate, may be the vehicles of the unseen. Arguments against such possibilities have surely, once for all, been silenced, for Christians at any rate, by the Incarnation and the Sacramental system, of which the whole principle is that the Infinite and Eternal did once, and does still, express itself under forms of inanimate nature, in terms of time and space.

'With regard to another point, perhaps I need not remind you that a thunderstorm broke over Canterbury on the day and hour of the actual murder of the Archbishop.'